9/03 - 3
2105 - 4

CSD

Just Imagine

SUSAN ELIZABETH PHILLIPS

Just Imagine

Previously published as *Risen Glory*

Published in large print by arrangement with Avon Books, an imprint of HarperCollins Publishers Inc., in the United States and Canada.

Wheeler Large Print Book Series.

Set in 16 pt Plantin.

Library of Congress Cataloging-in-Publication Data Available

Phillips, Susan Elizabeth.
Just imagine / Susan Elizabeth Phillips.
p. (large print) cm.(Wheeler large print book series)
ISBN 1-58724-238-9 (hardcover)
1. Large type books. I. Title. II. Series.

To my husband Bill,
with love and appreciation

PART ONE

A Stable Boy

When duty whispers low, Thou must,
The youth replies, I can.

RALPH WALDO EMERSON
"VOLUNTARIES III"

1

The old street vendor noticed him at once, for the boy was out of place in the crowd of well-dressed stockbrokers and bankers who thronged the streets of lower Manhattan. Cropped black hair that might have held a hint of curl had it been clean stuck out in spikes from beneath the brim of a battered felt hat. A patched shirt unbuttoned at the neck, perhaps in deference to the early July heat, covered narrow, fragile shoulders, while a strap of leather harness held up a pair of greasy, oversized britches. The boy wore black boots that seemed too big for one so small, and he held an oblong bundle in the crook of his arm.

The street vendor leaned against a pushcart filled with trays of pastries and watched the boy shove his way through the crowd, as if it were an enemy to be conquered. The old man saw things others missed, and something about the boy caught his imagination. "You there, *ragazzo*. I got a pastry for you. Light as the kiss of an angel. *Vieni qui.*"

The lad jerked up his head, then gazed longingly at the trays of confections the old man's wife made fresh each day. The peddler could almost hear him counting the pennies concealed in the bundle he clutched so protectively. "Come, *ragazzo*. It is my gift to you." He held up a fat apple tart. "The gift of an old man to a new arrival in this, the most important city in the world."

The boy stuck a defiant thumb into the waistband of his trousers and approached the cart. "Jes' what makes you reckon I'm a new arrival?"

His accent was as thick as the smell of Carolina jasmine blowing across a cotton field, and the old man concealed a smile. "Perhaps it is only a silly fancy, eh?"

The boy shrugged and kicked at some litter in the gutter. "I'm not sayin' I am, and I'm not sayin' I'm not." He punched a grimy finger in the direction of the tart. "How much you want for that?"

"Did I not say it was a gift?"

The boy considered this, then gave a short nod and held out his hand. "Thank you kindly."

As he took the bun, two businessmen in frock coats and tall beaver hats came up to the cart. The boy's gaze swept contemptuously over their gold watch fobs, rolled umbrellas, and polished black shoes. "Damn fool Yankees," he muttered.

The men were engaged in conversation and didn't hear, but as soon as they left, the old man frowned. "I think this city of mine is not a good place for you, eh? It has only been three months since the war is over. Our President is dead. Tempers are still high."

The boy settled on the edge of the curb to consume the tart. "I didn't hold much with Mr. Lincoln. I thought he was puerile."

"Puerile? *Madre di Dio!* What does this word mean?"

"Foolish like a child."

"And where does a boy like you learn such a word?"

The boy shaded his eyes from the late-afternoon sun and squinted at the old man. "Readin' books is my avocation. I learned that particular word from Mr. Ralph Waldo Emerson. I'm an admirer of Mr. Emerson." He began nibbling delicately around the edge of his tart. " 'Course, I didn't know he was a Yankee when I started to read his essays. I was mad as skunk piss when I found out. By then it was too late, though. I was already a disciple."

"This Mr. Emerson. What does he say that is so special?"

A fleck of apple clung to the tip of the boy's grimy index finger, and he flicked it with a small pink tongue. "He talks about character and self-reliance. I reckon self-reliance is the most important attribute a person can have, don't you?"

"Faith in God. That is the most important."

"I don't hold much with God anymore, or even Jesus. I used to, but I reckon I've seen too much these last few years. Watched the Yankees slaughter our livestock and burn our barns. Watched them shoot my dog, Fergis. Saw Mrs. Lewis Godfrey Forsythe lose her husband and her son Henry on the same day. My eyes feel old."

The street vendor looked more closely at the boy. A small, heart-shaped face. A nose that tilted up ever so slightly at the end. It seemed somehow a sin that manhood would soon coarsen those delicate features. "How old are you, *ragazzo?* Eleven? Twelve?"

Wariness crept into eyes that were a surprising shade of deep violet. "Old enough, I guess."

"What about your parents?"

"My mother died when I was born. My daddy died at Shiloh three years ago."

"And you, *ragazzo?* Why have you come here to my city of New York?"

The boy popped the last bit of tart into his mouth, tucked the bundle back under his arm, and stood. "I've got to protect what's mine. Thank you kindly for that tart. It's been a real pleasure makin' your acquaintance." He began to walk away, then hesitated. "And just so you know... I'm not a boy. And my name's Kit."

As Kit made her way uptown toward Washington Square according to the directions she'd received from a lady on the ferry, she decided she shouldn't have told the old man her name. A person bent on murder shouldn't go around advertising herself. Except it wasn't murder. It was justice, even though the

Yankee courts wouldn't see it that way if she got caught. She'd better make certain they never found out that Katharine Louise Weston of Risen Glory Plantation, near what was left of Rutherford, South Carolina, had ever been within spitting distance of their damn city.

She clutched the bundle more tightly. It held her daddy's six-shot Pettingill's self-cocking army percussion revolver; a train ticket back to Charleston; Emerson's *Essays, First Series*; a change of clothing; and the money she'd need while she was here. She wished she could get it over with today so she could go back home, but she needed time to watch the Yankee bastard and get to know his ways. Killing him was only half the job. The other half was not getting caught.

Up until now, Charleston was the largest city she'd seen, but New York wasn't anything like Charleston. As she walked through the noisy, bustling streets, she had to admit there were some fine sights. Beautiful churches, elegant hotels, emporiums with great marble doorways. But bitterness kept her from enjoying her surroundings. The city seemed untouched by the war that had torn apart the South. If there was a God, she hoped He'd see to it that William T. Sherman's soul roasted in hell.

She was staring at an organ grinder instead of paying attention to where she was going, and she bumped into a man hurrying home.

"Hey, boy! Watch out!"

"Watch out yourself," she snarled. "And I'm

not a boy!" But the man had already disappeared around the corner.

Was everybody blind? Since the day she'd left Charleston, people had been mistaking her for a boy. She didn't like it, but it was probably for the best. A boy wandering alone wasn't nearly as conspicuous as a girl. Folks back home never mistook her. Of course, they'd all known her since she was born, so they knew she didn't have any patience with girlish gewgaws.

If only everything weren't changing so fast. South Carolina. Rutherford. Risen Glory. Even herself. The old man thought she was a child, but she wasn't. She'd already turned eighteen, which made her a woman. It was something her body wouldn't let her forget, but her mind refused to accept. The birthday, along with her sex, seemed accidental, and like a horse confronted with too high a fence, she'd decided to balk.

She spotted a policeman ahead and slipped into a group of workers carrying toolboxes. Despite the tart, she was still hungry. Tired, too. If only she were back at Risen Glory right now, climbing one of the peach trees in the orchard, or fishing, or talking to Sophronia in the kitchen. She closed her fingers around a scrap of paper in her pocket to reassure herself it was still there, even though the address printed on it was permanently stamped in her memory.

Before she found a place to stay for the night, she needed to see the house for herself.

Maybe she'd catch a glimpse of the man who threatened everything she loved. Then she'd get ready to do what no soldier in the entire army of the Confederate States of America had been able to. She'd pull out her gun and kill Major Baron Nathaniel Cain.

Baron Cain was a dangerously handsome man, with tawny hair, a chiseled nose, and pewter-gray eyes that gave his face the reckless look of a man who lived on the edge. He was also bored. Even though Dora Van Ness was beautiful and sexually adventurous, he regretted his dinner invitation. He wasn't in the mood to listen to her chatter. He knew she was ready, but he lingered over his brandy. He took women on his terms, not theirs, and a brandy this old shouldn't be rushed.

The house's former owner had kept an excellent wine cellar, the contents of which, along with the home itself, Cain owed to iron nerves and a pair of kings. He pulled a thin cigar from a wooden humidor the housekeeper had left for him on the table, clipped the end, and lit it. In another few hours he was due at one of New York's finest clubs for what was sure to be a high-stakes poker game. Before then, he'd enjoy Dora's more intimate charms.

As he leaned back in his chair, he saw her gaze linger on the scar that disfigured the back of his right hand. It was one of several that he'd accumulated, and all of them seemed to excite her.

"I don't think you've heard a word I've said all evening, Baron." Her tongue flicked her lips, and she gave him a sly smile.

Cain knew that women considered him handsome, but he took little interest in his looks and certainly no pride. The way he saw it, his face had nothing to do with him. It was an inheritance from a weak-willed father and a mother who'd spread her legs for any man who caught her eye.

He'd been fourteen when he'd begun to notice women watching him, and he'd relished the attention. But now, a dozen years later, there'd been too many women, and he'd grown jaded. "Of course I heard you. You were giving me all the reasons I should go to work for your father."

"He's very influential."

"I already have a job."

"Really, Baron, that's hardly a job. It's a social activity."

He regarded her levelly. "There's nothing social about it. Gambling is the way I earn my living."

"But—"

"Would you like to go upstairs, or would you rather I took you home now? I don't want to keep you out too late."

She was on her feet in an instant and, minutes later, in his bed. Her breasts were full and ripe, and he couldn't understand why they didn't feel better in his hands.

"Hurt me," she whispered. "Just a little."

He was tired of hurting, tired of the pain he

couldn't seem to escape even though the war was over. His mouth twisted cynically. "Whatever the lady wants."

Later, when he was alone again and dressed for the night, he found himself wandering through the rooms of the house he'd won with a pair of kings. Something about it reminded him of the house where he'd grown up.

He'd been ten when his mother had run off, leaving him with his debt-ridden father in a bleak Philadelphia mansion that was falling into disrepair. Three years later his father had died, and a committee of women came to take him to an orphan asylum. He ran away that night. He had no destination in mind, only a direction. West.

He spent the next ten years drifting from one town to another, herding cattle, laying railroad track, and panning for gold until he discovered he could find more of it over a card table than in the creeks. The West was a new land that needed educated men, but he wouldn't even admit that he knew how to read.

Women fell in love with the handsome boy whose sculptured features and cold gray eyes whispered a thousand mysteries, but there was something frozen inside him that none of them could thaw. The gentler emotions that take root and flourish in a child who has known love were missing in him. Whether they were dead forever or merely frozen, Cain didn't know. Didn't much care.

When the war broke out, he crossed back over the Mississippi River for the first time in twelve years and enlisted, not to help preserve the Union, but because he was a man who valued freedom above everything else, and he couldn't stomach the idea of slavery. He joined Grant's hard-bitten troops and caught the general's eye when they captured Fort Henry. By the time they reached Shiloh, he was a member of Grant's staff. He was nearly killed twice, once at Vicksburg, then four months later at Chattanooga, charging Missionary Ridge in the battle that opened the way for Sherman's march to the sea.

The newspapers began to write of Baron Cain, dubbing him the "Hero of Missionary Ridge" and praising him for his courage and patriotism. After Cain made a series of successful raids through enemy lines, General Grant was quoted as saying, "I would rather lose my right arm than lose Baron Cain."

What neither Grant nor the newspapers knew was that Cain lived to take risks. Danger, like sex, made him feel alive and whole. Maybe that was why he played poker for a living. He could risk everything on the turn of a card.

Except it had all begun to pale. The cards, the exclusive clubs, the women—none of those things meant as much as they should. Something was missing, but he had no idea what it was.

*   *   *

Kit jerked awake to the sound of an unfamiliar male voice. Clean straw pressed against her cheek, and for an instant she felt as if she were home again in the barn at Risen Glory. Then she remembered it had been burned.

"Why don't you turn in, Magnus? You've had a long day." The voice was coming from the other side of the stable wall. It was deep and crisp, with none of the elongated vowels and whispered consonants of her homeland.

She blinked, trying to see through the darkness. Memory washed over her. Sweet Jesus! She had fallen asleep in Baron Cain's stable.

She inched up on one elbow, wishing she could see better. The directions the woman on the ferry had given her had been wrong, and it had been dark before she'd found the house. She'd huddled in some trees across the way for a while, but nothing had happened, so she'd come around to the back and climbed the wall that surrounded the house in order to see better. When she'd spotted the open stable window, she'd decided to slip inside to investigate. Unfortunately, the familiar scents of horses and fresh straw had proved too much for her, and she'd fallen asleep in the back of an empty stall.

"You plannin' to take Saratoga out tomorrow?" This was a different voice, the familiar, liquid tones reminiscent of the speech of former plantation slaves.

"I might. Why?"

"Don't like the way that fetlock's healin'. Better give her a few more days."

"Fine. I'll take a look at her tomorrow. Good night, Magnus."

"Night, Major."

Major? Kit's heart pounded. The man with the deep voice was Baron Cain! She crept to the stable window and peered over the sill just in time to see him disappear inside the lighted house. Too late. She'd missed her chance to get a glimpse of his face. A whole day wasted.

For a moment she felt a traitorous tightening in her throat. She couldn't have made a bigger mess of things if she'd tried. It was long after midnight, she was in a strange Yankee city, and she'd nearly got herself found out the first day. She swallowed hard and tried to restore her spirits by forcing her battered hat more firmly down on her head. It was no good crying over milk that was already spilled. For now, she had to get out of here and find a place to spend the rest of the night. Tomorrow she'd take up her surveillance from a safer distance.

She fetched her bundle, crept to the doors, and listened. Cain had gone into the house, but where was the man called Magnus? Cautiously she pushed the door open and peered outside.

Light from the curtained windows filtered over the open ground between the stable and the carriage house. She slipped out and listened, but the yard was silent and deserted. She knew the iron gate in the high brick wall was locked, so she'd have to get out the same way she'd come in, over the top.

The open stretch of yard she'd have to run across made her uneasy. Once more she glanced toward the house. Then she took a deep breath and ran.

The moment she was free of the stable, she knew something was wrong. The night air, no longer masked by the smell of horses, carried the faint, unmistakable scent of cigar smoke.

Her blood raced. She dug in her heels and threw herself at the wall, but the vine she grabbed to help her over came away in her hand. She clawed frantically for another one, dropped her bundle, and pulled herself up the wall. Just as she reached the top, something jerked hard on the seat of her trousers. She flailed at the empty air and then slammed, belly-first, to the ground. A boot settled into the small of her back.

"Well, well, what do we have here?" the boot's owner drawled overhead.

The fall had knocked the wind out of her, but she still recognized that deep voice. The man who was holding her down was her sworn enemy, Major Baron Nathaniel Cain.

Her rage shimmered in a red haze. She dug her hands into the dirt and struggled to get up, but he didn't budge.

"Git your damn foot off me, you dirty son of a bitch!"

"I don't think I'm quite ready to do that," he said with a calmness that enraged her.

"Let me up! You let me up right now!"

"You're awfully feisty for a thief."

"Thief!" Outraged, she slammed her fists into the dirt. "I never stole anything in my life. You show me a man who says I have, and I'll show you a damn liar."

"Then what were you doing in my stable?"

That stopped her. She searched her brain for an excuse he might believe. "I—I came here lookin'...lookin'...for a job workin' in your stable. Nobody was around, so I went inside to wait for somebody to show up. Musta fallen asleep."

His foot didn't budge.

"W-when I woke up, it was dark. Then I heard voices, and I got scared somebody would see me and think I was tryin' to hurt the horses."

"It seems to me that somebody looking for work should have had enough sense to knock on the back door."

It seemed that way to Kit, too.

"I'm shy," she said.

He chuckled and slowly the weight lifted from her back. "I'm going to let you up now. You'll regret it if you try to run, boy."

"I'm not a—" She caught herself just in time. "I'm not about to run," she amended, scrambling to her feet. "Haven't done anything wrong."

"I guess that remains to be seen, doesn't it?"

Just then the moon came out from behind a cloud, and he was no longer a looming, menacing shadow but a flesh-and-blood man. She sucked in her breath.

He was tall, broad-shouldered, and lean-hipped. Although she didn't usually pay attention to such things, he was also the handsomest man she'd ever seen. The ends of his necktie dangled from the open collar of his white dress shirt, which was held together with small onyx studs. He wore black trousers and stood easily, a hand lightly balanced on his hip, his cigar still clenched between his teeth.

"What do you have in there?" He jerked his head toward the base of the wall where her bundle lay.

"Nothin' of yours!"

"Show me."

Kit wanted to defy him, but he didn't look like he'd take well to that, so she pulled the bundle from the weeds and opened it. "A change of clothes, a copy of Mr. Emerson's *Essays*, and my daddy's six-shot Pettingill's revolver." She didn't mention the train ticket back to Charleston tucked inside the book. "Nothin' of yours in here."

"What's a boy like you doing with Emerson's *Essays?*"

"I'm a disciple."

There was a slight twitching at the corner of his lips. "You have any money?"

She bent over to rewrap her bundle. " 'Course I've got money. You think I'd be so puerile as to come to a strange city without it?"

"How much?"

"Ten dollars," she said defiantly.

"You can't live for long in New York City on that."

He'd be even more critical if he knew she really had only three dollars and twenty-eight cents. "I told you I was lookin' for a job."

"So you did."

If only he weren't quite so big. She hated herself for taking a step backward. "I'd better be goin' now."

"You know trespassing is against the law. Maybe I'll turn you over to the police."

Kit didn't like being backed into a corner, and she stuck up her chin. "Hit don't make no nevermind to me what you do. I ain't done nothin' wrong."

He crossed his arms over his chest. "Where are you from, boy?"

"Michigan."

At first she didn't understand his burst of laughter, and then she realized her mistake. "I guess you found me out. I'm really from Alabama, but with the war just over, I'm not anxious to advertise that."

"Then you'd better keep your mouth shut." He chuckled. "Aren't you a little young to be carrying a gun?"

"Don't see why. I know how to use it."

"I'll just bet you do." He studied her more closely. "Why did you leave home?"

"No jobs anymore."

"What about your parents?"

Kit repeated the story she'd told the street vendor. When she was done, he took his time thinking it over. She had to force herself not to squirm.

"My stable boy quit last week. How'd you like to work for me?"

"For you?" she murmured weakly.

"That's right. You'd take your orders from my head man, Magnus Owen. He doesn't have your lily-white skin, so if that's going to offend your Southern pride, you'd better tell me now, and we won't waste any more time." When she didn't reply, he continued. "You can sleep over the stable and eat in the kitchen. Salary is three dollars a week."

She kicked at the dirt with the toe of her scuffed boot. Her mind raced. If she'd learned anything today, she'd learned that Baron Cain wouldn't be easy to kill, especially now that he'd seen her face. Working in his stable would keep her close to him, but it would also make her job twice as dangerous.

Since when had danger ever bothered her?

She tucked her thumbs into the waist of her trousers. "Two bits more, Yankee, and you got yourself a stable boy."

Her room above the stable smelled agreeably of horses, leather, and dust. It was comfortably furnished with a soft bed, an oak rocker, and a faded rag rug, as well as a washstand that she ignored. Most important, it possessed a window that looked out over the back of the house so she could keep watch.

She waited until Cain had disappeared inside before she kicked off her boots and climbed into bed. Despite her nap in the stable, she was tired. Even so, she didn't fall asleep right away. Instead, she found herself wondering how her life might have turned out if her daddy hadn't made that trip to Charleston when she was eight years old and taken it into his head to get married again.

From the moment Garrett Weston had met Rosemary, he'd been moonstruck, even though she was older than he and her blond beauty had hard edges any fool could have spotted. Rosemary didn't make a secret of the fact that she couldn't stand children, and the day Garrett brought her home to Risen Glory, she'd pleaded the need for a newlywed's privacy and sent eight-year-old Kit to spend the night in a cabin near the slave quarters. Kit had never been allowed back.

If she forgot that she no longer had the run of the house, Rosemary reminded her with a stinging slap or a boxed ear, so Kit confined herself to the kitchen. Even the sporadic lessons she received from a neighborhood tutor were conducted in the cabin.

Garrett Weston had never been an attentive father, and he barely seemed to notice that his only child was receiving less care than the children of his slaves. He was too obsessed with his beautiful, sensual wife.

The neighbors were scandalized. *That child is running wild! Bad enough if she was a boy, but even a fool like Garrett Weston should know enough not to let a girl run around like that.*

Rosemary Weston had no interest in local society, and she ignored their pointed hints that Kit needed a governess or, at the very least, acceptable clothing. Eventually, the neighborhood women sought out Kit themselves with their daughters' cast-off dresses and lectures on proper female behavior. Kit ignored the lectures and traded the dresses for britches and boys' shirts. By the time she was ten, she could shoot, cuss, ride a horse bareback, and had even smoked a cigar.

At night when loneliness overwhelmed her, she reminded herself that her new life had advantages for a girl who'd been born with an adventurous heart. She could climb the peach trees in the orchard any time she wanted and swing from ropes in the barn. The men of the community taught her how to ride and fish. She'd sneak into the library before her stepmother emerged from her bedroom in the morning and forage for books with no worries of censorship. And if she scraped her knee or caught a splinter in her foot, she could always run to Sophronia in the kitchen.

The war changed everything. The first shots had been fired at Fort Sumter a month before her fourteenth birthday. Not long after that, Garrett Weston had turned over the management of the plantation to Rosemary and joined the Confederate army. Since Kit's stepmother never rose before eleven and hated the outdoors, Risen Glory began to fall into disrepair. Kit tried desperately to take her father's place, but the war had put an end to the market for Southern cotton, and she was too young to hold it all together.

The slaves ran off. Garrett Weston was killed at Shiloh. Bitterly, Kit received the news that he'd left the plantation to his wife. Kit had received a trust fund from her grandmother a few years earlier, but that meant nothing to her.

Not long after, Yankee soldiers marched through Rutherford, burning everything in their path. Rosemary's attraction to a handsome young lieutenant from Ohio and her subsequent invitation for him to join her in her bedroom spared the house at Risen Glory, although not the outbuildings. Shortly after Lee's surrender at Appomattox. Rosemary died in an influenza epidemic.

Kit had lost everything. Her father, her childhood, her way of life. Only the land was left. Only Risen Glory. And as she curled into the thin mattress above the stable owned by Baron Cain, she knew that was all that counted. No matter what she had to do, she'd get it back.

She fell asleep imagining how it would be when Risen Glory was finally hers.

The stable held four horses, a matched pair for the carriage and two hunters. Some of Kit's tension eased the next morning as a large bay with a long, elegant neck nuzzled her shoulder. Everything would be all right. She'd keep her eyes open and bide her time. Baron Cain was dangerous, but she had the advantage. She knew her enemy.

"His name is Apollo."

"What?" She spun around to see a young man with rich chocolate skin and large, expressive eyes standing on the other side of the half door that separated the stalls from the center aisle of the stable. He was in his early-to-mid-twenties and tall, with slim shoulders and a slight, supple build. A black-and-white mongrel waited patiently near his heels.

"That bay. His name is Apollo. He's the major's favorite mount."

"You don't say." Kit opened the door and stepped out of the stall.

The mongrel sniffed her while the young man looked her over critically. "I'm Magnus Owen. Major said he hired you last night after he caught you sneakin' out of the stable."

"I wasn't sneakin'. Well, not exactly. That major of yours has a naturally suspicious nature, is all." She looked down at the mongrel. "That your dog?"

"Yep. I call him Merlin."

"Looks like a no-account dog to me."

Magnus's smooth, high forehead puckered indignantly. "Now, why do you want to say somethin' like that, boy? You don't even know my dog!"

"I spent yesterday afternoon asleep in that stall over there. If Merlin was any kinda dog, he'd of been mighty annoyed about that." Kit reached down and absentmindedly scratched behind his ears.

"Merlin wasn't here yesterday afternoon," Magnus said. "He was with me."

"Oh. Well, I guess I'm just inherently prejudiced. The Yankees killed my dog, Fergis. Best dog I ever knew. I mourn him to this day."

Magnus's expression softened a little. "What's your name?"

She paused for a moment, then decided it would be easier to use her own first name. Behind Magnus's head she spotted a can of Finney's Harness Oil and Leather Preserver. "Name's Kit. Kit Finney."

"A mighty funny name for a boy."

"My folks were admirers of Kit Carson, the Injun fighter."

Magnus seemed to accept her explanation and was soon outlining her duties. Afterward, they went into the kitchen for breakfast, and he introduced her to the housekeeper.

Edith Simmons was a stout woman with thinning salt-and-pepper hair and strong opinions. She'd been cook and housekeeper for the former owner and had agreed to stay on only when she'd discovered that Baron Cain was unmarried and there'd be no wife to tell her how to do her job. Edith believed in thrift, good food, and personal hygiene. She and Kit were natural-born enemies.

"That boy is too dirty to eat with civilized people!"

"I won't argue with you there," Magnus replied.

Kit was too hungry to argue for very long, so she stomped into the pantry and splashed some water on her face and hands, but she refused to touch the soap. It smelled girlish, and Kit had been fighting everything feminine for as long as she could remember.

As she devoured the sumptuous breakfast, she studied Magnus Owen. From the way Mrs. Simmons deferred to him, it was obvious that he was an important figure in the household, unusual for a black man under any circumstances, but especially for one who was so young. Something tugged at Kit's memory, but it wasn't until they'd finished eating that she realized what it was. Magnus Owen reminded her of Sophronia, the cook at Risen Glory and the only person in the world Kit loved. Both Magnus and Sophronia acted as if they knew everything.

A pang of homesickness struck her, but she pushed it away. She'd be at Risen Glory soon enough, bringing the plantation back to life.

That afternoon when she finished her work, she sat in the shade near the front door of the stable, her arm draped across Merlin, who'd fallen asleep with his nose resting on her thigh. The dog didn't stir as Magnus approached.

"This animal's worthless," she whispered. "If you was an ax murderer, I'd be dead by now."

Magnus chuckled and lowered himself beside her. "I got to admit, Merlin isn't much of a watchdog. But he's young still. He was only a pup when the major found him rootin' around in the alley behind the house."

Kit had seen Cain only once that day, when

he'd curtly ordered her to saddle Apollo. He'd been too full of himself to take a few minutes to pass the time of day. Not that she wanted to talk to the likes of him. It was just the principle of the thing.

The Yankee newspapers called him the Hero of Missionary Ridge. She knew he'd fought at Vicksburg and Shiloh. Maybe he was even the man who'd killed her daddy. It didn't seem right that he was alive when so many brave Confederate soldiers were dead. And it was even more unjust that every breath he drew threatened the only thing she had left in the world.

"How long've you known the major?" she asked cautiously.

Magnus plucked a blade of grass and began to chew on it. "Since Chattanooga. He almost lost his life savin' mine. We been together ever since."

An awful suspicion began to grow inside Kit. "You weren't fightin' for the Yankees, were you, Magnus?"

" 'Course I was fightin' for the Yankees!"

She didn't know why she should be so disappointed, except that she liked Magnus. "You told me you were from Georgia. Why didn't you fight for your home state?"

Magnus removed the blade of grass from his mouth. "You got a lot of nerve, boy. You sit here with a black man and, cool as a cucumber, ask him why he didn't fight for the people who was keepin' him in chains. I was twelve years old when I got freed. I came North. I got a job and went to school. But I wasn't really free, do you understand me? There wasn't a single Negro in this country could really be free as long as his brothers and sisters was slaves."

"It wasn't primarily a question of slavery," she explained patiently. "It was a question of whether a state has the right to govern itself without interference. Slavery was just incidental."

"Mighta been incidental to you, white boy, but it wasn't incidental to me."

Black folks sure were touchy, she thought as he rose and walked away. But later, while she put out the second feed for the horses, she was still mulling over what he'd said. It reminded her of several heated conversations she'd had with Sophronia.

Cain vaulted from Apollo's back with a gracefulness unusual for a man of his size. "Take your time cooling him out, boy. I don't want a sick horse." He tossed Kit the bridle and began to stride toward the house.

"I know my job," she called out. "Don't need no Yankee telling me how to take care of a hot, sweaty horse."

The words were no sooner out of her mouth than she wished she could snatch them back. Today was only Wednesday, and she couldn't risk getting fired yet.

She'd already learned that Sunday was the only night Mrs. Simmons and Magnus didn't sleep in the house. Mrs. Simmons had the day off and stayed with her sister, and Magnus spent the night in what Mrs. Simmons described as a drunken and debauched manner unfit for young ears. Kit needed to hold her tongue for four days. Then, when Sunday night came, she was going to kill the Yankee bastard who was gazing down at her with those cool gray eyes.

"If you think you'd be happier working for somebody else, I can always find another stable boy."

"Didn't say I wanted to work for anybody else," she muttered.

"Then maybe you'd better try a little harder to hold your tongue."

She kicked the dirt with the dusty toe of her boot.

"And, Kit?"

"Yeah?"

"Take a bath. People are complaining about the way you smell."

"A bath!" Kit's outrage nearly choked her, and she could barely hold onto her temper.

Cain seemed to be enjoying her struggle. "Was there anything else you wanted to say to me?"

She clenched her teeth and thought about the size of the bullet hole she intended to leave in his head. "No, sir," she mumbled.

"Then I'll need the carriage at the front door in an hour and a half."

As she walked Apollo around the yard, she released a steady stream of profanity. Killing that Yankee was going to give her more pleasure than anything she'd done in all her eighteen years. What business was it of his whether she took a bath or not? She didn't hold with baths. Everybody knew they made you susceptible to influenza. Besides, she'd have to take off her clothes, and she hated seeing her body ever since she'd grown breasts because they didn't fit who she wanted to be.

A man.

Girls were soft and weak, but she'd erased that part of herself until she'd become strong and tough as any man. As long as she didn't lose sight of that, she'd be just fine.

She was still feeling out of sorts as she stood between the heads of the matched gray carriage horses and waited for Cain to emerge from the house. She'd splashed water on her face and changed into her spare set of clothes, but they weren't any cleaner than the ones she'd abandoned, so she didn't see what difference it made.

As Cain came down the steps, he took in his stable boy's patched breeches and faded blue shirt. If anything, he decided the kid looked worse. He studied what he could see of the boy's face beneath the brim of that mangled hat and decided his chin might be a little cleaner. He probably shouldn't have hired the scamp, but the boy made him smile like nothing else had for longer than he could remember.

Unfortunately, the afternoon's activity would be less amusing. He wished he hadn't let Dora maneuver him into taking her for a drive through Central Park. Even though they'd both known the rules from the start, he was beginning to believe she wanted a more permanent relationship, and he suspected she'd take advantage of the privacy their ride offered to press him. Unless they had company...

"Climb in the back, boy. It's about time you saw something of New York City."

"Me?"

He smiled at the boy's astonishment. "I don't see anybody else around. I need somebody to hold the horses." And to forestall an invitation from Dora to be a permanent member of the Van Ness family.

Kit gazed up into the Yankee's gray, Rebel-killing eyes, then swallowed hard and swung herself into the leather-upholstered seat. The less time she spent in his presence, the better, but he had her trapped.

As he expertly maneuvered the carriage through the streets, Cain pointed out the city's attractions, and her pleasure in the new sights began to overcome her caution. They passed Delmonico's famous restaurant and Wallach's Theatre, where Charlotte Cushman was appearing in *Oliver Twist.* Kit glimpsed the fashionable shops and hotels that surrounded the lush greenery of Madison Square, and, farther north, she studied the glittering mansions of the wealthy.

Cain drew up in front of an imposing brownstone. "Watch the horses, boy. I won't be long."

At first Kit didn't mind the wait. She surveyed the houses around her and watched the sparkling carriages with their well-dressed occupants flash by. But then she thought of Charleston, reduced to rubble, and the familiar bitterness rose inside her.

"A perfect day for a drive. And I have the most amusing story to tell you."

Kit looked up to see an elegant woman with shining blond curls and a pretty, pouting mouth come down the steps on Cain's arm. She was dressed in strawberry silk and held a lacy white parasol to protect her pale skin from the afternoon sun. A tiny froth of a bonnet perched on top of her head. Kit detested her on sight.

Cain helped the woman into the carriage and politely assisted her with her skirts. Kit's opinion of him sank even lower. If this was the kind of woman he fancied, he wasn't as smart as she'd figured.

She put her scuffed boot on the iron step and swung herself into the rear seat. The woman jerked around in astonishment. "Baron, who is this filthy creature?"

"Who're you callin' filthy?" Kit sprang from the seat, her hands balled into fists.

"Sit down," Cain barked.

She glared at him, but his Rebel-murdering expression didn't flicker. With a glower, she sank back into the seat, then gave the evil eye to the back of that pert strawberry-and-white bonnet.

Cain eased the carriage into the traffic. "Kit is my stable boy, Dora. I brought him along to stay with the horses in case you wanted to walk in the park."

The ribbons on Dora's bonnet fluttered. "It's much too warm to walk."

Cain shrugged. Dora adjusted her parasol and settled into a silence that screamed her displeasure, but to Kit's satisfaction, Cain paid no attention.

Unlike Dora, Kit wasn't prone to sulking, and she gave in to the pleasure of the bright summer afternoon and the landmarks he continued to point out. This was the only chance she'd ever get to see New York City, and even if she had to do it with her sworn enemy, she intended to enjoy it.

"This is Central Park."

"I don't see why they call it that. Any fool can tell it's at the north edge of the city."

"New York is growing fast," Cain replied. "Right now there's mainly open land around the park. A few shanties, some farms. But it won't be long before the city takes over."

Kit was about to voice her skepticism when Dora spun in her seat and fixed her with a withering glare. The message clearly said Kit wasn't to open her mouth again.

Fixing a simpering smile on her face, Dora turned back to Cain and patted his forearm with a hand gloved in strawberry lace. "Baron, I have a most amusing story to tell you about Sugar Plum."

"Sugar who?"

"You remember. My darling little pug."

Kit made a face and leaned back in the seat. She watched the play of light as the carriage slipped along the tree-lined promenade that ran through the park. Then she found herself studying Dora's bonnet. Why would anybody wear something so silly? And why couldn't Kit keep her eyes off it?

Two women riding in a black landau passed in the other direction. Kit noticed how eagerly they gazed at Cain. Women sure did seem to make fools of themselves over him. He knew how to handle horses, she'd give him that. Still, that didn't count much with a lot of women. They were more interested in how a man looked.

She tried to study him objectively. He was a handsome son of a bitch, no doubt about that. His hair was the same color as wheat right before harvest time, and it curled a little over the back of his collar. As he turned to make a comment to Dora, his profile stood out against the sky, and she decided there was something pagan about it, like the drawing she'd seen of a Viking—a smooth, high brow, a straight nose, and an aggressive line to the jaw.

"...then Sugar Plum pushed the raspberry bonbon away with her nose and picked a lemon one instead. Isn't that the sweetest thing you've ever heard?"

Pugs and raspberry bonbons. The woman was a damn fool. Kit sighed loudly.

Cain glanced back at her. "Is something wrong?"

She tried to be polite. "I don't hold much with pugs."

There was a slight movement at the corner of Cain's mouth. "Now, why is that?"

"You want my honest opinion?"

"Oh, by all means."

Kit darted a disgusted glare at Dora's back. "Pugs are sissy dogs."

Cain chuckled.

"That boy is impertinent!"

Cain ignored Dora. "You prefer mutts, Kit? I've noticed you spend a lot of time with Merlin."

"Merlin spends time with me, not the other way around. I don't care what Magnus says. That dog's 'bout as worthless as a corset in a whorehouse."

"Baron!"

Cain made a queer, croaking noise before he recovered his composure. "Maybe you'd better remember there's a lady present."

"Yessir," Kit muttered, although she didn't see what that had to do with anything.

"That boy doesn't know his place," Dora snapped. "I'd fire any servant who behaved so outrageously."

"I guess it's a good thing that he works for me, then."

He hadn't raised his voice, but the rebuke was clear, and Dora flushed.

They were nearing the lake, and Cain pulled the carriage to a stop. "My stable boy isn't an ordinary servant," he continued, his tone somewhat lighter. "He's a disciple of Ralph Waldo Emerson."

Kit looked away from a family of swans gliding between the canoes to see if he was making fun of her, but he didn't seem to be.

Instead, he laid his arm over the back of the leather seat and turned to face her. "Is Mr. Emerson the only writer you read, Kit?"

Dora's indignant huff made Kit garrulous. "Oh, I read 'bout everything I can lay my hands on. Ben Franklin, of course, but most everybody reads him. Thoreau, Jonathan Swift. Edgar Allan Poe when I'm in the mood. I don't hold much with poetry, but otherwise I have a generally voracious appetite."

"So I see. Maybe you just haven't read the right poets. Walt Whitman, for example."

"Never heard of him."

"He's a New Yorker. Worked as a nurse during the war."

"I don't reckon I could stomach a Yankee poet."

Cain lifted an amused brow. "I'm disappointed. Surely an intellectual like yourself wouldn't let prejudice interfere with an appreciation for great literature."

He was laughing at her, and she felt her hackles rising. "It surprises me you even know the name of a poet, Major, 'cause you don't look much like a reader to me. But I guess that's the way it is with big men. All the muscle goes to their bodies, not sparin' much for the brain."

"Impertinent!" Dora shot Cain an I-told-you-so look.

Cain ignored it and studied Kit more closely. The boy had guts, he'd give him that. He couldn't be older than thirteen, the same age Cain had been when he'd run away. But Cain had nearly reached his adult height at that time, while Kit was small, only a couple of inches over five feet.

Cain noted how delicate the boy's grimy features were: the heart-shaped face, the small nose with its decided upward tilt, and those thickly lashed violet eyes. They were the kind of eyes women prized, but they looked foolish on a boy and would look even more outlandish when Kit grew to be a man.

Kit refused to flinch under his scrutiny, and Cain felt a spark of admiration. The daintiness of his features probably had something to do with his pluck. Any boy who looked so delicate must have been forced to do a lot of fighting.

Still, the kid was too young to be on his own, and Cain knew he should turn him over to an orphan asylum. But even as he considered the idea, he understood he wouldn't do it. There was something about Kit that reminded Cain of himself at that age. He was feisty and stubborn, walking through life daring somebody to take a swing at him. It would be like clipping the wings of a bird to put that boy in an orphanage. Besides, he was good with the horses.

Dora's need to be alone with him finally overcame her aversion to exercise, and she asked him to walk to the lake. There, the scene that he had hoped to avoid was played out with tiresome predictability. It was his fault. He had let sex overcome good judgment.

It was a relief to get back to the carriage where

Kit had struck up a conversation with the man who rented the canoes and two brightly painted ladies of the night out for a stroll before they went to work.

The kid sure could talk.

That evening after dinner Kit sprawled in her favorite spot outside the stable door, her arm propped on Merlin's warm back. She found herself remembering something strange Magnus had told her earlier when she'd been admiring Apollo.

"The Major won't keep him long."

"Why not?" she'd said. "Apollo's a real beauty."

"He sure is. But the Major doesn't let himself get tied to things he likes."

"What do you mean?"

"He gives away his horses and his books before he can get too attached to them. It's just the way he is."

Kit couldn't imagine it. Those were the things that kept you anchored to life. But maybe the major didn't want to be anchored.

She scratched her scalp under her hat, and an image of Dora Van Ness's pink-and-white bonnet flashed through her mind. It was foolish. The bonnet wasn't anything more than a few pieces of lace and a trail of ribbons. Yet she couldn't get it out of her mind. She kept imagining what she'd look like wearing it.

What was wrong with her? She pulled off her

own battered hat and slammed it on the ground. Merlin looked up in surprise.

"Don't pay me no nevermind, Merlin. All these Yankees are makin' me queer in the head. As if I don't have enough distractin' me without thinkin' 'bout bonnets."

Merlin stared at her with soulful brown eyes. She didn't like admitting it, but she was going to miss him when she went home. She thought of Risen Glory waiting for her. By this time next year, she'd have that old plantation back on its feet.

Deciding that the mysterious human crisis was over, Merlin put his head back down on her thigh. Idly, Kit fingered one of his long, silky ears. She hated this city. She was sick of Yankees and the sound of traffic even at night. She was sick of her old felt hat, and most of all, she was sick of people calling her "boy."

It was ironic. All her life she'd hated everything that had to do with being female, but now that everybody thought she was a boy, she hated that, too. Maybe she was some kind of mutation.

She tugged absentmindedly at a dirty spike of hair. Every time that Yankee bastard had called her "boy" today, she'd gotten a sick, queasy feeling. He was so arrogant, so sure of himself. She'd seen Dora's watery eyes after they'd come back from their walk to the lake. The woman was a fool, but Kit had felt a moment of sympathy for her. In different ways, they were both suffering because of him.

She trailed her fingers over the dog's back and reviewed her plan. It wasn't foolproof, but all in all, she was satisfied. And determined. She'd get only one chance to kill that Yankee devil, and she didn't intend to miss.

The next morning, Cain tossed a copy of Walt Whitman's *Leaves of Grass* at her.

"Keep it."

2

Hamilton Woodward stood as Cain walked through the mahogany doors of his private law office. So this was the Hero of Missionary Ridge, the man who was emptying the pockets of New York's wealthiest financiers. Not a flashy dresser, that much was in his favor. His pin-striped waistcoat and dark maroon cravat were expensive but conservative, and his pearl-gray frock coat was superbly tailored. Still, there was something not quite respectable about the man. It was more than his reputation, although that was damning enough. Perhaps it was the way he walked, as if he owned the room he'd just entered.

The attorney came around the side of his desk and extended his hand. "How do you do, Mr. Cain. I'm Hamilton Woodward."

"Mr. Woodward." As Cain shook hands, he made an assessment of his own. The man was middle-aged and portly. Competent. Pompous. Probably a lousy poker player.

Woodward indicated a leather armchair drawn up in front of his desk. "I apologize for asking you to see me on such short notice, but this matter has been delayed long enough. Through no fault of my own, I might add. I only learned of it yesterday. I assure you, no one associated with this firm would be so cavalier about something this important. Especially when it concerns a man to whom we all owe so great a debt. Your courage during—"

"Your letter said only that you wanted to speak with me on a matter of great importance," Cain cut in. He disliked people praising his wartime exploits, as if what he'd done were something to be unfurled like a flag and hung out for public display.

Woodward picked up a pair of spectacles and settled the wire stems over his ears. "You are the son of Rosemary Simpson Cain—later Rosemary Weston?"

Cain hadn't made his living at the poker tables by telegraphing his feelings, but it was difficult to hide the ugly emotions that sprang up inside him. "I wasn't aware she'd remarried, but yes, that's my mother's name."

"*Was* her name, don't you mean?" Woodward glanced at a paper in front of him.

"She's dead, then?" Cain felt nothing.

The attorney's plump jowls jiggled in distress. "I do apologize. I assumed you knew. She passed on nearly four months ago. Forgive me for having broken the news so abruptly."

"Don't trouble yourself with apologies. I haven't seen my mother since I was ten years old. Her death means nothing to me."

Woodward shuffled the papers before him, not appearing to know how to respond to a man who reacted so coldly to the death of his mother. "I, uh, have a letter sent to me by a Charleston attorney named W. D. Ritter, who represents your mother's estate." He cleared his throat. "Mr. Ritter's asked me to contact you so you can be advised of the terms of her will."

"I'm not interested."

"Yes, well, that remains to be seen. Ten years ago your mother married a man named Garrett Weston. He was the owner of Risen Glory, a cotton plantation not far from Charleston, and when he was killed at Shiloh, he left the plantation to your mother. Four months ago she died of influenza, and she seems to have left the plantation to you."

Cain didn't betray his surprise. "I haven't seen my mother in sixteen years. Why would she do that?"

"Mr. Ritter included a letter that she wrote to you shortly before her death. Perhaps it will explain her motives." Woodward withdrew a sealed letter from the folder in front of him and passed it across the desk.

Cain put it in the pocket of his coat without glancing at it. "What do you know about the plantation?"

"It was apparently quite prosperous, but the war took its toll. With work, it might be reclaimed. Unfortunately, there's no money attached to this bequest. And there's also the matter of Weston's daughter, Katharine Louise."

This time Cain didn't bother to hide his surprise. "Are you telling me I have a half sister?"

"No, no. She's a stepsister. You aren't related by blood. The girl is Weston's child from his previous marriage. She does, however, concern you."

"I can't imagine why."

"Her grandmother left her quite a lot of money, fortunately in a Northern bank. Fifteen thousand dollars, to be exact, to be held in trust until her twenty-third birthday or until she marries, whichever event occurs first. You've been appointed administrator of her trust and her guardian."

"Guardian!" Cain erupted from the deep seat of the leather chair.

Woodward shrank back in his own chair. "What else was your mother to do? The girl is barely eighteen. There's a substantial sum of money involved and no other relatives."

Cain leaned forward over the gleaming mahogany surface of the desk. "I'm not going to take responsibility for an eighteen-year-old girl or a run-down cotton plantation."

Woodward's pitch rose a notch. "That's up to you, of course, although I do agree that giving a man as—as worldly as yourself guardianship over a young woman is somewhat irregular. Still, the decision is yours. When you go to Charleston to inspect the plantation, you can speak with Mr. Ritter and advise him of your decision."

"There is no decision," Cain said flatly. "I didn't ask for this inheritance, and I don't want it. Write your Mr. Ritter and tell him to find another patsy."

Cain was in a black mood by the time he arrived home, and his mood wasn't improved when his stable boy failed to appear to take the carriage.

"Kit? Where the hell are you?" He called twice before the boy raced out. "Damn it! If you're working for me, I expect you to be here when I need you. Don't keep me waiting again!"

"And howdy to you, too," Kit grumbled.

Ignoring her, he leaped from the carriage and strode across the open yard to the house. Once inside, he went straight to the library and splashed some whiskey into a glass. Only after he'd drained it did he pull out the letter Woodward had given him and break the red wax seal.

Inside was a single sheet of paper covered with small, nearly indecipherable handwriting.

March 6, 1865

Dear Baron,
I can imagine your surprise at receiving a letter from me after so many years, even if it is a letter from the grave. A morbid thought. I am not resigned to dying. Still, my fever will not

break, and I fear the worst. While I have strength, I will dispose of those few responsibilities I have left.

If you expect apologies from me, you will receive none. Life with your father was exceptionally tedious. I am also not a maternal woman, and you were a most unruly child. It was all very tiresome. Still, I must admit to having followed the newspaper stories of your military exploits with some interest. It pleased me to learn you are considered a handsome man.

None of this, however, concerns my purpose in writing. I was very attached to my second husband, Garrett Weston, who made life pleasant for me, and it is for him that I write this letter. Although I've never been able to abide his hoydenish daughter, Katharine, I realize she must have someone to watch out for her until she comes of age. Therefore, I have left Risen Glory to you with the hope that you will act as her guardian. Perhaps you will decline. Although the plantation was once the finest in the area, the war has done it no good.

Whatever your decision, I have discharged my duty.

Your mother,
Rosemary Weston

After sixteen years, that was all.

Kit heard the clock on the Methodist church in the next block chime two as she knelt in front of the open window and stared toward the dark house. Baron Cain wasn't going to live to see the dawn.

The predawn air was heavy and metallic, warning of a storm, and even though her room was still warm from the afternoon's heat, she shivered. She hated thunderstorms, especially those that broke at night. Maybe if she'd had a parent to run to for comfort when she'd been a child, her fear would have passed. Instead, she'd huddled in her cabin near the slave quarters, alone and terrified, certain that the earth was going to split open at any minute and gobble her up.

Cain had finally gotten home half an hour ago. Mrs. Simmons, the maids, and Magnus were gone for the night, so he was in the house alone, and as soon as he'd had time to fall asleep, the way would be clear.

The distant rumble of thunder jangled her. She tried to convince herself that the weather would make her work easier. It would hide any noise she might make when she slipped into the house through the pantry window she'd unlocked earlier. But the thought didn't comfort her. Instead, she imagined herself as she'd be in an hour or so, running through the dark streets with a thunderstorm crashing around her. *And the earth splitting open to gobble her up.*

She jumped as lightning flashed. To distract herself, she tried to concentrate on her plan. She'd cleaned and oiled her daddy's revolver and reread Mr. Emerson's essay "Self-Reliance" to bolster her courage. Then she'd bundled her possessions and hidden them in the back of the carriage house so she could grab them quickly.

After she killed Cain, she'd make her way to the docks off Cortlandt Street, where she'd catch the first ferry for Jersey City. There she'd find the train station and begin her journey back to Charleston, knowing the long nightmare that had begun when that Charleston lawyer had come to her was finally over. With Cain dead, Rosemary's will would become meaningless and Risen Glory would be hers. All she had to do was find his bedroom, aim her gun, and pull the trigger.

She shivered. She'd never actually killed a man, but she could think of no better place to start than with Baron Cain.

He should be asleep by now. It was time. She picked up her loaded revolver and crept down the stairs, being careful not to disturb Merlin as she left the stable. A clap of thunder made her shrink against the door. She reminded herself she wasn't a child and shot across the yard to the house, then scrambled through the shrubbery to get to the pantry window.

She tucked the revolver into the waistband of her breeches and tried to open the window. It didn't budge.

She pushed again, harder this time, but nothing happened. The window was locked.

Stunned, she leaned against the house. She'd known her plan wasn't foolproof, but she hadn't expected to be thwarted so soon.

Mrs. Simmons must have discovered the unfastened latch before she left.

The first drops of rain began to fall. Kit wanted to run back to her room and hide under the covers until the storm passed, but she summoned her courage and circled the house, looking for another way inside. The rain fell harder, striking her through her shirt. A maple tree thrashed in the wind. Near its branches she spotted an open second-story window.

Her heart pounded. The storm roared above her, and her breath came in short, panicky gasps. She forced herself to grab the lowest branch of the tree and pull herself up.

A bolt of lightning split the skies, and the tree quivered. She clung to the branch, terrified by the force of the storm and cursing herself for being so lily-livered. Setting her teeth, she forced herself higher into the tree. Finally, she began edging out onto the branch that seemed to grow closest to the house, although the driving rain made it impossible to see how far it went.

She whimpered as another thunderclap left the stink of brimstone in the air. *Don't swallow me up!* She willed herself to move farther out. The limb pitched in the wind then began to sag under her weight.

The skies lit with another lightning bolt. Right then, she saw that the branch didn't grow close enough for her to reach the window. Despair washed over her.

She blinked her eyes, wiped her nose on her sleeve, and worked her way back down the tree.

As she reached the bottom, lightning struck so close that her ears rang. Trembling, she pressed her spine against the trunk. Her clothes stuck to her skin, and the brim of her hat hung like a sodden pancake around her head. Tears she refused to shed burned hot behind her lids. Was this the way it would end? Risen Glory taken from her because she was too weak, too chickenhearted, too *girly* to get into a house?

She jumped as something brushed her legs. Merlin stared up at her, his head cocked to the side. She sank to her knees and buried her face in his wet, musty fur. "You no-account dog..." Her arms trembled as she drew the animal closer. "I'm as worthless as you."

He scraped her wet cheek with his rough tongue. Another blast of lightning struck. He howled, and Kit jumped to her feet, fear igniting her determination. Risen Glory was hers! If she couldn't get into the house through a window, she'd get in through the door!

Half crazed from the storm and her own desperation, she raced toward the back door, fighting the wind and rain, too desperate to pay attention to the tiny voice that told her to give up and try again another day. She threw herself against the door, and when the lock didn't give, she began pounding it with her fists.

Tears of fury and frustration choked her. "*Let me in!* Let me in, you Yankee son of a bitch!"

Nothing happened.

She continued to pound, cursing and kicking.

A jagged bolt of lightning shot from the

sky and struck the maple that had so recently sheltered her. Kit screamed and threw herself inside.

Directly into the arms of Baron Cain.

"What in the hell..."

The heat from his naked, sleep-warmed chest seeped through her cold, wet shirt, and for a moment, all she wanted to do was stay where she was, right there against him, until she could stop shivering.

"Kit, what's wrong?" He grabbed her shoulders. "Has something happened?"

She jerked back. Unfortunately, Merlin was behind her. She stumbled over him and sprawled down on the hard kitchen floor.

Cain studied the tangled heap at his feet. His mouth quirked. "I take it this thunderstorm is a little too much for you."

She tried to tell him he could go straight to Hades, but her teeth were chattering so hard she couldn't talk. She'd also landed on the revolver tucked in her britches, and a sharp pain shot through her hip.

Cain stepped over them to shut the door. Unfortunately, Merlin chose that moment to shake himself off.

"Ungrateful mutt." Cain grabbed a towel from a hook near the sink and began rubbing it over his chest.

Kit realized her revolver would be visible under her clothes as soon as she stood up. While Cain was preoccupied drying off, she slipped it out of her britches and hid it behind a basket of apples near the back door.

"I don't know which of you is more scared," Cain grumbled as he watched Merlin disappear down the hallway that led to Magnus's room. "But I wish you both could have waited till morning."

"I'm sure not scared of a little damn rain," Kit retorted.

Just then there was another crash, and she leaped to her feet, her face turning pale.

"My mistake," he drawled.

"Just because I—" She broke off and swallowed as she finally got a good look at him.

He was nearly naked, wearing only a pair of dun-colored trousers slung low on his hips, with the top two buttons left unfastened in his haste to get to the door. She'd been around her share of scantily clad men working in the fields or at the sawmill, but now it was as if she'd never seen a one of them.

His chest was broad and muscular, lightly furred. A raised scar slashed one shoulder, and another jutted over his bare abdomen from the open waistband of his trousers. His hips were narrow and his stomach flat, bisected by a thin line of tawny hair. Her eyes inched lower to the point at which the legs of his trousers met. What she saw there fascinated her.

"Dry yourself off."

She lifted her head and saw him staring at her, a towel extended in his hand, his expression puzzled. She grabbed the towel and reached under the collapsed brim of her hat to dab at her cheeks.

"It might be easier if you'd take your hat off."

"I don't want to take it off," she snapped, unsettled by her reaction. "I like my hat."

With a growl of exasperation, he headed into the hallway, only to reappear with a blanket. "Get rid of those wet clothes. You can wrap up in this."

She stared at the blanket and then at him. "I'm not takin' off my clothes!"

Cain frowned. "You're cold."

"I'm not cold!"

"Your teeth are chattering."

"Are not!"

"Damn it, boy, it's three o'clock in the morning, I lost two hundred dollars at poker tonight, and I'm tired as hell. Now get out of those damned clothes so we can both get some sleep. You can use Magnus's room tonight, and I'd better not hear another sound from you till noon."

"Are you deaf, Yankee? I said I wasn't takin' off any clothes!"

Cain wasn't used to anybody standing up to him, and the grim set of his jaw told her she should have killed him right away. As he took a step forward, she shot toward the basket of apples where she'd hidden her gun, only to jerk to a stop when he caught her arm.

"Oh, no, you don't!"

"Let me go, you son of a bitch!"

She started swinging, but Cain was holding her at arm's length. "I told you to take off those wet clothes, and you're going to do what I say so I can get some damn sleep!"

"You can rot in hell, Yankee!" She swung

again, but her blow bounced off as harmlessly as thistledown.

"Stop it before you get hurt." He shook her once as a warning.

"Go fuck yourself!"

Her hat flew off as she felt herself being lifted off the floor. There was a clap of thunder, Cain sank down onto a kitchen chair, and she found herself upended over his outstretched knee.

"I'm going to do you a favor." His open palm slammed down on her bottom.

"Hey!"

"I'm going to teach you a lesson your father should have taught you."

Once again his hand came down, and she cried out, more from indignation than from pain. "Stop it, you rotten Yankee bastard!"

"Never cuss at people who are bigger than you are..."

He gave her another hard, stinging smack.

"Or stronger than you are..."

Her bottom began to burn.

"And most of all..."

The next two smacks left her bottom on fire.

"...don't cuss at me!" He pushed her off his lap. "Now, do we understand each other or not?"

She sucked in her breath as she landed on the floor. Fury and pain swirled in a haze around her, clouding her vision, so she didn't see him reaching for her. "You're going to get out of these clothes."

His hand clamped her wet shirt. With a howl of rage, she leaped to her feet.

The old, worn fabric ripped in his hand.

After that, everything happened at once. Cool air touched her flesh. She heard the faint patter of buttons skittering across the wooden floor. She looked down and saw her small breasts exposed to his gaze.

"What in the—"

A sense of horror and humiliation suffocated her.

He released her slowly and took a step back. She grabbed for the torn edges of her shirt and tried to pull them together.

Eyes the color of frozen pewter stared down at her. "So. My stable boy isn't a boy after all."

She clutched the shirt and tried to hide her humiliation behind belligerence. "What difference does it make? I needed a job."

"And you got one by passing yourself off as a boy."

"You're the one who assumed I was a boy. I never said any such thing."

"You never said any different, either." He picked up the blanket and tossed it to her. "Dry yourself off while I get myself a drink." He moved toward the hallway door. "I'll expect some answers when I come back, and don't even think about running away, because that'd be your biggest mistake yet."

After he disappeared, she flung down the blanket and raced toward the basket of apples to retrieve the revolver. She sat at the table to hide it in her lap. Only then did she gather her tattered shirttails together and tie them in a clumsy knot at her waist.

Cain stalked back just as she realized how unsatisfactory the result was. He'd ripped her undershirt along with her shirt, and a deep V of exposed flesh extended down to the knot.

Cain took a sip of whiskey and stared at the girl. She was sitting at the wooden table, her hands folded out of sight in her lap, the soft fabric of her shirt clearly outlining a pair of small breasts. How could he have believed for a moment that she was a boy? Those delicate bones should have been a giveaway, along with her eyelashes, which were thick enough to sweep the floor.

The dirt had thrown him off. The dirt and the cussing, not to mention that pugnacious attitude. What a scamp.

He wondered how old she was. Fourteen or so? He knew a lot about women, but not about girls. When did they start growing breasts? One thing for sure...she was too young to be on her own.

He set down his whiskey tumbler. "Where's your family?"

"I told you. They're dead."

"You don't have any relatives at all?"

"No."

Her composure annoyed him. "Look, a child your age can't run around New York City alone. It isn't safe."

"The only person who's given me trouble since I got here's been you."

She had a point, but he ignored it. "Regardless. Tomorrow I'll take you to some people who'll be responsible for you until you're older. They'll find a place for you to live."

"Are you talkin' 'bout an orphanage, Major?"

It irritated him that she seemed amused. "Yes, I'm talking about an orphanage! You sure as hell—heck—aren't going to stay here. You need some place to live until you're old enough to look after yourself."

"Doesn't seem to me I've had too much trouble up till now. Besides, I'm not exactly a child. I don't think orphanages take in eighteen-year-olds."

"Eighteen?"

"You havin' trouble hearing?"

Once again she'd managed to shock him. He stared down the length of the table at her—ragged boy's clothing, a grimy face and neck, short black hair that was stiff with dirt. In his experience, eighteen-year-olds were nearly women. They wore dresses and took baths. But then, nothing about her bore the slightest resemblance to a normal eighteen-year-old.

"Sorry to spoil all your nice plans for an orphanage, Major."

She had the nerve to smirk, and he was suddenly glad he'd spanked her. "Now, you listen to me, Kit—or is your name phony, too?"

"No. It's my real name, all right. Leastways it's what most everybody calls me."

Her amusement faded, and he felt a prickling at the base of his spine, the same sensation he'd felt before a battle. Odd.

He watched her jaw set. "Except my last name's not Finney," she said. "It's Weston. Katharine Louise Weston."

It was her last surprise. Before Cain could react, she was on her feet, and he was looking down into the barrel of an army revolver.

"Son of a bitch," he muttered.

Without taking her eyes from him, she came around the edge of the table. The gun pointing at his heart was steady in her small hand, and everything fell into place.

"Doesn't seem to me you're so particular about cussin' when you're the one doin' it," she said.

He took a step toward her and was immediately sorry. A bullet whizzed by his head, just missing his temple.

Kit had never fired a gun indoors, and her ears rang. She realized her knees were shaking, and she tightened her grip on the revolver. "Don't move unless I tell you, Yankee," she spat out with more bravado than she felt. "Next time it'll be your ear."

"Maybe you'd better tell me what this is all about."

"It's self-evident."

"Humor me."

She hated the faint air of mockery in his voice. "It's about Risen Glory, you black-hearted son of a bitch! It's mine! You've got no right to it."

"That's not what the law says."

"I don't care about the law. I don't care about wills or courts or any of that. What's right is right. Risen Glory is mine, and no Yankee's takin' it from me."

"If your father'd wanted you to have it, he'd have left it to you instead of Rosemary."

"That woman made him blind and deaf as well as a fool."

"Did she?"

She hated the cool, assessing look in his eyes, and she wanted to hurt him as she'd been hurt. "I suppose I should be grateful to her," she sneered. "Hadn't of been for Rosemary's easy ways with men, the Yankees would've burned the house as well as the fields. Your mother was well known for sharin' her favors with anybody who asked."

Cain's face was expressionless. "She was a slut."

"That's God's truth, Yankee. And I'm not goin' to let her get the best of me, even from the grave."

"So now you're going to kill me."

He sounded almost bored, and her palms began to sweat. "Without you standin' in my way, Risen Glory will be mine, just what should of happened in the first place."

"I see your point." He nodded slowly. "All right, I'm ready. How do you want to go about it?"

"What?"

"Killing me. How are you going to do it? Do you want me to turn around so you won't have to look me in the face when you pull the trigger?"

Outrage overcame her distress. "What kind

of fool jackass thing is that to say? You think I could ever respect myself again if I shot a man in the back?"

"Sorry, it was just a suggestion."

"A damn fool one." A trickle of sweat slid down her neck.

"I was trying to make it easier for you, that's all."

"Don't you worry about me, Yankee. You worry about your own immortal soul."

"All right, then. Go to it."

She swallowed. "I intend to."

She lifted her arm and sighted down the barrel of her revolver. It felt as heavy as a cannon in her hand.

"You ever killed a man, Kit?"

"You be quiet!" The trembling in her knees had grown worse, and her arm was beginning to shake. Cain, on the other hand, looked as relaxed as if he'd just awakened from a nap.

"Hit me right between the eyes," he said softly.

"Shut up!"

"It'll be fast and sure that way. The back of my head will blow off, but you can handle the mess, can't you, Kit?"

Her stomach roiled. "Shut up! Just shut up!"

"Come on, Kit. Get it over with."

"Shut up!"

The gun exploded. Once, twice, three times, more. And then the click of an empty chamber.

Cain hit the floor with the first shot. As the

kitchen once again fell silent, he looked up. On the wall behind where he'd been standing, five holes formed the outline of a man's head.

Kit stood with her shoulders slumped, her arms at her sides. The revolver dangled uselessly from her hand.

He eased himself up and walked over to the wall that had received the lead balls originally intended for him. As he studied the perfect arc, he slowly shook his head. "I'll say this for you, kid. You're one hell of a shot."

For Kit, the world had come to an end. She'd lost Risen Glory, and she had no one to blame but herself.

"Coward," she whispered. "I'm a damn, lily-livered coward of a girl."

3

Cain made Kit sleep in a small, second-story bedroom that night instead of in her pleasant leather- and dust-scented room above the stalls. His orders were precise. Until he decided what to do with her, she couldn't work with the horses. And if she tried to run away, he'd bar her from Risen Glory forever.

The next morning, she fled back to the stable and huddled miserably in the corner with a book called *The Sybaritic Life of Louis XV*, which she'd sneaked out of the library several days earlier. After a while, she dozed off and dreamed of thunderstorms, bonnets, and the King of France romping with his mistress, Madame de Pompadour, across the cotton-laced fields of Risen Glory.

When she awoke, she felt groggy and heavy-limbed. She slumped dejectedly outside Apollo's stall with her elbows resting on the greasy knees of her britches. In all her planning, she'd never anticipated what it would feel like to look an unarmed man square in the eye and pull the trigger.

The stable door opened, letting in the feeble light of an overcast afternoon. Merlin scampered across the floor and flung himself at Kit, nearly knocking her hat off in his exuberance. Magnus followed at a more leisurely pace, his boots stopping near her own.

She refused to lift her eyes. "I'm not in the mood for conversation right now, Magnus."

"Can't say I'm surprised. The major told me what happened last night. That was some trick you pulled, *Miss* Kit."

It was the form of address she was accustomed to hearing at home, but he made it sound like an insult. "What happened last night was between me and the major. It's none of your business."

"I don't like misjudging people, and as far as I'm concerned, there's nothin' about you that's any of my business anymore." He picked up an empty bucket and left the stable.

She threw down her book, grabbed a brush,

and headed into the stall that housed a russet mare named Saratoga. She didn't care what Cain's orders were. If she didn't keep busy, she'd go crazy.

She was running her hands down Saratoga's hind legs when she heard the door open. Jumping up, she whirled around to see Cain standing in the center aisle of the stable, regarding her with granite-hard eyes.

"My orders were clear, Kit. No work in the stable."

"The good Lord gave me two strong arms," she retorted. "I'm no good at sittin' idle."

"Grooming horses isn't an appropriate activity for a young lady."

She stared at him hard, trying to see if he was making fun of her, but she couldn't read his expression. "If there's work to be done, I believe in doin' it. A sybaritic life doesn't appeal to me."

"Stay away from the stable," he said tightly.

She opened her mouth to protest, but he was too quick for her. "No arguments. I want you cleaned up and in the library after dinner so I can talk to you." He turned on his heel and strode out the stable door, his powerful, long-legged gait too graceful for a man of his size.

Kit reached the library first that evening. In token obedience to Cain's orders, she'd scrubbed the middle of her face, but she felt too vulnerable to do any more. She needed to feel strong now, not like a girl.

The door opened, and Cain came into the room. He was dressed in his customary at-home uniform of fawn trousers and white shirt, open at the throat. His eyes flicked over her. "I thought I told you to get cleaned up."

"I washed my face, didn't I?"

"It's going to take a lot more than that. How can you stand to be so filthy?"

"I don't hold much with baths."

"Seems to me there are a lot of things you don't 'hold much' with. But you're taking a bath before you spend another night here. Edith Simmons is threatening to quit, and I'll be damned if I lose a housekeeper because of you. Besides, you stink up the place."

"I do not!"

"Hell you don't. Even if it's only temporary, I *am* your guardian, and right now you're taking orders from me."

Kit froze. "What you talkin' about, Yankee? What do you mean, 'guardian'?"

"And here I thought there wasn't anything that got past you."

"Tell me!"

She thought she saw a flash of sympathy in his eyes. It disappeared as he explained the details of the guardianship and the fact that he was also the administrator of her trust fund.

Kit barely remembered the grandmother who'd set aside the money for her. The trust fund had been a constant source of resentment to Rosemary, and she'd forced Garrett to consult one lawyer after another about breaking it, to no avail. Although Kit supposed she should be grateful to her grandmother, the money was useless. She needed it now, not in five years or when she got married, which she wouldn't ever do.

"The guardianship is Rosemary's joke from the grave," Cain concluded.

"That damn lawyer didn't say anything to me about a guardian. I don't believe you."

"I've seen your temper firsthand. Did you give him a chance to explain?"

With a sinking heart, she remembered how she'd forced him out of the house as soon as he'd told her about Cain's inheritance, even though he'd said there was more.

"What did you mean earlier about it bein' a temporary state?"

"You don't think I'm going to let myself be saddled with you for the next five years, do you?" The Hero of Missionary Ridge actually shuddered. "Early tomorrow morning, I'm leaving for South Carolina to get this mess straightened out. Mrs. Simmons will watch over you until I get back. It shouldn't be much more than three or four weeks."

She clasped her hands behind her back so he couldn't see that they'd started to tremble. "How're you plannin' on straightening things out?"

"I'm going to find you another guardian, that's how."

She dug her fingernails into her palms, terrified to ask her next question, yet knowing she had to. "What's goin' to happen...to Risen Glory?"

He studied the toe of his boot. "I'm going to sell it."

Something like a growl erupted from Kit's throat. "No!"

He raised his head and met her eyes. "I'm sorry, Kit. It's for the best."

Kit heard the note of steel in his voice, and felt the few fragile remnants of the only world she knew snap. She didn't even notice when Cain left the room.

Cain needed to get ready for a high-stakes game in one of the Astor House's private dining rooms. Instead, he wandered to the bedroom window. Not even the prospect of the late-night invitation he'd received from a famous opera singer lifted his spirits. It all seemed like too much trouble.

He thought about the violet-eyed scamp under his roof. Earlier, when he'd told her he was selling Risen Glory, she'd looked as though he'd shot her.

His rumination was interrupted by the shatter of glass and his housekeeper's scream. He swore and dashed into the hall.

The bathroom was a shambles. Broken glass lay near the copper tub, and clothing was scattered across the floor. A container of talc had spilled over the marble basin and dusted the black walnut wainscoting. Only the water in the tub was undisturbed, pale gold in the light of the gas jets.

Kit was holding Mrs. Simmons at bay with a

mirror. She had the handle clenched in one fist like a saber. Her other hand gripped a towel around her naked body as she backed the unfortunate housekeeper to the door. "Nobody's givin' me a bath! You get out of here!"

"What the hell's going on?"

Mrs. Simmons grabbed him. "That hoyden's trying to murder me! She threw a bottle of witch hazel! It just missed my head." She fanned her face and moaned. "I can feel an attack of my neuralgia coming on."

"Go lie down, Edith." Cain's flint-hard eyes found Kit. "I'll take over."

The housekeeper was too upset to protest the impropriety of leaving him alone with his naked ward, and she fled down the hallway muttering darkly of neuralgia and hoydens.

For all of Kit's bravado, he could see that she was frightened. Briefly he considered relenting, but he knew he wouldn't be doing her a favor. The world was a dangerous place for women, but it was doubly treacherous for naive little girls who believed they were as tough as men. Kit had to learn how to bend or she'd break, and right now he seemed to be the only one who could teach her that lesson.

Slowly, he unfastened the cuffs of his shirt and began rolling them up.

Kit watched the tanned, muscular forearms emerging as he turned up his sleeves. She took a quick step backward, her eyes glued to his arms. "What do you think you're doing?"

"I told you to take a bath."

Dry-mouthed, she drew her eyes away. It was

hard enough facing down Baron Cain when she was fully clothed. Now, with only a towel wrapped around her, she'd never felt so vulnerable. If he hadn't locked away her gun, she could have pulled the trigger without a second thought.

She licked her lips. "You'd...you'd better stop that right now."

His eyes drilled into hers. "I told you to take a bath, and that's what you're going to do."

She raised the tortoiseshell mirror. "Don't come any closer. I mean it. When I threw that witch hazel bottle at Mrs. Simmons, I intended to miss. This time I won't!"

"It's time you grew up," he said too quietly.

Her heart pounded. "I mean it, Yankee! Not a step farther."

"You're eighteen—old enough to act like a woman. It's one thing to go after me, but you went after someone who never did you any harm."

"She took my clothes away when I wasn't paying attention! And...and then she dragged me in here."

Kit still didn't know how Mrs. Simmons had managed to get her to the bathroom, except that after Cain announced that he was selling Risen Glory, she'd gone numb. It was only when the old lady started pulling away her clothes that Kit had come to her senses.

He spoke again, using the calm voice she found more frightening than his roar. "You should have remembered your manners. Since you didn't, I'll put you in that tub."

She flung the mirror against the wall as a distraction and darted past him.

He caught her before she'd gone three steps. "You don't want to learn, do you?"

"Let me go!"

Glass crunched under the soles of his shoes as he snatched her up in his arms and dropped her in the tub, towel and all.

"You filthy, stinkin'—"

That was as far as she got before he caught the top of her head and pushed her under the water.

She came up sputtering. "You dirty—"

He pushed her back under.

"You—"

He did it again.

Kit couldn't believe what was happening. He didn't keep her under long enough to drown her, but that didn't matter. It was the indignity. And if she couldn't hold her tongue, she'd be going under again. She glared at him as she came up, but she somehow managed to keep silent.

"Had enough yet?" he asked mildly.

She wiped her eyes and mustered her dignity. "Your behavior is puerile."

He began to smile, only to stop as he gazed into the tub.

That was when she realized that she'd lost her towel.

She drew up her knees to hide her body. "You get out of here right now!" Water splashed over the rim as she tried to retrieve the towel from the bottom of the tub.

He took a quick backward step toward the door, then stopped.

She hovered over her knees and struggled with the sodden towel.

He cleared his throat. "Can you, uh, take it from here?"

She thought she detected a flush spreading over those hard cheekbones. She nodded and yanked at the heavy towel.

"I'll get one of my shirts for you to put on. But if I find a speck of dirt when you're finished, we'll start all over again."

He disappeared without closing the door. She gritted her teeth and imagined buzzards eating his eyeballs.

She washed herself twice, dislodging grime that had been comfortably residing in the nooks and crannies of her body for some time. Then she scrubbed her hair. When she was finally satisfied that even Jesus's Mother couldn't find any dirt on her, she stood to grab a dry towel but saw that the tub was surrounded with broken glass like a moat around a medieval castle.

This was what came of taking baths.

She cussed as she wrapped the sodden towel around herself, then shouted toward the open door. "Listen up, Yankee! I need you to throw me a dry towel, but you'd better keep your eyes shut, or I swear I'll murder you in your sleep, then cut you open and eat your liver for breakfast."

"It's nice to know that soap and water haven't spoiled your sweet disposition." He reappeared in the doorway, eyes wide open. "I was worried about that."

"Yeah, well, you just worry about holdin' onto your internal organs."

He grabbed a towel from the shelf across the bathroom, but instead of handing it to her like a decent person, he gazed down at the broken glass. *"Every faculty which is a receiver of pleasure has an equal penalty for its abuse.* Ralph Waldo Emerson, in case you don't recognize the quote."

Only after he'd passed over the towel did she feel safe in responding. "Mr. Emerson also wrote, *Every hero becomes a bore at last.* If I didn't know better, I'd think you inspired those very words."

Cain chuckled, somehow glad to see she still had her spirit. She was thin as a filly, all bony arms and long, skinny legs. Even the hint of dark fleece he'd glimpsed when her towel had fallen off in the tub had been somehow childlike.

As he turned away, he remembered her small, coral-tipped breasts. They'd seemed less innocent. The image made him uncomfortable, and he spoke more gruffly than he intended. "Are you dry yet?"

"Dry as I'm goin' to get with you standin' there."

"Wrap up. I'm turning around."

"And here I was just thinkin' how nice it is not having to look at your ugly face."

Aggravated, he stalked over to the tub. "I should make you walk through this glass in your bare feet."

"Couldn't be any more painful than enduring your bumptious company."

He snatched her from the tub, carried her out into the hall, and set her hard on her feet. "I put a shirt in your bedroom. Tomorrow Mrs. Simmons will take you shopping for some decent clothes."

She regarded him suspiciously. "Just what do you consider decent clothes?"

He knew what was coming next, and he braced himself. "Dresses, Kit."

"Have you *lost your mind?*"

She looked so outraged that he nearly smiled, but he wasn't that stupid. Time to draw in the reins. "You heard me. And while I'm gone, you'll do exactly what Mrs. Simmons tells you. If you give her any trouble, I'm leaving orders with Magnus to lock you in your room and throw away the key. I mean it, Kit. When I get back I'd better hear that you behaved yourself. I intend to turn you over to your new guardian clean and respectably dressed."

The emotions that played over her face ranged from indignation to anger, then settled into something that looked uncomfortably like despair. Water from the dripping ends of her hair splashed like tears onto her thin shoulders, and her voice was no longer its normal bellow. "Are you really gonna do it?"

"Of course I'll find another guardian for you. You should be happy about that."

Her knuckles turned white as she clutched the towel. "That's not what I mean. Are you really goin' to sell Risen Glory?"

Cain hardened himself against the suffering in that small face. He had no intention of being burdened with a run-down cotton plantation, but she wouldn't understand that. "I'm not keeping the money, Kit. It'll go into your trust fund."

"I don't care about that money! You can't sell Risen Glory."

"I have to. Someday maybe you'll understand."

Kit's eyes darkened into killing pools. "The biggest mistake I made was not blowin' your head off."

Her small, towel-draped figure was strangely dignified as she walked away from him and shut her bedroom door.

4

"Do you mean to tell me there isn't anyone in this entire community who'd be willing to take over the guardianship of Miss Weston? Not even if I pay her expenses?" Cain studied the Reverend Rawlins Ames Cogdell of Rutherford, South Carolina, who studied him in return.

"You must understand, Mr. Cain. We've all known Katharine Louise a good deal longer than you have."

Rawlins Cogdell prayed that God would

forgive him for the satisfaction he was taking in putting a spoke in this Yankee's wheel. The Hero of Missionary Ridge, indeed! How galling it was to be forced to entertain such a man. But what else was he to do? These days blue-uniformed occupation troops were everywhere, and even a man of God had to be careful not to offend.

His wife, Mary, appeared in the doorway with a plate holding four tiny finger sandwiches, each one spread with a thin glaze of strawberry preserves. "Am I interrupting?"

"No, no. Come in, my dear. Mr. Cain, you do have a treat in store for you. My wife is famous for her strawberry preserves."

The preserves were from the bottom of the last jar his wife had put up two springs ago when there was still sugar, and the bread was sliced from a loaf that had to last them the rest of the week. Still, Rawlins was pleased she was offering it. He would sooner starve than let this man know how poor they all were.

"None for me, my dear. I'll save my appetite for dinner. Please, Mr. Cain, take two."

Cain wasn't nearly as obtuse as Cogdell believed. He knew what a sacrifice the offering on the chipped blue willowware plate was. He took a sandwich even though there was nothing he wanted less and made the required compliments. Damn all Southerners. Six hundred thousand lives had been lost because of their stiff-necked pride.

Cain believed their arrogance was a product

of the disease of the slave system. The planters had lived like omnipotent kings on isolated plantations, where they held absolute authority over hundreds of slaves. It had given them a terrible conceit. They'd believed they were all-powerful, and defeat had changed them only superficially. A Southern family might be starving, but tea sandwiches would still be offered to a guest, even a despised one.

The Reverend Cogdell turned to his wife. "Please sit down, my dear. Perhaps you can help us. Mr. Cain finds himself on the horns of a dilemma."

She did as her husband requested and listened as he outlined Cain's connection with Rosemary Weston and the fact that he wanted to transfer his guardianship of Kit. When her husband was finished, she shook her head.

"I'm afraid what you want is impossible, Mr. Cain. There are a number of families who would have been only too happy to take Katharine Louise in during her formative years. But it's too late for that. My goodness, she's eighteen now."

"Hardly a Methuselah," Cain said dryly.

"Standards of behavior are different in South Carolina than they are in the North." Her rebuke was softly spoken. "Girls of good family are raised from birth in the gracious traditions of Southern womanhood. Not only has Katharine Louise never shown any inclination to conform to these traditions, but she mocks them. The families of our community would be concerned about the influence Katharine would have on their own daughters."

Cain felt a spark of pity for Kit. It couldn't have been easy growing up with a stepmother who hated her, a father who ignored her, and a community that disapproved of her. "Isn't there anyone in this town who feels affection for her?"

Mary's small hands fluttered in her lap. "Gracious, Mr. Cain, you misunderstand. We're all deeply fond of her. Katharine Louise is a generous and warmhearted person. Her hunting skills have put food in the mouths of our poorest families, and she never fails to cheer us up. But that doesn't alter the fact that she conducts herself outside even the most liberally defined boundaries of acceptable behavior."

Cain had played too much poker not to know when he was beaten. Willard Ritter had given him letters of introduction to four families in Rutherford, and he'd been rejected by all of them. He finished his cursed jelly sandwich and took his leave.

As he rode back to Risen Glory on the bony mare he'd hired at a livery stable in Charleston, he faced the unpleasant truth. Like it or not, he was stuck with Kit.

The plantation house came into view. It was a handsome, two-story structure of stucco-covered brick that sat at the end of a twisting overgrown drive. Despite the general air of neglect from peeling paint and broken shutters, the place was sturdy. The house had weathered to a warm shade of cream with bricks and mortar visible beneath the stucco. Live oaks heavy with Spanish moss shaded each end and draped the tiled roof. Azaleas, smilax, and holly spilled from overgrown beds, while magnolias scattered their waxy leaves across the knee-high grass of the front yard.

But it wasn't the house that had caught Cain's interest when he'd arrived two days ago. Instead, he'd spent the afternoon inspecting the ruins of the burned outbuildings, crawling over broken machinery, setting aside rusted tools, and occasionally stopping in an empty field to pick up a handful of rich soil. It trickled through his fingers like warm silk. Once again he found himself thinking about New York City and how it had begun to suffocate him.

Cain turned his horse over to Eli, the bent old man and former slave who'd met him with a shotgun the day Cain had arrived at Risen Glory.

"That's far enough," he'd said. "Miz Kit told me to shoot anybody steps foot on Risen Glory."

"Miss Kit needs to have her britches tanned," Cain had replied, not adding that he'd already done the job.

"You sure enough right 'bout that. But I still have to shoot you if you come any closer."

Cain could have disarmed the old man without difficulty, but he'd wanted his cooperation, so he'd taken the time to explain his relationship to Kit and Rosemary Weston. When Eli understood that Cain wasn't one of the fancy scalawags who'd been preying on the countryside, he'd put down his shotgun and welcomed him to Risen Glory.

The middle of the house curved in a graceful bow. Cain stepped into the wide center hallway that had been designed to carry a breeze. Parlors, a music room, and a library opened off it, everything shabby and dust-shrouded. The handsome teak table in the dining room bore fresh gouges. Sherman's troops had carted it outside and used it to butcher the plantation's remaining livestock.

Cain caught the scent of fried chicken. Eli couldn't cook, and as far as he knew, there was no one else in the house. The former slaves, enticed by the promise of forty acres and a mule, had gone off after the Union army. He wondered if the mysterious Sophronia had returned. Eli had made several references to Risen Glory's cook, but Cain hadn't yet seen her.

"Evenin', Major."

Cain stopped in his tracks as a small, much-too-familiar figure appeared at the end of the hallway. Then he began to curse.

Kit's hands twisted nervously at her sides. She wasn't moving any closer until he'd had a chance to adjust.

She'd left Cain's house in New York the same way she'd entered it. Over the back wall. She'd taken her bundle with her, along with *The Sybaritic Life of Louis XV*, which was the inspiration for the desperate plan she'd conceived the day after Cain left.

Now she plastered a smile on her face that

was so big and fat it made her cheeks ache. "I sure hope you're hungry, Major. I got some fried chicken and hot buttermilk biscuits just beggin' for somebody with an appetite. I even scrubbed down the table in the dining room so we could eat there. 'Course, it's kinda scratched up, but it's a gen-u-wine Sheraton. You ever heard of Sheraton, Major? He was a Englishman and a Baptist to boot. Doesn't that seem strange to you? Seems like only Southerners should be Baptists. I—"

"What in the hell are you doing here?"

She'd known he'd be mad, but she'd hoped he wouldn't be quite this mad. Frankly, she wasn't sure she was up to it. She'd endured the train trip back to Charleston, a bone-jarring wagon ride, and, just today, a fifteen-mile hike that had left her with blisters and a sunburn. The last of her money had gone to buy food for tonight's dinner. She'd even taken a bath in the kitchen and changed into a clean shirt and britches so she didn't smell. She was surprised to discover that she liked being clean. Taking baths hadn't turned out to be such a bad idea after all, even if it did mean she had to look at her naked breasts.

She attempted a simper even though it about curdled her stomach. "Cookin' dinner for you, Major. That's what I'm doin'."

He clenched his teeth. "No. What you're doing is getting ready to *die*. Because I'm going to *kill you!*"

She didn't exactly believe him, but she

didn't entirely disbelieve him, either. "Don't you yell at me! You'd of done the same thing!"

"What are you talking about?"

"You wouldn't have stayed up there in New York City while somebody was takin' away the only thing in your life you ever cared about! You wouldn't have sat in that fancy bedroom readin' books and tryin' on ugly dresses while it all slipped away. You'd of got yourself back to South Carolina as fast as you could, just like me. And then you'd have done anything you had to so you could keep what was yours."

"And I'm getting a pretty good idea what you've decided to do." In two long strides, he closed the distance between them. Before she could jump back, he began to rake his hands over her body.

"Stop that!"

"Not till you're disarmed."

She gasped as he touched her breasts. A tingle of sensation shot through her, but he didn't seem affected. He moved on to her waist and her hips.

"Stop it!"

He found the knife strapped to her calf. "Were you planning to use this on me when I was asleep?"

"If I didn't have the guts to kill you with a gun, I'd hardly do it with a knife, now, would I?"

"I suppose you were carrying it to open cans?"

"You took my gun. I couldn't travel without some kind of protection."

"I see." He set the knife out of her reach. "Then if you're not planning to kill me, what do you have in mind?"

This wasn't going the way Kit had hoped. She wanted to tell him to stop towering over her, but she wasn't that much of a fool. "Why don't we eat dinner first, and then I'll tell you? Food's hard to come by. No sense in lettin' everything get all dried out."

He took a moment making up his mind. "All right, we'll eat. But afterward we're having a serious talk."

She hurried toward the kitchen. "Supper'll be on the table in a minute."

Cain should have confronted her right away, but he was hungry, damn it. He hadn't eaten a decent meal since he'd left New York.

He disposed of her knife, then stalked back into the dining room. Kit appeared with a platter of fried chicken she placed on the table, and he finally noticed what had escaped him earlier. Everything about her was clean. From her cropped hair to the plaid shirt with a button missing at the neck to the dark brown britches that hung loosely on her small hips, she was scrubbed up as shiny as a new penny. He hadn't imagined anything short of force convincing her to bathe voluntarily. She was obviously prepared to go to drastic lengths to please him.

Not that she was going to have any success. He still couldn't believe she'd done this. But then, why not? She didn't understand the meaning of caution.

"Sit down and eat, Major. I sure hope you're hungry."

Cain had to admit it was a great meal. The chicken was fried a gold brown and steam rose from the buttermilk biscuits when he split them open. Even the dandelion greens were richly flavored.

When he'd eaten his fill, he leaned back in the chair. "You didn't do this by yourself."

"'Course I did. Normally Sophronia would have helped, but she's not here."

"Sophronia's the cook?"

"She also looked after me when I was growing up."

"She didn't do a very good job of it."

Those violet eyes narrowed. "I've got half a mind to comment on your upbringing, too."

The food had mellowed him, so this time she didn't get his dander up. "Everything was delicious."

She rose to fetch a bottle of brandy she'd put on the sideboard earlier. "Rosemary hid this before the Yankees came. Thought you might like to have a glass to celebrate your arrival at Risen Glory."

"Trust my mother to take better care of the liquor than she did of her stepdaughter." He took the bottle and began prying out the cork. "How did Risen Glory get its name? It's unusual."

"It happened not long after my granddaddy built the house." Kit leaned against the sideboard. "A Baptist preacher man came to the door askin' for a meal, and even though my grandma was strict Methodist, she fed him. They got to talkin', and when he heard the plantation didn't have a name yet, he said they should call it Risen Glory on account of it was almost Easter Sunday. It's been Risen Glory ever since."

"I see." He fished a piece of cork from his glass of brandy. "I think it's time you tell me what you're doing here."

Her stomach lurched. She watched him take a sip, his eyes staying on her the whole time. He never missed anything.

She moved toward the open doors that led from the dining room to the overgrown garden. It was dark and quiet outside, and she could smell honeysuckle in the night breeze. She loved it all so much. The trees and brooks, the sights and smells. Best of all, she loved watching the fields dance white with cotton. Soon, they'd be that way again.

Slowly she turned back to him. Everything depended on the next few minutes, and she had to do it right. "I came here to make a proposal to you, Major."

"I resigned my commission. Why don't you just call me Baron?"

"If it's all the same, I'll just go on callin' you 'Major'."

"I suppose it's better than some of the other things you've called me." He kicked back in the chair. Unlike a proper Southern gentleman, he'd hadn't worn a cravat to the table, and his collar was open. For a moment she found herself staring at the strong muscles in his neck. She forced herself to look away.

"Tell me about this proposal of yours."

"Well..." She tried to suck in some air. "As you might of guessed, your part of the bargain would be to hang onto Risen Glory until I can buy it back from you."

"I figured that."

"You wouldn't be stuck with it forever," she hastened to add. "Just for five years, until I can get to the money in my trust fund."

He studied her. She caught her bottom lip between her teeth. This was going to be the hardest part. "I realize you'd expect somethin' in return."

"Of course."

She hated the flicker of amusement in his eyes. "What I'm preparin' to offer is a little unorthodox. But if you think about it, I know you'll see that it's fair." She gulped.

"Go on."

She squeezed her eyes shut, took a deep breath, and let it out. "I'm offerin' to be your mistress."

He choked.

She got the rest out in a rush. "Now, I know this might be taking you by surprise, but even you've got to admit I'm a lot better company than those sorry excuses for females in New York City. I don't giggle and bat my eyes. I couldn't flirt even if I wanted to, and you sure won't ever hear me talkin' about pugs. Best part is, you wouldn't have to worry about goin' to all those balls and stuffy dinner parties most women like. Instead, we could spend our time hunting and fishing and riding horses. We could have a real good time."

Cain started to laugh.

Kit yearned to have her knife back. "You mind tellin' me what you think is so damn *humorous?*"

He finally managed to control himself. He set down his glass and rose from the table. "Kit, do you know why men keep mistresses?"

"Of course I do. I read *The Sybaritic Life of Louis XV*."

He regarded her quizzically.

"Madame de Pompadour," she explained. "She was Louis XV's mistress. I got the idea from readin' 'bout her."

She didn't tell him Madame de Pompadour had also been the most powerful woman in France. She'd managed to control the king and the country just by using her wits. Kit could surely manage to control the fate of Risen Glory if she was the major's mistress. Besides, she didn't have anything but herself to bargain with.

Cain started to say something, stopped, shook his head, then downed what was left of his brandy. When he was done, he looked like he was starting to get mad all over again. "Being a man's mistress involves more than hunting and fishing. Do you have any idea what I'm talking about?"

Kit felt herself flush. This was the part she hadn't let herself dwell on, the part the book hadn't covered at all.

Being raised on a plantation had exposed her to the rudimentary facts of animal reproduction, but it had also left her with a lot of questions that Sophronia refused to answer. Kit suspected she didn't have all the details right, but she knew enough to understand the whole process was disgusting. Still, it would have to be part of the bargain. For some reason, mating was important to men, and women were expected to put up with it, although she couldn't imagine Mrs. Cogdell letting the reverend climb up on her back like that.

"I know what you're talkin' about. And I'm prepared to let you mate with me." She glowered. "Even though I'm gonna *hate it!*"

Cain laughed; then his expression clouded as if he might be thinking about that damn spanking again. He yanked a cheroot from his pocket and stalked out the garden doors to light it.

She followed him outside and found him standing by an old rusty bench, gazing out toward the orchard. She waited for him to say something. When he didn't, she spoke. "Well, what about it?"

"It's the most ridiculous thing I've ever heard."

The glow from his cheroot cast a flickering shadow over his face, and panic welled inside her. This was her only chance to keep Risen Glory. She had to convince him. "Why is it so ridiculous?"

"Because it is."

"You tell me why!"

"I'm your stepbrother."

"Bein' my stepbrother doesn't mean a damn thing. It's purely a legal relationship."

"I'm also your guardian. I couldn't find a single person in this county who was willing to take you off my hands, and judging by your recent behavior, I guess that's no surprise."

"I'll do better! And I'm a real good shot. I can put all the meat on the table you want."

That started him cussing again. "Men aren't looking for somebody who can put meat on the table when they're choosing a mistress, damn it! They want a woman who looks and acts and *smells* like a woman."

"I smell real good! Go on. Smell me!" She lifted her arm so he could get a good whiff, but all he cared about was being mad.

"They want a woman who knows how to smile, and say pretty things, and make love. Now, that leaves you out!"

Kit swallowed her last morsel of pride. "I could learn."

"Oh, for God's sake!" He stalked to the other side of the overgrown gravel path. "I've made up my mind."

"Please! Don't—"

"I'm not selling Risen Glory."

"Not sellin'..." Kit couldn't seem to find her breath, and then a great wave of happiness washed over her. "Oh, Major! That's...that's the most wonderful thing I ever heard!"

"Hold on. There's one condition."

Kit felt a sharp prickle of warning. "No conditions! We don't need any conditions."

He stepped into the amber pool of light spilling out from the dining room. "You have to return to New York and go to school."

"School!" Kit was incredulous. "I'm eighteen years old. I'm too old for school. Besides, I'm already self-educated."

"Not that kind of school. A finishing school. A place that teaches deportment and etiquette and all those other female accomplishments you don't know a damn thing about."

"Finishing school?" She was horrified. "Now, that's the stupidest, most puerile—" She saw the storm clouds gathering in his expression and changed tack. "Let me stay here. Please. I won't be any trouble. Swear to Jesus. I can sleep out back, and you won't even know I'm around. I can make myself useful all kinds of ways. I know this plantation better than anyone. Please let me stay."

"You're going to do as I say."

"No, I—"

"If you don't cooperate, I'll sell Risen Glory so fast you won't know what happened. Then you won't have a prayer of ever getting your hands on it."

She felt sick. Her hatred of him coalesced into a hard, tight ball. "How...how long would I have to go to this school?"

"Until you can behave like a lady, so I guess that's up to you."

"You could keep me there forever."

"All right. Let's say three years."

"That's way too long. I'll be twenty-one by then."

"You've got a lot to learn. Take it or leave it."

She regarded him bitterly. "And then what happens? Will I be able to buy Risen Glory back from you with the money in my trust fund?"

"We'll discuss that when the time comes."

He could keep her away from Risen Glory for years, exiled from everything she loved. She turned away and rushed back into the dining room. She remembered how she'd humiliated herself by offering to be his mistress, and her hatred choked her. When her exile was over and Risen Glory was safe, he was going to pay for this.

"What'll it be, Kit?" he said from behind her.

She could barely force out the words. "You don't give me much choice, do you, Yankee?"

"Well, well, well." A woman's voice, throaty and seductive, rippled in from the hallway. "Will you jes' look at what that child brought back with her from New York City."

"Sophronia!" Kit pitched herself across the dining room and into the arms of the woman who stood in the doorway. "Where you been?"

"Rutherford. Jackson Baker took sick."

Cain stared at the newcomer with surprise. So this was Kit's Sophronia. She was hardly what he'd envisioned.

He'd imagined someone much older, but she looked as if she were in her early twenties, and she was one of the most exotically beautiful women he'd ever seen. Slim and tall, she towered over Kit. She had high, chiseled cheekbones, pale caramel skin, and slanted golden eyes that slowly lifted as he studied her.

Their gazes met and held over the top of Kit's head. Sophronia untangled herself and walked toward him, moving with a languid sensuality that made her simple blue cotton dress seem like a gown of the finest silk. When she was directly in front of him, she stopped and held out her slim hand.

"Welcome to Risen Glory, Boss Man."

Sophronia acted hateful all the way back north on the train. Everything was "yes, sir" and "no, sir" to Cain, smiling at him and taking his side against Kit.

"That's because he's right," Sophronia said when Kit confronted her about it. "It's time you started to act like the woman you were born to be."

"And it's time you started remembering whose side you're supposed to be on."

Sophronia and Kit loved each other more than anyone else on earth, despite being black and white. Which didn't mean they didn't argue. And those arguments only accelerated after they reached New York.

The minute Magnus laid eyes on Sophronia, he started walking around in a daze, and Mrs. Simmons wouldn't stop talking about Sophronia being so wonderful. After three days, Kit was sick of it. Then her already bad mood plummeted even further.

"I look like a jackass!" The dun-colored felt hat sat like a squashed gravy boat on Kit's ragged hair. The material of her ocher jacket was of good quality, but cut too big in the shoulders, and the ugly brown serge dress dragged on the carpet. She looked like she'd dressed up in a spinster aunt's clothes.

Sophronia splayed her long fingers on her hips. "What d'you expect? I told you those clothes Mrs. Simmons bought for you was too big, but you wouldn't pay me no nevermind. You ask me, this is what you get for thinkin' you know so much more than everybody else."

"Just because you're three years older than me and we're in New York City doesn't mean you can act like some kind of queen."

Sophronia's elegant nostrils quivered. "You think you can say anything you want to me. Well, I'm not your slave no more, Kit Weston. You understand me? I don't belong to you. I don't belong to anybody 'cept Jesus!"

Kit didn't like hurting Sophronia's feelings, but sometimes she could be pigheaded. "It's just that you don't ever show any gratitude. I taught you your sums. I taught you how to read and write, even though it was against the law. I hid you from Jesse Overturf that night he wanted to lie with you. And now you're taking that Yankee's side against mine every chance you get."

"Don't you talk to me 'bout gratitude. I spent years keepin' you out of Miz Weston's sight.

And every time she caught you and locked you in that closet, it was me who let you out. I took a whippin' for you. So I don't want to hear anything about gratitude. You're a noose around my neck. Suffocating me. Cutting off my life's breath. If it wasn't for you—"

Abruptly Sophronia broke off as she heard footsteps approaching outside the door. Mrs. Simmons appeared and announced that Cain was waiting below to take Kit to the school he'd chosen.

Just like that, the two combatants found themselves locked in each other's arms. Finally Kit pulled away, picked up her ugly, gravy-boat hat, and walked to the door. "You be careful, hear?" she whispered.

"You mind yourself at that fancy school," Sophronia whispered back.

"I will."

Sophronia's eyes clouded with tears. "We'll be seeing each other again before you know it."

PART TWO

A Templeton Girl

Manners are the happy way of doing things.

RALPH WALDO EMERSON
"CULTURE"

5

The Templeton Academy for Young Ladies sat on Fifth Avenue like a great gray stone whale. Hamilton Woodward, Cain's attorney, had recommended it. Although the school didn't normally take girls as old as Kit, Elvira Templeton had made an exception for the Hero of Missionary Ridge.

Kit stood hesitantly on the threshold of the third-floor room she'd been assigned and studied the five girls wearing identical navy blue dresses with white collars and cuffs. They were clustered around the room's only window to gaze down at the street. It didn't take her long to figure out what they were staring at.

"Oh, Elsbeth, isn't he the handsomest man you ever saw?"

The girl identified as Elsbeth sighed. She had crisp, brown curls and a pretty, fresh face. "Imagine. He was right here in the Academy, and none of us were allowed to go downstairs. It's so unfair!" And then, with a giggle: "My father says he's not really a gentleman."

More giggles.

A beautiful, blond-haired girl who reminded Kit of Dora Van Ness spoke up. "Madame Riccardi, the opera singer, went into a decline when he told her he was moving to South Carolina. Everybody's heard about it. She's his mistress, you know."

"Lilith Shelton!" The girls were deliciously horrified, and Lilith regarded them disdainfully.

"You're all such innocents. A man as sophisticated as Baron Cain has dozens of mistresses."

"Remember what we decided," another girl said. "Even if she is his ward, she's a Southerner, so we all have to hate her."

Kit had heard enough. "If that means I won't ever have to talk to you silly bitches, that's just fine with me."

The girls spun around and gasped. Kit felt their eyes taking in her ugly dress and awful hat. One more item to add to the ledger of hatred she was keeping against Cain. "Get out of here! All of you. And if I catch any of you in here again, I'll kick your skinny asses straight to hell!"

The girls fled the room with horrified shrieks. All but one. The girl they'd called Elsbeth. She stood trembling and terrified, her eyes wide as teacups, her pretty lips trembling.

"Are you deaf or something? I told you to get out."

"I...I c-can't."

"Why the hell not?"

"I...I live here."

"Oh." For the first time, Kit noticed the room had two beds.

The girl was sweet-faced, one of those people with a naturally kind disposition, and Kit couldn't find it in her heart to bully her. At the same time, she was the enemy. "You'll have to move."

"Mrs....Mrs. Templeton won't let me. I—I already asked."

Kit cursed, yanked up her skirts, and sank down on the bed. "How come you were lucky enough to get me?"

"My—my father. He's Mr. Cain's attorney. I'm Elsbeth Woodward."

"I'd say I was pleased to make your acquaintance, but both of us know it'd be a lie."

"I'd...I'd better go."

"You do that."

Elsbeth scampered from the room. Kit lay back on the pillow and tried to figure out how she was going to survive the next three years.

The Templeton Academy used a system of demerits to maintain order. For every ten demerits a girl acquired, she was confined to her room all day Saturday. By the end of her first day, Kit had accumulated eighty-three. (Taking the Lord's name in vain was automatically ten.) By the end of her first week, she'd lost count.

Mrs. Templeton called Kit into her office and threatened her with expulsion if she didn't start following all the rules. Kit had to participate in her classes. She'd been given two uniforms, and she was to start wearing them at once. Her grammar must improve immediately. Ladies didn't say "ain't" or "I reckon." Ladies referred to objects as "unimportant," not "useless as toad spit." And most of all, ladies didn't curse.

Kit remained stoic during the interview, but inside, she was panicky. If the old biddy expelled her, Kit would have broken her agreement with Cain and lost Risen Glory forever.

She vowed to hold onto her temper, but as the days passed, it grew more and more difficult. She was three years older than her classmates, but she knew less than any of them. They snickered at her cropped hair behind her back and giggled when she caught her skirts on a chair. One day the pages of her French book were glued together. Another day her nightgown was tied in knots. She'd gone through life with her fists swinging, and now her future depended on keeping her temper. Instead of retaliating, she collected the insults and stored them away to reexamine late at night as she lay in bed. Someday she'd make Baron Cain pay for every slur.

Elsbeth continued to behave like a frightened mouse whenever she was around Kit. Although she refused to join in Kit's persecution, she was too timid to make the other girls stop. Still, her kind heart couldn't ignore the injustices, especially as she grew to realize that Kit wasn't as ferocious as she seemed.

"It's hopeless," Kit confessed to her one night after she'd tripped over the skirt of her uniform in dance class and sent a Chinese vase crashing from a pedestal. "I'll never learn to dance. I talk too loud, I hate wearing skirts, the only musical instrument I can play is a jew's harp, and I can't look at Lilith Shelton without cussing."

Elsbeth's teacup eyes rounded in worry. "You have to be nicer to her. Lilith is the most popular girl in school."

"And the nastiest."

"I'm sure she doesn't mean to be that way."

"I'm sure she does. You're so nice yourself, you don't recognize ugliness in other people. You don't even seem to be noticin' it in me, and I'm 'bout as bad as they come."

"You're not bad!"

"Yes, I am. But not as bad as all the mean-minded girls who go to this school. I reckon you're the only decent person here."

"That's not true," Elsbeth said earnestly. "Most of them are awfully nice if you just give them a chance. You're so ferocious that you scare them."

Kit's spirits lifted a little. "Thank you. Truth is, I don't know how I could scare anybody. I'm a failure at everything I've done here. I can't imagine how I'm gonna last three years."

"Father didn't tell me you had to stay so long. You'll be twenty-one. That's too old to be in school."

"I know, but I don't have any choice." Kit

fidgeted with the gray woolen coverlet. Ordinarily she didn't believe in sharing confidences, but she was feeling lonelier than she could remember. "Did you ever love somethin' so much you'd do just about anything to keep it safe?"

"Oh, yes. My little sister, Agnes. She's not like other children. Even though she's almost ten, she can't read or write, but she's so sweet, and I'd never let anybody hurt her."

"Then you understand."

"Tell me, Kit. Tell me what's wrong."

And so Kit told her about Risen Glory. She described the fields and the house, talked about Sophronia and Eli, and tried to make Elsbeth see the way the trees changed color depending on the time of day.

Then she told her about Baron Cain. Not everything. Elsbeth would never understand her masquerade as a stable boy or the way she'd tried to kill him, let alone her offer to be his mistress. Still, she told her enough.

"He's evil, and I can't do anything about it. If I get expelled, he'll sell Risen Glory. And if I do manage to last three years here, I'll still have to wait till I'm twenty-three to get control of the money in my trust fund so I can buy it back. The longer I wait, the harder that's going to be."

"Isn't there any way you can use your money before then?"

"Only if I get married. Which I ain't."

Elsbeth was an attorney's daughter. "If you did marry, your husband would control your money. It's the way the law works. You couldn't spend it without his permission."

Kit shrugged. "It's all academic. There's no man in the world I'd shackle myself to. Besides, I was raised all wrong to be a wife. Only thing I can do right is cook."

Elsbeth was sympathetic, but she was also practical. "That's why we're all here. To learn how to be proper wives. The girls from the Templeton Academy are known for making the most successful marriages in New York. That's part of what's so special about being a Templeton girl. Men come from all over the East to attend the graduation ball."

"It doesn't make any difference to me if they come from Paris, France. You'll never see me at any ball."

But Elsbeth had been struck with inspiration, and she wasn't paying attention. "All you have to do is find the right husband. Somebody who wants to make you happy. Then everything will be perfect. You won't be Mr. Cain's ward any longer, and you'll have your money."

"You're a real sweet girl, Elsbeth, but I've got to tell you that's the most ridiculous idea I ever heard. Getting married would just mean I'd be handing another man my money."

"If you picked the right man, it'd be the same as having it yourself. Before you get married, you could make him promise to buy you Risen Glory for a wedding present." She clapped her hands, caught up in her vision. "Just imagine how romantic it would be. You could go back home right after your honeymoon."

Honeymoons and husbands... Elsbeth might have been speaking another language. "That's plain foolishness. What man's goin' to marry me?"

"Stand up!" Elsbeth's voice held the same note of command as Elvira Templeton's, and Kit rose reluctantly.

Elsbeth tapped her finger on her cheek. "You're awfully thin, and your hair is horrible. Of course it'll grow," she added politely, "and it is a beautiful color, all soft and inky. Even now it'd look quite nice if it were cut a little straighter. Your eyes are too big for your face, but I think that's because you're so thin." Slowly she circled Kit. "You're going to be quite pretty someday, so I don't think we'll have to worry about that."

Kit scowled. "Just what *will* we have to worry about?"

But Elsbeth was no longer intimidated by her. "Everything else. You have to learn to talk and to walk, what to say and, even more important, what not to say. You'll have to learn everything the Academy teaches. You're lucky that Mr. Cain provided you with such a generous clothing allowance."

"Which I don't need. What I need is a horse."

"Horses won't help you get a husband. But the Academy will."

"I don't know how. I haven't exactly made a success of it so far."

"No, you haven't." Elsbeth's sweet smile grew impish. "But then, you haven't had me helping you, either."

The idea was silly, but Kit felt her first spark of hope.

As the weeks passed, Elsbeth was as good as her word. She trimmed Kit's hair with manicure scissors and tutored her in the subjects in which she'd fallen behind. Eventually Kit stopped knocking over vases in dancing class and discovered she had a flair for needlework—not embroidering fancy samplers, which she detested, but adding flamboyant touches to garments such as school uniforms. (Ten demerits.) She was a whiz at French, and before long, she was tutoring the girls who had once mocked her.

By Easter, Elsbeth's plan for her to find a husband no longer seemed so ridiculous, and Kit began to fall asleep dreaming that Risen Glory was hers forever.

Just imagine.

Sophronia was no longer the cook at Risen Glory, but the plantation's housekeeper. She tucked Kit's letter away in the inlaid mahogany desk where she kept the household records and pulled her shawl more tightly around her shoulders to ward off the February chill. Kit had been at the Templeton Academy for seven months now, and she finally seemed resigned to her fate.

Sophronia missed her. Kit was blind in a lot of ways, but she also understood things other people didn't. Besides, Kit was the only person in the world who loved her. Still, they somehow always managed to quarrel, even in letters, and this was the first correspondence Sophronia had received from her in a month.

Sophronia thought about sitting down to answer it right away, but she knew she'd put it off, especially after the last time. Her letters only seemed to make Kit mad. You'd think she'd be glad to hear how well Risen Glory was doing now that Cain was running the place, but she accused Sophronia of siding with the enemy.

Sophronia gazed around the comfortable rear sitting room. She took in the new rose damask upholstery on the settee and the way the delft tiles bordering the fireplace sparkled in the sunlight. Everything shone with beeswax, fresh paint, and care.

Sometimes she hated herself for working so hard to make this house beautiful again. Working her fingers to the bone for the man, just as if there'd never been a war and she was still a slave. But now she was getting paid. Good wages, too, better than any other housekeeper in the county. Still, Sophronia wasn't satisfied.

She moved toward her reflection in the gilt pier glass that hung between the windows. She'd never looked better. Regular meals had softened the chiseled bones in her face and rounded out the sharp angles of her body. She wore her long hair smoothly coiled and piled high on the back of her head. The sophisticated style added to her already considerable height of nearly six feet, and that pleased her. With her exotically slanted golden eyes and her pale caramel skin, she looked like one of the Amazon women pictured in a book she'd found in the library.

She frowned as she studied her simple dress. She wanted dressmaker gowns. She wanted perfumes and silks, champagne and crystal. But most of all, she wanted her own place, one of those pretty pastel houses in Charleston where she'd have a maid and feel safe and protected. She knew exactly how to go about getting that place in Charleston, too. She had to do what terrified her the most. Instead of being a white man's house-keeper, she had to become his mistress.

Every night when she served Cain his dinner, she let her hips sway seductively, and she forced her breasts against his arm when she set food before him. Sometimes she forgot her fear of white men long enough to notice how handsome he was, and she'd recall that he'd been kind to her. But he was too big, too powerful, too much a man for her to feel easy with him. Regardless, she made her lips moist and her eyes inviting, practicing all the tricks she'd forced herself to learn.

An image of Magnus Owen appeared in her mind. Damn that man! She hated the way he looked at her out of those dark eyes, as if he felt sorry for her. Sweet, blessed Jesus, if that wasn't enough to make a body laugh. Magnus Owen, who wanted her so bad he couldn't stand it, had the gall to feel sorry for her.

An involuntary shudder swept through her as she though of pale white limbs wrapping themselves around her golden brown ones. She pushed the image aside and gnawed on her resentment.

Did Magnus Owen really think she'd let him touch her? Him or any other black man? Did Magnus think she'd been studying hard, grooming herself, listening to the white ladies in Rutherford until she could sound exactly like them, just so she'd end up with a black man who couldn't protect her? Not likely. Especially a black man whose eyes seemed to pierce into the farthest reaches of her soul.

She made her way to the kitchen. Soon, now, she'd have everything she wanted—a house, silk gowns, safety—and she was going to earn it in the only way she knew how, satisfying a white man's lust. A white man who was powerful enough to protect her.

That night it turned rainy. Howling February winds swept down the chimneys and rattled the shutters as Sophronia paused outside the library. In one hand she held a silver tray bearing a bottle of brandy and a single glass. With her other hand she unfastened the top buttons of her dress to reveal the swells of her breasts. It was time to make her next move. She took a deep breath and entered the room.

Cain glanced up from the ledgers on the desk. "You must have been reading my mind."

He uncoiled his rugged, long-limbed frame from the leather chair, rose, and stretched. She didn't let herself step back as he came out from behind the desk, moving like a great golden lion. He'd been working from dawn to dusk for months, and he looked tired.

"It's a cold night," she said, setting the tray on the desk. "I thought you might need something to keep you warm." She forced her hand to the open V of her dress so he couldn't mistake her meaning.

He gazed at her, and she felt the familiar stirrings of panic. Once again she reminded herself how kind he'd been, but she also knew there was something dangerous about him that frightened her.

His eyes flicked over her, then lingered on her breasts. "Sophronia..."

She thought of silk gowns and a pastel house. A house with a sturdy lock.

"Shh..." She stepped up to him and splayed her fingers over his chest. Then she let her shawl drop on her bare arm.

For the past seven months, his life had been filled with hard work and little pleasure. Now his lids dropped and he closed his long, tapered fingers around her arm. His hand, bronzed by the Carolina sun, was darker than her own flesh.

He cupped her chin. "Are you sure about this?"

She forced herself to nod.

His head dipped, but in the instant before their lips met, there was a noise behind them. They turned together and saw Magnus Owen standing in the open doorway.

His gentle features twisted as he saw her ready

to submit to Cain's embrace. She heard a rumble deep in his throat. He charged into the room and threw himself at the man he considered his closest friend, the man who had once saved his life.

The suddenness of the attack took Cain by surprise. He staggered backward and barely managed to keep his balance. Then he braced himself for Magnus's assault.

Horrified, she watched as Magnus came at him. He swung, but Cain sidestepped and lifted his arm to block the blow.

Magnus swung again. This time he found Cain's jaw and sent him sprawling. Cain got back up, but he refused to retaliate.

Gradually Magnus regained some semblance of sanity. When he saw Cain wasn't going to fight, his arms sagged to his sides.

Cain looked deep into Magnus's eyes, then gazed across the room at Sophronia. He bent down to right a chair that had been upended in the struggle and spoke gruffly. "You'd better get some sleep, Magnus. We have a big day tomorrow." He turned to Sophronia. "You can go. I won't be needing you anymore." The deliberate way he emphasized his words left no doubt about his meaning.

Sophronia rushed from the room. She was furious with Magnus for upsetting her plans. At the same time, she feared for him. This was South Carolina, and he'd struck a white man, not once but twice.

She barely slept that night as she waited for the devils in white sheets to come after him, but nothing happened. The next day, she saw him working side by side with Cain, clearing brush from one of the fields. The fear she'd felt turned into seething resentment. He had no right to interfere in her life.

That evening, Cain instructed her to leave his brandy on the table outside the library door.

6

*F*resh spring flowers filled the ballroom of the Templeton Academy for Young Ladies. Pyramids of white tulips screened the empty fireplaces, while cut-glass vases stuffed with lilacs lined the mantels. Even the mirrors had been draped with swags of snowy azaleas.

Along the ballroom's perimeter, clusters of fashionably dressed guests gazed toward the charming rose-bedecked gazebo at the end of the ballroom. Soon the most recent graduates of the Templeton Academy, the Class of 1868, would pass through.

In addition to the parents of the debutantes, guests included members of New York's most fashionable families: Schermerhorns and Livingstons, several Jays, and at least one Van Rensselaer. No socially prominent mother would permit a marriageable son to miss any of the events surrounding the graduation of the latest crop of Templeton girls, and certainly not the Academy's final ball, the best place in New York to find a suitable daughter-in-law.

The bachelors had gathered in groups around the room. Their ranks had been thinned by the war, but there were still enough present to please the mothers of the debutantes.

The younger men were carelessly confident in their immaculate white linen and black tailcoats, despite the fact that some of their sleeves hung empty, and more than one who hadn't yet celebrated his twenty-fifth birthday walked with a cane. The older bachelors' coffers overflowed from the profits of the booming postwar economy, and they signaled their success with diamond shirt studs and heavy gold watch chains.

Tonight was the first time the gentlemen from Boston, Philadelphia, and Baltimore would have the privilege of viewing the newest crop of Manhattan's most desirable debutantes. Unlike their New York counterparts, these gentlemen hadn't been able to attend the teas and sedate Sunday afternoon receptions that had led up to this evening's ball. They listened attentively as the local bachelors speculated on the winners in this year's bridal sweepstakes.

The beautiful Lilith Shelton would grace any man's table. And her father was to settle ten thousand on her.

Margaret Stockton had crooked teeth, but she'd bring eight thousand to her marriage bed, and she sang well, a pretty quality in a wife.

Elsbeth Woodward was only worth five

thousand at the outside, but she was sweet-natured and most pleasant to look at, the sort of wife who wouldn't give a man a moment's trouble. Definitely a favorite.

Fanny Jennings was out of the running. The youngest Vandervelt boy had already spoken with her father. A pity, since she was worth eighteen thousand.

On and on it went, one girl after another. As the conversation began to drift to the latest boxing match, a Bostonian visitor interrupted. "Isn't there another I've heard talk about? A Southern girl? Older than the rest?" Twenty-one, he'd heard.

The men of New York avoided each other's eyes. Finally one of them cleared his throat. "Ah, yes. That would be Miss Weston."

Just then the orchestra began to play a selection from the newly popular *Tales from the Vienna Woods*, a signal that the members of the graduating class were about to be announced. The men fell silent as the debutantes appeared.

Dressed in white ball gowns, they came through the gazebo one by one, paused, and sank into a graceful curtsy. Following the appropriate applause, they glided down steps strewn with rose petals onto the ballroom floor and took the arm of their father or brother.

Elsbeth smiled so prettily that her brother's best friend, who until that moment had thought of her only as a nuisance, began to think again. Lilith Shelton tripped ever so slightly on the hem of her skirt and wanted to die, but she was a Templeton Girl, so she didn't let her mortification show. Margaret Stockton, even with her crooked teeth, looked fetching enough to garner the attention of a member of the less prosperous branch of the Jay family.

"Katharine Louise Weston."

There was an almost imperceptible movement among the gentlemen of New York City, a slight tilting of heads, a vague shifting of positions. The gentlemen of Boston, Philadelphia, and Baltimore sensed that something special was about to happen and fixed their attention more closely.

She came toward them from the shadows of the gazebo, then stopped at the top of the steps. They saw at once that she wasn't like the others. This was no tame tabby cat to curl up by a man's hearth and keep his slippers warm. This was a woman to make a man's blood surge, a wildcat with lustrous black hair caught back from her face with silver combs, then falling in a riotous tangle of thick dark curls down her neck. This was an exotic cat with widely spaced violet eyes so heavily fringed, the very weight of her lashes should have held them closed. This was a jungle cat with a mouth too bold for fashion but so ripe and moist that a man could only think of drinking from it.

Her gown was fashioned of white satin with a billowing overskirt caught up by bows the same shade of violet as her eyes. The neckline was heart-shaped, softly outlining the contours of her breasts, and the bell-shaped sleeves ended in a wide cuff of Alençon lace. The gown was beautiful and expensive, but she wore it almost carelessly. One of the lavender bows had come undone at the side, and the sleeves must have gotten in her way, because she'd pushed them a bit too high on her delicate wrists.

Hamilton Woodward's youngest son stepped forward as her escort for the promenade. The more critical guests observed that her stride was a shade too long—not long enough to reflect badly on the Academy, just long enough to be noted. Woodward's son whispered something to her. She tilted her head and laughed, showing small, white teeth. Each man who watched wanted that laugh to be his alone, even as he told himself that a more delicate young lady would perhaps not laugh quite so boldly. Only Elsbeth's father, Hamilton Woodward, refused to look at her.

Under cover of the music, the gentlemen from Boston, Philadelphia, and Baltimore demanded to know more about this Miss Weston.

The gentlemen from New York were vague at first. Some talk that Elvira Templeton shouldn't have let a Southerner into the Academy so soon after the war, but she was the ward of the Hero of Missionary Ridge.

Their comments grew more personal. Quite something to look at. Hard to keep your eyes off her, in fact. But a dangerous sort of wife, don't you think? Older. A bit wild. Wager she wouldn't take the bit well at all. And how could a man hope to keep his mind on business with a woman like that waiting for him at home?

If she waited.

Gradually the gentlemen from Boston, Philadelphia, and Baltimore learned the rest of it. In the past six weeks Miss Weston had captured the interest of a dozen of New York's most eligible bachelors, only to reject them. These were men from the wealthiest families—men who would one day run the city, even the country—but she didn't seem to care.

As for those she did seem to favor... That was what galled the most. She picked the least likely men. Bertrand Mayhew, for example, who came from a good family but was virtually penniless and hadn't been able to make a decision on his own since his mother died. Then there was Hobart Cheney, a man with neither money nor looks, only an unfortunate stammer. The delicious Miss Weston's preferences were incomprehensible. She was passing over Van Rensselaers, Livingstons, and Jays for Bertrand Mayhew and Hobart Cheney.

The mothers were relieved. They very much enjoyed Miss Weston's company—she made them laugh and was sympathetic to their ailments. But she wasn't quite up to scratch as a daughter-in-law, was she? Forever tearing a flounce or losing a glove. Her hair was never entirely neat, always a lock tumbling about at her ears or curling at her temples. As for the bold way she looked one in the eye...refreshing, but at the same time discomposing. No, Miss

Weston wouldn't make the right sort of wife for their sons at all.

Kit was aware of the opinion the society matrons had of her, and she didn't blame them for it. As a Templeton Girl, she even understood. At the same time, she didn't let it distract her from entertaining her partners with the breathless Southern conversation she'd perfected by calling up memories of the women in Rutherford. Now, however, her partner was poor Hobart Cheney, who was barely capable of maintaining a conversation under the best of circumstances, let alone when he was counting dance steps so vigorously under his breath, so she remained silent.

Mr. Cheney stumbled, but Elsbeth had coached her well for the past three years, and Kit led him back into the steps before anyone noticed. She also gave him her brightest smile so he wouldn't realize he was actually following her. Poor Mr. Cheney would never know how close he'd come to being her chosen husband. If he'd been a trifle less intelligent, she might have picked him because he was a sweet man. As it was, Bertrand Mayhew presented the better choice.

She glimpsed Mr. Mayhew standing off by himself, waiting for the first of two dances that she had promised him. She felt the familiar heaviness that settled over her whenever she looked at him, spoke with him, or even thought of him.

He wasn't much taller than she, and his belly protruded below the waistband of his trousers like a woman's. At forty, he'd lived his life in the shadow of his mother, and now that she was dead, he desperately needed a woman to take her place. Kit had decided she would be that woman.

Elsbeth was upset, pointing out that Kit could have any of a dozen eligible men who were both richer than Bertrand Mayhew and less distasteful. But Elsbeth understood. To get Risen Glory back, Kit needed power from her marriage, not riches, and a husband who expected her to behave like a properly submissive wife was of no use to her at all.

Kit knew it wouldn't be difficult to persuade Bertrand to use the money in her trust fund to buy back Risen Glory, nor would she have trouble convincing him to live there permanently. Because of that, she suppressed the part of her that wished she could have found a husband who was less repugnant. After the midnight supper, she would take him to the reception room to see the newest collection of stereoscopic views of Niagara Falls, and then she would lead him to the question. It wouldn't be difficult. Dealing with men had proved to be surprisingly easy. Within a month she would be on her way to Risen Glory. Unfortunately, she'd be married to Bertrand Mayhew.

She wasted no thought on the letter she'd received from Baron Cain the day before. She seldom heard from him, and then only to reprimand her over one of the quarterly reports he received from Mrs. Templeton. His letters were always formal and so dictatorial that she couldn't risk reading them in front of Elsbeth because they made her fall back on her old habits of profanity.

After three years, the mental ledger of her grievances against him had grown thick with entries. His latest letter ordered her without explanation to remain in New York until further notice. She intended to ignore it. Her life was about to become her own, and she'd never again let him stand in her way.

The music ended with a flourish, and instantly Bertrand Mayhew appeared at her side. "Miss—Miss Weston? I was wondering—that is to say, did you remember—"

"Why, if it isn't Mr. Mayhew." Kit tilted her head and gazed at him through her lashes, a gesture she had practiced for so long under Elsbeth's tutelage that it had become second nature. "My dear, dear Mr. Mayhew. I was afraid—terrified, in fact—that you'd forgotten me and gone off with one of the other young ladies."

"Oh, my, no! Oh, Miss Weston, how could you ever imagine I would do something so ungentlemanly? Oh, my stars, no. My dear mother would never have—"

"I'm sure she wouldn't." She excused herself prettily from Hobart Cheney, then linked her arm through Mr. Mayhew's, well aware that the gesture was overly familiar. "Now, now. No long face, you hear? I was only teasing."

"Teasing?" He looked as baffled as if she'd just announced she was going to ride naked down Fifth Avenue.

Kit repressed a sigh. The orchestra began to play a lively gallop, and she let him lead her into the dance. At the same time, she tried to shake off her depression, but a glimpse of Elsbeth's father made that difficult.

What a pompous fool! Over Easter, one of the lawyers at Hamilton Woodward's firm had drunk too much and accosted Kit in the Woodwards' music room. One touch of those slobbery lips, and she'd planted her fist in his belly. That would have been the end of it, but Mr. Woodward happened to come into the room just then. His business partner had lied and said Kit had been the aggressor. Kit had angrily denied it, but Mr. Woodward hadn't believed her. Ever since, he'd tried unsuccessfully to break up her friendship with Elsbeth, and all evening he'd been shooting her scalding glances.

She forgot about Mr. Woodward as she spotted a new couple entering the ballroom. Something familiar about the man caught her attention, and as the couple made their way to Mrs. Templeton to pay their respects, she recognized him. *Oh, my...*

"Mr. Mayhew, would you escort me over to Mrs. Templeton? She's speaking with someone I know. Someone I haven't seen for years."

The gentlemen from New York, Boston, Philadelphia, and Baltimore noticed that Miss Weston had stopped dancing and looked to see what had caught her attention. With no small amount of envy, they studied the man who'd just entered the ballroom. What was it about the pale, thin stranger that had brought such an attractive flush to the cheeks of the elusive Miss Weston?

Brandon Parsell, former cavalry officer in South Carolina's famous "Hampton's Legion," had something of the look of an artist about him, even though he was a planter by birth and knew nothing about art beyond the fact that he liked that fellow who painted horses. His hair was brown and straight, combed from a side part over a fine, well-molded brow. He had a neatly trimmed mustache and conservative side whiskers.

It wasn't the kind of face that inspired easy camaraderie with members of his own sex. It was, instead, a face that women liked, as it brought to mind novels about chivalry and called up memories of sonnets, nightingales, and Grecian urns.

The woman at his side was Eleanora Baird, the plain, somewhat overdressed daughter of his employer. He acknowledged her introduction to Mrs. Templeton with a courtly bow and a well-chosen compliment. Listening to his easy Southern drawl, no one would have guessed the loathing he felt for all of them: the glittering guests, the imposing hostess, even the Northern spinster whom duty required he escort that evening.

And then—from nowhere, it seemed—he felt a sharp pang of homesickness, a longing for the walled gardens of Charleston on a Sunday afternoon, a yearning for the quiet night air of Holly Grove, his family's former home. There was no reason for the crush of emotion that tightened his chest, no reason beyond the faint, sweet scent of Carolina jasmine borne on a rustle of white satin.

"Ah, Katharine, my dear," Mrs. Templeton called out in that strident Northern accent that jangled Brandon's ears. "I have someone I'd like you to meet. A countryman of yours."

Slowly he turned toward the evocative jasmine perfume and, as quickly as a missed heartbeat, lost himself in the beautiful, willful face that met his gaze.

The young woman smiled. "Mr. Parsell and I are already acquainted, although I see by his expression that he doesn't remember me. Shame, Mr. Parsell. You've forgotten one of your most faithful admirers."

Although Brandon Parsell didn't recognize the face, he knew the voice. He knew those gently blurred vowels and soft consonants as well as he knew the sound of his own breathing. It was the voice of his mother, his aunts, and his sisters. The voice that, for four long years, had soothed the dying and defied the Yankees and sent the gentlemen out to fight again. It was the voice that had gladly offered up husbands, brothers, and sons to the Glorious Cause.

The voice of all the gently bred women of the South.

It was the voice that had cheered them on at Bull Run and Fredericksburg, the voice that had steadied them in those long weeks on the bluffs at Vicksburg, the voice that had cried bitter tears into lavender-scented handkerchiefs, then whispered "Never mind" when they lost Stonewall Jackson at Chancellorsville.

It was the voice that had spurred on Pickett's men in their desperate charge at Gettysburg, the voice they'd heard as they lay dying in the mud at Chickamauga, and the voice they would not let themselves hear on that Virginia Palm Sunday when they'd surrendered their dreams at Appomattox Court House.

Yet, despite the voice, there was a difference in the woman who stood before him from the women who waited at home. The white satin ball gown she wore rustled with newness. No brooch had been artfully placed to conceal a darn that was almost, but not quite, invisible. There were no signs that a skirt originally designed to accommodate a hoop had been taken apart and reassembled to give a smaller, more fashionable silhouette. There was another difference, too, in the woman who stood before him from the women who waited at home. Her violet eyes did not contain any secret, unspoken reproach.

When he finally found his own voice, it seemed to come from a place far away. "I'm afraid you have the advantage, ma'am. It's hard for me to believe I could have forgotten such a memorable face, but if you say it's so, I'm not disputing it, just begging your forgiveness for my poor memory. Perhaps you'll enlighten me?"

Elvira Templeton, accustomed to the plainer speech of Yankee businessmen, blinked twice before she remembered her manners. "Mr. Parsell, may I present Miss Katharine Louise Weston."

Brandon Parsell was too much a gentleman to let his shock show, but even so, he couldn't find the words to frame a proper response. Mrs. Templeton continued with the amenities, introducing Miss Baird and, of course, Mr. Mayhew. Miss Weston seemed amused.

The orchestra began to play the first strains of *The Blue Danube* waltz. Mr. Parsell came out of his stupor and turned to Mr. Mayhew. "Would you very much mind fetching a cup of punch for Miss Baird, sir? She was just remarking on her thirst. Miss Weston, can an old friend claim the honor of this waltz?" It was an uncharacteristic breach of etiquette, but Parsell couldn't bring himself to care.

Kit smiled and presented her gloved hand. They moved out onto the ballroom floor and into the steps of the dance. Brandon finally broke the silence. "You've changed, Kit Weston. I don't believe your own mammy would recognize you."

"I never had a mammy, Brandon Parsell, as you very well know."

He laughed aloud at her feistiness. He hadn't realized how much he missed talking to a woman whose spirit hadn't been broken. "Wait until I tell my mother and my sisters I've seen you. We heard Cain had shipped you to a school up North, but none of us speaks to him, and Sophronia hasn't said much to anybody."

Kit didn't want to talk about Cain. "How are your mother and sisters?"

"As well as can be expected. Losing Holly Grove's been hard on them. I'm working at the bank in Rutherford." His laugh was self-deprecating. "A Parsell working in a bank. Times do change, don't they, Miss Kit Weston?"

Kit took in the clean, sensitive lines of his face and observed the way his neatly trimmed mustache brushed the upper curve of his lip. She didn't let her pity show as she breathed in the faint smells of tobacco and bay rum that clung so pleasantly to him.

Brandon and his sisters had been at the center of a carefree group of young people some five or six years older than she. When the war started, she remembered standing at the side of the road and watching him ride toward Charleston. He'd sat his horse as if he'd been born in a saddle, and he'd worn the gray uniform and plumed hat so proudly that her throat had congealed with fierce, proud tears. To her, he'd symbolized the spirit of the Confederate soldier, and she'd yearned for nothing more than to follow him into battle and fight at his side. Now Holly Grove lay in ruins and Brandon Parsell worked in a bank.

"What are you doing in New York, Mr. Parsell?" she asked, trying to steady herself against the faint giddiness attacking her knees.

"My employer sent me here to attend to some

family business for him. I'm returning home tomorrow."

"Your employer must think highly of you if he's willing to trust you with family affairs."

Again the self-deprecating sound that was nearly, but not quite, a laugh. "If you listen to my mother, she'll tell you that I'm running the Planters and Citizens Bank, but the truth is, I'm little more than an errand boy."

"I'm sure that's not so."

"The South has been raised on self-delusion. It's like mother's milk to us, this belief in our invincibility. But I, for one, have given up self-delusion. The South isn't invincible, and neither am I."

"Is it so very bad?"

He moved her toward the edge of the ballroom. "You haven't been to Rutherford for years. Everything's different. Carpetbaggers and scalawags are running the state. Even though South Carolina's about to be readmitted to the Union, Yankee soldiers still patrol the streets and look the other way when respectable citizens are accosted by riffraff. The state legislature's a joke." He spat out the last word as if it were venomous. "Living here, you can't have any idea what it's like."

She felt guilty, as if she had somehow shirked her duty by deserting the South to go to school in New York. The music ended, but she wasn't ready for the dance to be over. And maybe Brandon wasn't, either, because he made no move to release her. "I imagine you already have a partner for the supper dance."

She nodded, then heard herself saying, "But since you're a neighbor and leaving New York tomorrow, I'm certain Mr. Mayhew won't object to stepping aside."

He lifted her hand and brushed the back of it with his lips. "Then he's a fool."

Elsbeth swooped down on her the moment he took his leave and dragged her to the sitting room that had been set aside for the ladies to tidy themselves.

"Who is he, Kit? All the girls are talking about him. He looks like a poet. Oh, my! Your bows are coming untied, and you already have a spot on your skirt. And your hair..." She pushed Kit down in front of the mirror and snatched out the filigreed silver combs she'd given her last year as a birthday present. "I don't know why you wouldn't let me put it up for tonight. It looks so wild like this."

"For the same reason I wouldn't let you lace me into a corset. I don't like anything that takes away my freedom."

Elsbeth gave her an impish smile. "You're a woman. You're not supposed to have any freedom."

Kit laughed. "Oh, Elsbeth, what would I have done without you these last three years?"

"Gotten expelled."

Kit reached up and squeezed her hand. "Have I ever said thank you?"

"A hundred times. And I'm the one who should thank you. If it hadn't been for you,

I'd never have learned to stand up for myself. I'm sorry Father's being so beastly. I'll never forgive him for not believing you."

"I don't want to come between you and your father."

"I know you don't." Elsbeth renewed her attack on Kit's hair. "Why do I bother to scold you for being so untidy? You hardly do anything the way a young lady is supposed to, yet half the men in New York are in love with you."

Kit made a face in the mirror. "Sometimes I don't like the way they look at me. As if I'm not wearing any clothes."

"I'm sure you're imagining it." Elsbeth finished securing the combs and wound her arms around Kit's shoulders. "It's just that you're so beautiful, they can't help looking at you."

"Silly." Kit laughed and jumped up from her chair. "His name is Brandon Parsell, and he's taking me in to supper."

"Supper? I thought Mr. Mayhew..."

But it was too late. Kit had already left.

A waiter came by with a third tray of petits fours. Kit started to reach for one, then caught herself just in time. She'd already had two, and she'd eaten every bite of the food she'd piled onto her plate. If Elsbeth had noticed—as most assuredly she had—Kit would receive another lecture. Templeton Girls ate sparingly at social occasions.

Brandon took the accusingly empty plate from

her and set it aside. "I confess to enjoying a pipe after dinner. Would you be agreeable to showing me the garden? That is, if you don't mind the smell of tobacco."

Kit knew she should be with Bertrand Mayhew now, showing him stereoptic views of Niagara Falls and leading him to a marriage proposal, but she couldn't summon the will to excuse herself. "I don't mind at all. When I was younger, I smoked tobacco myself."

Brandon frowned. "As I recall, your childhood was unfortunate and best forgotten." He led her toward the doors that opened into the school's garden. "It's amazing how well you've managed to overcome the adversity of your upbringing, not to mention being able to live for so long with these Yankees."

She smiled as he led her along a brick path hung with paper lanterns. She thought of Elsbeth, Fanny Jennings, Margaret Stockton, and even Mrs. Templeton. "They're not all bad."

"What about the Yankee gentlemen? How do you feel about them?"

"Some are pleasant, others not."

He hesitated. "Have you received any proposals of marriage?"

"None that I've accepted."

"I'm glad."

He smiled, and without quite knowing how it happened, they were standing still. She felt the whisper of a breeze ruffling her hair. His hands settled on her shoulders. Gently he drew her toward him.

He was going to kiss her. She knew it would happen, just as she knew she would let him.

Her first real kiss.

A frown creased his forehead. He released her abruptly. "Forgive me. I nearly forgot myself."

"You were going to kiss me."

"I'm ashamed to admit it's all I've been able to think about since I first set eyes on you. A man who presses his attentions on a lady is no gentleman."

"What if the lady's willing?"

His expression grew tender. "You're an innocent. Kisses lead to greater liberties."

She thought of Eve's Shame and the lecture on marital relations that all the senior girls had to endure before they graduated. Mrs. Templeton spoke of pain and duty, of obligation and endurance. She advised them to let their husbands have their way, no matter how shocking and horrible it might seem. She suggested they recite verses from the Bible or a bit of poetry while it was going on. But never once did she tell them exactly what Eve's Shame involved. It was left to their fertile imaginations.

Lilith Shelton reported that her mother had an aunt who'd gone insane on her wedding night. Margaret said she'd heard there was blood. And Kit had exchanged anxious glances with Fanny Jennings, whose father raised Thoroughbreds on a farm near Saratoga. Only Kit and Fanny had seen the shuddering of a reluctant mare as she was covered by a trumpeting stallion.

Brandon reached inside his pocket for a pipe and a worn leather tobacco pouch. "I don't know how you've been able to stand living in this city. It's not much like Risen Glory, is it?"

"Sometimes I thought I'd die of homesickness."

"Poor Kit. You've had a rough time of it, haven't you?"

"Not as bad as you. At least Risen Glory is still standing."

He wandered toward the garden wall. "It's a fine plantation. Always has been. Your daddy might not have had much sense where womenfolk were concerned, but he knew how to grow cotton." There was a hollow, hissing sound as he drew on his pipe. He relit it and gazed over at her. "Can I tell you something I've never confided to another livin' soul?"

A little thrill went through her. "What's that?"

"I used to have a secret hankering for Risen Glory. It's always been a better plantation than Holly Grove. It's a cruel twist of fate that the best plantation in the country is in the hands of a Yankee."

She realized her heart was racing, even as her mind spun with new possibilities. She spoke slowly. "I'm going to get it back."

"Remember what I said about self-delusion. Don't make the same mistakes as the others."

"It's not self-delusion," she said fiercely. "I've learned about money since I've been in the North. It's the great equalizer. And I'll have it. Then I'm buying Risen Glory back from Baron Cain."

"It'll take a lot of money. Cain has some crazy idea about spinning his own cotton. He's building a mill right there at Risen Glory. The steam engine just arrived from Cincinnati."

This was news Sophronia hadn't passed on, but Kit couldn't concentrate on it now. Something too important was at stake. She thought about it for only a moment. "I'll have fifteen thousand dollars, Brandon."

"Fifteen thousand!" In a land that had been stripped of everything, this was a fortune, and for a moment he simply gaped at her. Then he shook his head. "You shouldn't have told me that."

"Why not?"

"I—I wanted to call on you after you returned to Risen Glory, but what you've told me casts a shadow over my motivations."

Kit's own motivations were so much more shadowy that she laughed. "Don't be a goose. I could never doubt your motivations. And yes, you may call on me at Risen Glory. I intend to return as soon as I can make the arrangements."

Just like that, she made her decision. She couldn't marry Bertrand Mayhew, not yet anyway, not until she'd had time to see where this exciting new possibility might lead her. She didn't care what Cain had written in his letter. She was going home.

That night as she fell asleep, she dreamed

of walking through the fields of Risen Glory with Brandon Parsell at her side.

Just imagine.

PART THREE

A Southern Lady

We boil at different degrees.

RALPH WALDO EMERSON
"ELOQUENCE"

7

The carriage tilted as it swung into the long, winding drive that led to Risen Glory. Kit tensed with anticipation. After three years, she was finally home.

The deep grooves that had rutted the drive for as long as she could remember had been leveled and the surface spread with fresh gravel. Weeds and undergrowth had been cut back, making the road wider than she recalled. Only the trees had resisted change. The familiar assortment of buckthorn, oak, black gum, and sycamore welcomed her. In a moment she'd be able to see the house.

But when the carriage rounded the final curve, Kit didn't even glance that way. Something more important had caught her attention.

Beyond the gentle slope of lawn, beyond the orchard and the new outbuildings, beyond the house itself, stretching as far as her eyes could see, were the fields of Risen Glory. Fields that looked as they had before the war, with endless rows of young cotton plants stretching like green ribbons across the rich, dark soil.

She banged the roof of the carriage, startling

her companion, so that she let go of the peppermint drop she'd been about to slip into her mouth and lost it in the frilly white folds of her dress.

Dorthea Pinckney Calhoun gave a shriek of alarm.

A Templeton Girl, even a rebellious one, understood that she couldn't travel so far without a companion, let alone stay in the same house with an unmarried man. The fact that he was her cursed stepbrother made no difference. Kit wouldn't do anything that could give Cain an excuse to send her back, and since he didn't want her here in the first place, he'd be looking for a reason.

It hadn't been hard to find a penniless Southern woman anxious to return to her homeland after years of exile with a widowed Northern sister-in-law. Miss Dolly was a distant relative of Mary Cogdell, and Kit had gotten her name through a letter she received from the minister's wife. With her tiny stature and her faded blond corkscrew curls, Miss Dolly resembled an aged china doll. Although she was well past fifty, she favored ancient gowns heavy with frills and wide skirts beneath which she never wore any fewer than eight petticoats.

Kit had already discovered she was a natural coquette, batting the lashes of her wrinkled eyelids at any man she judged to be a gentleman. And she always seemed to be in motion. Her hands in their lacy, fingerless mitts fluttered; her faded curls bobbed, her pastel sashes and antique fringes were never still. She talked of cotillions and cough remedies and a set of porcelain temple dogs that had disappeared along with her girlhood. She was sweet, harmless, and, as Kit had soon discovered, slightly mad. Unable to accept the defeat of her glorious Confederacy, Miss Dolly had permitted herself the small luxury of slipping back in time so that she could forever live in those first days of the war when hopes were high and thoughts of defeat unthinkable.

"The Yankees!" Miss Dolly exclaimed as the carriage jolted to a stop. "They're attacking us! Oh, my... Oh, my, my..."

In the beginning, her habit of referring to events that had happened seven years before as if they were occurring that very day had been unnerving, but Kit had quickly realized Miss Dolly's genteel madness was her way of coping with a life she hadn't been able to control.

"Nothing like that," Kit reassured her. "I stopped the carriage. I want to walk."

"Oh, dear. Oh, my dear, that won't do at all. Marauding troops are everywhere. And your complexion—"

"I'll be fine, Miss Dolly. I'll meet you at the house in a few minutes."

Before her companion could protest further, Kit stepped out of the carriage and waved the driver on. As the vehicle pulled away, she climbed a grassy hillock so she could get an unrestricted view of the fields beyond the house. Lifting her veil, she shaded her eyes from the late-afternoon sun.

The plants were about six weeks old. Before long, the buds would open into creamy four-petaled flowers that would give birth to the cotton bolls. Even under her father's efficient management, Risen Glory hadn't looked this prosperous. The outbuildings that had been destroyed by the Yankees had been rebuilt, and a new whitewashed fence stretched around the paddock. Everything about the plantation looked well tended and prosperous.

Her gaze came to rest on the house from which she'd been exiled when she was so young. The front still bowed in a graceful arch, and the color was the same shade of warm cream that she remembered, tinted now by the rose-colored light of the fading sun.

But there were differences. The red tile roof had been repaired near the twin chimneys, the shutters and front door held a fresh coat of shiny black paint, and, even from a distance, the window glass sparkled. Compared to the lingering devastation she'd seen from the window of the train, Risen Glory was an oasis of beauty and prosperity.

The improvements should have gratified her. Instead, she felt a mixture of anger and resentment. All this had happened without her. She settled the beaded veil back over her face and headed for the house.

Dolly Calhoun waited by the carriage steps, her Cupid's-bow mouth quivering from having been deserted just as she'd arrived at her destination. Kit gave her a reassuring smile, then stepped around the trunks to pay the driver from the last of her allowance money. As he pulled away, she took Miss Dolly's arm and helped her up the front steps, then lifted the brass knocker.

The young maid who answered the door was new, and that deepened Kit's resentment. She wanted to see Eli's dear, familiar face, but the old man had died the previous winter. Cain hadn't permitted her to return home to see him buried. Now she had new resentments to join the old, familiar ones.

The maid glanced curiously at them and then at the array of trunks and bandboxes piled on the piazza.

"I'd like to see Sophronia," Kit said.

"Miz Sophronia's not here."

"When do you expect her?"

"The Conjure Woman took sick this mornin' and Miz Sophronia went to check up on her. Don't know when she's comin' back."

"Is Major Cain here?"

"He'll be comin' in from the fields any minute now, but he ain't here yet."

Just as well, Kit thought. With any luck, they'd be settled in before he arrived. She clasped Miss Dolly gently by the arm and steered her through the doorway, past the astonished maid. "Please see that our trunks are taken upstairs. This is Miss Calhoun. I'm sure she'd appreciate a glass of lemonade in her room. I'll wait in the front sitting room for Major Cain."

Kit saw the maid's uncertainty, but the girl didn't have the courage to challenge a well-dressed visitor. "Yes, ma'am."

Kit turned to her companion, more than a little worried about how she would react to sleeping under the same roof with a former officer in the Union army. "Why don't you lie down until supper, Miss Dolly? You've had a long day."

"I think I will, you sweet darlin'." Miss Dolly patted Kit's arm. "I want to look my best this evening. I only hope the gentlemen won't talk about politics all through dinner. With General Beauregard in command at Charleston, I'm sure none of us need to worry about those murderous Yankees."

Kit gave Miss Dolly a gentle prod toward the bewildered maid. "I'll look in on you before dinner."

After they disappeared upstairs, Kit finally had time to take in her surroundings. The wooden floor shone with polish, and an arrangement of spring flowers sat on the hall table. She remembered how Rosemary's slovenliness had galled Sophronia.

She crossed the hall and entered the front sitting room. The freshly painted ivory walls and apple-green moldings were spare and cool, and new, yellow silk taffeta curtains rippled in the breeze from the open windows. The furniture, however, was the comfortable hodgepodge Kit remembered, although the chairs and settees had been reupholstered, and the room smelled of lemon oil and beeswax instead of mildew. Tarnish no longer marred the silver candlesticks, and the grandfather's clock was working for the first time in Kit's memory. The mellow, rhythmic ticking should have relaxed her, but it didn't. Sophronia had done her job too well. Kit felt like a stranger in her own home.

Cain watched Vandal, his new chestnut, being led into the stable. He was a good horse, but Magnus was mad as hell that Cain had gotten rid of Apollo to buy him. Unlike Magnus, Cain didn't let himself get attached to any of the horses. He'd learned as a child not to get attached to anything.

As he strode from the stable toward the house, he found himself thinking about all he'd accomplished in three years. Despite the problems of living in a conquered land with neighbors who shunned him, he hadn't once regretted his decision to sell his house in New York and come to Risen Glory. He'd had a little experience growing cotton in Texas before the war, and Magnus had been raised on a cotton plantation. With the help of a healthy supply of agricultural pamphlets, the two of them had managed to produce a paying crop last year.

Cain didn't pretend to feel a deep affinity for the land, just as he didn't get sentimental over the animals, but he was enjoying the challenge of restoring Risen Glory. Building the new spinning mill on the northeast corner of the plantation was more fulfilling to him.

He'd gambled everything he had on the mill. As a result, he was as close to broke as he'd been since he was a kid, but he'd always liked taking risks. For the moment, he felt content.

He was scraping his boots by the back door when Lucy, the maid Sophronia had recently hired, came flying out. "It wasn't my fault, Major. Miz Sophronia didn't tell me nobody was comin' today when she went off to see the Conjure Woman. This lady showed up askin' for you, and then she just took herself off to the sitting room, bold as brass."

"Is she still there?"

"Yes. And that's not all. She brung—"

"Damn!" He'd received a letter the week before announcing that a member of the Society to Protect Widows and Orphans of the Confederacy would be calling on him for a contribution. The respectable citizens of the neighborhood ignored him unless they needed money; then some matronly woman would show up and observe him with pursed lips and nervous eyes while she tried to get him to empty his pockets. He'd begun to suspect the charities were merely a face-saving excuse to get a glimpse inside the lair of the evil Hero of Missionary Ridge. It amused him to watch those same women try to discourage the flirtatious glances that came his way from their daughters when he was in town, but he restricted his female companionship to infrequent trips to the more experienced women of Charleston.

He stalked into the house and down the hallway toward the sitting room. He didn't care that he was dressed in the same tobacco-brown trousers and white shirt he'd worn all day in the fields. He'd be damned if he'd change his clothes to receive another one of these tiresome women. But what he saw when he entered the sitting room wasn't what he'd expected...

The woman stood at the window looking out. Even with her back to him, he saw that she was well dressed, unusual for the women of the community. Her skirt rippled ever so slightly as she turned.

He caught his breath.

She was exquisite. Her dove-gray gown was trimmed with rose piping, and a waterfall of pale gray lace fell from her throat over a pair of supple, round breasts. A small hat the same soft rose shade as the trim of her gown perched on her inky-dark hair. The tip of the short gray plume that dipped from the brim came level with her brow.

The rest of the woman's features were covered by a black veil as light as a spider's web. Tiny, sparkling dewdrops of jet clung to its honeycombed surface, with only a moist red mouth visible beneath. That and a small pair of jet earbobs.

He didn't know her. He'd have remembered such a creature. She must be one of the respectable daughters of the neighborhood who'd been so carefully tucked away from him.

She remained quietly confident under his open appraisal. What household calamity had resulted in so enticing a morsel being sent to take her mother's place in the den of the infamous Yankee?

His gaze touched that ripe mouth peeking from beneath her veil. Beautiful and intriguing. Her parents would have done better to keep this one safely locked away.

While Cain was studying her so intently, Kit was conducting her own perusal from behind the honeycombed cells of her veil. Three years had passed. She was older now, and she studied him through more mature eyes. What she saw wasn't reassuring. He was more outrageously handsome than she remembered. The sun had bronzed the planes of his face and streaked his crisp, tawny hair. The darker hair at his temples gave his face the rugged look of a man who belonged outdoors.

He was still dressed for the fields, and the sight of that muscular body unsettled her. The white shirt that stretched across his chest was rolled up at the sleeves, revealing tanned, hard-tendoned forearms. Brown trousers clung to his hips and hugged the powerful muscles of his thighs.

The spacious room in which they were standing seemed to have shrunk. Even standing still, he radiated an aura of power and danger. Somehow she'd managed to forget that. What curious, self-protective mechanism had made her reduce him in her mind to the level of other men? It was a mistake she wouldn't make again.

Cain was aware of her scrutiny. She seemed to have no intention of being the first to speak, and her composure indicated a degree of self-confidence that intrigued him. Curious to test its limits, he broke the silence with deliberate brusqueness.

"You wanted to see me?"

She felt a stab of satisfaction. He didn't know who she was. The veiled hat had given her this one small advantage. The masquerade wouldn't last for long, but while it did, she'd have time to size up her opponent with wiser eyes than those of an immature eighteen-year-old who'd known both too much and too little.

"This room is quite beautiful," she said coolly.

"I have an excellent housekeeper."

"You're fortunate."

"Yes, I am." He walked farther into the room, moving with the easy rolling gait of a man who spent much of his time on horseback. "She usually takes care of calls like yours, but she's out on some kind of errand."

Kit wondered who he thought she was and what he meant. "She's gone to see the Conjure Woman."

"The Conjure Woman?"

"She makes spells and tells futures." After three years at Risen Glory, he didn't even know this much. Nothing could have offered more proof that he didn't belong here. "She's sick, and Sophronia's gone to see her."

"You know Sophronia?"

"Yes."

"So you live nearby?"

She nodded but didn't elaborate. He indicated a chair. "You didn't give Lucy your name."

"Lucy? Do you mean your maid?"

"I see there's something you don't know."

She ignored the chair he'd indicated and walked to the fireplace, deliberately turning her back to him. He noticed that she moved with a bolder step than most women. She also didn't try to position herself in a way that showed off her fashionable gown to best advantage. It was as if her clothing were merely something to toss on in the morning and, once she'd done up the fastenings, to forget.

He decided to press her. "Your name?"

"Is it important?" Her voice was low, husky, and distinctly Southern.

"Maybe."

"I wonder why."

Cain was intrigued as much by the provocative way she avoided answering his question as by the faint fragrance of jasmine that drifted from her skirts and tugged at his senses. He wished she'd turn back around so he could get a closer look at the captivating features he could only glimpse behind the veil.

"A lady of mystery," he mocked softly, "coming into the enemy's lair without a zealous mother to serve as chaperone. Not wise at all."

"I don't always behave wisely."

Cain smiled. "Neither do I."

His gaze slipped from that silly dab of a hat to the coil of silky dark hair resting on the nape of her neck. What would it look like unfastened and tumbling over naked white shoulders? His jolt of arousal told him he'd been without a woman too long. Although even if he'd had a dozen the night before, he knew this woman would still have stirred him.

"Should I expect a jealous husband to come banging on my door looking for his wayward wife?"

"I have no husband."

"No?" He suddenly wanted to test the limits of her self-confidence. "Is that why you're here? Has the supply of eligible men in the county dipped so low that well-bred Southern ladies are forced to scout in the Yankee's lair?"

She turned. Through her veil he could just make out flashing eyes and a small nose with delicately flaring nostrils.

"I assure you, Major Cain, I'm not here to scout for a husband. You have an elevated opinion of yourself."

"Do I?" He moved closer. His legs brushed her skirt.

Kit wanted to step back, but she held her ground. He was a predator, and like all predators, he fed off the weakness of others. Even the smallest retreat would be a victory for him, and she wouldn't show him any vulnerability. At the same time, his nearness made her feel slightly dizzy. The sensation should have been unpleasant, but it wasn't.

"Tell me, mystery lady. What else would a respectable young woman be doing visiting a man by herself?" His voice was deep and teasing, and his gray eyes glimmered with a devilry that made her blood rush faster. "Or is it possible that the respectable young lady isn't as respectable as she seems to be?"

Kit drew up her chin and met his gaze. "Don't judge others by your own standards."

If she'd only known, her unspoken challenge stirred him more than anything else could have. Were those eyes behind the honeycombed veil blue or a darker, more exotic color? Everything about this woman intrigued him. She was no simpering coquette or hothouse orchid. Rather, she reminded him of a wild rose, growing tangled and unruly in the deepest part of the woods, a wild rose with prickly thorns ready to draw blood from any man who touched her.

The untamed part of him responded to the same quality he sensed in her. What would it be like to work his way past those thorns and pluck this wild rose of the deep wood?

Even before he moved, Kit understood that something was about to happen. She wanted to break away, but her legs wouldn't respond. As she gazed up into that chiseled face, she tried to remember this man was her deadly enemy. He controlled everything that was dear to her: her home, her future, her very freedom. But she'd always been a creature of instinct, and her blood had begun to roar so loudly in her head that it was blotting out her reason.

Slowly Cain lifted his scarred hand and cupped the side of her neck. His touch was surprisingly gentle and maddeningly exciting. She knew she had to pull back, but her legs, along with her will, refused to obey.

He lifted his thumb and slid it upward along the curve of her jaw and under the edge of the honeycombed veil. It dipped into the valley behind the lobe of her ear. He caressed the silky hollow, sending quivers coursing through her.

He brushed the delicate shells of her ears and the tendrils of curl that feathered around her small jet earbob. His quiet breathing rippled the bottom edge of her veil. She tried to move away, but she was paralyzed. Then he lowered his lips.

His kiss was gentle and persuading, nothing at all like the wet, grinding assault from Hamilton Woodward's friend. Her hands lifted of their own accord and clasped his sides. The feel of warm-muscled flesh through the thin material of his shirt became part of the kiss. She lost herself in a swelling sea of sensation.

His lips opened and began to move over her closed ones. He curved his hand along the delicate line of her spine to the small of her back. The narrow space between their bodies disappeared.

Her head swam as his chest pressed her breasts, and his hips settled against the flatness of her stomach. The moist tip of his tongue began its gentle sorcery, sliding leisurely between her lips.

The shocking intimacy inflamed her. A

wild rush of hot sensation poured through every part of her body.

And through his.

They lost their identities. For Kit, Cain no longer had a name. He was the quintessential man, fierce and demanding. And for Cain, the mysterious veiled creature in his arms was everything that a woman should be...but never was.

He grew impatient. His tongue began to probe more deeply, determined to slip past the barrier of her teeth and gain full access to the sweet interior of her mouth.

The unaccustomed aggression brought a flicker of sanity to Kit's fevered mind. Something was wrong....

He brushed the side of her breast, and reality returned in a cold, condemning rush. She made a muffled sound and sprang back.

Cain was more shaken than he cared to admit. He'd found the thorns of his wild rose much too soon.

She stood before him, breasts heaving, hands balled into fists. With a pessimistic certainty that the rest of her face could never live up to the promise of her mouth, he reached out and pushed the veil up onto the brim of her hat.

Recognition didn't come instantly. Maybe it was because he took in the separate features of her face instead of the whole. He saw the smooth, intelligent forehead, the thick, dark slashes of eyebrows, the heavily lashed violet eyes, the determined chin. All of it, together with that wild-rose mouth from which he'd drunk so deeply, spoke of a vivid, unconventional beauty.

Then he felt an uneasiness, a nagging sense of familiarity, a hint of something unpleasant lurking on the other side of his memory. He watched the nostrils of her small, straight nose quiver like the wings of a hummingbird. She set her jaw and lifted her chin.

In that instant, he knew her.

Kit saw his pale gray irises rim with black, but she was too stricken by what had passed between them to step away. What had happened to her? This man was her mortal enemy. How could she have forgotten that? She felt sick, angry, and more confused than she'd ever been.

A disturbance came from the hallway—a series of rapid clicks, as if a sack of parched corn was being spilled on the wooden floor. A streak of black-and-white fur darted into the room, then skidded to a stop. *Merlin.*

The dog cocked his head to study her, but it didn't take him nearly as long to guess her identity as it had Cain. With three barks of recognition, he raced over to greet his old friend.

Kit fell to her knees. Oblivious to the damage his dusty paws were inflicting on her dove-gray traveling dress, she hugged him and let him lap her face. Her hat fell to the carpet, loosening her carefully arranged hair, but she didn't care.

Cain's voice intruded on their reunion like a

polar wind over a glacier. "I see finishing school hasn't improved you. You're still the same headstrong little brat you were three years ago."

Kit looked up at him and said the first thing that came to mind. "You're just mad because the dog's smarter than you are."

8

Not long after Cain had stalked out of the sitting room, Kit heard a familiar voice. "Lucy, did you let that dog in the house again?"

"He slipped past me, Miz Sophronia."

"Well, he won't slip past me!"

Kit smiled as she heard the approach of brisk, efficient footsteps. She hugged Merlin and whispered, "I won't let her get you."

Sophronia swept into the room, then drew to a sudden halt. "Oh, I'm sorry. Lucy didn't say we had a visitor."

Kit looked up and gave her a mischievous grin.

"Kit!" Sophronia's hand flew to her mouth. "Lord! Is it really you?"

With a laugh, Kit sprang to her feet and raced toward her. "It's me, all right."

The women hugged each other while Merlin circled them, barking at their skirts.

"It's so good to see you. Oh, Sophronia, you're even more beautiful than I remember."

"Me! Look at you. You look like you just stepped out of *Godey's Lady's Book*."

"It's all Elsbeth's doing." Kit laughed again and grabbed Sophronia's hand. They sank down on the settee, where they tried to catch up on three years of separation.

Kit knew it was her fault their correspondence had been so infrequent. Sophronia didn't like to write letters, and the few she'd sent were so full of praise for what Cain was doing at Risen Glory that Kit's replies had been scathing. Finally Sophronia had stopped writing.

Kit remembered her earlier agitation over all the improvements Sophronia had made to the house. Now that seemed petty, and she praised her for everything she'd done.

Sophronia drank in Kit's words. She knew the old house was shining under her care, and she was proud of her accomplishments. At the same time, she began to feel the familiar combination of love and resentment that always plagued her where Kit was concerned.

For so long, Sophronia had been the only one watching out for Kit. Now Kit was a woman with friendships and experiences Sophronia couldn't share. She was also beautiful, poised, and at home in a world Sophronia would never enter.

The old hurts began to throb.

"Don't think because you're home now you can start stickin' your nose in my business and tellin' me how to run this house."

Kit merely chuckled. "I wouldn't think of

it. All I care about is the land. The fields. I can't wait to see everything."

Sophronia's resentment faded and worry took its place. Putting the major and Kit under the same roof was going to lead to trouble.

Rosemary Weston's old bedroom had been redecorated in blush pink and soft moss green. It reminded Kit of the inside of a ripe watermelon, close to the bottom where the pink meat joined the pale iridescence of the rind. She was glad the cool, pretty room would be hers, even though it was second-best to the bedroom Cain occupied. The fact that both shared a common sitting room made her uneasy, but at least it would allow her to keep a closer watch on him.

How could she have let him kiss her like that? The question she'd been trying to avoid asking felt like a fist in her stomach. True, she'd pushed him away, but not before he'd thoroughly kissed her. If it had been Brandon Parsell, she could have understood, but how could she have done such a thing with Baron Cain?

She remembered Mrs. Templeton's lecture on Eve's Shame. Surely only an unnatural woman would abandon herself like that with her most bitter enemy. Maybe there was something wrong with her.

Nonsense. She'd merely been exhausted from the trip, and Miss Dolly's chatter was enough to drive anyone into doing something irrational.

Determined not to think of it again, she stripped off her dress and stood in chemise and petticoat to freshen up at the washstand. Bathing was her favorite luxury. She could hardly believe she'd once hated it so. What a silly child she'd been. Silly about everything except her hatred for Cain.

She cursed softly under her breath, a habit even Elsbeth hadn't been able to stop. Before Cain had stormed out of the sitting room, he'd ordered her to meet him in the library after dinner. She wasn't looking forward to the interview. At the same time, he needed to understand he was no longer dealing with an immature eighteen-year-old.

Lucy had unpacked her trunks, and for a moment Kit considered throwing on one of her oldest dresses and dashing outside to reacquaint herself with her home. But she had to be downstairs soon, ready to do battle again. Morning would be time enough.

She chose a frock with sprigs of gay blue forget-me-nots scattered over a white background. The skirt was drawn up in soft folds to reveal an underskirt in the same blue as the flowers. Cain had provided a generous clothing allowance, damn his soul, and Kit had a beautiful wardrobe. Much of the thanks went to Elsbeth, who said Kit's taste was too erratic and hadn't trusted her to shop alone. The truth was, unless Elsbeth rode herd, Kit generally grew bored and settled for whatever the shopkeepers placed before her.

Impatiently she pulled out her hairpins.

That morning, she'd dressed her hair in the Spanish style, parted in the center and pulled into a simple coil at the nape of her neck. With a few tendrils escaping here and there and her small jet earbobs, the sophisticated style had been perfect for her first encounter with Cain. But she couldn't tolerate the confinement any longer. Now she brushed her hair out until it crackled, then caught it back from her face with the silver filigreed combs Elsbeth had given her. It tumbled in a riot of curls that spilled over her shoulders. After dabbing jasmine scent at her wrists, she was ready to fetch Miss Dolly.

As she knocked at her door, she wondered how her fragile companion would handle sitting at dinner with a Yankee war hero. She knocked a second time, and when there was no response, pushed open the door.

Miss Dolly sat huddled in a rocking chair in the corner of the darkened room. Tears streaked her wrinkled cheeks, and she held the tattered fragment of what had once been a baby-blue handkerchief.

Kit dashed to her side. "Miss Dolly! What's wrong?"

The older woman didn't seem to hear. Kit knelt before her. "Miss Dolly?"

"Hello, darlin'," she said vaguely. "I didn't hear you come in."

"You've been crying." Kit clasped the woman's bird-frail hands. "Tell me what's wrong."

"Nothing, really. Silly memories. Making rag babies with my sisters when we were children. Playin' under the grape arbor. Reminiscence is part of old age."

"You're not old, Miss Dolly. Why, just look at you in your pretty white dress. You look as fresh as a spring day."

"I do try to keep myself pretty," Miss Dolly acknowledged, straightening a little in her chair and making a dab at her wet cheeks. "It's just that sometimes, on days like today, I find myself thinkin' about things that happened a long time ago, and it makes me sad."

"What kind of things?"

Miss Dolly patted Kit's hand. "Now, now, darlin'. You don't want to hear my ramblin's."

"You don't ramble," Kit assured her, even though only a few hours earlier, that very habit had been driving her to distraction.

"You've got a good heart, Katharine Louise. I knew it the moment I set eyes on you. I was so glad when you asked me to accompany you back to South Carolina." Her ribbons dipped as she shook her head. "I didn't like it in the North. Everybody had such loud voices. I don't like Yankees, Katharine. I don't like them at all."

"You're upset about meeting Major Cain, aren't you?" Kit rubbed the back of Miss Dolly's hand. "I shouldn't have brought you here. I was only thinking of myself, not of how it would affect you."

"Now, now. Don't you be blamin' your sweet self for a silly old woman's foolishness."

"I won't let you stay if it's going to make you unhappy."

Miss Dolly's eyes widened in alarm. "But I don't have anywhere else to go!" She pushed herself up from the rocking chair and began to cry again. "Silly foolishness...that's all this is. I'll—I'll just freshen up, and then we'll go right downstairs for dinner. I won't be a minute. Not a...not a minute."

Kit rose and embraced the woman's frail shoulders. "Calm yourself, Miss Dolly. I won't send you away. Not as long as you want to stay with me. I promise."

Hope flickered in her companion's eyes. "You won't send me away?"

"Never." Kit smoothed the puffy white sleeves of Miss Dolly's gown, then gave her powdery cheek a kiss. "Make yourself pretty for dinner."

Miss Dolly glanced nervously toward the hallway that lay beyond the safe haven of her room. "All—all right, darlin'."

"Please don't worry about Major Cain." Kit smiled. "Just pretend you're entertaining General Lee."

After ten minutes of primping, Miss Dolly decided she was ready, but Kit was so happy to see the older woman's spirits restored that she didn't mind the wait. As they descended the stairs, Miss Dolly began fussing over her. "Hold still a minute, darlin'. The overskirt on your pretty dress isn't caught up properly." She clucked her tongue while she adjusted the garment. "I do wish you'd be a little more careful with your appearance. I don't mean to be critical, but you don't always look quite as neat as a young lady should."

"Yes, ma'am." Kit assumed her most docile expression, the one that had never fooled Elvira Templeton but seemed to do the trick with Miss Dolly. At the same time, she made up her mind to murder Baron Cain with her bare hands if he did anything tonight to frighten Miss Dolly.

Just then he came out of the library. He was dressed informally in a pair of black trousers and a white shirt, his hair still damp from his bath. She relished the fact that he was too boorish to dress for dinner, even though he'd known there'd be ladies at the table.

He looked up and saw them coming toward him. Something she couldn't decipher flickered in his eyes.

Her heart began to pound. The memory of that lunatic kiss washed over her. She took a deep breath. The evening that lay ahead would be hard enough. She had to forget what had happened and keep her wits about her. Cain's appearance was going to terrify Miss Dolly.

She turned to soothe her, only to see the old woman's lips curving in a coquettish smile. Miss Dolly extended one lace-encased hand and made her descent into the hallway as gracefully as a debutante.

"My dear, dear General. I can't tell you what an honor this is for me, sir. You will never know the hours I've spent on my poor knees, prayin' for your safety. Never in my wildest dreams did I ever imagine I'd have the honor of meeting you." She thrust her tiny hand into Cain's large one. "I'm Katharine's chaperone, Dorthea Pinckney Calhoun, of the Columbia Calhouns." And then she dropped a deep curtsy that would have done any Templeton Girl proud.

Cain stared in bewilderment at the top of her frilly cap. She bobbed back up, her head barely coming to his middle shirt button. "If there's anything, anything at all, I can do to make you comfortable during your stay here at Risen Glory, General, you need only ask. From this moment, this very *instant*, consider me your devoted servant."

Miss Dolly's eyelids batted at him with such alarming speed Kit was afraid she'd blind herself.

Cain turned to Kit for enlightenment, but Kit was mystified. He cleared his throat. "I believe—I'm afraid, madam, that you've made a mistake. I'm not entitled to the rank of general. Indeed, I hold no military office at all now, although some still refer to me by my former rank of major."

Miss Dolly gave a trill of girlish laughter. "Oh, my, my! Silly me! You've caught me like a kitten in the cream." She lowered her voice to a conspiratorial whisper. "I forget that you're in disguise. And a very good one it is, I might add. No Yankee spy could ever recognize you, although it's a shame you had to shave off your beard. I do admire beards."

Cain's patience snapped and he turned on Kit. "What's she talking about?"

Miss Dolly pressed her fingers to his arm. "Now, now, no need to fret. I promise when we're in company I'll be very discreet, and only address you as Major, dear General."

Cain's voice sounded a warning. "Kit...."

Miss Dolly clucked her tongue. "There, there, General. I don't want you to worry your head for an instant about Katharine Louise. A more loyal daughter of the Confederacy does not exist. She would never betray your true identity to anyone. Isn't that so, darlin'?"

Kit tried to reply. She even opened her mouth. But nothing seemed to come out.

Miss Dolly plucked up the chicken-skin fan that dangled from her bony wrist and tapped Kit's arm. "Tell the general that's so, darlin', this very instant. We mustn't let him worry unnecessarily about betrayal. The poor man has enough on his mind without adding to his burden. Go on, now. Tell him he can trust you. Tell him."

"You can trust me," Kit croaked.

Cain glared at her.

Miss Dolly smiled and sniffed the air. "If my nose isn't betraying me, I do believe I smell chicken fricassee. I'm more than a little partial to fricassee, 'deed I am, especially if it contains just a tiny dash of nutmeg."

She linked her arm through Cain's and turned toward the dining room. "You know, General, there's a strong possibility that we're distantly related. According to my great-aunt, Phoebe Littlefield Calhoun, her father's branch of the family is connected through marriage to the Virginia Lees."

Cain stopped dead in his tracks. "Are you trying to tell me, madam— Do you actually believe that I am General Robert E. Lee?"

Miss Dolly opened her Cupid's-bow mouth to respond, only to close it with a giggle. "Oh, no, you shan't catch me that easily, General. And it's naughty of you to test me, especially after I informed you that you could rely on my discretion. You're Major Baron Nathaniel Cain. Katharine Louise told me that quite clearly."

And then she favored him with a broad, conspiratorial wink.

Cain scowled throughout dinner, and Kit's normal appetite deserted her. Not only did she have to endure his company and the memory of their kiss, but she knew she'd planted the seed of Miss Dolly's latest madness. Miss Dolly, however, had no difficulty filling the strained silence. She chirped on about fricassees, distant relations, and the medicinal qualities of chamomile until Cain's face looked like a storm cloud. Over dessert, he came to a full state of alert when she suggested an informal poetry recitation in the parlor.

"Worst luck, Miss Calhoun." His gaze traveled down the table. "Katharine Louise has brought along some secret dispatches from New

York City. I'm afraid I need to meet with her privately." One tawny brow shot upward. "And *immediately*!"

Miss Dolly beamed. "Why, of course, dear General. You needn't say another word. You go on. I'll just sit here and enjoy this delicious ginger cake. Why, I haven't—"

"You're a true patriot, madam." He pushed back his chair and gestured toward the door. "The library, *Katharine Louise.*"

"I...uh..."

"Now."

"Hurry along, my dear. The general is a busy man."

"And about to get busier," he said pointedly.

Kit rose and swept past him. Fine. It was time they had a showdown.

The library at Risen Glory was much as Kit remembered. Comfortable chairs with sagging leather seats sat at angles to the old mahogany desk. The generous windows kept everything light and cheerful despite the somber leather-bound books that lined the shelves.

It had always been her favorite room at Risen Glory, and she resented the unfamiliar humidor sitting on the desk as well as the Colt army revolver that rested in a red-lined wooden box next to it. Most of all, she resented the portrait of Abraham Lincoln that hung above the mantelpiece in place of "The Beheading of John the Baptist," a painting that had been there for as long as she could remember.

Cain slouched into the chair behind the desk, propped his heels on the mahogany surface, and crossed his ankles. His posture was deliberately insolent, but she didn't let him see that it annoyed her. Earlier that afternoon when she'd been veiled, he'd treated her as a woman. Now he wanted to treat her as his stable boy. He'd soon see it wouldn't be that easy to ignore the years that had passed.

"I told you to stay in New York," he said.

"So you did." She pretended to study the room. "That portrait of Mr. Lincoln is out of place at Risen Glory. It insults my father's memory."

"From what I hear, your father insulted his own memory."

"True. But he was still my father, and he died bravely."

"There's nothing brave about death." The angular planes of his face grew harsh in the dim lamplight of the room. "Why did you disobey my orders and leave New York?"

"Because your orders were unreasonable."

"I don't have to explain myself."

"So you seem to think. I fulfilled our agreement."

"Did you? Our agreement was for you to conduct yourself properly."

"I completed my time at the Academy."

"It's not your activities at the Academy that concern me." Without taking his feet from the desktop, he leaned forward and extracted a letter from a drawer. Then he slapped it on the desk. "Interesting reading, although I wouldn't want to show it to anyone who's easily shocked."

She picked it up. Her stomach twisted when she saw the signature. *Hamilton Woodward.*

> *It is my sad duty to report that last Easter, while a guest in our house, your ward behaved in a manner so shocking, I can barely report it. On the evening of our annual dinner party, Katharine brazenly attempted to seduce one of my partners. Fortunately, I interrupted in time. The poor man was stunned. He has a wife and children, and is prominent in local charities. Her wanton behavior makes me fear that she might be afflicted with the sickness of nymphomania...*

She crumpled the letter and threw it on his desk. She had no idea what nymphomania was, but it sounded horrible. "This letter's a lie. You can't believe it."

"I was reserving judgment until I had a chance to travel to New York at the end of the summer and speak with you personally. That was why I told you to stay where you were."

"We had an agreement. You can't set that aside just because Hamilton Woodward is a fool."

"Is he?"

"Yes." She felt the color burning in her cheeks.

"You're telling me you don't make a habit of offering your favors?"

"Of course not."

His eyes drifted to her mouth, forcing her

to recall what had happened between them only a few hours earlier.

"If this letter's such a lie," he said quietly, "how do you explain slipping into my arms so easily this afternoon? Was that your idea of proper conduct?"

She didn't know how to defend something she couldn't understand herself, so she went on the attack. "Maybe you're the one who should explain. Or do you always assault the young women who come into this house?"

"Assault?"

"Consider yourself lucky I was fatigued by my journey," she said as haughtily as she could manage. "Otherwise my fist would have ended up in your belly. Which is what I did to Mr. Woodward's friend."

He dropped his feet to the carpet. "I see."

He didn't believe her. "It's interesting that you're so concerned about my behavior, but you don't seem to be giving any thought to your own."

"It's not the same thing. You're a woman."

"Ah, I see. And that makes a difference?"

He looked prickly. "You know exactly what I mean."

"If you say so."

"I say you're going back to New York!"

"And I say I'm not."

"It isn't up to you to decide."

That was truer than she could bear to admit, and she thought quickly. "You want to get rid of me, isn't that right? And put an end to this ridiculous guardianship?"

"More than you'll ever know."

"Then you'll let me stay at Risen Glory."

"Forgive me if I don't see the connection."

She tried to speak calmly. "There are several gentlemen who wish to marry me. I simply need a few weeks to make up my mind which one I'm going to choose."

His face clouded. "Make up your mind in New York."

"How can I? It's been a confusing three years, and this is the most important decision of my life. I have to consider it carefully, and I need familiar surroundings to do that. Otherwise I'll never be able to decide, and neither of us wants that." The explanation was thin at best, but she gave it all the sincerity she could muster.

His glower grew darker. He moved toward the fireplace. "Somehow I can't see you as a devoted wife."

She couldn't see herself that way either, but still his comment offended her. "I don't know why not." She summoned an image of Lilith Shelton as she'd held court with her opinions about men and marriage. "Marriage is what every woman wants, isn't it?" She adopted the same wide-eyed vacuousness she'd seen so often on her former classmate's face. "A husband to take care of her, pretty clothes, a piece of jewelry on her birthday. What more could a woman want from life?"

Cain's eyes grew wintry. "Three years ago when you were my stable boy, you were a thorn in my side, but you were brave and hardworking. That Kit Weston wouldn't have been interested in selling herself for clothes and jewelry."

"That Kit Weston hadn't been forced by her guardian to attend a finishing school devoted to turning young girls into wives."

She'd made her point. He reacted with a bored shrug and leaned against the mantelpiece. "It's all in the past."

"That past has molded who I am now." She took a deep breath. "I intend to marry, but I don't want to make the wrong choice. I need time, and I'd like to have that time here."

He studied her. "These young men..." His voice dropped in pitch and developed an unsettling huskiness. "Do you kiss them like you kissed me yesterday?"

She needed all her willpower not to look away. "It was the fatigue from my journey. They're much too gentlemanly to have pressed themselves as you did."

"Then they're fools."

She wondered what he meant by that. He moved away from the fireplace. "Very well. You can have one month, but if you haven't made up your mind by then, you're going back to New York, husband or not. And another thing..." He tilted his head toward the hallway. "That crazy woman has to go. Let her rest for a day, then put her on the train. I'll make sure she's compensated."

"No! I can't."

"Yes, you can."

"I promised her."

"That was your mistake."

He looked so unbending. What argument could she offer that would convince him? "I can't stay here without a chaperone."

"It's a little late to worry about respectability."

"Perhaps for you, but not for me."

"I don't think she'll be much of a chaperone. As soon as any of the neighbors talk to her, they'll realize she's crazy as a loon."

Kit rose in hot defense. "She's not crazy!"

"You could have fooled me."

"She's just a little...different."

"More than a little." Cain regarded her suspiciously. "Just how did she get the idea that I was General Lee?"

"I...might have inadvertently mentioned something."

"You told her I was General Lee?"

"No, of course not. She was afraid to meet you, and I was trying to tease her into a better mood. I had no idea she'd take me seriously." Kit explained what had happened when she went to Miss Dolly's room.

"And now you expect me to go along with this charade?"

"It won't be hard," Kit pointed out reasonably. "She does most of the talking."

"That's not good enough."

"It'll have to be." She hated pleading with him, and the words nearly stuck in her throat. "Please. She doesn't have anyplace else to go."

"Damn it, Kit! I don't want her here."

"You don't want me here, either, but you're letting me stay. What difference does one more person make?"

"A big difference." His expression turned calculating. "You want a lot from me, but I haven't heard you offer anything in return."

"I'll exercise your horses," she said quickly.

"I was thinking of something more personal."

She swallowed. "I'll mend your clothes."

"You were more imaginative three years ago. Of course, you weren't as...experienced then as you are now. Do you remember the night you offered to be my mistress?"

She slid the tip of her tongue over her dry lips. "I was desperate."

"How desperate are you now?"

"This discussion is highly improper," she managed to reply with all the starch of Elvira Templeton.

"Not as improper as that kiss this afternoon." He came closer, and his voice was low, slightly husky. For a moment she thought he was going to kiss her again. Instead, his lips curled into a smile full of mockery. "Miss Dolly can stay for now. I'll make up my mind later how you can repay me."

As he left the room, she stared at the door and tried to decide whether she'd won or lost.

That night, Cain lay motionless in the dark, one arm crooked behind his head, and stared at the ceiling. What kind of game had he been playing with her this evening? Or was she the one playing the game?

Her kiss this afternoon had made it clear she was no innocent, but was she as wanton as Woodward's letter would have him believe? He didn't know. For now, he would simply have to wait and watch.

In his mind he saw a wild-rose mouth with bruised, petal-soft lips, and desire rushed through him, hot and thick.

One thing he knew for certain. The time when he could regard her as a child was gone forever.

9

Kit was up early the next morning despite her restless night. She pulled on khaki britches that would have scandalized Elsbeth, then shrugged into a boy's shirt and drew it closed over her lace-edged chemise. She regretted the shirt's long sleeves, but her arms would be brown as a butternut if she left them exposed to the sun. She consoled herself that the white material was as thin and fine as the fabric of her undergarments and would undoubtedly be cool.

She tucked her shirttails into her britches and fastened the short row of buttons snugly over the front. As she drew on her boots, she enjoyed the way the soft brown leather molded to her feet and calves. They were the first pair of good riding boots she'd ever owned, and she couldn't wait to try them out.

She arranged her hair in a single long braid at the back. Tendrils curled at her temples and in front of the tiny silver ear studs she'd fastened in her lobes. To shade her face, she'd bought a boy's black felt hat with a flat brim and a thin leather cord that fastened beneath her chin.

When she finished dressing, she frowned at her reflection in the cheval glass. Despite her masculine dress, no one could mistake her for a boy. The soft material of the shirt outlined her breasts with more definition than she'd anticipated, and the slim cut of the boy's britches clung to womanly hips.

What did it matter? She intended to wear her unorthodox outfit only when she rode on Risen Glory land. Anyplace else, she'd wear her new riding habit no matter how much she detested its confinement. She grimaced as she remembered that she'd also have to ride sidesaddle then, something she'd done only on occasional outings in Central Park. How she'd hated it. The sidesaddle had robbed her of the sense of power she loved and left her feeling awkward and unbalanced.

She let herself out of the house quietly, passing up breakfast and a morning chat with Sophronia. Her old friend had come to her room last night. Although Sophronia listened politely to Kit's stories, she'd volunteered little about the changes in her own life. When Kit had pressed her for details, she'd relayed neighborhood gossip that revealed nothing of herself. Only when Kit had asked her about Magnus Owen did she seem to be the Sophronia of old, haughty and snappish.

Sophronia had always been an enigma, but now she seemed even more so. It wasn't just the outward changes produced by pretty clothes and a good diet. Sophronia seemed to resent her. Maybe the feeling had always been there, but Kit had been too young to understand it. What made it even more puzzling was that, beneath that resentment, Kit felt the old, familiar force of Sophronia's love.

She delicately sniffed the air as she walked across the open yard behind the house. It smelled exactly as she remembered it, of good, rich earth and fresh manure. She even caught the faint scent of skunk, not altogether unpleasant at a distance. Merlin came out to greet her, and she stopped to scratch his ears and throw a stick for him to fetch.

The horses weren't yet in the paddock, so she let herself into the stable, a new building erected on the foundation of the one the Yankees had burned. The heels of her boots clicked on the stone floor, which was swept as cleanly as when Kit had attended to it.

There were ten stalls, four of which were currently filled, two with carriage horses. She inspected the other horses and dismissed one immediately, an old sorrel mare who was obviously gentle but had no sparkle. She'd be a good mount for a timid rider, but Kit wasn't timid.

The other horse excited her. He was a midnight-black gelding with a white blaze running down the center of his head. He was a large, powerful-looking animal, nearly eighteen hands, and his eyes were alert and lively.

She reached out a hand to stroke the long, elegant neck. "What's your name, boy?"

The animal whinnied softly and tossed his powerful head.

Kit smiled. "I have an idea we're going to be good friends."

Just then the stable door opened, and she turned to see a young boy, perhaps eleven or twelve, come in.

"Are you Miz Kit?"

"Yes. Who are you?"

"I'm Samuel. The major told me if you came to the stable today, I'm s'posed to tell you he wants you to ride Lady."

Kit looked suspiciously toward the old sorrel mare. "Lady?"

"Yes, ma'am."

"Sorry, Samuel." She stroked the gelding's silky mane. "We'll saddle this one instead."

"That's Temptation, ma'am. And the major was most particular. He said for you to leave Temptation alone and ride Lady, and he said if I let you leave this stable on Temptation, he was goin' to have my hide, and then you'd have to live with that on your conscience."

Kit fumed at Cain's blatant manipulation. She doubted he'd see through on his threat to hurt Samuel, but the man still had the heart of a marauding Yankee, so she couldn't take the chance. She gazed longingly at Temptation. Never had a horse been better named.

"Saddle Lady." She sighed. "I'll talk to Mr. Cain."

As she'd suspected, Lady was more interested in grazing than racing. Kit soon gave up trying to urge the mare beyond a sedate trot and turned her attention to the changes around her.

All but a few of the old slave cabins had been destroyed. That was the part of Risen Glory she didn't let herself think about, and she was glad to see them gone. The cabins that were left had been painted and repaired. Each had its own garden, and flowers grew near the front doors. She waved at the children playing in the shade of the same buckthorns where she'd once played.

When she came to the edge of the first planted field, she dismounted and walked over to inspect it. The young cotton plants were covered with tight buds. A lizard slithered in the dirt near her boots, and she smiled. Lizards and toads, along with martins and mockingbirds, preyed on the bollworms that could be so destructive to the cotton plants. It was too early to tell, but it looked as if Cain had the beginnings of a good crop. She felt a mixture of pride and anger. This should be her crop, not his.

As she stood looking out across the land she knew so well, she felt a flutter of panic. It was far more prosperous than she'd imagined. What if she didn't have enough money in her trust fund to buy the plantation back? Somehow she had to get access to the plantation's books. She refused to consider the awful possibility that he might not be willing to sell.

She strode over to Lady, who was nibbling away at a patch of new clover, and snatched up the bridle she hadn't bothered to secure. She used a stump to climb back into the saddle, then headed toward the pond, where she'd spent so many happy summer hours swimming. It was just as she remembered, with its clean spring-fed water and willow-lined bank. She promised herself a swim as soon as she was certain she wouldn't be disturbed.

She rode on to the tiny cemetery where her mother and her grandparents were buried and paused outside the iron fence. Only her father's body was missing, buried in a mass grave in Hardin County, Tennessee, not far from Shiloh Church. Rosemary Weston lay alone by the far corner of the fence.

Kit grimly set out toward the southeast corner of the property and the new spinning mill she'd heard about from Brandon Parsell. Just before she cleared the last stand of trees, she saw a big chestnut tied off to the side and decided it must be Vandal, the horse Samuel had told her about while he was saddling Lady. The gelding was a fine animal, but she missed Apollo. She remembered what Magnus had told her about Cain.

The major doesn't let himself get too attached to things—horses, the towns where he lives, even his books.

She rounded the trees and caught her first sight of the new spinning mill. The South had always shipped most of its bulk cotton to England for processing and weaving. In the years since the war, a handful of men had built a few scattered mills that took the ginned cotton and spun it into thread. As a result, compact cotton spools could be shipped to England for weaving instead of the bulky cotton bales, yielding a thousand times the value for the same tonnage. It was an idea whose time had come. Kit just wished it hadn't come on Risen Glory's land.

Last night, Kit had questioned Sophronia about Cain's mill and learned there wouldn't be any power looms for weaving. This would be a spinning mill only. It would take the ginned cotton, clean it, card it to straighten the fibers, then pull and twist them into yarn.

Now she saw an oblong brick building, two and a half stories tall, with many windows. The building was smaller than the pictures she'd seen of the big New England textile mills along the Merrimack River, but huge and threatening on Risen Glory's land. It would make everything so much more complicated.

The mill was alive with hammering and the voices of the workers. Three men worked on the roof, while another climbed the ladder leaning against the side of the building with a stack of shingles on his back.

They'd all shed their shirts. As one of them straightened, a wave of muscles rippled on his back. Even though he was turned away, she recognized him. She rode closer to the building and dismounted.

A burly man pushing a wheelbarrow saw her and nudged the man next to him. Both of them stopped what they were doing to stare at her. Gradually the construction site fell silent as, one by one, the men stepped out of the building or peered through open windows to see the young woman dressed in boy's clothing.

Cain grew conscious of the silence and looked down from his perch on the roof. At first he saw only the top of a flat-brimmed hat, but he didn't need to see the face beneath it to recognize his visitor. One look at the slim, womanly body so clearly revealed by that white shirt and those khaki britches that hugged a pair of long, slim legs told him everything he needed to know.

He swung his foot onto the ladder and descended. When he reached the bottom he turned to Kit and studied her. God, she was beautiful.

Kit felt her cheeks flaming with embarrassment. She should have worn the modest riding habit she hated. Instead of reprimanding her as she'd expected, Cain seemed to be enjoying her outfit. The corner of his mouth crinkled.

"You might be wearing britches, but you sure don't look like my stable boy anymore."

His good mood irked her. "Stop it."

"What?"

"Smiling."

"I'm not supposed to smile?"

"Not at me. It looks ridiculous. Don't smile at anyone. Your face was born to scowl."

"I'll try to remember that." He took her arm and nudged her toward the mill door. "Come on. I'll show you around."

Although the construction of the building was nearly completed, the steam engine that would power the machinery was the only equipment that had been installed. Cain described the overhead belt drive and spindles, but she had a hard time concentrating. He should have put his shirt on before he'd decided to act as her tour guide.

She met a middle-aged man with ginger hair and whiskers whom Cain introduced as Jacob Childs, a New Englander he'd hired away from a mill in Providence. For the first time, she learned that Cain had made several trips North during the past few years to visit the textile mills there. It galled her that he'd never once stopped at the Academy to check on her, and she told him so.

"I didn't think of it," he replied.

"You're a terrible excuse for a guardian."

"I won't argue with you there."

"Mrs. Templeton could have been beating me, for all you knew."

"Not likely. You'd have shot her. I wasn't worried."

She saw his pride in the mill, but as they moved back into the yard, she couldn't find it in her to compliment him. "I'd like to talk to you about Temptation."

Cain appeared distracted. She glanced

down to see what he was looking at and realized her curves were more apparent in the sunlight than they'd been in the dim interior of the building. She moved into the shade and pointed an accusing finger at Lady, who was decapitating a patch of buttercups.

"That horse is nearly as old as Miss Dolly. I want to ride Temptation."

Cain seemed to have to force his attention back to her face. "He's too much horse for a woman. I know Lady's old, but you'll have to make do."

"I've been riding horses like Temptation since I was eight years old."

"Sorry, Kit, but that horse is a handful, even for me."

"But we're not talking about you," she said smoothly. "We're talking about someone who knows how to ride."

Cain seemed more amused than angry. "You think so?"

"What do you say we see? You on Vandal and me on Temptation. We'll start at the gate next to the barn, race past the pond to the maple grove, and finish right here."

"You're not going to bait me."

"Oh, I'm not baiting you." She gave him a silky smile. "I'm challenging you."

"You do like to live dangerously, don't you, Katharine Louise?"

"It's the only way."

"All right. Let's see what you've got."

He was going to race her. She gave a silent cheer as he grabbed his shirt from a sawhorse.

While he buttoned it, he issued orders to the men who'd been standing around staring at her. Then he picked up a worn Western hat with a stained sweatband that testified to years of comfortable wear and set it on his head.

"I'll meet you at the stable." He rode from the clearing without bothering to wait for her.

Lady was eager for the oats that awaited her, and she made the homeward journey a little faster, but they still arrived well after Cain. Temptation was already saddled when Kit got there, and Cain was checking the cinch strap. Kit dismounted and handed Lady's bridle to Samuel. Then she walked over to Temptation and ran a hand down his muzzle.

"Ready?" Cain said shortly.

"I'm ready."

He gave her a leg up, and she swung into the saddle. When Temptation felt her weight, he began to prance and sidestep, and it took all her skill to keep him under control. By the time the horse had finally settled down, Cain had mounted Vandal.

As she rode from the yard, Kit was intoxicated by the sensation of leashed power in the animal beneath her, and she could barely resist giving him his head. She reluctantly reined in when she reached the gate near the barn.

"The first one who makes it back to the mill wins," she said to Cain.

He tipped up the brim of his hat with his thumb. "I'm not racing you."

"What do you mean?" Kit needed to race him. She wanted to compete with him at something where his size and strength wouldn't give him an advantage. On horseback, the differences between a man and a woman would disappear.

"Exactly what I said."

"Is the Hero of Missionary Ridge afraid to get beat by a woman in front of his men?"

Cain squinted slightly in the blaze of the late-morning sun. "I don't have anything to prove, and you're not going to bait me."

"Why did you come here if you weren't going to race?"

"You were doing a little bragging back there. I wanted to see if any of it was true."

She rested her hand across the pommel and smiled. "I wasn't bragging. I was stating facts."

"Talk's cheap, Katharine Louise. Let's see what you can do with a horse."

Before she could respond, he set off. She watched as he let Vandal break from an easy trot into a canter.

He rode well for a large man, so relaxed and easy he seemed to be an extension of his horse. She realized he was every bit as good a rider as she. Another black mark to chalk up against him.

She leaned over Temptation's sleek black neck. "All right, boy. Let's show him."

Temptation proved to be everything she'd hoped. At first she kept him abreast of Vandal and held him to a canter, but then, when she sensed the horse straining to go faster, she let him have his head. Veering away from the planted fields, she turned him into an open meadow. They tore across it at a fierce gallop, and as she felt the raw strength of the animal beneath her, everything else disappeared. There was no yesterday or tomorrow, no ruthless man with cold gray eyes, no kiss she couldn't explain. There was only the magnificent animal that had become part of her.

She spotted a low hedge ahead. With the barest pressure of her knees, she turned the horse toward it. As they thundered closer, she leaned forward in the saddle, keeping her knees tight to his flanks. She felt a great surge of power as Temptation effortlessly cleared the barrier.

Reluctantly she slowed him to a trot and turned back. She'd done enough for now. If she pushed the horse harder, Cain would accuse her of being reckless, and she wasn't going to give him an excuse to keep this horse from her.

He waited for her at the top of the meadow. She reined in beside him and wiped the perspiration from her cheeks with her sleeve.

His saddle creaked slightly as he moved. "That was quite an exhibition."

She kept silent, waiting for his verdict.

"Did you ride at all when you were in New York?" he asked.

"I wouldn't call it riding."

With a tug on the reins, he turned Vandal toward the stable. "Then you're going to be sore as hell tomorrow."

Was that all he was going to say? She watched his retreating back, then tapped her heels against Temptation's flanks and caught up with him. "Well?"

"Well, what?"

"Are you going to let me ride this horse or not?"

"I don't see why not. As long as you don't put a sidesaddle on him, you can ride him."

She smiled and resisted the urge to turn Temptation back toward the meadow for another gallop.

She reached the yard before Cain and dismounted while Samuel held the bridle. "You'd better take your time cooling him out," she told the youngster. "And put a blanket on him. I rode him hard."

Cain drew up in time to hear her orders. "Samuel's nearly as good a stable boy as you were, Kit." He smiled and dismounted. "But he doesn't look half as fine in britches."

For two and a half years, Sophronia had been punishing Magnus Owen for standing between herself and Baron Cain. Now the door of the rear sitting room she used as an office swung open.

"I heard you wanted to see me," he said. "Is somethin' wrong?"

The time he'd served as Risen Glory's overseer had wrought subtle changes in him. The muscles beneath his soft butternut shirt and dark brown trousers had grown sleek and hard, and there was a taut wiriness about him that had been lacking before. His face was still smooth and handsome, but now, as happened whenever he was in Sophronia's presence, subtle lines of tension etched his features.

"Nothing's wrong, Magnus," Sophronia replied, her manner deliberately condescending. "I understand you're goin' into town later this afternoon, and I wanted you to pick up some supplies for me." She didn't rise from the desk as she extended the list. Instead, she made him come to her.

"You called me in from the fields just so I could be your errand boy?" He snatched the list from her hand. "Why didn't you send Jim for this?"

"I didn't think about it," she replied, perversely glad that she had been able to ruffle his even temper. "Besides, Jim's busy washin' windows for me."

Magnus's jaw tightened. "And I suppose washin' windows is more important than takin' care of the cotton that's supportin' this plantation?"

"My, my. You do have a high opinion of yourself, don't you, Magnus Owen?" She rose from her chair. "You think this plantation's goin' to fall apart just because the overseer had to come in from the fields for a few minutes?"

A tiny vein began to throb at the side of his forehead. He lifted a work-roughened hand and splayed it on his hip. "You got some airs about you, woman, that are gettin' mighty unpleasant. Somebody needs to take you down a peg or two before you get yourself in real trouble."

"Well, that somebody sure enough won't be you." She held her chin high and swept past him into the hallway.

Magnus was generally so even-tempered it was hard to get a rise out of him, but now his hand whipped out and caught her arm. She gave a small gasp as he pulled her back into the sitting room and slammed the door.

"That's right," he drawled in the sweet, liquid tones of his plantation childhood. "I keep forgettin' Miz Sophronia's too good for the rest of us po' black folk."

Her golden eyes sparked with anger at his mockery. He pressed her body against the door with his own.

"Let me go!" She shoved at his chest, but even though they were the same height, he was much stronger, and she might as well have been trying to move an oak tree with a puff of thistledown.

"Magnus, let me go!"

Maybe he didn't hear the edge of panic in her plea, or maybe he'd been goaded by her once too often. Instead of releasing her, he pinned her shoulders to the door. The heat of his body burned through her skirt. "Miz Sophronia thinks just 'cause she acts like she's white, she's goin' to wake up some mornin' and find out she *is* white. Then she won't ever have to talk to none of us black folk again, except maybe to give us orders."

She turned her head and pressed her eyes closed, trying to shut out his scorn, but Magnus wasn't finished with her. His voice grew softer, but his words were no less wounding.

"If Miz Sophronia was only white, then she wouldn't ever have to worry none about a black man wantin' to take her in his arms and make her his woman and have chil'ren by her. She wouldn't have to worry about a black man wantin' to sit by her and hold her when she felt lonesome, or about growin' old lyin' in a big old feather bed. No, Miz Sophronia wouldn't have to worry about none of that. She's too fine for all that. She's too *white* for all that!"

"Stop it!" Sophronia lifted her hands and held them over her ears to shut out his cruel words.

He stepped back to free her, but she couldn't move. She stood frozen, her spine rigid, her hands clamped to her ears. Tears coursed down her cheeks.

With a muffled groan, Magnus took her stiff body in his arms and began stroking her and crooning into her ear. "There, now, girl. It's all right. I'm sorry I made you cry. Last thing I want is to hurt you. There, now, everything's goin' to be all right."

Gradually the tension ebbed from her body, and for a moment she sagged against him. He was so solid. So safe.

Safe? The thought made her jerk away. She drew back her shoulders and stood proud and haughty, despite the tears she couldn't quite stop shedding. "You got no right to talk to me like that. You don't know me, Magnus Owen. You just think you do."

But Magnus had his own pride. "I know you've got nothing but smiles for any rich white man looks your way, but you won't spare a glance for a black man."

"What can a black man give me?" she said fiercely. "Black man's got no *power*. My mother, my grandmother, her mother before her—black men loved them all. But when the white man came skulkin' through the cabin door in the middle of the night, not one of those black men could keep him from havin' her. Not one of those black men could keep his children from being sold away. Not one of them could do more than stand by and watch the women they loved being tied naked to a post and whipped until their backs ran red with blood. Don't you talk to me about black men!"

Magnus took a step toward her, but when she turned away, he walked to the window instead. "Times are different now," he said gently. "The war's over. You're not a slave any longer. We're all free. Things have changed. We can vote."

"You're a fool, Magnus. You think just because the white man says you can vote, things are goin' to be any different? It doesn't mean nothin'."

"Yes, it does. You're an American citizen now. You're protected by the laws of this country."

"Protected!" Sophronia's spine stiffened

with contempt. "There's no protection for a black woman except what she makes for herself."

"By selling her body to any rich white man who comes along? Is that how?"

She whirled around, lashing him with her tongue. "You tell me what else a black woman has to barter with. Men have been usin' our bodies for centuries and givin' us nothin' in return for it except a passel of children we couldn't protect. Well, I want more than that, and I'm goin' to have it, too. I'm goin' to have me a house and clothes and fine food. And I'm goin' to be *safe!*"

He flinched. "Sellin' yourself into another kind of slavery? Is that how you think you're gettin' your safety?"

Sophronia's eyes didn't waver. "It's not slavery when I choose the master and set the terms. And you know as well as I do that I'd have it all by now if it wasn't for you."

"Cain wasn't goin' to give you what you wanted."

"You're wrong. He would of given me anythin' I asked for if you hadn't spoiled it."

Magnus rested his hand on the carved back of the rose damask settee. "There's no man in the world I respect more than him. He saved my life, and I guess I'd do about anythin' he asked me. He's fair and honest, and every man who works for him knows it. He never asks anybody to do anythin' he hasn't done himself. The men admire him for that, and so do I. But he's a hard man with women,

Sophronia. I never saw one yet could bring him to heel."

"He wanted me, Magnus. If you hadn't busted in on us that night, he would've given me whatever I asked for."

Magnus came toward her and touched her shoulder. She recoiled instinctively, even though his touch felt strangely comforting.

"And if he had?" Magnus asked. "Would you've been able to hide that shiver that comes over you every time a man so much as touches your arm? Even though he's rich and white, would you've been able to forget that he's also a man?"

He'd struck too close to her nightmares. She turned away and headed blindly toward the desk. When she was finally sure she could speak without her voice betraying her, she said coldly, "I've got work to do. If you won't get the supplies for me, I'll send Jim to town."

At first she didn't think he'd answer, but he finally nodded. "I'll get your supplies." Then he turned on his heel and left her alone.

Sophronia stared at the vacant doorway, and for a moment she was filled with a nearly overpowering longing to fling herself after him. The instinct faded. Magnus Owen might be a plantation overseer, but he was still a black man, and he could never keep her safe.

10

Kit's muscles ached as she descended the stairs the next morning. In contrast to the britches she'd worn the day before, she was dressed in a demure outfit of palest lilac voile with a delicate white lace shawl tossed around her shoulders. From her fingers dangled the lavender sashes of a floppy leghorn hat.

Miss Dolly stood by the front door waiting for her. "Now, aren't you pretty as a picture. Just fasten up that button on your glove, darlin', and straighten your skirts."

Kit smiled and did as she was told. "You look awfully pretty yourself."

"Why, thank you, darlin'. I do try to keep myself nice, but it's not as easy as it once was. I no longer have youth entirely on my side, you know. But just look at you. Not a single gentleman will be able to keep his mind on the Lord with you sittin' in the congregation lookin' like a piece of Easter candy waitin' to be devoured."

"Makes me hungry just watching her," drawled a lazy voice from behind them.

Kit dropped the lavender hat ribbons she'd been trying to arrange into a bow.

Cain was leaning against the doorjamb of the library. He was dressed in a pearl-gray morning coat with charcoal trousers and waistcoat. A thinly striped burgundy cravat set off his white shirt.

Her eyes narrowed at his formal dress. "Where are you going?"

"To church, of course."

"Church! We didn't invite you to go to church with us!"

Miss Dolly's hand flew to her throat. "Katharine Louise Weston! I'm shocked! Whatever can you be thinking of, addressing the general so rudely? I asked him to escort us. You'll have to forgive her, General. She spent too long on horseback yesterday, and she could barely walk when she got out of bed this morning. It's made her peevish."

"I understand completely." The merriment in his eyes made his expression of sympathy suspect.

Kit plucked up the sashes of her hat. "I wasn't peevish." She was all thumbs with him watching, and she couldn't manage a respectable bow.

"Maybe you'd better tie that before she destroys the ribbons, Miss Calhoun."

"Certainly, General." Miss Dolly clucked her tongue at Kit. "Here, darlin'. Tilt up your chin and let me."

Kit was forced to submit to Miss Dolly's ministrations while Cain watched in amusement. Finally the bow was arranged satisfactorily, and they made their way out the front door to the carriage.

Kit waited until Cain had helped Miss Dolly in before she hissed at him. "I'll bet this is the first time you've set foot inside that church since you've been here. Why don't you stay home?"

"Not a chance. I wouldn't miss your reunion with the good people of Rutherford for anything in the world."

Our Father who art in heaven...

Jewel-like puddles of sunlight streamed through the stained-glass windows and settled over the bowed heads of the congregation. In Rutherford, they still talked about what a miracle it was that those windows had escaped the spawn of Satan, William Tecumseh Sherman.

Kit felt uncomfortable sitting in her lilac finery amidst the faded dresses and prewar bonnets of the other women. She'd wanted to show herself off to good advantage, but she hadn't stopped to consider how poor everyone was. She wouldn't forget again.

She found herself thinking about her real church, the simple clapboard structure not far from Risen Glory that had served as the spiritual home for the slaves from the surrounding plantations. Garrett and Rosemary had refused to make the weekly trip to the white community's church in Rutherford, so Sophronia had taken Kit with her every Sunday. Even thought Sophronia was a child herself, she'd been determined that Kit hear the Word.

Kit had loved that church, and now she couldn't help but compare this sedate service with the joyful worship of her childhood. Sophronia would be there now, along with Magnus and the others.

Her reunion with Magnus had been subdued. Although he'd seemed happy to see her, the old informality between them was gone. She was now a white woman, fully grown, and he was a black man.

A fly buzzed a lazy figure eight in front of her, and she stole a glance at Cain. His attention was turned politely toward the pulpit, his expression as inscrutable as ever. She was glad that Miss Dolly was seated between them. Sitting any closer to him would have ruined the morning.

On the other side of the church sat a man whose attention wasn't as firmly fixed on the pulpit. Kit gave Brandon Parsell a slow smile, then tilted her head just enough so that her straw hat brim shielded her face. Before she left the church, she would make certain he found a chance to speak with her. She had only a month, and she couldn't waste a day of it.

The service ended, and the members of the congregation couldn't wait to speak with her. They'd heard the New York City finishing school had transformed her from a hoyden to a young lady, and they wanted to see for themselves.

"Why, Kit Weston, just look at you..."

"And aren't you a fine lady now."

"My stars, even your own daddy wouldn't recognize you."

As they greeted her, they faced a dilemma. Acknowledging her meant that they'd have to greet her Yankee guardian, the man Rutherford's leading families had been so diligently shunning.

Slowly, first one person and then another nodded to him. One of the men asked him about his cotton crop. Della Dibbs thanked him for his contribution to the Bible Society. Clement Jakes asked whether or not he thought it would rain soon. The conversations were reserved, but the message was clear. It was time the barriers against Baron Cain came down.

Kit knew they'd later remark to each other that it was only for Kit Weston's sake they'd acknowledged him, but she suspected they welcomed the excuse to draw him into their insular circle, if only because it would give them a fresh topic of conversation. It would occur to none of them that Cain might not wish to be drawn in.

Standing off to the side of the church, a woman with an air of sophistication that set her apart watched what was happening with some amusement. So this was the notorious Baron Cain... The woman was a newcomer to the community, having lived in a large brick house in Rutherford for only three months, but she'd heard all about the new owner of Risen Glory. Nothing she'd heard, however, had prepared her for her first sight of him. Her eyes swept from his shoulders down to his narrow hips. He was magnificent.

Veronica Gamble was a Southerner by birth, if not by inclination. Born in Charleston, she had married the portrait painter Francis Gamble when she was barely eighteen. For the next fourteen years, they'd divided their time between Florence, Paris, and Vienna, where Francis had charged outrageous prices for flattering portraits of the wives and children of the aristocracy.

When her husband had died the previous winter, Veronica was left comfortably well off, if not wealthy. On a whim, she'd decided to return to South Carolina and the brick house that her husband had inherited from his parents. It would give her time to assess her life and decide what she wanted to do next.

In her early thirties, she was striking in appearance. Her auburn hair was pulled softly back from her face and fell in lustrous curls over the nape of her neck. Setting off its coppery hues were a pair of slanted eyes, almost as green as her fashionable Zouave jacket. On any other woman her full bottom lip would have been obtrusive, but on her it was sensual.

Although Veronica was considered a great beauty, her thin nose was a bit too long, her features too angular for true beauty. No man, however, seemed to notice. She had wit, intelligence, and the intriguing quality of watching those around her with an amused eye while she waited to see what life had in store.

She eased toward the doors at the back of the church, where the Reverend Cogdell was greeting his flock as they filed out. "Ah, Mrs. Gamble. How pleasant to have you with us this morning. I don't believe you've met Miss Dorthea Calhoun. And this is Mr. Cain of Risen

Glory. Where has Katharine Louise gone? I wanted you to meet her, too."

Veronica Gamble had no interest in either Miss Dorthea Calhoun or anyone named Katharine Louise. But she was very much interested in the dazzling man who stood next to the pastor, and she gracefully inclined her head. "I've heard a great deal about you, Mr. Cain. Somehow I'd expected horns."

Rawlins Cogdell winced, but Cain laughed. "I wish I'd been as fortunate to have heard of you."

Veronica slipped her gloved hand into the crook of his arm. "The matter is easily remedied."

Kit had heard Cain's laughter, but she ignored it to focus her attention on Brandon. His regular features were even more attractive than she'd remembered, and the stray lock of straight brown hair that tumbled over his forehead as he talked was endearing.

He couldn't have been more different from Cain. Brandon was polite where Cain was rude. And she didn't have to worry about him mocking her. He was every inch a Southern gentleman.

She studied his mouth. What would it feel like to kiss it? Very exciting, she was certain. Much more pleasant than Cain's assault the day she'd arrived.

An assault she'd done nothing to stop.

"I've thought about you quite often since we met in New York," Brandon said.

"I'm flattered."

"Would you like to ride with me tomorrow? The bank closes at three. I could be at Risen Glory within the hour."

Kit gazed up at him through her lashes, an effect she'd practiced to perfection. "I'd enjoy riding with you, Mr. Parsell."

"Until tomorrow, then."

With a smile, she turned away to acknowledge several young men who'd been patiently waiting for a chance to speak with her.

As they vied for her attention, she noticed Cain deep in conversation with an attractive auburn-haired woman. Something about the attentive way the woman was gazing up at him grated on Kit. She wished he'd glance in her direction so he could see her so well surrounded by masculine company. Unfortunately, he didn't seem to notice.

Miss Dolly had been engaged in animated conversation with the Reverend Cogdell and his wife, Mary, who was her distant relative and the one who'd recommended her as a chaperone. Kit realized the Cogdells were looking increasingly bewildered. She hastily excused herself and hurried to Miss Dolly's side.

"Are you ready to leave, Miss Dolly?"

"Why, yes, darlin'. I haven't seen the Reverend Cogdell and his dear wife, Mary, in years. What a joyous reunion, hampered only by the recent events at Bull Run. Oh, but that's old folk's conversation, darlin'. Nothin' for you to worry your pretty young head about."

Cain must have sensed disaster, too, for he materialized at Kit's side. "Miss Calhoun, the carriage is waiting for us."

"Why, thank you, General—" Miss Dolly gasped and pressed her fingers to her mouth. "I—I mean Major, of course. Silly me." With her ribbons all aflutter, she scampered toward the carriage.

The Reverend Cogdell and his wife stared after her in open-mouthed astonishment.

"She thinks I'm General Lee living in disguise at Risen Glory," Cain said bluntly.

Rawlins Cogdell began to wring his pale, thin hands in agitation. "Major Cain, Katharine, I do apologize. When my wife recommended Dolly Calhoun for the post of chaperone, we had no idea— Oh, dear, this will never do."

Mary Cogdell's small brown eyes were filled with remorse. "This is all my fault. We'd heard she was nearly destitute, but we had no idea she was feebleminded."

Kit opened her mouth to protest, but Cain cut her off. "You needn't worry about Miss Calhoun. She's settling in comfortably."

"But Katharine can't possibly stay at Risen Glory with you under these circumstances," the minister protested. "Dolly Calhoun is hardly a proper chaperone. Why, she must have spoken to a dozen people today. By this afternoon everyone in the county will know about her. This won't do. It won't do at all. The gossip will be dreadful, Mr. Cain. You're far too young a man—"

"Kit is my ward," he said.

"Nonetheless, there's no blood bond between you."

Mary Cogdell gripped her prayer book. "Katharine, you're an innocent young woman, so I'm sure it hasn't occurred to you how this will look to others. You simply can't stay at Risen Glory."

"I appreciate your concern," Kit replied, "but I've been away from my home for three years, and I don't intend to leave again so quickly."

Mary Cogdell looked at her husband helplessly.

"I assure you that Miss Dolly is a stickler for the proprieties," Cain surprised her by saying. "You should have seen her fussing over Kit this morning."

"Still..."

Cain inclined his head. "If you'll excuse us, Reverend Cogdell, Mrs. Cogdell. Please don't trouble yourself any further." He took Kit's arm and led her toward the carriage, where Miss Dolly was already waiting.

Rawlins Cogdell and his wife watched the carriage drive away. "There's going to be trouble there," the minister said. "I can feel it in my bones."

Kit heard the crunch of gravel and knew Brandon had arrived. She rushed to the cheval glass to check her reflection and saw a proper young lady in a riding habit gazing back at her. There were no boy's clothes for her today, and no Temptation, either. She'd resigned herself to a sidesaddle and poor Lady.

That morning, while the sky was still the pale, soft pink of the underside of a seashell, she'd raced across the fields on Temptation. The wild, exhilarating ride was much different from what she could expect this afternoon.

She had to admit her new riding habit was flattering, no matter how much she disliked the idea of wearing it. Made of crimson broadcloth trimmed in black braid, the jacket fit her snugly in the bodice and accented her waist. The full skirt fell in graceful folds to the hem, which was decorated with a deep border of black braid in a swirling pattern that looked like a chain of script *L*'s.

She checked to make certain there were no hanging threads or hooks that had escaped her notice. The four black frogs that held together the front of the jacket were all fastened, and her hat was on straight. It was black, a feminine version of a man's stovepipe, but with a lower, softer crown and a wisp of crimson veiling trailing from the back. She'd fastened her hair in a neat bun at the nape of her neck and even polished her boots.

Satisfied that she looked her best, she snatched up her riding crop and left the room, giving no thought at all to the black kid riding gloves lying in her glove box. When she reached the hallway, she heard voices coming from the piazza. To her consternation, she saw Cain standing in the drive talking to Brandon.

Once again she was struck by the contrast

between the two men. Cain was much bigger, but that wasn't all that set them apart. Brandon was properly dressed in hat, coat, and trousers, with a bottle-green four-in-hand showing above the top of his vest. The clothes were old and no longer of the most fashionable cut, but they were neatly pressed, and he wore them well.

As for, Cain, he was bareheaded and wearing an open-collared shirt rolled at the sleeves and a pair of muddy trousers. He stood in an easy slouch, one hand stuffed into his pocket, a dirty boot propped on the bottom step. Everything about Brandon indicated culture and breeding, while Cain looked like a barbarian.

Her eyes lingered on him a moment longer before she clutched her riding crop more tightly and walked forward. Lady waited patiently next to the mounting block. The old sidesaddle Kit had found in the attic rested on the horse's back.

Kit gave Cain a cool nod and Brandon a smiling greeting. The admiration in his eyes told her that the efforts she'd taken with her appearance hadn't been in vain. Cain, however, seemed to be enjoying some private joke, one she quickly realized was at her expense.

"You watch yourself today, Kit. Lady can be a real handful."

She gritted her teeth. "I'm sure we'll get along fine."

Brandon made a motion to help her mount, but Cain was quicker. "Allow me."

Brandon turned away with obvious displeasure to mount his own horse, and Kit placed her fingers in Cain's outstretched hand. It felt strong and much too competent. After she'd settled into the sidesaddle, she looked down to see him gazing at her cumbersome skirts.

"Now who's the hypocrite?" he asked softly.

She gazed over at Brandon and gave him a blinding smile. "Now, Mr. Parsell, don't you ride too fast for me, y'hear? I've been up North for so long, my riding skills are rusty, 'deed they are."

Cain snorted and walked away, leaving her with the pleasant sensation that she'd had the last word.

Brandon suggested they ride to Holly Grove, his former home. As they trotted down the drive toward the road, Kit watched him covertly studying the planted fields that stretched out on both sides of them. She could only hope he was already making plans.

Holly Grove had been put to the torch by the same soldiers who'd spared Risen Glory. After the war, Brandon had returned to a crumbled ruin and blackened chimneys already overgrown with wild grape vines and blackberry brambles. He hadn't been able to pay the punishing taxes on the land, and everything had been confiscated. Now it stood idle.

They dismounted near what had once been the smokehouse. Brandon tied the horses, then took Kit's arm and led her toward the ruins of the house. They'd been chatting pleasantly as they rode, but now he fell silent. Kit's heart swelled with pity.

"It's all gone," he finally said. "Everything the South believed in. Everything we fought for."

She gazed at the devastation. If Rosemary Weston hadn't taken that Yankee lieutenant into her bedroom, this would have been the fate of Risen Glory.

"The Yankees laugh at us, you know," he went on. "They laugh because we believe in chivalry and honor. But look what happens when there's no chivalry and when honor's turned into a joke. They take away our land, tax us until we can't buy bread. Radical Reconstruction is the Almighty's curse on us." He shook his head. "What have we done to deserve so much evil?"

Kit stared up at the twin chimneys, like great ghostly fingers. "It was the slaves," she heard herself saying. "We're being punished for keeping human beings in slavery."

"Poppycock! You lived with the Yankees too long, Kit. Slavery is God's plan. You know what the Bible says."

She did know. She'd heard it preached often enough from the pulpit of the slave church by white ministers the plantation owners sent to remind their people that God approved of their enslavement. God had even issued instructions regarding a slave's obligations to his master. Kit remembered Sophronia sitting by her side during these sermons, stiff and pale, unable to reconcile what she was hearing with the loving Jesus she knew.

Brandon took her arm and led her back along the overgrown path, away from the house. Their mounts were peacefully grazing in the clearing near the smokehouse. Kit walked over to a tree that had fallen long ago in a storm and sat on the trunk.

"It was a mistake bringing you here," Brandon said as he came up beside her.

"Why?"

He stared off toward the blackened chimneys in the distance. "This makes the differences between us all the more apparent."

"Does it? Neither of us has a home. Remember that Risen Glory's not mine. Not yet, anyway."

He gave her a searching look. She plucked at a piece of tree bark. "I only have a month, and then Cain's going to force me to go back to New York."

"I can't tolerate the idea of your living in the same house with that man," he said, sitting next to her on the tree trunk. "Everybody who came into the bank today was talking about it. They say Miss Calhoun's not a fit chaperone. You watch yourself with Cain, you hear? He's not a gentleman. I don't like him. Don't like him at all."

She was warmed by Brandon's concern. "Don't worry. I'll be careful."

And then she deliberately tilted her face up to him, slightly parting her lips. She couldn't let this excursion end without kissing him. It was something she had to do so she could erase Cain's brand on her mouth.

And on your senses, a small voice whispered.

It was true. Cain's kiss had set fires in her blood, and she needed to prove to herself that Brandon Parsell could spark those same fires.

His eyes were partially shadowed by the brushed beaver brim of his gray hat, but she could see him looking at her mouth. She waited for him to come closer, but he didn't move. "I want you to kiss me," she finally said.

He was shocked by her forwardness. She saw it in his frown. His attitude irritated her even as it endeared him to her.

She reached up and gently lifted off his hat, noticing as she laid it aside that there was a small red line across the upper part of his forehead from the band. "Brandon," she said quietly, "I only have a month. There isn't time for me to be coy."

Even a gentleman couldn't ignore so bold an invitation. He leaned forward and pressed his mouth to hers.

Kit noticed that his lips were fleshier than Cain's. They were also sweeter, she decided, since they remained politely closed. This was a tender kiss compared with Cain's. A pleasant kiss. His lips were dry, but his mustache seemed a little rough.

Her mind was wandering, and she brought her attention back to what she was doing by lifting her arms and throwing them enthusiastically around his neck.

Were his shoulders a little narrow? It must be her imagination, because they were very solid. He began trailing kisses across her cheek and the line of her jaw. His mustache scratched the sensitive skin, and she winced.

He pulled back from her. "I'm sorry. Have I frightened you?"

"No, of course not." She swallowed her disappointment. The kiss hadn't proved anything. Why couldn't he set aside his scruples and do the job right?

No sooner had she thought this than she admonished herself. Brandon Parsell was a gentleman, not a Yankee barbarian.

He dropped his head. "Kit, you must know that I wouldn't hurt you for anything in the world. I apologize for my lack of restraint. Women like you are to be cherished and shielded from the more sordid aspects of life."

She felt another prickle of irritation. "I'm not made of glass."

"I know that. But I also want you to know that if anything...permanent were to happen between us, I would never debase you. I'd bother you as little as possible with my own needs."

This was something she understood. When Mrs. Templeton had spoken about Eve's Shame, she'd told them there were husbands who were most considerate of their wives, and they should pray to marry such a man.

She was suddenly glad Brandon's sweet kisses hadn't stirred a raging fire in her. Her response to Cain had been nothing more than a reaction to the strange emotions of being home again.

Now she was more certain than ever that she wanted to marry Brandon. He was everything a woman could want in a husband.

He made her put on her hat so she wouldn't get sunburned and gently chastised her for forgetting her gloves. As he fussed over her, she smiled and flirted, playing the Southern belle to perfection.

She reminded herself that he was accustomed to a different sort of woman, one who was quiet and retiring like his mother and his sisters, and she tried to restrain her normally impulsive tongue. Still, she managed to shock him with her opinions about Negro suffrage and the Fifteenth Amendment. As two small furrows etched themselves between his eyes, she knew she had to make him understand.

"Brandon, I'm a well-educated woman. I have opinions and ideas. I've also been on my own for a long time. I can't be what I'm not."

His smile didn't quite erase the furrows. "Your independence is one of the things I most admire about you, but it's going to take a while for me to get used to it. You're not like the other women I know."

"And do you know a lot of women?" she teased.

Her question made him laugh. "Kit Weston, you're a minx."

Their conversation on the ride back to Risen Glory was a happy combination of gossip and reminiscences. She promised to go on a picnic with him and let him escort her to church on Sunday. As she stood on the porch and waved good-bye, she decided that, all in all, the day had gone well.

Unfortunately, the evening did not.

Miss Dolly waylaid her before dinner. "I need your sweet young eyes to sort through my button box. I have a pretty mother-of-pearl in there somewhere, and I simply must find it."

Kit did as she was asked, even though she needed a few minutes alone. The sorting was accompanied by chatter, twittering, and fluttering. Kit learned which buttons had been sewn on which dresses, where the garments had been worn and with whom, what the weather had been like on that particular day, as well as what Miss Dolly had eaten.

At dinner, Miss Dolly requested that all the windows be closed, despite the fact that the evening was warm, because she'd heard rumors of a diphtheria outbreak in Charleston. Cain managed Miss Dolly well and the windows remained open, but he ignored Kit until dessert.

"I hope Lady behaved for you today," he finally said. "The poor horse looked terrified when you marched toward her with all those skirts on. I think she was afraid you'd suffocate her."

"You're not nearly as amusing as you seem to think. My riding habit is the height of fashion."

"And you hate wearing it. Not that I blame you. Those things should be outlawed."

Her opinion exactly. "Nonsense. They're very comfortable. And a lady always likes to look her best."

"Is it just my imagination, or does your accent get thicker whenever you want to irritate me?"

" 'Deed I hope not, Major. That would be most impolite of me. Besides, you're in South Carolina now, so you're the one with the accent."

He smiled. "Point taken. And did you enjoy your ride?"

"I had a wonderful time. There aren't many gentlemen as pleasant to be with as Mr. Parsell."

His smile faded. "And where did you and Mr. Parsell ride?"

"To Holly Grove, his old home. We enjoyed catching up on old times."

"That's all you did?" he asked pointedly.

"Yes, it's all," she retorted. "Not every man's interests when they're with young women are as narrow as yours."

Miss Dolly frowned at the sharpness in Kit's voice. "You're dawdlin' over your dessert, Katharine Louise. If you're finished, let's go to the sitting room and leave the general to his cigar."

Kit was enjoying irritating Cain too much to leave. "I'm not quite finished yet, Miss Dolly. Why don't you go? I don't mind the smell of cigar smoke."

"Well, if you don't mind..." Miss Dolly set her napkin on the table and rose, then stood at her chair as if she were gathering her courage. "Now, watch your manners, darlin'. I know you don't mean anything by it, but sometimes you seem a bit sharp when you speak to the general. You mustn't let your natural high spirits keep you from giving him his proper respect." Her duty done, she fluttered from the room.

Cain looked after her with some amusement. "I must admit, Miss Dolly's beginning to grow on me."

"You're really a terrible person, do you know that?"

"I admit I'm no Brandon Parsell."

"You're certainly not. Brandon's a gentleman."

He leaned back in his chair and studied her. "Did he behave like a gentleman with you today?"

"Of course he did."

"And what about you? Were you a lady?"

Her pleasure in their bantering faded. He still hadn't forgotten that ugly letter from Hamilton Woodward. She didn't like how much it bothered her to know he questioned her virtue. "Of course I wasn't a lady. What fun would that be? I took off my clothes and offered myself to him. Is that what you want to know?"

Cain pushed back his plate. "You've grown into a beautiful woman, Kit. You're also reckless. It's a dangerous combination."

"Mr. Parsell and I talked *politics*. We discussed the indignities the federal government's been forcing on South Carolina."

"I can just hear the two of you now. Sighing over what the Yankees have done to your poor state. Moaning over all the injustices of the occupation—none of it the South's fault, of course. I'm sure you two made quite a pair."

"How can you be so callous? You can see the horrors of Reconstruction all around you. People've had their homes taken from them. They've lost savings. The South is like a piece of glass being ground underneath a Yankee bootheel."

"Let me remind you of a few painful facts you seem to have forgotten." He picked up the brandy decanter at his elbow, but before he could pour from it, he shoved the stopper back into the neck. "It wasn't the Union that started this war. Southern guns fired on Fort Sumter. You lost the war, Kit. And you lost it at the expense of six hundred thousand lives. Now you expect everything to be just like it was." He regarded her with disgust. "You talk about the horrors of Reconstruction. The way I see it, the South should be thankful the federal government has been as merciful as it has."

"Merciful?" Kit leaped to her feet. "Do you call what's happened here merciful?"

"You've read history. You tell me." Now Cain was on his feet, too. "Name any other conquering people who've dealt so leniently with the ones they've conquered. If this had been any country but the United States, thousands of men would have been executed for treason after Appomattox, and thousands more would be rotting in prisons right now. Instead, there was a general amnesty, and now the Southern states are being readmitted to the Union. My God, Reconstruction is a slap on the wrist for what the South has done to this country."

Her knuckles were white where they gripped the back of the chair. "It's too bad there wasn't enough bloodshed to satisfy you. What kind of man are you to wish the South more misery than it's already had?"

"I don't wish it any more misery. I even agree with the leniency of federal policies. But you'll have to forgive me if I can't work up much righteous indignation because people in the South have lost their homes."

"You want your pound of flesh."

"Men have died in my arms," he said quietly. "And not all of those men wore blue uniforms."

She released her grip on the chair and rushed from the room. When she reached her bedroom, she sank onto the chair at her dressing table.

He didn't understand! He was seeing everything from the Northern perspective. But even as she mentally listed all the reasons he was wrong, she found it difficult to reclaim her old sense of righteousness. He'd seemed so sad. Her head had begun to pound, and she wanted to go to bed, but there was a job she'd already put off for too long.

Late that night after everyone was asleep, she made her way downstairs to the library, and to the calf-bound ledgers in which Cain kept the plantation's accounts.

11

The next few weeks brought a steady stream of callers. In better times the women would have dressed in their prettiest gowns and arrived at Risen Glory in fine carriages. Now they came in wagons drawn by plow horses, or they sat on the front seats of broken-down buggies. Their gowns were shabby and their bonnets rusty with age, but they carried themselves as proudly as ever.

Self-conscious about the extravagance of her wardrobe, Kit dressed plainly for her first callers. But she soon discovered that the women were disappointed by her simple gowns. They made pointed references to the pretty lilac frock she'd worn to church, and had her hat been trimmed in taffeta or satin? They'd heard the gossip about her clothes passed from maid to cook to the grizzled old woman who sold she-crab from a tub off the back of a pushcart. Kit Weston's wardrobe was rumored to contain beautiful gowns of every color and description. The women were starved for beauty, and they wanted to see them all.

Once Kit understood, she didn't have the heart to disappoint them further. She dutifully wore a different dress every day and, with several of the younger women, abandoned subterfuge altogether and invited them to her bedroom so they could see for themselves.

It saddened her to realize that the clothes meant more to her visitors than they did to her. The dresses were pretty, but they were such a bother with their hooks, laces, and overskirts that always caught on furniture. She wished she could give the green muslin to the pretty young widow who'd lost her husband at Gettysburg, and the periwinkle silk to Prudence Wade, who'd been left scarred by smallpox. But the women were as proud as they were poor, and she knew better than to offer.

Not all her callers were women. A dozen men of various ages made their way to her door in as many days. They invited her on buggy rides and picnics, surrounded her after church, and nearly got into a fight over who was to accompany her to a Chautauqua lecture on phrenology. She managed to turn them down without hurting their feelings by telling them she'd already promised to attend with Mr. Parsell and his sisters.

Brandon was increasingly attentive, even though she frequently shocked him. Still, he remained at her side, and she was certain he intended to ask her to marry him soon. Half of her month was over, and she suspected he wouldn't wait much longer.

She'd seen little of Cain, even at meals, since the night of their disquieting conversation about Reconstruction. The machinery for the mill had arrived, and they were busy storing it under tarps in the barn and sheds until they were ready to install it. Whenever he was nearby, she was uncomfortably conscious of him. She flirted outrageously with her male admirers if she thought he was watching. Sometimes he seemed amused, but at other times a darker emotion flickered across his features that she found disquieting.

Gossip traveled quickly, and it wasn't long before Kit learned that Cain had been seen in the company of the beautiful Veronica Gamble. Veronica was a source of mystery and speculation to the local women. Even though she was Carolina-born, her exotic lifestyle after her marriage made her a foreigner. There was a rumor that her husband had painted a picture of her lying stark naked on a couch, and that it was hanging on her bedroom wall as bold as brass.

One evening Kit came downstairs for supper and found Cain in the sitting room reading a newspaper. It had been nearly a week since he'd appeared for a meal, so she was surprised to see him. She was even more surprised to find him dressed in formal black and white, since she'd never known him to wear anything but casual dress in the dining room.

"Are you going out?"

"Sorry to disappoint you, but I'm eating in this evening." He put down his paper. "We have a guest for dinner."

"A guest?" Kit looked down at her muddy gown and ink-stained fingers in dismay. "Why didn't you tell me?"

"It didn't occur to me."

Kit's whole day had gone badly. Sophronia had been cranky that morning, and they'd quarreled about nothing. Then Reverend Cogdell and his wife had come calling. They'd recounted all the gossip that Kit's stay at Risen Glory without a proper chaperone was producing and urged her to live with them until someone more suitable could be found. Kit had been doing her best to reassure them that Miss Dolly was up to the task when her companion had fluttered into the room and insisted they roll bandages for the Confederate wounded. When they'd left, Kit had helped Sophronia clean the Chinese wallpaper in the dining room with bread crusts. Then she'd spilled a bottle of ink while she was writing to Elsbeth. Afterward, she'd gone for a walk.

There'd been no time to change for dinner, but since she wasn't expecting anyone except Miss Dolly at the table, she hadn't been concerned about the condition of her plain muslin dress. Miss Dolly would scold her, but she scolded her about her appearance even when Kit was dressed up. Again she glanced at the ink stains on her fingers and the mud on her skirt from kneeling to free a baby field sparrow caught in a tangle of brambles.

"I'll need to change," she said just as Lucy appeared at the door.

"Miz Gamble's here."

Veronica Gamble swept into the room. "Hello, Baron."

He smiled. "Veronica, it's good to see you again."

She wore a stylish jade-green evening gown with an underskirt of bronze-and-black striped satin. A border of overlapping black lace trimmed the décolletage and set off the pale, opalescent skin of a natural redhead. Her hair was swept up into a sophisticated arrangement of curls and braids caught in a crescent of bronze silk laurel leaves. The difference in their appearances couldn't have been more apparent, and Kit self-consciously smoothed her skirt, which did nothing to improve it.

She realized Cain was watching her. There was something oddly satisfied in his expression. He almost seemed to be enjoying comparing her unkempt appearance with Veronica's perfection.

Miss Dolly swept into the room. "Why, I didn't know we were having company tonight."

Cain performed the introductions. Veronica replied graciously, but that didn't ease Kit's resentment. Not only was the other woman elegant and sophisticated, but she radiated an inner self-confidence Kit didn't think she'd ever possess. Next to her, Kit felt callow, awkward, and unattractive.

Veronica, in the meantime, was engaging Cain in conversation about the newspaper he'd been reading.

"...that my late husband and I were great supporters of Horace Greeley."

"The abolitionist?" Miss Dolly began to quiver.

"Abolitionist and newspaper editor," Veronica replied. "Even in Europe, Mr. Greeley's editorials supporting the Union cause were much admired."

"But, my dear Mrs. Gamble..." Miss Dolly gasped like a guppy. "Surely you don't mean—I understood you were born in Charleston."

"That's true, Miss Calhoun, but I somehow managed to rise above it."

"Oh, my, my..." Miss Dolly pressed her fingertips to her temples. "I do believe I've developed a headache. I'm sure I won't be able to eat a bite of dinner. I think I'll just go to my room and rest."

Kit watched in dismay as she fled from the room. Now she was alone with them. Why hadn't Sophronia told her that Mrs. Gamble was expected so Kit could have taken a tray in her room? It was outrageous for Cain to expect her to dine with his mistress.

The thought made her chest hurt.

She told herself it was outraged propriety.

Veronica sat on the settee while Cain took his place in a green-and-ivory-upholstered chair next to her. He should have looked ridiculous on such a delicate piece of furniture, but he seemed as comfortable as if he were astride Vandal or perched on the roof of his cotton mill.

Veronica told Cain a story about a comic mishap at a balloon ascension. He tossed back his head and laughed, showing even, white teeth. The two of them might have been alone for all the notice they were taking of Kit.

She rose, unwilling to watch them together any longer. "I'll see if dinner's ready."

"Just a minute, Kit."

Cain uncoiled from his chair and walked toward her. Something calculated in his expression made her wary.

His eyes roamed over her crumpled frock. Then he reached for her. She started to back away, only to have him catch a lock of hair in his fingers near one of her silver combs. When his hand came away, he was holding a piece of twig.

"Climbing trees again?"

She flushed. He was treating her as if she were nine years old and deliberately embarrassing her in front of their sophisticated guest.

"Go ask Sophronia to hold dinner until you've had time to change out of that dirty frock." With a dismissive look, he turned to Veronica. "You'll have to forgive my ward. She's only recently graduated from finishing school. I'm afraid all her lessons haven't yet sunk in."

Kit's cheeks burned with mortification, and angry words bubbled inside her. Why was he doing this? He didn't care about soiled frocks and tangled hair. She knew that about him. He loved the outdoors like she did and had little patience for formality.

She fought to hold onto her temper. "I'm afraid you'll have to excuse me from dinner this evening, Mrs. Gamble. I, too, seem to have developed a headache."

"A veritable epidemic." Veronica's voice was softly mocking.

Cain's jaw set stubbornly. "We have a guest. Headache or not, I'll expect you back downstairs in ten minutes."

Kit choked on her rage. "Then I'm afraid you'll be disappointed."

"Don't try to defy me."

"Don't issue orders you can't enforce." Somehow she summoned the self-control not to run from the room, but once she reached the hallway, she picked up her skirts and fled. As she approached the top of the stairs, she fancied she could hear the sound of Veronica Gamble's laughter coming from behind her.

But Veronica wasn't laughing. Instead, she was studying Cain with great interest and a small measure of sadness. So *that* was the way it was. Ah, well...

She'd hoped their relationship would move beyond friendship into intimacy. But now she saw it wasn't meant to be, at least in the foreseeable future. She should have known. He was too magnificent a man not to be difficult.

She felt a flash of pity for his ward. For all

her extravagant beauty, the young woman didn't yet know her own mind, and she certainly didn't know his. Kit was much too inexperienced to understand why he'd deliberately embarrassed her. But Veronica understood. Cain was attracted to the girl, and he didn't like it. He was fighting his attraction by bringing Veronica here tonight, hoping that seeing the two women side by side would convince him he was drawn to Veronica instead of to Kit. But it wasn't to be.

Cain had won this round. The young woman had barely managed to hold onto her temper. Still, Kit Weston was nobody's fool, and Veronica had a feeling the game was far from over.

She tapped her fingernail on the upholstered arm of the settee and wondered if she should permit Cain to use her as a pawn in the struggle he was waging with himself. It was a foolish question, and it made her smile. Of course she'd permit it.

Life was dull here, and it wasn't in her nature to be jealous of another woman over something as natural as sex. Besides, it was all so deliciously amusing.

"Your ward is high-spirited," she said, just to stir the pot.

"My ward needs to learn submission." He poured a glass of sherry for her and, with an apology, excused himself.

She heard him taking the stairs two a time. The sound excited her. It reminded her of the glorious arguments she and Francis used to have, arguments they sometimes fought with deliciously angry sex. If only she could see what was about to happen in the room upstairs...

She sipped at her sherry, more than prepared to wait them out.

Cain knew he was behaving badly, but he didn't care. For weeks he'd been keeping himself away from her. As far as he could tell, he was the only single man in the community who wasn't jumping to her tune. Now it was time they had a reckoning. He was just sorry Veronica had to be subjected to Kit's rudeness.

And to his own.

But he wouldn't dwell on that. "Open this door."

Even as he rapped the panels with his knuckles, he knew he was making a mistake by coming up here after her. But if he let her defy him now, he'd lose any chance he had of keeping her under control.

He told himself this was for her own good. She was willful and stubborn, a danger to herself. Whether he liked it or not, he was her guardian, which meant he had a responsibility to guide her.

But he didn't feel like a guardian. He felt like a man who was losing a struggle with himself.

"Go away!"

He twisted the knob and let himself in.

She stood by the window, the last of the sunlight casting her exquisite face into shadow. She was a wild, beautiful creature, and she tempted him beyond bearing.

As she turned, he froze in place. She'd been unbuttoning her dress, and the sleeves had fallen down on her shoulders so he could see the soft rounds of her breasts visible above her chemise. His mouth went dry.

She didn't try to clutch the bodice together as a modest young woman should. Instead, she gave him glare for glare. "Get out of my room. You have no right to come charging in here."

He remembered Hamilton Woodward's letter accusing her of seducing his business partner. When Cain had received it, he had no reason not to believe it, but now he knew better. Kit's claim that she'd punched the bastard was undoubtedly true. If only he were as certain that she was turning aside Parsell's advances.

He tore his eyes away. "I'm not going to be disobeyed."

"Then you'd better bark out your orders to someone else."

"Watch it, Kit. I tanned that rump of yours once before, and it won't bother me to do it again."

Instead of backing away, she had the gall to take a step toward him. His hand itched, and he found himself imagining exactly how that backside would feel, bare beneath his palm. Then he imagined sliding his hand around that sweet curve—not to hurt, but to please.

"If you want to see what a knife feels like in your belly, just go ahead and try it, Yankee."

He almost laughed. He outweighed her by nearly a hundred pounds, but the little wildcat still thought she could challenge him.

"You've forgotten something," he said. "You're my ward. I make the decisions and you do as I say. Is that understood?"

"Oh, it's understood, all right, Yankee. It's understood that you're an arrogant ass! Now get out of my room."

As she jabbed her finger toward the door, the strap of her chemise fell over her opposite shoulder. The thin fabric caught at the crest of her breast, clung to that sweet peak for a moment, and then dropped, exposing the dark coral tip.

Kit saw him lower his gaze a moment before she felt the currents of cool air tickling her flesh. She looked down and drew in her breath. She snatched the front of her chemise and pulled it back up.

Cain's eyes turned from slate to pale smoke, and his voice was husky. "I liked it better the other way."

As quickly as that, the battle between them shifted to new ground.

Her fingers grew clumsy on the fabric of her chemise as he came closer. All her survival instincts urged her to run from the room, but the most she could manage was to turn away.

He came up behind her and traced the curve of her neck with his thumb. "You're so damned beautiful," he whispered. He gathered her curls into his hands and gently untangled them from the strap of her chemise.

Her skin prickled. "You shouldn't..."

"I know."

He leaned down and pushed her hair away. His breath feathered the skin at her collarbone.

"I don't—I don't want you to..."

He gently bit the soft flesh at the side of her neck. "Liar," he whispered.

She closed her eyes and let her back rest against his chest. She felt the cool, wet spot on her neck where his tongue had touched her flesh.

His hands moved up over her ribs and then, incredibly, over her breasts. Her skin turned hot and cold at once. She shuddered as he caressed her through her chemise, shuddered at how good it felt and at her insanity in submitting to such an intimacy.

"I've wanted to do this ever since you got back," he whispered.

She made a soft, helpless sound when he slipped his hands inside her dress, inside her chemise...and touched her.

Nothing had ever felt as good as those callused palms on her breasts. She arched against him. He brushed the tips and she moaned.

A knock sounded at the door.

She sucked in her breath and jerked away, scrambling to pull up her bodice.

"Who is it?" Cain barked out impatiently.

The door flew back on its hinges.

Sophronia stood on the other side, two pale smudges of alarm over her cheekbones. "What are you doing in her room?"

Cain's eyebrow slashed upward. "That's between Kit and me."

Sophronia's amber eyes took in Kit's disheveled state, and her hands knotted into fists in the skirt of her dress. She bit into her bottom lip as if she were trying to hold back all the words she didn't dare say in front of him. "Mr. Parsell is downstairs," she finally managed. The fabric of her skirt crumpled in her fists. "He has a book to lend you. I put him in the sitting room with Mrs. Gamble."

Kit's own fingers were stiff from the tight grip she had on her bodice. Slowly she relaxed them and nodded to Sophronia. Then she addressed Cain with as much composure as she could muster. "Would you invite Mr. Parsell to join us for dinner? Sophronia can help me finish dressing. I'll be downstairs in a few minutes."

Their eyes locked, stormy violet clashing with the gray of winter sleet. Who was the winner and who the loser in the battle that had just been fought between them? Neither of them knew. There was no resolution, no healing catharsis. Instead, their antagonism crackled even more powerfully than it had before.

Cain left without a word, but his expression clearly indicated it wasn't over between them.

"Don't say a word!" Kit began peeling off her dress, tearing a seam in her clumsiness. How could she have let him touch her like that? Why hadn't she pushed him away? "I need the gown in the back of my wardrobe. It's covered in muslin."

Sophronia didn't move, so Kit pulled it from the wardrobe herself and tossed it on the bed.

"What's happened to you?" Sophronia hissed. "The Kit Weston I used to know wouldn't lock herself in a bedroom with a man who's not her husband."

Kit turned on her. "I didn't invite him!"

"I'll bet you didn't tell him to leave, either."

"You're wrong. He was angry with me because he wanted me to have dinner downstairs with Mrs. Gamble, and I refused."

Sophronia jabbed her finger toward the gown on the bed. "Then why do you want that?"

"Brandon's here, so I've changed my mind."

"Is that why you're getting dressed up? For Mr. Parsell?"

Sophronia's question took her aback. Whom *was* she getting dressed up for? "Of course it's for Brandon. And for Mrs. Gamble. I don't want to look like a country bumpkin in front of her."

Sophronia stiff features softened almost imperceptibly. "You can lie to me, Kit Weston, but just don't lie to yourself. You'd better make certain you're not doing this for the major."

"Don't be ridiculous."

"Leave him to Mrs. Gamble, honey." Sophronia walked over to the bed and pulled the muslin off the gown. At the same time, she repeated the words Magnus had said to her only a few weeks earlier. "He's a hard man with women. There's something as cold as ice inside him. Any woman who tries to get past that ice will only end up with a bad case of frostbite." She settled the gown over Kit's head.

"You don't need to tell me all this."

"When the major looks at a beautiful woman, all he sees is a body to bring him pleasure. If a woman understands that about him, like I expect Mrs. Gamble does, she can enjoy herself and there won't be any hard feelings afterward. But any woman who's fool enough to fall in love with him is only going to end up with a broken heart."

"This has nothing to do with me."

"Doesn't it?" Sophronia did up the fastenings. "The reason the two of you fight so much is because you're just alike."

"I'm not anything like him! You know better than anyone how much I hate him. He's standing in the way of everything I want from life. Risen Glory's mine. It's where I belong. I'll die before I let him keep it. I'm going to marry Brandon Parsell, Sophronia. And as soon as I can, I'm buying this plantation back."

Sophronia took a brush to her tangles. "And what makes you think the major will sell it to you?"

"Oh, he'll sell, all right. It's just a matter of time."

Sophronia began to draw her hair into a neat knot, but Kit shook her head. She'd wear it free tonight, with only the silver combs. Everything about her must be as different from Veronica Gamble as possible.

"You got no way of knowing he'll sell," Sophronia said.

Kit wasn't about to confess her late-night forages through the plantation's calf-bound ledgers, adding and subtracting her way through pages of boldly entered figures. It hadn't taken her long to discover that Cain had overextended himself. He was hanging onto Risen Glory and his spinning mill by the most fragile of threads. The smallest disaster could send him under.

Kit didn't know much about spinning mills, but she did know about cotton. She knew about unexpected hailstorms, about hurricanes and droughts, about insects that fed off the tender bolls until nothing was left. Where cotton was concerned, disaster was bound to strike sooner or later, and when it did, she'd be ready. She'd buy the plantation right out from under him. And she'd buy it at her own price.

Sophronia was staring at her and shaking her head.

"What's wrong?"

"Are you really wearing that dress downstairs for dinner?"

"Isn't it wonderful?"

"It's made for a ball, not for dinner at home."

Kit smiled. "I know."

The gown had been so outrageously expensive that Elsbeth had protested. She'd argued that Kit could put her clothing allowance to better use buying several more modest gowns. Besides, it was too conspicuous, she'd said, so extravagantly beautiful that, even on the most demure female—which Kit certainly was not—it would draw more attention than, perhaps, a well-brought-up young lady should wish to attract.

Such subtleties were lost on Kit. She only knew that it was glorious and she had to have it.

The overskirt of the dress was a billowing cloud of silver organdy caught up over gleaming white satin shot with silver thread. Crystal bugle beads covered the tight-fitting bodice, sparkling like night snow under a starry winter sky. More beads spangled the skirt all the way to the hem.

The neckline was low, falling well off her shoulders. She glanced down and saw that the tops of her exposed breasts were still faintly rosy from Cain's hands. She quickly looked away and put on the necklace that went with the gown, a choker of crystal bugle beads drizzling onto her skin like melting ice chips.

The very air around her seemed to crackle as she moved. She slipped on satin slippers with spool-shaped heels, the ones she'd worn at the Templeton ball. They were eggshell instead of the stark white of the gown, but she didn't care.

"Don't worry, Sophronia. Everything's going to be fine." She gave Sophronia a quick peck on the cheek and made her way downstairs, the gown shimmering around her in a crystalline cloud of ice and snow.

Veronica Gamble's smooth forehead betrayed nothing of her thoughts as Kit swept into the sitting room. So the little kitten had decided to fight. She wasn't surprised.

The gown was outrageously inappropriate for the occasion and quite wonderful. Its remote ice-maiden perfection served as a perfect foil for the girl's vivid beauty. Mr. Parsell, who'd so blatantly wrangled a dinner invitation, seemed stunned by her appearance. Baron looked like a thundercloud.

The poor man. He would have done better to have left her in that dirty dress.

Veronica wondered what had happened between the two of them in the room upstairs. Kit's face was flushed, and Veronica's observant eyes caught a small red mark on her neck. They hadn't made love, that was certain. Cain was still as tightly coiled as a jungle beast about to spring.

Veronica sat on Cain's right during dinner, with Kit at the foot of the table and Brandon next to her. The meal was delicious: fragrant jambalaya accompanied by oyster patties smothered in a cucumber-curry sauce, green peas flavored with mint, beaten biscuits, and, for dessert, rich slabs of cherry pie. Veronica was certain she was the only one who noticed the food.

She was excessively attentive to Baron throughout the meal. She leaned close to him and told him her most amusing stories. She laid her fingers lightly on his sleeve and occasionally squeezed his hard-muscled arm with deliberate intimacy.

He gave her his total attention. If she hadn't

known better, she would have believed he didn't notice the subdued laughter coming from the other end of the table.

After dinner, Cain suggested the men take their brandy in the sitting room with the women instead of remaining at the dinner table. Brandon agreed with more eagerness than was polite. Throughout the meal, Cain had barely been able to conceal his boredom with Brandon's stuffiness, while Brandon couldn't quite hide his contempt for Cain.

In the sitting room, Veronica deliberately took a place on the settee next to Kit, even though she knew the girl had taken a dislike to her. Yet Kit was courteous and thoroughly entertaining once they began to talk. She was exceptionally well read for a young woman, and when Veronica suggested that Kit borrow her copy of a scandalous new book by Gustave Flaubert that she'd just finished reading, Brandon sent her a thunderous look of disapproval.

"You don't approve of Kit reading *Madame Bovary*, Mr. Parsell? Then perhaps we'd better leave it on my shelf for the time being."

Cain regarded Brandon with amusement. "I'm sure Mr. Parsell isn't so stodgy as to object to an intelligent young woman improving her mind. Or are you, Parsell?"

"Of course he's not," Kit said too quickly. "Mr. Parsell is one of the most progressive men I know."

Veronica smiled. A most entertaining evening, indeed.

Cain crossed the hall and let himself into the library. Without bothering to light the lamp on his desk, he pulled off his coat and opened the window. The guests had left some time ago, and Kit had excused herself immediately afterward. Cain had to get up at dawn tomorrow, and he knew he should go to bed, but too many old memories had come back to nag at him tonight.

He gazed out into the darkness with unseeing eyes. Gradually the nighttime rasp of crickets and the soft, wheezy cry of a distant barn owl became less real than the bitter voices of the past.

His father, Nathaniel Cain, was the only son of a wealthy Philadelphia merchant. He lived in the same brownstone mansion in which he'd been born and was a competent, if unexceptional, businessman. He was nearly thirty-five when he married sixteen-year-old Rosemary Simpson. She was too young, but her parents had been anxious to rid themselves of their troublesome daughter, especially to such a well-heeled bachelor.

From the beginning, it was a marriage made in hell. She hated her pregnancy, had no interest in the son who was born exactly nine months after her wedding night, and grew to regard her adoring husband with contempt. Over the years she embarrassed him in public and cuckolded him in private, but he never stopped loving her.

He blamed himself for her restlessness. If only he hadn't forced a child on her so soon, she might have been more content. As time passed, however, he ceased blaming himself for her misdeeds and blamed only the child.

It took her nearly ten years to run through his fortune. She left him for a man who had been one of his employees.

Baron had observed it all, a bewildered, lonely child. In the months after his mother's departure, he stood by helplessly, watching his father being consumed by his unhealthy obsession for his faithless wife. Filthy, unshaven, drowning in alcohol, Nathaniel Cain sealed himself inside the lonely, decaying mansion and constructed elaborate fantasies of everything his wife had not been.

Only once had the boy rebelled. In a fit of anger, he'd spewed out all his resentment against the mother who'd abandoned them both. Nathaniel Cain had beaten him until his nose streamed with blood and his eyes had swollen shut. Afterward, he didn't seem to remember what had happened.

The lesson Cain had learned from his parents had been a hard one, and he'd never forgotten it. He'd learned that love was a weakness that twists and perverts.

Hard-earned lessons were the best-remembered. He gave away books when he finished them, traded horses before he could grow too fond of them, and stood by the window of the library at Risen Glory staring out at the hot, still night thinking about his father, his mother...and Kit Weston.

He found little comfort in the fact that so

many of the emotions she aroused in him were angry ones. It bothered him that she made him feel anything at all. But since the afternoon she'd invaded his house, veiled, mysterious, and wildly beautiful, he hadn't been able to get her off his mind. And today, when he'd touched her breasts, he'd known there'd never been a woman he'd wanted more.

He glanced over at his desk. His papers didn't seem to have been disturbed tonight, so she hadn't slipped in when he'd gone out to the stable to check on the horses. He probably should have locked up the ledgers and bankbooks after he'd found evidence of her snooping, but he'd felt a perverse sense of satisfaction in witnessing her dishonesty.

Her month was almost up. If tonight was any indication, she'd be marrying that idiot Parsell soon. Before that happened, he had to find a way to free himself from the mysterious hold she had on him.

If only he knew how.

He heard a soft sound in the hallway. She was roaming again, and tonight he was in no mood for it. He stalked across the carpet and twisted the doorknob.

Kit spun around as the library door crashed open. Cain stood on the other side. He looked rough, elegant, and thoroughly untamed.

She wore only a thin nightdress. It covered her from neck to toe, but after what had passed between them in her bedroom earlier, she felt too exposed.

"Insomnia?" he drawled.

Her bare feet and unbound hair made her feel like a hoyden, especially after spending the evening with Veronica Gamble. She wished she'd at least put on her slippers before she'd come downstairs "I—I didn't eat much at dinner. I was hungry, and I wanted to see if there was any cherry pie left."

"I wouldn't mind a piece myself. We'll look together." Even though he spoke casually, she sensed something calculating in his expression, and she wished she could keep him from following her to the kitchen. She should have stayed in her room, but she'd barely eaten anything for dinner, and she'd hoped a late-night snack would fill her stomach enough so she could sleep.

Patsy, the cook, had left the pie under a towel on the table. Kit cut a small piece she no longer wanted for herself, then handed Cain the pie plate. He grabbed a fork and carried everything over to the kitchen door. As she sat at the table, he opened it to let in the night air, then leaned against the doorframe to eat.

After only a few bites, he set aside the pie. "Why are you wasting your time with Parsell, Kit? He's a stiff."

"I knew you'd say something unpleasant about him." She jabbed her fork at the crust. "You were barely civil all evening."

"While you, of course, were a model of courtesy to Mrs. Gamble."

Kit didn't want to talk about Veronica Gamble. The woman confused her. Kit disliked her, yet she was also drawn to her.

Veronica had traveled everywhere, read everything, and met fascinating people. Kit could have talked to her for hours.

She felt the same kind of confusion when she was with Cain.

She toyed with one of the cherries. "I've known Mr. Parsell since I was a child. He's a fine man."

"Too fine for you. And I mean that as a compliment, so pull in your claws."

"Must be one of those Yankee compliments."

He moved away from the door, and the walls of the kitchen seemed as if they were closing in on her. "Do you really think that man would ever let you ride a horse in britches? Or trounce through the woods in your skirts? Do you think he'll let you curl up on the sofa with Sophronia's head in your lap, or show Samuel how to shoot marbles, or flirt with every man you see?"

"Once I marry Brandon, I won't flirt with anyone."

"Flirting's in your nature, Kit. Sometimes I don't even think you know you're doing it. I've been told that Southern women acquire the knack in the womb, and you don't seem to be any exception."

"Thank you."

"That wasn't a compliment. You need to look elsewhere for a husband."

"Strange. I don't remember asking your opinion."

"No, but your future bridegroom will have

to ask for my permission—that is, if you want to see the money in your trust."

Kit's heart skipped a beat. The stubborn set of Cain's jaw frightened her. "That's only a formality. You'll give your permission to whomever I choose."

"Will I?"

The pie clotted in Kit's stomach. "Don't toy with me about this. When Mr. Parsell asks permission to marry me, you'll grant it."

"I can't fulfill my responsibility as your guardian if I believe you're making a mistake."

She shot to her feet. "Were you fulfilling your responsibility this evening in my room when you...when you touched me?"

A sizzle of electricity coursed between them.

He looked down, then slowly shook his head. "No. No, I wasn't."

The memory of his hands on her breasts was too recent, and she wished she hadn't brought it up. She turned away. "Where Brandon's concerned, I know my mind."

"He doesn't care about you. He doesn't even like you very much."

"You're wrong."

"He desires you, but he doesn't approve of you. Ready cash is hard to come by in the South. What he wants is your trust fund."

"That's not true." She knew Cain was right, but she denied it. She had to make certain he wouldn't stand in the way of her marriage.

"Marrying that stiff-necked bastard would be the biggest mistake of your life," he said finally, "and I'm not going to be part of it."

"Don't say that!"

But as she stared at that implacable face, she felt Risen Glory slipping away from her. The panic that had been nibbling at her all evening clamped down hard. Her plan...her dreams. Everything was slipping away. She couldn't let him do this. "You have to let him marry me. You don't have any choice."

"I sure as hell do."

She heard her voice coming from far away, almost as if it didn't belong to her. "I didn't want to tell you this, but..." She licked her dry lips. "The relationship between Mr. Parsell and myself has progressed...too far. There must be a wedding."

Everything went still between them. She watched as he took in her meaning. The planes of his face grew hard and unrelenting. "You've given him your virginity."

Kit managed a slow, unsteady nod.

Cain heard a noise roaring inside his head. A great internal howl of outrage. It echoed in his brain, clawed at his skin. At that moment he hated her. Hated her for not being what he'd believed—wild and pure. Pure for him.

The nearly forgotten echo of his mother's scathing laughter rattled in his head as he fled the stifling confines of the kitchen and stormed outside.

12

Magnus drove the buggy home from church with Sophronia at his side and Samuel, Lucy, and Patsy in the back. When they'd first left church, he'd tried to make conversation with Sophronia, but she'd been brusque, and he'd soon given up. Kit's return had upset her, although he didn't understand why. There was something strange about that relationship.

Magnus looked over at her. She sat at his side like a beautiful statue. He was tired of all the mysteries surrounding her. Tired of his love for her, a love that was bringing him more misery than happiness. He thought of Deborah Williams, the daughter of one of the men working on the cotton mill. Deborah had made it clear that she wanted Magnus's attention.

Damn it! He was ready to settle down. The war was behind him, and he had a good job. Risen Glory's small, neat overseer's house situated at the edge of the orchard pleased him. His days of hard drinking and easy women were over. He wanted a wife and children. Deborah Watson was pretty. Sweet-natured, too, unlike the vinegar-tongued Sophronia. She'd make a good wife for him. But instead of cheering him up, the idea made him feel even more unhappy.

Sophronia didn't smile at him often, but when she did, it was like a rainbow unfolding. She read newspapers and books, and she understood things in a way that Deborah never could. Most of all, he'd never heard Deborah sing when she was going about her work the way Sophronia did.

He noticed a crimson-and-black buggy coming toward them. It was too new to belong to any of the locals. Probably a Northerner's. A carpetbagger, most likely.

Sophronia straightened, and he looked more closely at the vehicle. As it drew nearer, he recognized the driver as James Spence, the owner of the new phosphate mine. Magnus hadn't had any contact with the man, but from what he'd heard, he was a good businessman. He paid an honest day's wage and didn't cheat his customers. Still, Magnus didn't like him, probably because Sophronia so obviously did.

Magnus saw that Spence was a good-looking man. He tipped a biscuit-colored beaver hat, revealing a thick head of black hair, parted neatly in the center, and a set of trim side whiskers. "Good morning, Sophronia," he called out. "Nice day, isn't it?" He didn't even glance at the other occupants.

"Mornin', Mr. Spence," Sophronia replied with a sassy smile that set Magnus's teeth on edge and made him want to shake her.

Spence replaced his hat, the buggy passed, and Magnus remembered this wasn't the first time Spence had shown an interest in Sophronia. He'd seen the two of them talking when he'd driven her into Rutherford to shop.

His hands tightened involuntarily on the reins. It was time they talked.

The opportunity came late that afternoon, when he was sitting with Merlin on the front porch of his house, enjoying his day of leisure. A flicker of blue in the orchard caught his attention. Sophronia, in a pretty blue dress, was walking through the cherry trees, gazing up into the branches and probably trying to decide whether there was enough fruit left to justify another picking.

He rose and sauntered down the steps. Stuffing his hands into his pockets, he ambled into the orchard. "Looks like you might as well let the birds enjoy those cherries," he said when he reached her.

She hadn't heard him come up behind her, and she whirled around. "What do you mean, sneakin' up on me like that?"

"Wasn't sneakin'. I guess I'm just naturally light on my feet."

But Sophronia refused to respond to his bantering. "Go away. I don't want to talk to you."

"That's too bad, because I'm talkin' to you anyway."

She turned her back to him and began to walk toward the house. With a few quick steps, he planted himself in front of her. "We can talk here in the orchard"— he kept his voice as pleasant as could be—"or you can take my arm, and we'll walk over there to my house, and you can sit in that big ol' rockin' chair on my front porch while I say what I have to say."

"Let me by."

"You want to talk here? That's fine with me." He took her by the arm and steered her toward the gnarled trunk of the apple tree behind her, using his body to block any chance she had of sliding past him.

"You're makin' a fool of yourself, Magnus Owen." Her eyes burned with bright, golden fires. "Most men would've taken the hint by now. I don't like you. When are you goin' to get that through your thick skull? Don't you have any pride? Doesn't it bother you to be chasin' after a woman who doesn't care anything about you? Don't you know that half the time I'm laughin' at you behind your back?"

Magnus flinched, but he didn't move away. "You just go ahead and laugh at me all you want. My feelin's for you are honest, and I'm not ashamed of them." He rested the heel of his hand on the trunk near her head. "Besides, you're the one should be ashamed. You sat in church this mornin' cryin' out praises to Jesus, and then you walked out the door, and the first thing you did was make eyes at James Spence."

"Don't you judge me, Magnus Owen."

"That Northerner may be rich and goodlookin', but he's not your kind. When are you goin' stop fightin' what you are?"

Magnus's words made Sophronia ache, but not for anything would she let him see that. Instead, she tilted her head provocatively and rested it against the tree trunk. At the same time, she pushed her breasts ever so slightly forward.

A stab of triumph shot through her at his quick intake of breath and the way his eyes drank her in. It was time she punished him for trying to interfere with her life, and she was going to punish him in the way that would hurt the most. A little ache spread inside her at the thought of causing him pain. The same ache she felt whenever he looked at her, spoke to her, or turned those soft dark eyes in her direction. She fought her weakness.

"You jealous, Magnus?" She placed her hand on his arm and kneaded the warm, hard flesh beneath his sleeve. Touching a man usually gave her an ugly clawing feeling inside, especially if it was a white man she had to touch, but this was only Magnus, and he didn't scare her a bit. "You wishin' it was you instead of him I was smilin' at? Is that what's botherin' you, Mistuh Overseer?"

"What's bothering me is watching all those wars goin' on inside you and not being able to do anythin' about it," he said huskily.

"There aren't any wars goin' on inside me."

"There's no reason to lie to me. Don't you understand? Lyin' to me is just like lyin' to yourself."

His gentle words cracked the chrysalis of her self-protection. He saw it happening just as he could see through the sham of her seduction to the vulnerability behind it. He saw it all, and he still knew he had to kiss her. He damned himself as a fool for not having done it sooner.

Slowly, ever so slowly, he lowered his head,

determined not to frighten her, just as determined to have what he wanted.

The knowledge of what was to come flickered in her golden eyes. He saw a tremor of uneasiness, a hint of defiance.

He came nearer, then paused at the point of illusion, where his lips first sensed the warmth of hers. Instead of touching them, he feathered her skin with his warm breath.

She waited, whether as a challenge or in resignation, he didn't know.

Slowly, the illusion became reality. His lips brushed hers. Tenderly, he kissed her, yearning to heal with his mouth her hidden wounds, to destroy devils, tame demons, and show her a gentle world of love and softness where evil didn't exist. A world where tomorrow held laughter and hope that knew no color. A world where forever lived inside two loving hearts wedded in joy as one.

Sophronia's lips trembled under his. She felt like a trapped bird, frightened yet somehow knowing her captor wouldn't harm her. Slowly his healing magic seeped through her pores like warm summer sun.

He gently lifted her away from the tree and enfolded her in his arms. The maleness that had frightened her for so long didn't seem terrifying now. How soft his mouth was. Soft and clean.

Much too soon, he drew away from her. Her mouth felt abandoned, her skin cold despite the heat of the June afternoon. It was a mistake to meet his eyes, but she did it anyway.

She drew a deep, shattering breath at the love and tenderness she saw there. "Leave me alone," she whispered. "Please, leave me alone."

And then she fled, tearing across the orchard as if an army of devils were at her heels. But all the devils were inside her, and she couldn't outrun a single one of them.

Kit had forgotten how hot it could be in South Carolina, even in June. Heat haze shimmered in the air above the cotton fields, which were covered now with creamy white four-petal blossoms. Even Merlin had deserted her this afternoon, preferring to nap in the shadows of the hydrangeas that grew near the kitchen door.

Kit should have done the same thing. Her bedroom was shuttered like the rest of the house to keep out the afternoon heat, but she hadn't been able to rest there. Two days had passed since the Saturday night dinner party, but her encounter with Cain kept coming back to her.

She hated the lie she'd told him, but even now she couldn't think of anything else she might have said that would have guaranteed he'd give the permission she needed to marry. As for Brandon… She'd received a note asking her to accompany him to the Wednesday evening church social, and she was reasonably certain he'd propose to her then. No wonder she was in a fitful mood. Impulsively she turned Temptation into the trees.

The pond lay like a small, glimmering jewel

in the center of the woods, where it was safely tucked away from the bustle of the plantation. It had always been one of her favorite places. Even on the hottest August days, its spring-fed water was cold and clear, and the thick barrier of trees and underbrush acted like a fence around it. The spot was quiet and private, perfect for secret thoughts.

She led Temptation to the water's edge so he could drink his fill, then wandered around the pond's perimeter. The willows there had always reminded her of women who'd tossed their hair forward over their heads and let the ends dip into the water. She tugged at a switch and stripped the leaves into neat stacks in her fingers.

The lure of the water was irresistible. The workers never came near here, and Cain and Magnus had gone into town, so no one could disturb her. She threw her hat aside and tugged at her boots, then tossed off the rest of her clothes. When she was naked, she made a shallow dive from a rock at the edge and cut into the water like a silverfish. She came to the surface gasping at the cold, laughed, and dived under again.

Eventually she settled onto her back and let her hair unfold like a fan around her head. As she floated, she closed her eyes against the flaming copper ball of sun balanced on the treetops. She felt suspended in time, part of the water, the air, the land. The sun touched the hills of her body. The water lapped at the valleys. She felt almost content.

A bullfrog croaked. She rolled onto her stomach and swam in lazy circles. When she began to feel chilled, she headed into the shallower water at the edge and lowered her feet to the sandy bottom.

Just as she was about to step out, she heard Temptation nicker. From the border of the woods came the answering whistle of another horse. With a curse, she scrambled up the bank and dashed toward her clothes. There was no time for undergarments. She grabbed her khaki breeches and tugged them on over her dripping legs.

She heard the horse coming closer. Her fingers were too stiff from the chilly water to allow her to manage the buttons. She snatched up her shirt and shoved her wet arms into the sleeves. She was fumbling with the button between her breasts when the chestnut gelding broke through the line of trees, and Baron Cain invaded her private world.

He reined in near the spot where her undergarments still lay. Loosely crossing his hands on the pommel of the saddle, he looked down at her from the great height of Vandal's back. His eyes were shaded by the brim of his tan hat, leaving their expression unfathomable. His mouth was unsmiling.

She stood frozen. Her wetly translucent shirt revealed every inch of the skin it clung to. She might as well have been naked.

Cain slowly swung his leg over the saddle and dropped to the ground. While she struggled with the buttons on her breeches, she thought how wrong it was for such a large man to move so quietly.

His boots were dusty, and he wore his fawn trousers low on his narrow hips. His pale butternut shirt was open at the throat. His eyes remained shadowed under his hat brim, and not being able to see their expression made her even more uneasy.

As if he were reading her mind, he dropped the hat to the ground, where it landed next to her undergarments. She wished he'd left it on. The scorching heat in those gray eyes was threatening and dangerous.

"I—I thought you were going into town with Magnus."

"I was. Until I saw you heading out on Temptation."

"You knew I was here?"

"I would have shown up earlier, but I wanted to make sure we wouldn't be interrupted."

"Interrupted?" The button on her breeches refused to behave beneath her fingers. "What difference would that make?"

"Don't bother fastening it," he said quietly. "It's just going to come back off again." Mesmerized, she watched him lift his hands and slowly unbutton his own shirt.

"Don't do that." Her voice sounded breathless, even to her own ears.

He tugged his shirt free of the waistband of his trousers, then stripped it off and let it fall to the ground.

Oh, she knew what he was doing... She

knew, but she didn't know... "Sophronia's going to be expecting me," she said in a rush. "If I'm not back soon, she'll send somebody to look for me."

"Nobody's coming after you, Kit. I told them you wouldn't be back until late. We have all the time in the world."

"We have no time. I have...I have to go." But she didn't move. She couldn't.

He came closer, exploring her with his eyes. She felt him take in all the curves that her wet clothing outlined with such scrupulous attention to detail.

"Do you still want me to turn you over to Parsell?" he asked.

No! "Yes. Yes, of course I do."

"Then I will." His voice grew husky and seductive. "But first we have something to settle between us."

She shook her head, but she didn't try to back away. Instead, she heard herself say inanely, "This isn't proper."

"Most improper." His smile held a gentle note of mockery. "And neither of us cares."

"I care," she said breathlessly.

"Then why don't you climb up on Temptation right now and ride away?"

"I will." But she didn't move. She simply stood there and gazed at the muscles of his bare chest burnished by the late-afternoon light.

Their eyes locked, and he drew nearer. Even before he touched her, she felt the heat of his skin.

"We both know this has been between us ever

since the day you came here. It's time we put an end to it so we can get on with the rest of our lives."

Temptation whickered.

He brushed her cheek with his finger and spoke softly. "I'm going to have you now, Kit Weston."

His head dipped so slowly that he might have been moving in a dream. His lips touched her eyelids and closed each one with a soft, quieting kiss. She felt his breath on her cheek, and then his open mouth, like a warm cave, settled over hers.

The tip of his tongue gently played with her lips. It slid along them and tried to coax away the uncertainty that held them shut. Her breasts had been so cold. Now they crushed against the hard warmth of his bare chest. With a moan, she opened her mouth and let him in.

He explored every part of the velvet interior that she made so freely accessible. His tongue touched hers. Gradually, he coaxed her into his mouth until she finally took what he offered her.

Now she become the aggressor. She entwined her arms around his neck. Tasted. Invaded.

He made a muffled sound deep in his throat. She felt his hand slide between their bodies. He pushed aside the open V of her britches and flattened his palm on her stomach.

The intimacy inflamed her. She dug her fingers into his thick, tawny hair. He pushed his hand beneath her shirt and found her breast. As his thumb circled the small, tight bud at the center, she pulled her mouth away with a smothered cry. Would she go to hell for this? What she was letting him do… This man wasn't her husband but her dearest enemy.

She felt herself falling and realized he was taking her to the ground with him. He cushioned their landing, then rolled her onto her back.

The earth was soft and mossy beneath her. He tugged at the button between her breasts, pushed aside the wet fabric, and exposed her breasts.

"You're so beautiful," he said huskily. He lifted his gaze to her face. "So perfect. Wild and free." Locking his eyes with hers, he covered her nipples with his thumbs and began making a series of small circles.

She bit her lip to keep from crying out. The frenzied sensations spiraled inside her, growing hotter and wilder.

"Go ahead," he whispered. "Let yourself feel."

The sound she made came from a place deep inside her.

His smile was smoky and full of satisfaction. He kissed the hollow of her throat, then the nipples he was torturing so expertly with his fingers.

Fiery pinwheels whirled behind her eyes as he suckled her. Just when she knew she could bear it no longer, his mouth trailed to the patch of flat, smooth stomach exposed by the open V of her britches. He kissed her there, then drew them down over her hips.

Finally she lay beneath him, naked except for her open white shirt.

Every nerve in her body quivered. She was frightened. Ecstatic. Noises played inside her head.

"Open for me, sweet."

His hands guided her...pushing...separating... Oh, yes...

Feathers of air touched her intimately. Her thighs were spread. She was open to his gaze, and the first trickle of apprehension hit her. *Eve's Shame.* Now he would do to her this momentous, awful thing that men did to women.

There's pain... There's blood...

But this wasn't pain. He brushed the curls between her thighs, and it felt more wonderful than anything she'd ever imagined.

His breathing grew heavy in her ear, and the muscles in his shoulders quivered beneath her palms. Her apprehension returned. He was so powerful, and she was defenseless. He could tear her apart. Yet she lay here.

"Wait," she whispered.

His head came up, his eyes darkly glazed.

"I shouldn't be... I need..."

"What's wrong?"

Her fear of him evaporated, but not her anxiety. So much was wrong, and right then, she knew she had to tell him. "It wasn't true," she managed. "What I told you. I've—I've never been with a man."

His brow clouded. "I don't believe you. This is another one of your games."

"No..."

"I want the truth."

"I'm telling you the truth."

"There's one way to find out for certain."

She didn't understand, not even when she felt his hand between her thighs. She sucked in her breath as he pushed his finger inside her.

Cain felt her wince, heard her gasp of surprise, and something inside him twisted. The membrane was there, that tenacious survivor of her rough, unruly childhood. Taut as a drumhead, strong as she was strong, it protected her even as it damned him.

His vulnerability frightened him, and he hated that. He sprang to his feet and cried out, "Isn't there anything about you that's what it should be?"

She stared up at him from her bed in the moss. Her legs were still parted. Long and slender, they held the secrets she'd shared with no man. Even as he grabbed his shirt and hat, he wanted her with a ferocity that made him shake, and pain he refused to acknowledge consumed him.

He stalked across the patch of grass to the place where his horse was tied. Before he mounted, he washed all feeling from his face and turned to inflict some of his own torment on her. But he couldn't think of words cruel enough.

"This isn't over between us yet."

13

Brandon proposed to her at the Wednesday night church social. She accepted his offer of marriage, but, pleading a headache, declined his invitation for a walk around the church grounds. He pressed a kiss to her cheek, took her back to Miss Dolly, and told her he would be calling at Risen Glory later the next afternoon to secure Cain's permission.

Kit hadn't lied about having a headache. She was barely sleeping, and when she did sleep, she'd jolt awake to the memory of the strange, tortured expression she'd glimpsed on Cain's face when he'd discovered she still was a virgin.

Why had she allowed him to touch her like that? If it had been Brandon, she could have rationalized it. But Cain... Once again she was plagued with the notion that there was something very wrong with her.

The next afternoon, she rode Temptation hard and then changed into an old dress and took a long walk with Merlin. When she returned, she met Brandon coming down the front steps.

Ridges of disapproval engraved themselves between his eyes. "I hope no one's seen you in that dress."

She felt a spark of irritation, then put the blame on herself, where it belonged. She'd known he was coming this afternoon, but she hadn't thought to save time to change. She really was hopeless. "I was walking in the woods. Have you spoken with Cain?"

"No. Lucy said he's in the paddock. I'll speak with him there."

Kit nodded and watched him walk away. Her stomach pitched with anxiety. She had to find something to do or she'd go crazy. She made her way to the kitchen, where she greeted Patsy, then began mixing ingredients for a batch of Miss Dolly's favorite beaten biscuits.

Sophronia came in while she was working and watched with a frown as she banged the wooden mallet at the dough. "I'm glad I'm not those biscuits. For somebody who's supposed to be getting married soon, you don't look too happy about it."

Somehow they all knew what was happening. Even Lucy had found an excuse to come into the kitchen right behind Sophronia, who took coffee beans from a burlap bag in the pantry and put them in the big wooden grinder.

"Of course I'm happy." Kit took another whack at the dough. "I'm nervous, that's all."

"A bride's got a right to be nervous." Patsy picked up her paring knife and began peeling peaches for a cobbler.

Lucy had stayed by the window, and she saw him first. "Mr. Parsell's comin' back from the paddock."

Kit snatched up a muslin towel and wiped her doughy hands, then ran out the back door and raced toward Brandon, but as she saw his expression, her smile faded. "What's wrong?"

He didn't break his stride. "Cain refused his permission."

Kit felt as if the wind had been knocked out of her.

"He said he didn't think we'd suit each other. It's insufferable. A Parsell being dismissed like that by a Yankee ruffian."

Kit grabbed his arm. "We can't let him get away with this, Brandon. It's too important. I have to get Risen Glory back."

"He's your guardian. I don't see what we can do. He controls your money."

Kit barely noticed that neither of them spoke of love, only the plantation. She was too angered by his resignation. "You may be ready to give up, but I'm not."

"There's nothing more I can do. He's not going to change his mind. We'll just have to accept it."

She wouldn't listen. Instead, she turned away from him and strode determinedly toward the paddock.

Brandon watched her for a moment, then headed for the front of the house and his horse. As he mounted, he wondered if it might not all be for the best. Despite Kit's captivating beauty and her fertile plantation, there was something about her that made him uneasy. Maybe it had to do with the voices of too many of his ancestors whispering to him.

She's not at all the right sort of wife for a Parsell—even a penniless one.

*   *   *

Cain stood at the whitewashed fence, one foot propped on the bottom rail as he stared out at the grazing horses. He didn't bother to turn when Kit charged up behind him, although he would've needed to be deaf not to hear her angry footsteps.

"How could you do this? Why did you refuse Brandon?"

"I don't want you to marry him," Cain replied, not looking at her.

"Is this your punishment for what happened yesterday at the pond?"

"This has nothing to do with yesterday," he said so tonelessly she knew he was lying.

Her rage felt as if it were strangling her. "Damn you, Baron Cain! You're not going to control my life any longer. You send word to Brandon that you've changed your mind, or I swear to God, I'll make you pay!"

She was so small and he so large that her threat should have been ludicrous. But she was deadly serious, and they both knew it.

"Maybe you already have." He headed out across the paddock.

She stumbled toward the orchard, not seeing where she was going, knowing only that she had to be alone. That day at the pond... Why had she told him the truth?

Because if she hadn't, they wouldn't have stopped.

She wanted to believe she could make him

change his mind, but she knew as surely as she drew breath that he wouldn't. Her childhood hatred of being born female returned in a rush. How she hated being at the mercy of men. Would she now have to drag Bertrand Mayhew here from New York?

The memory of his fussy ways and soft, pudgy body was repulsive to her. Maybe one of the men who had showered attention on her since she'd returned... But Brandon had been the Holy Grail, and choosing any other made her despair.

How could Cain have done this to her?

The question haunted her for the rest of the evening. She refused dinner and sealed herself in her bedroom. Miss Dolly came to the door, and then Sophronia. She sent them both away.

Long after dark, there was a sharp knock from the adjoining sitting room. "Kit, come in here," Cain said. "I want to talk to you."

"Unless you've changed your mind, I don't have anything more to say to you."

"Either you can come in here or I'll join you in your bedroom. Which is it going to be?"

She pressed her eyes shut for a moment. Choices. He presented them to her and then took them away. Slowly she walked to the door and turned the knob.

He stood across the sitting room, a glass of brandy in his hand, his hair rumpled.

"Tell me you've changed your mind," she said.

"You know I haven't."

"Can you even imagine what it's like to have another person control your life?"

"No. That's why I fought for the Union cause. And I'm not trying to control your life, Kit. Despite what you think, I'm trying to do what's right."

"I'm sure that's what you've told yourself."

"You don't want him."

"I have nothing else to say to you."

She turned and headed back to her room, but he caught her in the doorway. "Stop being so stubborn and use your head! He's a weakling, not the kind of man who could ever make you happy. He lives in the past and whines because things aren't the way they used to be. He was born and bred for only one thing, and that's running a plantation on slave labor. He's the past, Kit. You're the future."

There was more truth in what he was saying than she would admit. But Cain didn't know the real reason she wanted to marry Brandon. "He's a fine man, and I would have been privileged to call him my husband."

He gazed down at her. "But would he have made your heart pound the way it did at the pond when I held you in my arms?"

No, Brandon would never have made her heart pound like that, and she'd have been glad of it. What she'd done with Cain made her feel weak. "It was fear that made my heart pound, nothing else."

He turned away. Took a sip of brandy. "This is no good."

"All you had to do was say yes, and you'd have been rid of me."

He lifted his glass and tossed down the rest of his drink. "I'm sending you back to New York. You're leaving on Saturday."

"What?"

Even before Cain turned and saw her stricken expression, he knew he'd driven a knife into her heart.

She was one of the most intelligent women he'd ever known, so why did she have to be so stupid about this? He knew she wouldn't listen to him, but he still tried to think of something he could say that would penetrate her stubborn will and make her see reason, but there was nothing. With a muffled curse, he left the sitting room and headed downstairs.

He sat in the library for some time, his head bowed, a muscle twitching in his cheek. Kit Weston had gotten under his skin, and it scared the hell out of him. All his life he'd watched men make fools of themselves over women, and now he was in danger of doing the same.

It was more than her wild beauty that stirred him, more than the sensuality she hadn't yet entirely claimed. There was something sweet and vulnerable about her that unearthed feelings inside him he hadn't known he possessed. Feelings that made him want to laugh with her instead of snarl, that made him want to make love with her until her face lit up with a joy meant for him alone.

He leaned his head back. He'd told her he

was sending her back to New York, but he couldn't do it. Tomorrow he'd tell her. And then he was going to do his best to start over with her. For once in his life, he was going to set his cynicism aside and reach out to a woman.

The thought made him feel young and foolishly happy.

The clock chimed midnight when Kit heard Cain go to his room. On Saturday she would have to leave Risen Glory. It was a blow so devastating, so unexpected, she couldn't comprehend how to deal with it. This time there would be no schemes to sustain her as there'd been during her three years at the Academy. He'd won. He'd finally beaten her.

Rage at her powerlessness overcame her pain. She wanted vengeance. She wanted to destroy something he cared about, to ruin him as he'd just ruined her.

But there was nothing he cared about, not even Risen Glory itself. Hadn't he turned the plantation over to Magnus while he completed his cotton mill?

The mill... She stopped her pacing. The mill was important to him, more important than the plantation, because it was his alone.

Devils of rage and hurt whispered to her what she could do. So simple. So perfect. So very wrong.

But no more wrong than what he'd done to her.

She found the slippers she'd kicked off hours earlier and stole from the room on bare feet. Noiselessly, she crept down the back hallways and staircases of the great house and out through the rear.

The night was clear, with just enough moonlight for her to see where she was going. She put on her slippers and made her way through the fringe of trees that surrounded the yard toward the outbuildings beyond the house.

The storage shed was dark inside. She reached into the pocket of her dress and pulled out the candle stub and matches she'd gathered from the kitchen. Once the candle was lit, she saw what she wanted and picked it up.

Even half full, the kerosene can was heavy. She couldn't risk saddling a horse, so she'd have to carry it on foot for almost two miles. She wrapped a rag around the handle so it wouldn't cut into her palm and let herself out of the shed.

The deep quiet of the Carolina night amplified the sound of the kerosene sloshing in the can as she walked along the dark road that led to the cotton mill. Tears slipped down her cheeks. He knew how she felt about Risen Glory. How he must hate her to banish her from her home.

She loved only three things in her life: Sophronia, Elsbeth, and Risen Glory. Her whole life had been marked by people trying to separate her from that home. What she planned to do was evil, but maybe so was she. Why else would so many people hate her so much? Cain. Her stepmother. Even her father hadn't cared enough to defend her.

Wrong. Wrong. Wrong. The kerosene sloshing in the can told her to turn back. Instead of listening, she clung to her despair. An eye for an eye, a tooth for a tooth. A dream for a dream.

There wasn't anything inside the cotton mill to steal, so the building wasn't locked. She hauled the can to the second floor. With her petticoat, she gathered up the sawdust lying around and piled it at the base of a supporting post. The outer walls were brick, but a fire set here would destroy the roof and the interior walls.

Wrong. Wrong. Wrong.

She wiped her tears on the sleeve of her dress and saturated the area with kerosene. With a sob of agony, she stepped back and threw in a lighted match.

It ignited in a quick, noisy explosion. She stumbled backward toward the stairs. Great tongues of flame lashed at the wooden post. Here was the vengeance that would comfort her when she left Risen Glory.

But the destruction she'd wrought appalled her. This was ugly and hateful. It only proved that she could inflict pain as well as Cain.

She grabbed an empty burlap sack and began beating at the flames, but the fire was burning too fast. A shower of deadly sparks rained on her. Her lungs burned. She stumbled down the stairs, gulping for air. At the bottom, she fell.

Billows of smoke swept down after her. The hem of her muslin dress began to smolder. She smothered out the embers with her hands and crawled to the door.

The great bell at Risen Glory began to ring just as she felt the clean air on her face. She pushed herself up from the ground and stumbled into the trees.

The men had the fire out before it could destroy the mill, but it had damaged the second floor and much of the roof. In the predawn light, Cain stood wearily off to the side, his face streaked with soot, his clothing scorched and smoke-blackened. At his feet lay what was left of a kerosene can.

Magnus came up beside him and silently surveyed the damage. "We were lucky," he finally said. "The rain we had yesterday kept it from spreading too fast."

Cain stabbed at the can with the toe of his boot. "Another week and we'd have been installing the machinery. The fire would have gotten that, too."

Magnus looked down at the can. "Who do you think did it?"

"I don't know, but I intend to find out." He looked up at the gaping roof. "I'm hardly the most popular man in town, so I guess I shouldn't be surprised that someone decided to get back at me. But why did they wait so long?"

"Hard to say."

"They couldn't have found a better way to hurt me. I sure as hell don't have the money to rebuild."

"Why don't you go back to the house and get some rest? Maybe things'll look better in the morning."

"In a minute. I want to take another look around first. You go ahead."

Magnus squeezed his shoulder and headed for the house.

Twenty minutes later Cain spotted it. He bent down on one knee at the bottom of the burned staircase and picked it up in his fingers.

At first he didn't recognize the piece of tarnished metal. The heat of the fire had melted the prongs together, and the delicate silverwork across the top had folded in on itself. But then, with a sudden wrenching in his gut, he knew it for what it was.

A silver filigree comb. One of a pair that he'd so often seen caught up in a wild tangle of black hair.

The twisting inside him turned to agony. The last time he'd seen her, both combs had been tucked into her hair.

He was crushed by a vise of raw emotion. He, of all men, should have known better than to let down the barriers he'd so carefully erected. As he stared at the misshapen piece of metal in his hand, something tender and fragile shattered inside him like a crystal teardrop. In its place was left cynicism, hatred, and self-loathing. What a weak, stupid fool he'd been.

He stood to pocket the comb, and as he walked out of his ruined mill, his face twisted with a vicious, deadly sense of purpose.

She'd had her revenge. Now it was his turn.

14

It was midafternoon before he found her. She was huddled beneath an old wagon that had been abandoned during the war in some brush at the northern edge of the plantation. He saw the soot streaks on her face and arms, the scorched places on her blue dress. Incredibly, she was asleep. He prodded her hip with the toe of his boot.

Her eyes flew open, but he was standing against the sun, and all she could see was a great menacing shape looming above her. Still, she didn't need to see more to know who he was. She tried to scramble to her feet, but he settled his boot on her skirt, pinning her to the ground.

"You're not going anyplace."

Something dropped in front of her. She looked down to see the melted silver hair comb.

"Next time you decide to burn something down, don't leave a calling card."

Her stomach churned. She managed a hoarse whisper. "Let me explain." It was a stupid thing to say. How could she explain? He already understood too well.

His head shifted slightly, blocking the sun for an instant. She winced as she glimpsed his eyes. They were hard, cold, and empty. Mercifully, he moved and the sun blinded her again.

"Did Parsell help you?"

"No! Brandon wouldn't do such a—" Brandon wouldn't, but she would. She wiped the back of her hand over her dry lips and tried to get up, but he wouldn't move his foot.

"I'm sorry." The words were so inadequate.

"I'm sure you're sorry that the fire didn't get it all."

"No, that's not— Risen Glory is my life." Her throat was raw from the smoke, and she needed water, but first she had to try to explain. "This plantation is all I ever wanted. I...needed to marry Brandon so I'd have control of the money in my trust fund. I was going to use it to buy Risen Glory from you."

"And how were you going to make me sell? Another fire?"

"No. What happened last night...it was..." She tried to breathe. "I saw the ledgers, so I knew you were overextended. All it would have taken was a bad season, and you'd have gone under. I wanted to be ready. I wasn't out to cheat you. I'd have given you a fair price for the land. And I didn't want the mill."

"So that's why you were so determined to get married. I guess even a Parsell isn't above marrying for money."

"It wasn't like that. We're fond of each

other. It's just..." Her voice trailed off. What was the use? He was right.

He lifted his foot from her skirt and walked over to Vandal. There was nothing he could do to her that was worse than what he'd already planned. Sending her back to New York would be like dying.

He came toward her again, a canteen in his hand. "Drink."

She took it from him and tilted the rim to her lips. The water was warm and metallic, but she drank her fill. Only when she handed the canteen back did she see what dangled from his fingers.

A long, thin cord.

Before she could move, he caught up her wrists and wrapped the cord around them.

"Baron! Don't do this."

He tied the ends to the axle of the old wagon and headed back to his horse without responding.

"Stop it. What are you doing?"

He vaulted into the saddle and spun the horse out. As suddenly as he had appeared, he was gone.

The afternoon passed with agonizing slowness. He hadn't fastened the cord so tightly that it cut into her wrists, but he'd done the job well enough that she couldn't free herself. Her shoulders ached from the strain of her position. Mosquitoes buzzed around her, and her stomach rumbled with hunger, but the thought of food made her nauseous. She was too filled with self-hatred.

He returned at dusk and dismounted with the slow, easy grace that no longer deceived her. He'd changed into a clean white shirt and fawn trousers, all of it at odds with her filthy condition. He pulled something from his saddlebags and moved toward her, the brim of his tan hat shadowing his face.

For a moment he gazed down; then he squatted beside her. With a few deft motions, the cords she'd struggled to untie came loose. As he released her wrists, she sagged against the wagon wheel.

He tossed her the canteen he'd brought with him, then opened the bundle he'd taken from his saddlebags. Inside was a soft roll, a chunk of cheese, and a slab of cold ham. "Eat," he said roughly.

She shook her head. "I'm not hungry."

"Do it anyway."

Her body had a more pressing demand than food. "I need some privacy."

He pulled a cheroot from his pocket and lit it. The blaze of the match cast a jagged, blood-red shadow across his face. The match went out. There was only the glowing ember at the tip and the ruthless slash of his mouth.

He jerked his head toward a clump of bushes barely six feet away. "Right there. No farther."

It was too close for privacy, but she'd lost the luxury of freedom when she'd piled the sawdust around the supporting post at the mill.

Her legs were stiff. She climbed awkwardly to her feet and stumbled toward the bushes. She prayed he'd move farther away, but he stayed where he was, and she added humiliation to all the other painful emotions she was feeling.

When she was done, she returned to the wagon and the food he'd brought. She had a hard time forcing it down, and she ate slowly. He made no attempt to hurry her, but leaned against the trunk as if he had all the time in the world.

It was dark when she was done. All she could see of him was the massive outline of his body and the burning tip of the cheroot.

He walked toward his horse. The moon came out from behind a cloud and washed them in silver light. It glittered on his brass belt buckle as he turned back to her. "Climb up. You and I have an appointment."

The flat, deadly tone of his voice chilled her. "What kind of appointment?"

"With a minister. We're getting married."

The world came to a thundering stop. "Married! Have you lost your mind?"

"You might say."

"I'd marry the devil first."

"We're one and the same. But then, you'll find that out."

The night was warm, but the cold certainty in his voice made her blood chill.

"You burned down my mill," he said, "and now you're going to pay to rebuild it. Parsell isn't the only one who'll marry you for the money in your trust."

"You're insane. I won't do it."

"You're not going to have any choice. Mount up. Cogdell's waiting for us."

Kit's knees went weak with relief. Reverend Cogdell was a friend. Once she told him what Cain had in mind, he'd never go along with this. She walked over to Vandal and began to mount.

"In front of me," he growled. "I've learned the hard way not to turn my back on you."

He swung her up, then mounted himself. He didn't speak until they'd left the clearing behind. "You'll get no help from Cogdell, if that's what you're hoping. I confirmed all his worst fears, and nothing will keep him from marrying us now."

Her heart skipped a beat. "What fears are you talking about?"

"I told him you were pregnant with my child."

She couldn't believe what she was hearing. "I'll deny it! You'll never get away with this."

"You can deny it all you want. I already told him you would. I explained everything to him. Since you found out you were pregnant, you haven't been acting rationally. You even tried to kill yourself last night in the fire. That's why I couldn't let you have your way any longer."

"No."

"I told him I'd been begging you for weeks to marry me so our child wouldn't be a bastard, but you wouldn't agree. He said he'd do the job tonight, no matter how much you protested. You can fight all you want, Kit, but in the end it won't do you any good."

"You're not going to get away with this."

There was the barest softening in his voice. "He cares for you, Kit. You'll spare him and yourself a lot of pain if you do what you're told."

"You go to hell!"

"Have it your way."

But even as she cursed him, she knew she'd lost. There was an awful kind of justice in it. She'd done something evil, and now she would pay for it.

Still, she made one last effort when she saw the minister and his wife waiting for them at the old slave church. She pulled away from Cain and ran to Mary Cogdell.

"Please... What Cain said isn't true. I'm not going to have a baby. We never—"

"There, there, dear. You're upset." Her kind brown eyes clouded with tears as she patted Kit's shoulder. "You need to calm down for the baby's sake."

That was when Kit knew she couldn't escape her fate.

The ceremony was mercifully brief. Afterward, Mary Cogdell kissed her cheek, and the minister urged her to obey her husband in all things. She dully listened to them tell Cain that Miss Dolly had settled in with them for the night, and she understood that Cain had gotten her out of the way.

He led her back outside to Vandal, and they set off for Risen Glory. The closer they got, the more her panic grew. What would he do to her when they were alone?

They reached the house. Cain dismounted and handed Vandal over to Samuel. Then he clasped Kit around the waist and lifted her to the ground. For a moment her knees threatened to buckle, and he steadied her. She recovered and pulled away.

"You have my money," she said as Samuel disappeared. "Leave me alone."

"And deny myself the pleasure of our wedding night? I don't think so."

Her stomach constricted. "There's not going to be a wedding night."

"We're married, Kit. And tonight I'm going to bed you."

Eve's Shame. If she hadn't been so exhausted, she might have argued with him, but she had no words left. All she could think about was running.

Lights shone in the darkness from Magnus's house at the edge of the orchard. She picked up her skirts and began to run toward it.

"Kit! Come back here!"

She ran faster. Trying to outrace him. Trying to outrace her own vindictiveness.

"Magnus!" she screamed.

"Kit, stop! It's dark. You're going to hurt yourself."

She raced into the orchard, jumping over the jutting roots that were as familiar to her as her own palm. Behind her, he cursed as he tripped over one of those same roots. Nevertheless, he gained on her.

"Magnus!" Again she screamed.

And then it was all over. From the corner of her eye she saw Cain hurl himself through the air. He tackled her from behind.

She cried out as they both fell to the ground. He pinioned her with his body.

She lifted her head and sank her teeth into the muscled flesh of his shoulder.

"Damn it!" He pulled her to her feet with a growl.

"What's going on here?"

Kit gave a sob of relief at the sound of Magnus's voice. She broke away and ran toward him. "Magnus! Let me stay at your house tonight."

He put his hand gently on her arm and turned to Cain. "What are you doin' to her?"

"Trying to keep her from killing herself. Or me. Right now, I don't know which one of us is in more danger."

Magnus looked at her questioningly.

"She's my wife," Cain said. "I married her not an hour ago."

"He forced me into it!" Kit exclaimed. "I want to stay at your house tonight."

Magnus frowned. "You can't do that. You belong to him now."

"I belong to myself! And both of you can go to hell."

She turned to run away, but Cain was too quick for her. Before she could move, he caught her and tossed her over his shoulder.

The blood rushed to her head. His grip tightened on her thighs. He began to stalk toward the house.

She punched him in the back and got a smack on her bottom for her efforts. "Stop that before I drop you."

Magnus's feet came into view walking beside them. "Major, that's a fine woman you've got there, and you're handling her a little rough. Maybe you'd better give yourself some time to cool down."

"That'd take the rest of my life." Cain turned the corner to the front of the house, his boots crunching on the gravel drive.

Magnus's next words sent Kit's already uneasy stomach pitching. "If you ruin her tonight, you're goin' to regret it the rest of your life. Remember what happens to a horse that gets broke too fast."

For a moment, stars swirled behind her eyelids. Then she heard the welcome sound of feet rushing down the front steps.

"Kit! Sweet Jesus, what's happened?"

"Sophronia!" Kit tried to jerk upright. At the same time, Sophronia grabbed Cain's arm.

"Put her down!"

Cain pushed Sophronia toward Magnus. "Keep her out of the house tonight." With that, he carried Kit up the steps and through the door.

Sophronia struggled inside the circle of Magnus's arms. "Let me go! I have to help her. You don't know what a man like that can do to a woman. White man. Thinks he owns the world. Thinks he owns her."

"He does." Magnus held her to him and stroked her. "They're married now, honey."

"Married!"

In calm, soothing tones, he told her what he'd

just heard. "We can't interfere with what takes place between a man and his wife. He won't hurt her."

As he said it, he hoped she wouldn't hear the faint thread of doubt in his voice. Cain was the most just man he knew, but tonight there had been something violent in his eyes. Despite this, he continued to comfort her as he led her across the dark orchard.

Only when they reached his house did she grow aware of their destination. Her head shot up. "Where do you think you're taking me?"

"Home with me," he said calmly. "We're goin' to go inside and have a little bite to eat. Then, if you feel like it, we'll sit in the kitchen and talk for a spell. Or if you're tired, you can go in the bedroom and sleep. I'll get myself a blanket and make a bed right out here on the porch with Merlin, where it's nice and cool."

Sophronia said nothing. She simply gazed at him.

He waited, letting her take her time. Finally she nodded and went into his house.

Cain slouched in the wing chair that rested near the open window of his bedroom. His shirt was open to the waist to catch the breeze; his ankles were crossed on a footstool in front of him. A glass of brandy dangled from the hand that hung over the arm of the chair.

He liked this room. It was comfortable,

with enough furniture to be functional but not enough to crowd him. The bed was large enough to accommodate his tall frame. Next to it was a washstand and across the room were a chest and a bookcase. In the winter the polished floorboards were covered with braided rugs for warmth, but now they were bare, the way he liked them.

He heard splashing from the copper tub behind the screen in a corner of the room, and his mouth tightened. He hadn't told Sophronia that the bath he'd asked her to have ready upon his return was for Kit, not himself. Kit had ordered him out of the room; then, when she'd seen he wasn't going, she'd stuck her nose in the air and disappeared behind the screen. Despite the fact that the water could no longer be warm, she wasn't in any hurry to get out.

Even without seeing her, he knew how she'd look when she rose from that tub. Her skin would glow golden in the light from the lamp, and her hair would curl over her shoulders, its inky blackness stark against the pale cream of her skin.

He thought about the trust fund he'd married her for. Marrying for money was something he would have despised another man for doing, yet it didn't bother him. He wondered why. And then he stopped wondering, because he didn't want to know the answer. He didn't want to acknowledge that this marriage had little to do with money or rebuilding the cotton mill. Instead, it was about that single moment of vulnerability when he'd abandoned the caution of a lifetime and decided to open his heart to a woman. For one moment, his thoughts had been tender, foolish, and ultimately more dangerous to him than all the battles of the war.

In the end it wouldn't be the cotton mill he was going to make her pay for, but that moment of vulnerability. Tonight, the antagonism between them would be sealed forever. Then he'd be able to go on with his life without being tantalized by phantom hopes for the future.

He raised the brandy to his lips, took a sip, then set the glass on the floor. He wanted to be stone-cold sober for what was about to happen.

From behind the screen, Kit heard the scrape of wooden legs across the bare floor and knew he'd grown impatient with waiting. She grabbed for a towel and, while she wrapped it around herself, wished she had something more substantial to cover her. But her own clothing was gone. Cain had disposed of her ruined garments after she'd taken them off.

Her head shot up as he pushed back one end of the folding screen. He stood resting one hand on top of the wooden frame.

"I'm not finished yet," she managed to say.

"You've had enough time."

"I don't know why you forced me to take my bath in your room."

"Yes, you do."

She clutched the towel more tightly. Once again she searched for some escape from what lay ahead, but there was an awful sense of inevitability about it. He was her husband now. If she tried to run, he'd catch her. If she fought him, he'd overpower her. Her only course lay in submission, just as Mrs. Templeton had advised in that distant life Kit had lived only a little more than a month ago. But submission had never been an easy course for her.

She gazed at the thin gold ring on her finger. It was small and pretty, with two tiny hearts at the top delicately outlined in diamond-and-ruby chips. He told her he'd gotten it from Miss Dolly.

"I don't have anything to put on," she said.

"You don't need anything."

"I'm cold."

Slowly, without taking his gaze from hers, he unbuttoned his shirt and passed it over.

"I don't want to take your shirt. If you'll move out of the way, I'll go to my room and get my robe."

"I'd rather stay here."

Obstinate, overbearing man! She gritted her teeth and stepped out of the tub. Holding the towel to her body with one hand, she reached for his shirt with the other. Clumsily, she slipped it on over the towel. Then she turned her back to him, dropped the towel, and rapidly fastened the row of buttons.

The long sleeves kept getting in her way, making the job more difficult. As the shirttails clung to her damp thighs, she was conscious of how thin the material was over her nakedness. She turned up the cuffs and edged past him. "I need to go to my room and comb out my hair or it'll tangle."

"Use my comb." He inclined his head toward the bureau.

She walked over and picked it up. Her face stared back at her from the mirror. She looked pale and wary, but she didn't look frightened. She should be, she thought, as she drew the comb through the long strands of wet hair. Cain hated her. He was powerful and unpredictable, stronger than she was, and he had the law on his side. She should be screaming for mercy now. Instead, she felt an odd agitation.

In the mirror's reflection she saw him slouch into the wing chair. He idly crossed one ankle over his knee. His eyes caught hers. She looked away and combed her hair more vigorously, sending droplets spattering.

She heard movement, and her gaze darted back to the mirror. Cain had picked up a glass from the floor and was lifting it to her reflection.

"Here's to wedded bliss, Mrs. Cain."

"Don't call me that."

"It's your name. Have you forgotten already?"

"I haven't forgotten anything." She took a deep breath. "I haven't forgotten that I've wronged you. But I've already paid the price, and I don't need to pay any more."

"I'll be the judge of that. Now put down that comb and turn around so I can look at you."

Slowly she did as he said, a queer excitement

building along with her dread. Her eyes settled on the scars that marred his chest. "Where did you get the scar on your shoulder?"

"Missionary Ridge."

"What about the one on your hand?"

"Petersburg. And I got the one on my gut fighting over a crooked poker game in a Laredo whorehouse. Now unbutton that shirt and come over here so I can take a better look at my newest piece of property."

"I'm not your property, Baron Cain."

"That isn't what the law says, Mrs. Cain. Women belong to the men who marry them."

"Keep telling yourself that if it makes you happy. But I don't belong to anybody except myself."

He rose and walked toward her with slow, deliberate steps. "Let's get something straight right from the start. I own you. And from now on, you'll do exactly what I say. If I want you to polish my boots, you'll polish them. If I tell you to muck out my stable, you'll do that, too. And when I want you in my bed, you'd better be flat on your back with your legs spread by the time I have my belt unbuckled."

His words should have made her stomach churn in fear, but there was something too calculated about them. He was deliberately trying to break her, and she wasn't going to let him do it.

"I'm terrified," she drawled.

She hadn't given him the reaction he wanted, so he came after her again. "When you married me, you lost your last bit of freedom. Now

I can do anything I want with you, short of killing you. And if I'm not too obvious about it, I can probably do that, too."

"If I don't get you first," she retorted.

"Not a chance."

She tried again to reason with him. "I did a terrible thing. It was wrong, but you have my money. It's triple what it should cost you to rebuild that mill, so let's put an end to this."

"Some things don't have a price." He rested one shoulder against a bedpost. "This should amuse you..."

She regarded him warily. Somehow she didn't think so.

"I'd already made up my mind not to send you back to New York. I was going to tell you in the morning."

She felt sick. She shook her head, hoping it wasn't true.

"Ironic, isn't it?" he said. "I didn't want to hurt you like that. But everything's changed now, and I don't much care about that." He reached out and began unfastening the buttons of her shirt.

She stood perfectly still, her earlier spark of confidence evaporating. "Don't do this."

"It's too late." He parted the shirt and gazed down at her breasts.

She tried not to say it, but she couldn't help it. "I'm afraid."

"I know."

"Will it hurt?"

"Yes."

She closed her eyes tight. He removed her shirt. She stood naked before him.

Tonight would be the worst, she told herself. When it was done, he'd have lost his power over her.

He caught her under the knees and carried her to his bed. She turned her head away as he began to strip off his clothing. Moments later, he lowered himself to the side of the bed. It sagged beneath his weight.

Something twisted inside Cain at the sight of her turned away from him. Her closed eyes... The resignation in that heart-shaped face... What had it cost her to admit her fear? Damn it, he didn't want her like this. He wanted her spitting and fighting. He wanted her cursing him and sparking his anger as only she knew how.

He cupped her knees to prod a reaction from her, but even then she didn't fight him. He pushed her legs apart and shifted his weight to kneel between them. Then he looked down at the secret part of her, bathed in lamplight.

She lay still as he separated the dark, silken threads with his fingers. His wild rose of the deep wood. Petals within petals. Protectively folded around the heart of her. His stomach knotted at the sight. He knew from the afternoon at the pond how small she was, how tight. He was flooded with a damning sense of tenderness.

From the corner of his eye he saw one delicate hand curl into a fist on the counterpane. He waited for her to swing at him, to fight him for what he was doing. Wished for it to happen. But she didn't move, and her very defenselessness undid him.

With a groan, he lay down and pulled her into his arms. She was trembling. Guilt as powerful as his desire ate at him. He'd never treated a woman so callously. This was part of the madness that had claimed him. "I'm sorry," he whispered.

He held her against his bare chest and stroked the damp locks of her hair. As he soothed her, his own desire raged, but he didn't give in to it, not until her trembling finally stopped.

Cain's arm felt solid and ironically comforting around her. She heard his breathing slow, but she knew he wasn't asleep, no more than she was. Moonlight silvered the quiet room, and she felt a strange sense of calm. Something about the quiet, something about the hell they'd been through and the hell that no doubt lay ahead, made questions possible.

"Why do you hate me so much? Even before the cotton mill. From the day I came back to Risen Glory."

He was quiet for a moment. Then he answered her. "I never hated you."

"I was destined to hate whoever inherited Risen Glory," she said.

"It always comes back to Risen Glory, doesn't it? Do you love this plantation so much?"

"More than anything. Risen Glory is all I've ever had. Without it, I'm not anything."

He brushed away a lock of hair that had fallen over her cheek. "You're a beautiful woman, and you have courage."

"How can you say that after what I did?"

"I guess we all do what we have to."

"Like forcing this marriage on me?"

"Like that." He was still for a moment. "I'm not sorry, Kit. No more than you are."

Her tension returned. "Why didn't you go ahead and do what you were going to? I wouldn't have stopped you."

"Because I want you willing. Willing and as hungry for me as I am for you."

She was too conscious of their nudity, and she turned away from him. "That won't ever happen."

She expected him to get angry. Instead, he propped himself up on the pillows and gazed down at her without attempting to touch her. "You have a passionate nature. I've tasted it in your kisses. Don't be afraid of it."

"I don't want a passionate nature. It's wrong for a woman."

"Who told you that?"

"Everybody knows it. When Mrs. Templeton talked to us about Eve's Shame, said that—"

"Eve's what?"

"Eve's Shame. You know."

"Good God." He sat up in bed. "Kit, do you know exactly what happens between a man and a woman?"

"I've seen horses."

"Horses aren't humans." He put his hands

on her shoulders and turned her toward him. "Look at me. Even though you hate me, we're married now, and there's no way I'm keeping my hands off you. But I want you to know what's happening between us. I don't want to scare you again."

Patiently, in language that was simple and direct, he told her about her own body and about his. And then he told her what happened when they were joined. When he was done, he got out of bed and walked naked over to the table where he picked up his brandy glass. Then he turned and stood quietly, letting her satisfy the curiosity she wouldn't confess to.

Kit's eyes drank in his body, so clearly illuminated in the moon-drenched room. She saw beauty of a kind she'd never before witnessed, a beauty that was lean and muscular, that spoke of strength and hardness and things she didn't entirely understand. Her eyes went to the center of him. He quickened under her gaze, and her apprehension returned.

He must have sensed her reaction, because he set down his glass and returned to her. This time his eyes held a challenge, and even though she was afraid, she'd never refused a challenge, not when it came from him.

The corner of his mouth twisted in what might have been a smile. Then he lowered his head and brushed his lips against hers. His touch was feather-light and soft, his mouth closed. There was no hard, probing tongue to remind her of the other, less friendly invasion that would soon take place.

Some of her tension dissolved. His lips found a path to her ear. He kissed the valley below it and then took the lobe with its tiny, silver stud gently between his teeth and teased it with his lips.

Her eyes drifted shut at the sensations he was arousing in her, then snapped open again when he clasped her wrists and stretched them above her head.

"Don't be afraid," he whispered, trailing his fingers down the soft underside of her arms. "It'll be good. I promise you." He paused at the crook of her elbow, brushing his thumb back and forth across the sensitive inner surface.

Everything that had passed between them should have made her wary, but as he traced delicate circles in the quivering hollows under her arms, she found the past evaporating and the exquisite sensations of the present taking her prisoner.

He slid the sheet to her waist and gazed at what was revealed. "Your breasts are beautiful," he muttered huskily.

A more gently reared woman would have lowered her arms, but Kit hadn't been gently reared, and modesty didn't occur to her. She saw his head dip, watched his lips part, felt his warm breath on her tender flesh.

She gave a moan as he circled the small nipple with his tongue. He transformed its softness into a tight, pulsing peak. She arched her body, and he opened his lips to encompass what she offered. Tenderly he suckled her.

She found herself lifting her arms to cradle

the back of his head in her palms and pull him closer. As his mouth tortured one nipple, he attended to the other with the tough, callused pad of his index finger, teasing the tip and then catching it with his thumb and squeezing it ever so gently.

Not knowing men, she couldn't understand what a tight rein he was keeping on his own passion as he pleasured her. All she knew was that the pull of his mouth on her breast was firing nerve endings deep inside her.

He pushed the sheet away and lay next to her. Once again his mouth found hers, but this time he didn't have to coax it open. Her lips were already parted for his pleasure. Still he took his time, letting her become accustomed to the feel of him.

As he played at her lips, Kit's own hands grew restless. One of her thumbs settled over his hard, flat nipple.

With a groan he plowed his hands into her damp, tangled hair and drew her head up off the pillow. He plunged his tongue into her mouth and took possession of the slippery-hot interior.

The wildness that had always been part of her nature met his passion. She arched beneath him, splaying her fingers over his chest.

The last vestige of his self-control snapped. His hands were no longer content with her breasts. They moved down her body to her belly and then into the dark, silky triangle.

"Open for me, sweet," he whispered huskily into her mouth. "Let me in."

She did open. It would have been unthinkable not to. But the access she offered was still not enough for him. He stroked the inner surface of her thighs until she thought she would go mad. Finally her legs were splayed wide enough to satisfy his desire.

"Please," she gasped.

He touched her then, his wild rose, the center of her. He gently opened her so it wouldn't be so difficult, taking his time even though he was nearly crazed from needing her as he'd never before needed a woman.

He moved on top of her, kissing her breasts, kissing her sweet young mouth. And then, unable to hold back any longer, he poised himself at the very center of her and slowly entered.

She stiffened. He soothed her with his kisses and then, with one smooth thrust, he broke through her maiden's veil and put innocence behind her.

She plummeted back to reality at the small, sharp pain. Until now, there had been only pleasure. This felt like a betrayal. His caresses had lied to her. They'd promised something magical, but in the end it had been a devil's promise.

His hand cupped her chin and turned her face. She glared up at him, too conscious of what was buried deep and massive inside her.

"It's all right, sweet," he murmured. "The hurt is over."

This time she didn't believe him. "Maybe for you. Get off!"

He smiled a smile that was deep and smoky. His hands returned to her breasts, and she felt the melting begin again.

He began to move inside her, and she no longer wanted him to leave. She dug her fingers into the hard muscles of his shoulders and buried her mouth in his neck so she could taste him with her tongue. His skin was sea salt and clean, and the stroking inside her was moving deeper, piercing womb and heart, melting her bones, her flesh, and even her soul.

She arched and strained and let him ride her through day and night, through space itself, clinging to him, to the sweet male of him, the hard shaft of him, driving deeper and deeper into her, carrying her higher, flinging her into the blinding brightness of the sun and moon where she hung for eternity and then shattered into a million slivers of light and darkness, answering his great cry with her own.

PART FOUR

Katharine Louise

Nothing can bring you peace but yourself.

RALPH WALDO EMERSON
"SELF-RELIANCE"

15

Kit was alone in the great rumpled bed when the noise in the hallway awakened her. She blinked against the sunlight, then bolted upright as she realized where she was. The sudden movement made her wince.

Sophronia rushed in without bothering to knock. "Kit! Honey, are you all right? Magnus wouldn't let me leave, or I'd have been here earlier."

Kit couldn't meet Sophronia's eyes. "I'm fine." She pushed back the covers. Her robe lay across the bottom of the bed. Cain must have put it there.

As she slipped into it, Sophronia stiffened. Kit saw her staring at the pale stain on the sheet. "You stayed with Magnus last night?" she said quickly, trying to divert her.

Sophronia pulled her gaze away from the bed and said unsteadily, "The major didn't give me much choice. Magnus slept on the porch."

"I see." Kit headed into her own room, just as if everything were normal. "A nice night for sleeping outdoors."

Sophronia followed her. Kit began to wash

in the water Lucy had left for her. The silence hung heavy between them.

It was Sophronia who broke it. “Did he hurt you? You can tell me.”

“I’m fine,” Kit repeated, too quickly.

Sophronia sat down on the side of the bed that hadn’t been slept in. “I never told you this. I didn’t want to, but now…”

Kit turned away from the washstand. “What’s wrong?”

“I—I know what it’s like to be…to be hurt by a man.” She twisted her hands in her lap.

“Oh, Sophronia…”

“I was fourteen the first time. He—he was a white man. I wanted to die afterward, I felt so dirty. And all that summer he’d find me, no matter how hard I tried to hide. ‘Gal,’ he’d call out. ‘You. Come over here.’ ”

Kit’s eyes filled with tears. She rushed to her friend’s side and knelt beside her. “I’m so sorry. I didn’t know.”

“I didn’t want you to.”

She drew Sophronia’s hand to her cheek. “Couldn’t you have gone to my father and told him what was happening?”

Sophronia’s nostrils flared, and she snatched her hand away. “He knew what was happening. White men always knew what was happening to the slave women they owned.”

Kit was glad she hadn’t eaten, because she would have vomited. She’d heard stories, but she’d always been able to convince herself that nothing like that could ever happen at Risen Glory.

"I'm not telling you this to make you cry." Sophronia took her thumb to one of Kit's tears.

Kit thought of the arguments about states' rights she'd made over the years to anyone who said the war had been fought over slavery. Now she understood why those arguments had been so important to her. They'd kept her from confronting a truth she hadn't been able to face. "It's so evil. So wicked."

Sophronia rose and moved away. "I'm doing my best to put it in the past. Right now, it's you I'm worried about."

Kit didn't want to talk about herself. She returned to the washstand, acting as if the world were just the same as it had been the day before. "You don't have to worry about me."

"I saw the expression on his face when he carried you into this house. It doesn't take much imagination to know you had a hard time of it. But listen to me, Kit. You can't keep all that ugliness stopped up inside you. You have to let it out before it changes you."

Kit tried to think of what she could say, especially after what Sophronia had revealed about herself. But how could she speak of something she didn't understand?

"No matter how terrible it was," Sophronia said, "you can talk to me about it. I understand, honey. You can tell me."

"No, you don't understand."

"I do. I know what it's like. I know how—"

"You don't." Kit turned. "This wasn't ugly

like what happened to you," she said softly. "It wasn't ugly or awful or anything like that."

"You mean that he didn't..."

Kit swallowed and nodded. "He did."

Sophronia's face turned ashen. "I—I guess I shouldn't have..." She ran out of words. "I need to get back to the kitchen. Patsy wasn't feelin' good yesterday." Her skirts made a soft whooshing sound as she left the room.

Kit stared after her, feeling sick and guilty. Finally she forced herself to finish dressing. She reached into her wardrobe and pulled out the first thing her fingers touched, a candy-striped dimity. She'd lost her silver comb, so she tied her curls back with a pumpkin-colored ribbon she found in her drawer. It clashed with her dress, but she didn't notice.

Just as she reached the foyer, the front door opened and Cain walked in with Miss Dolly. Kit was immediately swept into a peppermint-scented embrace.

"Oh, my sweet, sweet precious! This is the happiest day of my life, 'deed it is. To think that you and the major cherish tender feelin's for each other, and I didn't suspect a thing."

This was the first time she'd heard Miss Dolly voluntarily refer to Baron as "the major." She studied her more closely, which gave her an excuse to avoid looking at Cain.

"I've already chastised the major for keeping me in the dark, and I should chastise you, too, but I'm too consumed by happiness." The older woman clasped her hands to her ruffled bodice. "Just look at her, Major, in her pretty frock with a ribbon in her hair. Although you might want to find another color, Katharine Louise. That little pink satin you have, if it's not too badly crushed. Now I must go talk to Patsy about a cake." With a quick peck at Kit's cheek, she headed for the kitchen. When the clatter of her tiny heels on the wooden floor had receded, Kit was finally forced to look at her husband.

She might have been staring at a stranger. His face was empty of expression, his eyes distant. The passion they'd shared last night might have been something she'd imagined.

She searched for some trace of tenderness, some acknowledgment of the importance of what had passed between them. When she didn't find it, a chill went through her. She should have known this was how it would be with him. She'd been foolish to expect anything else. Still, she felt betrayed.

"Why is Miss Dolly calling you 'Major'?" She asked this question instead of the others she couldn't give voice to. "What did you say to her?"

He tossed his hat onto the hallway table. "I told her we were married. Then I pointed out that if she went on believing I was General Lee, she'd have to reconcile herself to the fact that you were living with a bigamist, since the general has been married for years."

"How did she react?"

"She accepted it, especially after I reminded

her that my own military record was nothing to be ashamed of."

"Your military record? How could you frighten her like that?" Finally she had a target on which to pin at least a small portion of her pain. "If you bullied her—"

"She wasn't frightened. She was quite pleased to hear how valiantly I was serving under General Beauregard."

"Beauregard fought for the Confederacy."

"Compromise, Kit. Maybe someday you'll learn the value of it." He headed for the stairs and then stopped. "I'm leaving for Charleston in an hour. Magnus will be here if you need anything."

"Charleston? You're leaving today?"

His eyes mocked her. "Were you expecting a honeymoon?"

"No, of course not. But don't you think it's going to look a little strange if you leave so soon after our—our wedding?"

"Since when have you cared what people think?"

"I don't. I was just thinking about Miss Dolly and her cake." Her anger ignited. "Go to Charleston. Go to hell for all I care."

She pushed past him and stalked out the front door. She half expected him to come after her, half hoped he would. She wanted a fight, a raging argument on which to blame her unhappiness. But the door remained shut.

She went to the live oak behind the house and leaned against one of the great drooping branches. How was she to survive being his wife?

* * *

For the next few days, she stayed away from the house as much as she could. At first light, she donned her britches and rode Temptation from one corner of the plantation to the next, everywhere but the spinning mill. She talked to the women about their gardens, the men about the cotton crop, and walked between the long rows of plants until the afternoon sun drove her into the refuge of the woods or to the banks of the pond.

But the pond was no longer a sanctuary. He'd spoiled that, too. As she sat beneath the willows, she thought about how he'd managed to take everything from her: home, money, and finally her body. Except she'd given that freely.

Sometimes the memory filled her with rage. Other times she'd feel edgy and restless. When that happened, she'd jump on Temptation and ride him until she was exhausted.

One day slid into another. Kit had never been a coward, but she couldn't find the courage to face her callers, so she left them to Miss Dolly. Although she didn't think the Cogdells would ever reveal the details of that awful wedding, the rest was bad enough. She'd married the enemy in a hurry-up affair that would leave them all counting on their fingers for months to come. Just as embarrassing was the fact that her husband had abandoned her the morning after their marriage, and she had no idea when he'd return.

Only once did she agree to receive company, and that was early Saturday afternoon, when Lucy announced that Mr. Parsell had come to call. Brandon knew how she felt about Cain, so he must realize that she'd been forced into the marriage. Maybe he'd thought of a way to help her.

She quickly changed from her britches into the dress she'd worn the day before and hurried downstairs. He rose from the settee to greet her.

"Mrs. Cain." He bowed formally. "I came to extend my felicitations as well as the best wishes of my mother and my sisters. I'm certain that you and Major Cain will be very happy."

Kit felt a hysterical bubble of laughter rising inside her. How like him it was to behave as if there'd never been anything between them but the most distant of friendships.

"Thank you, Mr. Parsell," she replied, somehow managing to match his tone. Propelled by her pride, she flawlessly played the role for which the Templeton Academy had trained her. For the next twenty minutes, she spoke of the condition of the roses that grew near the front of the house, the health of the president of the Planters and Citizens Bank, and the possibility of purchasing a new carpet for the church.

He responded to each topic and never once attempted to refer to any of the events that had transpired between them less than a week before. As he took his leave of her, precisely twenty minutes after his arrival, she wondered why it had taken her so long to admit to herself what an idiot he was.

She spent the evening curled in a chair in the rear sitting room, her old, battered copy of Emerson's *Essays* on her lap. Across from her was the mahogany desk where Sophronia worked on the housekeeper's records. Cain would expect her to take over now, but Sophronia wouldn't appreciate her interference, and Kit had no interest in counting linens. She didn't want to be mistress of the house. She wanted to be mistress of the land.

As night settled in, Kit sank deeper into despair. He could do anything he wanted to her plantation, and she couldn't stop him. He cared much more about the mill than the fields. Maybe he'd decide to slice up the fields to make way for a road. And he was a gambler. What if he squandered the money from her trust? What if he decided to sell off the land for ready cash?

The clock in the hallway chimed midnight and her thoughts grew darker. Cain had always been a wanderer. He'd already lived here for three years. How long would it be before he decided to sell Risen Glory and set off for someplace new?

She tried to tell herself Risen Glory was safe for now. Cain was preoccupied with the spinning mill, so he wasn't likely to do anything drastic right away. Even though it went against her nature, she had to bide her time.

Yes, Risen Glory was safe, but what about

her? What about that hot pounding in her blood when he touched her? Or the heightened awareness that shot through her every time she saw him? Was history repeating itself? Was Weston blood calling out to Cain blood as it had done once before in the union that had nearly destroyed Risen Glory?

"Katharine Louise, why aren't you in bed?" Miss Dolly stood in the doorway, her frilly nightcap askew, her face puckered with worry.

"Just restless. I'm sorry I woke you."

"Let me give you some laudanum, dear, so you can sleep."

"I don't need any."

"You need your rest, Katharine. Now, don't be stubborn."

"I'll be fine." She led Miss Dolly upstairs, but the older woman refused to leave her alone until Kit forced down several teaspoons of the laudanum.

She fell asleep, only to have her rest disturbed by opium-induced shadow-images. Toward dawn, a great tawny lion came to her. She smelled his male, jungle scent, but instead of feeling fear, she wove her fingers through his mane and pulled him closer.

Gradually, he changed into her husband. He whispered love words and began to caress her. Through the fabric of her dream, she felt his skin. It was warm and as moist as her own.

"I'll fill you now," her dream-husband whispered.

"Yes," she murmured. "Oh, yes."

He entered her then, and her body caught fire. She moved with him, and climbed with him, and just before the flames exploded, she called out his name.

The laudanum dream was still with her when she awakened the next morning. She gazed up at the pink-and-green silk bed hangings, trying to shake off the groggy aftereffects of the medicine. How real it had seemed...the lion who'd changed beneath her hands into—

She shot up in bed.

Cain stood at her washstand shaving before the mirror that hung above it. He wore only a white towel draped around his hips. "Good morning."

She glared at him. "Go into your own room to shave."

He turned and stared pointedly at her chest. "The scenery is better in here."

She realized the sheet had fallen to her waist, and she yanked it to her chin. Then she saw her nightgown lying crumpled on the floor. He chuckled at her sudden intake of breath. She lifted the sheet and stuck her head under it.

Sure enough. She wasn't imagining the dampness between her thighs.

"You were a wildcat last night," he drawled, clearly amused.

And he'd been a lion.

"I was drugged," she retorted. "Miss Dolly made me take laudanum. I don't remember anything."

"Then I guess you'll have to take my word

for it. You were sweet and submissive, and you did everything I wanted."

"Now who's dreaming?"

"I took what was mine last night," he said with deliberate relish. "It's a good thing that your freedom is a thing of the past. You obviously need a strong hand."

"And you obviously need a bullet in your heart."

"Get out of bed and get dressed, wife. You've been hiding out long enough."

"I haven't been hiding."

"That's not what I hear." He rinsed off his face, then reached for a towel to dry it. "I ran into one of our neighbors in Charleston yesterday. She took a great deal of pleasure in telling me you weren't receiving visitors."

"Forgive me if I wasn't anxious to listen to everyone clucking their tongues over the fact that I married a Yankee who abandoned me the morning after our wedding."

"That really rankles, doesn't it?" He tossed down the towel. "I didn't have any choice. The spinning mill has to be rebuilt in time for this year's crop, and I needed to make arrangements for the lumber and building supplies." He walked to the door. "I want you dressed and downstairs in half an hour. The carriage will be waiting."

She eyed him suspiciously. "What for?"

"It's Sunday. Mr. and Mrs. Cain are going to church."

"Church!"

"That's right, Kit. This morning you're

going to stop acting like a coward and face them all down."

Kit jumped up, taking the sheet with her. "I've never acted like a coward in my life!"

"That's what I'm counting on." He disappeared through the doorway.

She'd never admit it to him, but he was right. She couldn't keep hiding like this. Cursing under her breath, she threw aside the sheet and washed.

She decided to wear the blue-and-white muslin forget-me-not dress she'd worn on her first night back at Risen Glory. After she put it on, she pulled up her hair into a loose chignon, then perched a tiny confection of chip straw and blue satin on her head. For jewelry, she wore her detested wedding ring and eardrops set with moonstones.

It was a warm morning, and the worshipers hadn't gone inside yet. As the carriage from Risen Glory drew up, Kit watched their heads turn. Only the young children darting about in a final burst of energy were indifferent to the arrival of Baron Cain and his bride.

Cain helped Miss Dolly out, then reached inside the carriage to assist Kit. She stepped down gracefully, but as he began to release her arm, she moved closer to him. With what she hoped was an intimate smile, she slid first one hand and then the other up the length of his sleeve and clung to it in a pose of helpless and adoring femininity.

"Pushing it a bit, aren't you?" he muttered.

She gave him a blazing smile and whispered under her breath, "I'm just getting started. And you can go to hell."

Mrs. Rebecca Whitmarsh Brown reached her first. "Why, Katharine Louise, we didn't expect to see you this morning. It goes without saying that your very sudden marriage to Major Cain has surprised us all, hasn't it, Gladys?"

"It certainly has," her daughter answered tightly.

The young woman's expression clearly told Kit that Gladys's own eyes had been fixed on Cain, Yankee or not, and she didn't appreciate being passed over for a hoyden like Kit Weston.

Kit went so far as to press her cheek to his sleeve. "Why, Mrs. Brown, Gladys, I believe you're teasin' me, 'deed I do. Surely everyone in the entire county who possesses a pair of eyes guessed from the very beginnin' how Major Cain and I feel about each other. Although he, bein' a man, was much better able to hide his true emotions than I, a mere women, ever could."

Cain made an odd choking sound, and even Miss Dolly blinked.

Kit sighed and clicked her tongue. "I fought and fought our attraction—the major being a Yankee interloper and one of our most *evil* enemies. But as Shakespeare wrote, 'Love conquers all things.' Isn't that so, darlin'?"

"I believe Virgil wrote that, my dear," he replied dryly. "Not Shakespeare."

Kit beamed at the women. "Now, isn't he

just the smartest man? You wouldn't think a Yankee would know so much, would you? Most of them being dim-headed and all."

He squeezed her arm in what looked like a gesture of affection, but was, in fact, a warning to mind her manners.

She fanned her face. "Gracious, it certainly is warm. Baron, darlin', maybe you'd better take me inside where it's cooler. I seem to be feelin' the heat this morning."

The words were barely out of her mouth before a dozen pairs of eyes traveled to her waistline.

This time there was no mistaking Cain's wicked amusement. "Of course, my dear. Let's get you inside right away." He steered her up the steps, his arm around her shoulders as if she were a delicate, fruit-bearing flower in need of his protection.

Kit felt the churchgoers' eyes piercing her back, and she could hear them mentally ticking off the months. Let them count, she told herself. Soon they'd see for themselves that they were wrong.

And then a horrible thought struck her.

The Conjure Woman had lived in a ramshackle cabin on what had once been Parsell land for as long as anyone could remember. Some said old Godfrey Parsell, Brandon's grandfather, had bought her at a slave market in New Orleans. Others said she'd been born at Holly Grove and was part Cherokee. No one knew for certain how old she was, and no one knew her by any other name.

White and black alike, every woman in the county came to see her sooner or later. She could cure warts, predict the future, make love potions, and determine the sex of unborn babies. She was the only one Kit knew who could help.

"Afternoon, Conjure Woman. It's Kit Weston—Katharine Louise Cain now—Garrett Weston's daughter. You remember me?"

The door creaked open far enough for an old, grizzled head to protrude. "You Garrett Weston's young'un all grown up." The old woman let out a dry, rasping cackle. "Your daddy, he be burnin' in hellfire for sure."

"You're prob'ly right about that. May I come in?"

The old lady stood back from the door, and Kit stepped inside a room that was tiny and well-scrubbed, despite its clutter. Bunches of onions, garlic, and herbs hung from the rafters, odd pieces of furniture filled the corners, and an old spinning wheel sat near the cabin's only window. One wall of the room held crude wooden shelves bowed in the center from the weight of assorted crocks and jars.

The Conjure Woman stirred the fragrant contents of a kettle hanging by an iron hook over the fire. Then she lowered herself into a rocker next to the hearth. Just as if she were alone, she began to rock and hum in a voice as dry as fallen leaves.

"There is a balm in Gilead..."

Kit sat in the chair closest to her, a ladder-back with a sagging rush seat, and listened. Ever since that morning's church service, she'd tried to think of what she'd do if she had a baby. She'd be bound to Cain for the rest of her life. She couldn't let that happen, not while there was still a chance for her, some miracle that would give her freedom and make everything right again.

As soon as they'd returned from church, Cain had disappeared, but Kit hadn't been able to get away until much later that afternoon, when Miss Dolly retired to her bedroom to read her Bible and nap.

The Conjure Woman finally stopped singing. "Child, you lay your troubles on Jesus, you gonna feel a whole lot better."

"I don't think Jesus can do much about my troubles."

The old lady looked up at the ceiling and cackled. "Lord? You listenin' to this child?" Laughter rattled her bony chest. "She thinks You cain't help her. She thinks ol' Conjure Woman can help her, but Your son Jesus Christ cain't." Her eyes were beginning to water from her amusement, and she dabbed at them with the corner of her apron. "Oh, Lord," she cackled, "this child—she's so young."

Kit leaned forward and touched the old woman's knee. "It's just that I need to be certain, Conjure Woman. I can't have a baby. That's why I've come to you. I'll pay you well if you'll help me."

The old woman stopped her rocking and

looked Kit full in the face for the first time since she'd entered the cabin. "Chil'ren are the Lord's blessin'."

"They're a blessing I don't want." The heat in the small cabin was oppressive, and she rose. "When I was a child, I overheard the slave women talking. They said you sometimes helped them keep from having more children, even though you could have been put to death for it."

The Conjure Woman's yellowed eyes narrowed with something like contempt. "Those slave women gonna have their chil'ren sold away. You a white woman. You don't ever have to worry none about havin' your babies ripped out of your arms so you never see them again."

"I know that. But I can't have a baby. Not now."

Once again the old lady began to rock and sing. "There is a balm in Gilead to make the wounded whole. There is a balm in Gilead..."

Kit walked over to the window. It wasn't any use. The Conjure Woman wouldn't help her.

"That Yankee man. He got the devil in him, but he got goodness, too."

"A lot of devil and very little goodness, I think."

The old lady chuckled. "A man like that, he got strong seed. Ol' Conjure Woman needs strong med'cine to fight that seed." She struggled out of her chair and shuffled over to the wooden shelves, where she peered into first one container and then another. Finally, she poured a generous supply of grayish-white powder into an empty jelly jar and covered the top with a piece of calico she tied on with a string. "You stir a dab of this powder in a glass of water and drink all of it in the mornin', after he have his way with you."

Kit took the jar and gave her a swift, grateful hug. "Thank you." She pulled out several greenbacks she'd tucked into her pocket and pressed them into her hand.

"You just do what ol' Conjure Woman tells you, missy. Ol' Conjure Woman, she know what's best." And then she let out another wheezy cackle and turned back to the fire, chuckling at a joke known only to herself.

16

Kit was standing on a low stepladder in the library, trying to retrieve a book, when she heard the front door open. The grandfather's clock in the sitting room struck ten. Only one person slammed a door like that. All evening she'd been bracing herself for his return.

That afternoon, on her way back from the Conjure Woman's, she'd caught a glimpse of him in the distance. Since it was Sunday, he'd been working alone at the mill. He was stripped to the waist, unloading lumber he'd brought back from Charleston.

"Kit!"

The light from the library window had given her away, and from the sound of his bellow, he wasn't in a good mood.

The library door flew back on its hinges. His shirt was stained with sweat and his dirty nankeen trousers were tucked into boots that had undoubtedly left muddy tracks down the hallway. Sophronia wouldn't be happy about that.

"When I call you, I want you right away," he growled.

"If only I had wings," she said sweetly, but the man had no sense of humor.

"I don't appreciate having to look all over the house for you when I come home."

He was being so outrageous that she nearly laughed. "Perhaps I should wear a bell. Would you like something?"

"You're damn right I would. A bath, for one thing, and clean clothes. Then I want dinner. In my room."

"I'll get Sophronia." Even as she said it, she had a fairly good idea he'd take issue.

"Sophronia isn't my wife. She isn't the one who made me spend the last six hours unloading lumber I wouldn't have needed if you weren't so handy with a match." He leaned against the doorframe, blatantly daring her to defy him. "You'll take care of me."

She did her best to prod his ill humor by smiling. "My pleasure. I'll see about your bath."

"And dinner."

"But of course." As she swept past him

and headed for the kitchen, she played with a fantasy of jumping on Temptation and riding away forever, but it would take more than an evil-tempered husband to make her leave Risen Glory.

Sophronia was nowhere in sight, so she had Lucy get Cain's bath ready, then looked for something to feed him. She considered rat poison, but finally settled on the plate of food Patsy had kept warm on the back of the stove. She removed the towel so everything would be as cold as possible when he ate it.

Lucy appeared somewhat breathlessly at the door. "Mr. Cain says he wants you upstairs right now."

"Thank you, Lucy." As she carried the plate upstairs, she blew on the warm roast and potatoes, hoping to cool them off even more. She thought of dumping extra salt on top, but she didn't have the heart for it. He might be the devil incarnate, but he'd worked hard today. Lukewarm food was as far as she was prepared to go.

When she entered the room, she saw Cain sprawled in a chair, still fully dressed. He looked as grouchy as a lion with a thorn in its paw. "Where the hell have you been?"

"Seeing to your dinner, dearest."

He narrowed his eyes. "Help me off with my damned boots."

Even though his boots were mud-encrusted, he could have easily taken them off by himself, but he was spoiling for a fight. Normally she'd have been happy to oblige him, but since a fight was what he wanted, she chose to be perverse. "Of course, my lamb." She crossed over to him, turned her back, and straddled his leg. "If you brace yourself, it'll come off easier."

The only way he could brace himself would be to put his other muddy boot on her bottom. As she suspected, that was too much, even for him.

"Never mind, I'll take the damned things off myself."

"Are you sure? I live to be helpful."

He shot her a dark look, muttered something under his breath, and jerked off the boots. When he rose to take off his clothes, she busied herself by straightening the items on the top of the bureau.

She heard the sound of clothing dropping to the floor, then a splash as he lowered himself into the tub. "Come over here and scrub my back."

He knew he'd gotten the short end of their previous exchange, and now he intended to make up for it. She turned and saw him slouched low in the tub, his arm propped on the side, one wet calf dangling over the edge. "Take off your dress first so you don't get it wet."

This time he was certain she'd defy him, which would give him an excuse to be even more unpleasant. But he wasn't going to win that easily, especially when she wore a modestly cut chemise beneath, along with several petticoats. She avoided looking into the tub water as she unfastened her dress. "How considerate you are."

The water must have soothed him, because his eyes lost their hard look and developed an evil gleam. "Thank you for noticing. Now scrub my back."

She's scrub it, all right. She's scrub the skin off.

"Ouch!"

"Sorry," she said innocently from her position behind him. "I thought you were tougher."

"Don't forget my chest," he said by way of retaliation.

This would be awkward, and he knew it. She'd deliberately kept herself behind him, but it would be hard to wash his chest like that. She gingerly reached around him.

"You can't do a good job like that." He caught her wrist and pulled her to the side of the tub, soaking the front of her chemise in the process.

Avoiding looking down, she put the sponge to his chest and began soaping the mat of hair that stretched across it. She did her best not to linger over the white, lathery circles she made, but the swirling patterns icing those solid muscles enticed her. She wanted to paint in them.

One of her hairpins came out, and a lock of hair dipped into the water. Cain reached up to tuck it behind her ear. She sat back on her heels. His eyes drifted from her face to her breasts. She knew without looking that the water had made her chemise transparent.

"I'll—I'll set your plate on the table so you can eat after you've dried off."

"You do that," he said huskily.

She turned her back to him and took her time clearing off a small table by the fireplace. She could hear him drying off. When the sound stopped, she glanced cautiously at him.

He was dressed only in a pair of trousers, his hair damp and combed free of curl. She licked her lips nervously. The game had subtly shifted. "I'm afraid the food might be a little cold, but I'm sure it's delicious." She moved toward the door.

"Sit down, Kit. I don't like to eat alone."

She reluctantly took a seat across from him. He began to eat, and as she watched him, the four-poster bed in the corner of the room seemed to grow bigger in her imagination until it filled the room. She had to distract herself.

"I'm sure you're expecting me to take over Sophronia's responsibilities now, but—"

"Why would you want to do that?"

"I didn't say I wanted to. I can cook, but I'm terrible at the rest."

"Then let Sophronia do it."

She'd been prepared to rail at him for being unreasonable, but just like that, he'd knocked the wind out of her sails.

"There's only one household matter I want you to attend to, in addition to tending to me, of course."

She stiffened. Here it came. Something he knew she'd hate.

"A fox got one of the chickens last night. See if you can track it down. I'm sure you're a better shot than most of the men around here."

She simply stared at him.

"And if we want any game on the table, you'll have to put it there. I can't spare time from the mill right now to do it myself."

She couldn't believe what she was hearing, and she hated him for understanding her so well. She'd never have had this kind of freedom as Brandon's wife. But then, Brandon would never have looked at her as Cain was now doing.

The bed loomed larger. Her shoulders knotted with tension. She studied the sparkling prisms hanging from the lamp globe on the table, then ran her eyes over the books he kept near the bed.

The bed.

Her eyes settled on his hands. Broad-palmed, with lean, blunt-tipped fingers. Hands that had stroked her body and cupped every curve. Fingers that had explored her...

"Bread?"

She jumped. He held out a piece of bread he hadn't eaten.

"No. No, thank you." She struggled to hold onto her composure. "Miss Dolly was upset today. Now that I don't need a chaperone, she's afraid you'll send her away." She regarded him stubbornly. "I told her you'd do no such thing. I said she could stay here as long as she likes."

She waited for him to protest, but he merely

shrugged. "I guess Miss Dolly's ours now, whether we want her or not. Probably for the best. Since neither of us gives a damn about convention, she'll keep us respectable."

Kit shot up from the table. "Stop being so reasonable!"

"All right. Take off your clothes."

"No. I—"

"You didn't think a bath and food were all I'd want from you, did you?"

"If you expect more, you'll have to force me."

"Will I?" He leaned lazily back in the chair and scrutinized her. "Untie those laces. I want to watch you undress."

She was shocked to feel a flush of excitement, and she struggled against it. "I'm going to bed. Alone."

Even as Cain watched her march to the door, he could see the fight she was waging with herself. Now that she'd tasted passion, she wanted him as badly as he wanted her, but she'd fight him before she'd admit it.

She was so damned beautiful it made him hurt just looking at her. Was this weakness what his father had felt with his mother?

The thought chilled him. He'd meant to push Kit tonight until he sparked the temper that was always her undoing. He should have known she was too worthy an opponent to play so easily into his hands.

But it had been more than a desire to make her lose her temper that had prompted his churlish behavior. He'd wanted to inflict the small, humiliating wounds that would tell her how little he cared about her. Once she understood that, it would have been safe for him to take her in his arms and love her the way he wanted to.

He still intended to make love to her. But not the way he wanted it to be, not with tenderness and care. He wasn't that foolish.

He rose and made his way through the sitting room to her bedroom. She'd locked the door against him, of course. He hadn't expected anything else. With a little patience on his part, he could melt her resistance, but he didn't feel patient, and the lock gave with a single kick.

She still wore her underclothes, although she'd loosened the ribbon on her chemise, and her hair hung loose, black silk trailing over ivory shoulders. Her nostrils flared. "Go away! I'm not feeling well."

"You'll feel better soon." He swept her into his arms and carried her back to his bed, where she belonged.

"I won't do this!"

He dumped her on the bed. She landed in a pile of petticoats and fury. "You'll do whatever I tell you."

"I'll clean your boots, damn you, and I'll bring your dinner. But that's all."

He spoke calmly against the raging of his blood. "Who are you angriest at? Me for forcing the issue? Or you for wanting me to force it?"

"I'm not— I don't—"

"You do."

He rid them both of their clothes, and her

resistance melted with his first caresses. "Why does it have to be like this?" she whispered.

He buried his face in her hair. "Because we can't help it."

It was a meeting of bodies, not of souls. They each found satisfaction, but that was all. Exactly the way he wanted it.

Except afterward, he'd never felt emptier.

He rolled onto his back and stared at the ceiling. Scenes from his violent, unhappy childhood flashed before him. His father had lost more than his money to his wife. He'd lost his pride, his honor, and ultimately his manhood. And Cain was growing as obsessed with Kit as Nathaniel Cain had been with Rosemary.

The realization stunned him. His lust for this woman had blindsided him.

He drew a deep, agitated breath. Kit might desire him, but that desire wasn't as strong as her passion for Risen Glory. And beneath her desire, she hated him as much as ever.

Right then he knew what he had to do, and the knowledge was a knife in his gut. Desperately, he searched his mind for another way, but there wasn't any. He wouldn't let a woman steal his humanity, and that meant he couldn't touch her. Not tomorrow. Not next week. Not next month. Not until he'd broken the hold she had on him.

And that might take forever.

One week gave way to another, and they fell into a pattern of polite but distant coexistence, like two neighbors who nodded formally to each other over the fence but seldom stopped to chat. Cain hired extra men to work at the mill, and in little more than a month, the damage from the fire had been repaired. It was time to install the machinery.

As the days of summer ticked away, Kit's anger toward him yielded to confusion. He hadn't touched her since the Sunday night after he'd returned from Charleston. As long as she served him his meals when he came back from the mill, saw that his bath was ready, and superficially, at least, played the role of a dutiful wife, he treated her courteously. But he didn't take her into his bed.

She tramped through the woods in muddy boots and britches, the stock of his Spencer carbine tucked under one arm, a burlap bag holding quail or rabbits under the other. Although he wanted her waiting for him when he arrived home, he didn't care about proper female behavior the rest of the time. But even in the woods, she couldn't find contentment. She was too restless, too confused.

A letter arrived from Elsbeth:

My dearest, dearest Kit,

When I received your letter telling me of your marriage to Major Cain, I let out such a whoop, I quite terrified poor Mama, who feared I had injured myself. You minx! To think how you used to complain about him!

It is positively the most romantic histoire d'amour I have ever heard. And so perfect a solution to all of your troubles. Now you have both Risen Glory and a loving husband.

You must tell me if his proposal was as romantic as I have imagined it. In my mind I see you in your beautiful gown (the one you wore to our graduation ball) with Major Cain on his knee in front of you, his hands clasped imploringly to his breast just as we used to practice it. Oh, my dear Kit (my dear Mrs. Cain!), do tell me if my imagination has done justice to the event.

I hope you will be delighted with my own news, which I suspect will not come as a complete surprise. In October I shall be a bride just like you! I've told you in my letters that I've been spending much time with my brother's longtime friend, Edward Matthews. He is a little older than I and, until recently, thought of me as a child. I assure you, he no longer does!

Dearest Kit, I detest the distance between us. How I wish we could talk together as we used to and exchange confidences about the two men we love, your Baron and my darling Edward. Now that you are a married woman, I could ask you the questions I cannot bring myself to ask my own dear mama.

Can Eve's Shame really be as horrible as Mrs. Templeton suggested? I am beginning to suspect that she must be wrong, for I cannot imagine anything between my darling

Edward and myself that would be repulsive. Oh, dear, I shouldn't be writing of this, even to you, but it has been so much on my mind lately. I will close now before I am any more indiscreet. How I miss you!

Ta chère, chère amie,
Elsbeth

For a week, Elsbeth's letter stared accusingly at Kit from the top of her bureau. She sat down to answer it a dozen times, only to put away her pen. Finally she could postpone it no longer. The result was glaringly unsatisfactory, but it was the best she could do.

Dear Elsbeth,
How your letter made me smile. I'm so happy for you. Your Edward sounds perfect, just the husband for you. I know you will be the most beautiful bride in New York. If only I could see you.

I am amazed at how close your imagination hit upon the truth of Baron's marriage proposal. It was just as you imagined, down to the graduation gown.

Forgive me for such a short note, but I have a hundred things still to do this afternoon.

All my love,
Kit

P.S. Don't worry about Eve's Shame. Mrs. Templeton lied.

* * *

It was the end of August before Kit could bring herself to visit the spinning mill, and then only because she knew Cain wouldn't be there. It was harvest time, and he was in the fields with Magnus from dawn until long after dark, leaving Jim Childs in charge at the mill.

Even though Kit hadn't been near the mill since the awful night she'd tried to burn it down, it was never far from her thoughts. The mill threatened her. She couldn't imagine Cain being content to keep it small, but any expansion would be at the expense of the plantation. At the same time, she was fascinated by it. She was a Southerner born to cotton. Could the spinning mill perform the same miracle as the cotton gin? Or had it been a curse instead?

Like every other child of the South, she knew the story as well as she knew the lines in her own palms. The story had no boundaries of creed or color. It had been told by rich and poor alike, by free men and slaves. How the South was saved in ten short days. As she rode toward the mill, she remembered...

It was the end of the eighteenth century, and the devil seeds were killing the South. Oh, you could talk all you wanted about Sea Island cotton with its long, silky fibers and smooth seeds that slipped out as easily as the pit of a ripe cherry. But if you didn't own sandy soil along the coast, you might as well forget that

Sea Island cotton, because it wouldn't grow anyplace else.

There was tobacco, but it sucked the life out of the soil after a few years, leaving you with land that wouldn't grow anything.

Rice? Indigo? Corn? Good crops, but they wouldn't make a man rich. They wouldn't make a country rich. And that was what the South needed. A money crop. A crop that would make the whole world come banging on her door.

It was those devil seeds. The South could grow green seed cotton anywhere. It wasn't temperamental. It didn't need sandy soil or sea air. Green seed cotton grew like a weed. And it was worth about as much because those devil seeds clung to the short, tough fibers like burrs, they clung like glue, they clung like they'd been nailed in, they clung like the devil had put them there just so he could laugh at any man foolish enough to try to get them out.

A man had to work ten hours to separate one pound of cotton lint from three pounds of those devil seeds. Three pounds of seeds for one small pound of cotton lint. Ten hours' work. The devil was having a fine time in hell laughing at them all.

Where was the money crop going to come from? Where was the money crop that would save the South?

They stopped buying slaves and promised manumission to the slaves they owned. Too many mouths to feed. No money crop. The devil seeds.

And then a schoolteacher came to Savannah. A Massachusetts boy with a mind that worked differently from other men's. He dreamed machines. They told him about the devil seeds and those short, tough fibers. He went to the cleaning shed and watched how hard they fought to pull out the seeds.

Three pounds of seed for one pound of cotton lint. Ten hours.

The schoolteacher set to work. It took him ten days. Ten days to save the South. When he was done, he'd made a wooden box with some rollers and wire hooks. There was a metal plate with slots, and a crank on the side that turned like magic. The teeth hooked the cotton and pulled it through the rollers The devil seeds fell into the box. One man. One day. Ten pounds of cotton lint.

The miracle was made. A money crop. The South was Queen, and King Cotton was on the throne. The planters bought more slaves. They were greedy for them now. Hundreds of thousands of acres of land had to be planted with green seed cotton, and they needed strong backs for that. Promises of manumission were forgotten. Eli Whitney, the schoolteacher from Massachusetts, had given them the cotton gin. The miracle was made.

The miracle and the curse.

As Kit tied Temptation to the rail and walked toward the brick building, she thought how the gin that had saved the South had also destroyed it. Without the gin, slavery would have disappeared because it wouldn't have been economical, and there wouldn't have been a war. Would the spinning mill have the same disastrous effect?

Cain wasn't the only man who understood what it meant for the South to have its own mills instead of shipping the raw cotton to the Northeast or to England. And before long, there'd be more men. Then the South would control its cotton from beginning to end—grow it, gin it, spin it, and eventually weave it. The mills could bring back the prosperity the war had stripped away. But like the gin, the mills would bring changes, too, especially to plantations like Risen Glory.

Jim Childs showed her through the mill, and if he was curious about why the wife of his employer should suddenly reappear after a two-month absence, he gave no sign. As far as Kit knew, Cain hadn't told anyone that she was the person who'd tried to burn it down. Only Magnus and Sophronia seemed to have guessed the truth. When Kit left, she realized one part of her was anxious to see the huge machines at work when the mill finally opened in October.

On her way home, she caught sight of Cain standing beside a wagon filled with cotton. He was stripped to the waist, and his chest glistened with sweat. As she watched, he grabbed a full burlap sack from the shoulders of one of the workers and emptied it into the wagon. Then he took off his hat and ran his forearm over his brow.

The taut, sinewy tendons rippled across

the sheath of his skin like wind over water. He'd always been lean and hard-muscled, but the backbreaking work of plantation and mill had defined every muscle and tendon. Kit felt a sudden, piercing weakening inside her as she had a vision of that naked strength pressed over her. She shook her head to clear away the image.

After she returned to Risen Glory, she indulged in a frenzy of cooking, despite the fact that the weather during these final days of August was oppressive and the kitchen heavy with heat. By the end of the day, she'd produced a terrapin stew, corn rolls, and a jelly cake, but she still hadn't managed to shake her restlessness.

She decided to ride to the pond for a swim before dinner. As she left the stable on Temptation, she remembered that Cain was working in a field she'd have to cross to get there. He'd know exactly where she was going. Instead of upsetting her, the thought excited her. She tapped her heels into Temptation's flanks and set off.

Cain saw her coming. He even lifted his hand in a small, mocking salute. But he didn't go near the pond. She swam in the cool waters, naked and alone.

She awakened the next morning to her monthly courses. By afternoon, her relief that she wasn't pregnant had been displaced by racking pain. She was seldom sick with her monthlies, and never this badly.

At first she tried to ease the pain by walking,

but before long, she gave it up, stripped off her dress and petticoats, and went to bed. Sophronia dosed her with medicine, Miss Dolly read to her from *The Christian's Secret of a Happy Life*, but the pain didn't ease. She finally ordered them both out of the room so she could suffer in peace.

But she wasn't left alone for long. Near dinnertime, her door banged open and Cain strode in, still dressed from the fields.

"What's the matter with you? Miss Dolly told me you were sick, but when I asked her what was wrong, she began twitching like a rabbit and ran to her room."

Kit lay on her side, her knees clutched to her chest. "Go away."

"Not until you tell me what's wrong."

"It's nothing," she groaned. "I'll be all right tomorrow. Just go away."

"Like hell I will. The house is quiet as a funeral parlor, my wife is locked away in her bedroom, and nobody will tell me anything."

"It's my monthly time," Kit muttered, too sick to be embarrassed. "It's never this bad."

Cain turned and left the room.

Unsympathetic lout!

She clutched her stomach and moaned.

Less than half an hour later, she was surprised to feel the bed sag next to her. "Drink this. It'll make you feel better." Cain lifted her shoulders and held a cup to her lips.

She swallowed, then gasped for breath. "What is it?"

"Lukewarm tea with a heavy dose of rum. It'll take the edge off."

It tasted foul, but it was easier to drink it than to put up a fuss. As he gently laid her back on the bed, her head began to swim pleasantly. She was dimly aware of the smell of soap and realized he'd bathed before he'd come back to her. The gesture touched her.

He tugged at her sheet. Beneath it she wore only a plain schoolgirl's cotton chemise from her days at the Academy and a pair of expensive, delicately ruffled pantalets. Mismatched as usual.

"Close your eyes and let the rum do its work," he whispered.

Indeed, her eyelids were suddenly too heavy for her to hold open. As they fluttered shut, he touched the small of her back and began to massage her. His hands climbed gently along her spine, then down again. She was barely aware when he pushed the camisole out of his way and touched her skin directly. While she drifted off to sleep, she knew only that his touch seemed to have dulled the knife edge of pain.

The next morning, she found a great bunch of field daisies thrust into a drinking glass at her bedside.

17

Summer glided into fall and an air of tense expectancy hung over the house and its inhabitants. The harvest was in, and soon the mill would spring alive.

Sophronia moved belligerently through the days, increasingly snappish and difficult to please. Only the fact that Kit wasn't sharing Cain's bed brought her any comfort. It wasn't that she wanted Cain for herself—she'd gratefully relinquished her hold on that idea. Instead, it was a feeling that as long as Kit stayed away from Cain, Sophronia wouldn't have to face the awful possibility that a decent woman like Kit, a decent woman like *herself*, could find pleasure lying with a man. Because if that were possible, all her carefully arranged ideas about what was important and what wasn't would become meaningless.

Sophronia knew she was running out of time. James Spence was pressing her to make up her mind whether or not she'd be his mistress, safe and well protected in the small doll's house he'd found in Charleston, away from Rutherford's gossiping tongues. Never one to be idle, Sophronia now found herself staring out the window for long stretches of time, looking in the direction of the overseer's house.

Magnus waited, too. He sensed that

Sophronia was coming to some sort of crisis, and he steeled himself to face it. How much longer, he wondered, could he be patient? And how was he going to live with himself if she left him for James Spence with his fancy red buggy, his phosphate mine, and his skin as white as the underbelly of a fish?

Cain's problems were different, and yet the same. With the harvest in and the machinery installed in the mill, there was no longer any reason for him to work so hard. But he'd needed the numbing exhaustion of those long workdays to keep his body from realizing the great joke he was playing on it. Not since he was a kid had he been so long without a woman.

Most nights he was back at the house in time for dinner, and he couldn't decide whether she was deliberately driving him mad or it if was unintentional. Each night she appeared at the table smelling of jasmine, with her hair styled so that it reflected her mood. Sometimes she wore it impishly high on her head with wisps of curl framing her face like soft, inky feathers. Other times she'd arrange it in the severe Spanish style so few women could wear successfully, parted in the center and pulled into a heavy knot at the nape of her neck that just begged for his fingers to undo it. Either way, he had to struggle to take his eyes off her. It was ironic. He who'd never been faithful to a woman was now being faithful to a woman he couldn't make love with, not until he could put her in the proper place in his life.

Kit was as unhappy as Cain. Her body, once awakened, didn't want to go back to sleep. Strange, erotic fantasies plagued her. She found the book Cain had give her so long ago, Walt Whitman's *Leaves of Grass*. At the time, the poems had confused her. Now they stripped her bare. Never had she read poetry like this, sprawling verse stuffed with images that left her body burning:

Love-thoughts, love-juice, love-odor,
love-yielding,
love climbers, and the climbing sap,
Arms and hands of love, lips of love,
phallic thumb of
love, bellies press'd and glued together
with love....

She ached for his touch. She found herself rushing back to her bedroom in the afternoons for long, soaking baths and then dressing for dinner in her most attractive gowns. Before long, her clothes grew too tame. She cut off a dozen tiny silver buttons from the bodice of her cinnamon silk gown so that the neckline fell open to the middle of her breasts. Then she filled in the space with a string of glass beads the color of juniper berries. She replaced the belt on a pale yellow morning dress with a long swath of vermilion-and-indigo-striped taffeta. She wore bright pink slippers with a tangerine gown, then was unable to resist threading lime-colored ribbons through the sleeves. She was outrageous, enchanted. Sophronia said she was behaving like a peacock spreading its tail to attract a mate.

But Cain didn't seem to notice.

Veronica Gamble came to call on a rainy Monday afternoon nearly three months after Kit's wedding. Kit had volunteered to sift through the dusty clutter in the attic for a set of china no one could find, and once again she looked less than her best.

Other than exchanging a few courteous words when they saw each other at church or in town, Kit hadn't visited with Veronica since the disastrous dinner party. She'd sent her a polite thank-you note for the handsome, calf-bound copy of *Madame Bovary* that had been Veronica's wedding present—a most inappropriate gift, Kit had discovered as she was devouring every word. Veronica fascinated her, but she was also threatened by the older woman's self-assurance and cool beauty.

While Lucy served frosty glasses of lemonade and a plate of cucumber sandwiches, Kit dismally compared Veronica's well-cut biscuit-colored suit with her own soiled and rumpled cotton frock. Was it any wonder that her husband showed such obvious pleasure in Veronica's company? Not for the first time, Kit found herself wondering if all their meetings were taking place in public. The idea that they might be seeing each other privately made her ache.

"And how do you find married life?" Veronica asked after they'd exchanged pleasantries and Kit had consumed four cucumber sandwiches to the other woman's one.

"Compared to what?"

Veronica's laughter tinkled through the room like glass bells. "You're without doubt the most refreshing female in this decidedly tedious county."

"If it's so tedious, why do you stay here?"

Veronica fingered the cameo brooch at her throat. "I came here to heal my spirit. I'm certain that sounds melodramatic to someone as young as you, but my husband was very dear to me, and his death hasn't been easy for me to accept. In the end, though, I'm finding boredom almost as great an enemy as grief. When one has become accustomed to the company of a fascinating man, it's not easy to be alone."

Kit wasn't sure how to respond, especially since she sensed a subtle calculation behind the words, an impression that Veronica quickly reinforced.

"Enough! You cannot want to spend your afternoons listening to the maudlin reflections of a lonely widow when your own life is so new and young. Tell me how you're enjoying being married."

"I'm adjusting much like any other new bride," Kit answered carefully.

"What a conventional and proper response. I'm quite disappointed. I'd expected you to tell me with your customary bluntness to mind my own business, although I'm certain you shall do just that before I leave. I came here with the express purpose of prying into the intimacies of this most interesting marriage of yours."

"Really, Mrs. Gamble," Kit said weakly. "I'm sure I can't imagine why you'd care to do that."

"Because human mysteries make life amusing. And now I find one right in front of me." Veronica tapped her cheek with one oval fingernail. "Why, I ask myself, does the most attractive couple in South Carolina seem to be at loggerheads?"

"Mrs. Gamble, I—"

"Why do their eyes seldom meet in public? Why do they never touch each other in the casual way lovers do?"

"Really, I don't—"

"That, of course, is the most interesting question of all, because it makes me wonder if they truly are lovers."

Kit sucked in her breath, but Veronica waved her silent with a lazy flick of her hand. "Spare me any dramatics until you've heard me out. You may discover I'm doing you a favor."

A small, silent war took place inside Kit, with caution on one side and curiosity on the other. "Go on," she said as coolly as she could manage.

"There is something not quite right about this couple," Veronica continued. "The husband has a hungriness about him that is foreign to a well-satisfied man. While the wife.... Ah, the wife! She is even more interesting than the husband. She watches him when he isn't looking, drinking in his body in the most immodest fashion, letting her eyes caress him. It's most puzzling. The man is virile, the wife sensuous, and yet I am convinced the two are not lovers."

Having had her say, Veronica was now content to wait. Kit felt as if she'd been stripped bare. It was humiliating. And yet... "You came here with a purpose, Mrs. Gamble. I'd like to know what it is."

Veronica looked surprised. "But isn't it obvious? You can't be so naive that you don't realize I'm attracted to your husband." She tilted her head. "I'm here to give you fair warning. If you don't intend to make use of him, I certainly do."

Kit found herself almost calm. "You came here today to warn me that you intend to have a liaison with my husband?"

"Only if you don't want him, my dear." Veronica picked up her lemonade and took a delicate sip. "Despite what you may think, I formed an exceptional fondness for you the first time I met you. You remind me so much of myself at your age, although I hid my feelings better. Still, fondness can extend only so far, and in the end it will be better for your marriage if I share your husband's bed, instead of some scheming hussy who'll try to come between the two of you permanently."

Up until that moment, she had been speaking lightly, but now her green eyes bore uncompromisingly into Kit's like small, polished emeralds. "Believe me when I tell you this, my dear. For some reason that I can't possibly fathom, you've left your husband ripe for the picking, and it's only a matter of time until someone does just that. I intend that someone to be me."

Kit knew she should sweep indignantly from the room, but there was something about Veronica Gamble's utter frankness that triggered the part of her that had so little patience with dissemblance. This woman knew the answers to secrets that Kit could only glimpse.

She managed to keep her face expressionless. "For the sake of conversation, suppose some of what you say is true. Suppose...that I have...no interest in my husband. Or suppose—again for the sake of conversation—that...my husband has no...interest in me." Color flushed her cheeks, but she plunged determinedly on. "How might you suggest I go about...getting him interested?"

"Seduce him, of course."

There was a long, painful silence.

"And how," Kit asked stonily, "might one do that?"

Veronica considered for a moment. "A woman seduces a man by following her instincts without giving the slightest thought to what she's heard is proper or improper. Seductive dress, a seductive manner, a willingness to tantalize by giving a glimpse of promises to come. You're an intelligent woman, Kit. I'm certain if you put your mind to it, you'll find a way.

Just remember this. Pride has no place in the boudoir. It's a room devoted to giving, not holding back. Do I make myself clear?"

Kit nodded stiffly.

Having accomplished the purpose of her visit, Veronica gathered up her gloves and reticule and stood. "I warn you, my dear, you'd best learn your lessons quickly, for I shan't give you much time. You've had quite enough already."

She swept from the room.

A few moments later, as she mounted the steps to her carriage, Veronica smiled to herself. How Francis would have enjoyed this afternoon. It wasn't often that she got the chance to play fairy godmother, but she had to admit that she'd performed splendidly.

As she settled back into the tufted leather seat, her brow knitted ever so slightly. Now she had to make up her mind whether or not she would actually carry out her threat.

Kit finally had the excuse to do what she'd been wanting to for so very long. Dinner was torture, made worse by the fact that Cain seemed to be in the mood to prolong it. He talked about the mill and asked her opinion on what the market for cotton would be like within the year. As always when the subject was cotton, he listened attentively to her response.

Horrible man. He was so achingly handsome that she could barely look away from him, and why did he have to be so charming to Miss Dolly?

She escaped to her room as soon as she could. For a while, she paced. Finally she slipped out of her clothes, donned a faded cotton wrapper, and sat in front of her mirror to take the pins out of her hair. She was brushing it into a soft midnight cloud when she heard Cain climbing the stairs to his bedroom.

Her reflection showed an unnaturally pale face. She pinched her cheeks, then replaced her moonstone eardrops with a small pair of pearl studs. Afterward, she dabbed a touch of jasmine scent to the hollow of her throat.

When she was satisfied, she abandoned her wrapper for the black silk peignoir set that had been a wedding present from Elsbeth. It slid like oil over her naked flesh. The garment was starkly simple, with small capped sleeves and a rounded bodice that dipped so low it barely covered the peaks of her breasts. The skirt clung to her body in long, soft folds that outlined the shape of her hips and legs when she moved. Over the gown she donned the peignoir, made entirely of sheer black lace. With trembling fingers, she fastened the single small button at the throat.

Through the lace, her skin gleamed like winter moonlight, and as she walked, the peignoir fell open, something she was fairly certain Elsbeth hadn't taken into account when she'd bought the gift. The gown beneath shaped itself like a second skin to her body, outlining her breasts, clinging to the delicate indentation of her navel and, more seductively, to the small mound below.

She walked through the sitting room, her bare feet padding noiselessly on the carpet. When she reached the door to his bedroom, she nearly lost her nerve. Quickly, before that happened, she rapped on the door.

"Come in."

He was dressed in shirtsleeves and sitting in the wing chair next to the window, a sheaf of papers on the table by his side. He looked up, and when he saw how she was dressed, his eyes darkened to a deep, smoky gray. She walked toward him slowly, head high, shoulders proud, heart hammering.

"What do you want?" The charming man at the dinner table had been left behind. He sounded weary, suspicious, and hostile. Once again she wondered why he'd lost interest in her. Because he didn't find her appealing? If that was true, she was about to suffer a terrible humiliation.

She could have invented an excuse—a cut finger that needed his attention, a request to borrow a book—but he'd have seen right through it. She lifted her chin and met his gaze. "I want to make love with you."

She watched uneasily as his mouth curved in a small, mocking twist. "My beautiful wife. So forthright." His eyes grazed her body, so clearly defined against the thin fabric. "Let me be just as straightforward. Why?"

This wasn't the way she'd imagined it. She'd expected him to hold out his arms and take over. "We're—we're married. It's not right for us to be sleeping apart."

"I see." He tilted his head toward the bed. "It's a matter of observing the amenities, is that it?"

"Not exactly that."

"Then what?'

A slight sheen of perspiration gathered between her shoulder blades. "I just want to." Too late, she realized she couldn't do this. "Forget it." She turned toward the door. "Forget I ever said anything. It was a stupid idea." She reached for the knob just as his hand settled over hers.

"Giving up so easily?"

She wished she'd never started this, and she couldn't even blame her behavior on Veronica Gamble. She'd wanted to taste him, to touch him, to experience the mystery of lovemaking again. Veronica had merely given her the excuse.

She realized he'd moved away from her, and she looked up to see him leaning against the mantel of the fireplace.

"Go ahead," he said. "I'll wait for you to start."

"Start what?"

"A man can't perform on command. I'm afraid you'll have to arouse my interest."

Had she thought to drop her eyes, she would have seen that his interest was already well aroused, but she was too busy trying to fight down the queer jumble of feelings twisting about inside her. "I don't know how to do that."

He rested his shoulders against the mantelpiece and crossed his ankles indolently. "Experiment. I'm all yours."

She couldn't bear having him making fun of her. Her throat constricted, and she moved back to the door. "I've changed my mind."

"Coward," he said softly.

She turned in time to see the mockery fade from his expression and something different take its place, something both seductive and challenging. "I dare you, Kit Weston."

A wild pounding reverberated deep inside her. Follow your instincts, Veronica had advised. But how would she know what to do?

He lifted a brow in silent acknowledgment of her dilemma, and a rush of courage that defied logic surged through her. Slowly she raised her fingers to the single button that held the peignoir together. The garment slid to the floor in a cascade of black lace.

His eyes drank in her body. "You've never been one to refuse a dare, have you?" he said huskily.

Her mouth curved into a smile. She walked toward him slowly, feeling a sudden, unreasonable surge of self-confidence. As she moved, she let her hips sway ever so slightly so that the slim skirt of the gown clung even more revealingly. She stopped in front of him and stared into the smoky depths of his eyes. Without dropping her gaze, she reached up and rested the palms of her hands lightly on his shoulders.

She sensed his tension beneath her fingers, and it gave her a feeling of power she'd never known in his presence. She lifted herself on her toes and pressed her lips to the dancing pulse at the base of his throat.

He groaned softly and buried his face in her hair, but otherwise he kept his arms at his sides. Excitement at his uncharacteristic passivity quivered through her. She parted her lips and flicked at the pulse with the tip of her tongue until its rhythm beat faster and faster.

Greedy for more of him, she tugged at the buttons on his shirt. When it was open, she pushed the fabric out of her way and slipped her hands beneath. She splayed her fingers over the mat of hair on his chest and then touched her lips to the hard, flat nipple that she'd exposed.

With a strangled sound, he caught her in his arms and pulled her body against his. But it was her game now, and she'd make him play by her rules. With the soft, wicked laugh of a vixen, she eased out of his grasp and backed across the room.

Lifting her eyes to his, she wet her lips with the tip of her tongue. Then she slid the palms of her hands over her ribs, her waist, and the curve of her hips in deliberate provocation.

His nostrils flared. She heard his quickening breath. Slowly she slid her hands back up again, this time over the front of her. Thighs...stomach...ribs... *A woman seduces a man by following her instincts without giving the slightest thought to what she's heard is proper or improper.* She cupped her breasts in her palms.

A muffled exclamation escaped his lips.

The word was unintelligible, but he uttered it with a sense of wonder that made it seem a tribute.

Confident now of her power, she moved so that the bed was between them. She lifted her gown and climbed up onto the mattress. With a shake of her head, her hair tumbled forward over her shoulder. She smiled a smile that had been passed down from Eve and let her sleeve fall down on her arm. Beneath the veil of her hair lay one exposed breast.

It took all of Cain's self-control not to rush to the bed and devour her as she was meant to be devoured. He'd vowed to himself he wouldn't let this happen, but now he couldn't hold back. She was his.

But she wasn't done with him yet. Resting on her heels with the skirt of her gown puddled over her knees, she played with her tousled hair so the raven locks fell open and closed in an erotic game of peekaboo.

The last thread of Cain's self-restraint snapped. He had to touch her or die. He came to the edge of the bed and reached out with his scarred hand to push the dark curtain of her hair behind her shoulder. He gazed down at the perfectly formed breast with its taut crest. "You learn fast," he said thickly.

He reached for her breast, but once again she eluded him. She glided back against the pillows so that she was resting on one elbow, the black silk skirt of her gown loose across her thighs. "You wear too many clothes," she whispered.

His bottom lip curved. With a few deft motions, he unfastened the cuffs of his sleeves and pulled the garment off. She watched him undress. Her heart pounded with a wild, savage rhythm.

Finally he stood before her fiercely naked. "Now who's wearing too many clothes?" he murmured.

He knelt on the bed and placed his hand on her knee, just under the hem of her gown. But she sensed the gown excited him, and she wasn't surprised when he didn't remove it. Instead, he slid his hand beneath it and moved along the inner flesh of her thigh until he found what he was seeking. He touched her lightly once, then again, then once again, going deeper.

This time she was the one who moaned. As she arched her back, the black silk fell free from her other breast. He dipped his head to claim first one and then the other of her nipples. The double caress at her breasts and beneath her gown was more than she could bear. With a moan that came from her very soul, she shattered beneath his touch.

It could have been seconds or hours later before she came back to herself. He was stretched beside her, staring intently into her face. As she opened her eyes, he dipped his mouth to hers and kissed her lips.

"Fire and honey," he whispered.

She looked at him questioningly, but he only smiled and kissed her again. She returned his passion in full measure.

His mouth traveled to her breasts. Finally he pushed her gown high above her waist and moved on to her stomach.

She sensed what was to happen even before she felt the brush of his lips against the soft inner surface of her thigh. At first she thought she must be mistaken. The idea was too shocking. Surely she must be wrong. It couldn't be... He couldn't...

But he did. And she thought she would die from the pleasure he gave her.

After it was over, she felt as if she would never be the same again. He held her close and stroked her hair, idly curling the tendrils around his finger, giving her the time she needed to recover. Finally, when he could be patient no longer, he pressed himself over her.

She settled the heels of her hands on his chest and pushed him away.

Now the question was in his eyes as he lay back against the pillows, and she rose to her knees beside him. He watched her cross her arms modestly in front of her kneeling body, pick up the hem of her gown, and pull it off.

He took in her naked beauty for only a moment before she lay upon him. The curtain of her hair fell across them as she clasped his head between her small, strong hands.

She explored his mouth aggressively. She was boldly female, using her tongue to plunder and ravish, to take pleasure for herself and return it in abundance. Then she caressed the rest of him, touching her mouth to scars and muscles and hard, male flesh until there was only sensation between them. They came together, soared together...then fell apart.

Throughout the night they held each other, making love when they awakened, then dozing with their bodies still joined. Sometimes they talked, speaking of the pleasure of their bodies, but never once mentioning the things that held them apart. Even in their intimacy, they established limits that couldn't be crossed.

You may touch me here... You may touch me there... Oh, yes, oh, yes, and there... But do not expect more. Do not expect daylight to bring a change in me. There will be no changes. You will only hurt me... Take from me... Destroy me... I will give you my body, but do not, dare not, *expect more.*

In the morning, Cain growled at her when she crumpled the newspaper he wanted to read. Kit lashed out at him for setting a chair in her way.

The daytime barriers snapped back into place.

18

Sophronia made up her mind just before Christmas. James Spence met her beside the road that led to Rutherford and showed her a deed to a house in Charleston that had her name on it.

"It's a pretty pink stucco, Miz Sophronia,

with a fig tree in the front and a trellis all covered with wisteria in the back."

She took the deed, studied it carefully, and said she'd go with him.

As she gazed out the kitchen window at the wet, dreary December day that lay over the dormant fields of Risen Glory, she reminded herself that she was twenty-four years old. Her life had been standing still long enough. James Spence could give her everything she'd wanted for so long. He treated her politely, and he was handsome for a white man. He'd take good care of her, and in return, she'd take care of him. It wouldn't be all that much different from what she was doing now...except that she'd have to lie with him.

She shivered, then asked herself what difference it made. It wasn't as if she were a virgin. The house in Charleston would be hers—that was what was important—and she'd finally be safe. Besides, it was time to get away. Between Magnus, Kit, and the major, she'd go crazy if she had to stay at Risen Glory much longer.

Magnus watched her with those soft brown eyes of his. She hated the pity she saw in them, yet sometimes she found herself daydreaming about that Sunday afternoon when he'd kissed her in the orchard. She wanted to forget that kiss, but she couldn't. He hadn't tried to touch her again, not even the night Kit and the major had gotten married and she'd slept at his house. Why wouldn't he go away and leave her in peace?

She wished they'd all go away, even Kit. Ever since she'd gone back to the major's bed, there was something frantic about her. She rushed from one thing to another, never giving herself time to think. In the morning when Sophronia went to the henhouse to gather eggs, she could see Kit in the distance, riding Temptation as if there weren't any tomorrow, taking him over jumps that were too high, pushing them both to the limit. Even if was cold or rainy, she rode. It was almost as if she was afraid the land might have disappeared during the night while she and the major were carrying on in that big bedroom upstairs.

During the daytime, the air between them shimmered with tension. Sophronia hadn't heard Kit speak a civil word to him in weeks, and when the major talked to her, his voice sounded like it was frozen inside a block of ice. Still, at least he seemed to be trying. He'd given in on the matter of putting a road to the mill through those acres of scrub to the east, when everybody but Kit could see the land was useless and the road would save miles of traveling time.

This morning Sophronia had been afraid they'd come to blows. The major had been warning Kit for weeks to stop riding Temptation so recklessly. He'd finally put his foot down and told her she couldn't ride Temptation at all. Kit had called him names and threatened a few things no woman should even know about, much less mention. He'd stood there like a statue, not saying a word, just watching her with that stone-cold expression that sent shivers down Sophronia's spine.

But no matter how bad things were between them during the day, when nightfall came, the door of that big front bedroom would slam shut and not open again until morning.

Through the window, Sophronia saw Kit, dressed in those shameful britches, coming back from a walk. Sophronia's stomach coiled in dread. She couldn't put it off any longer. Her satchel was packed, and Mr. Spence would be waiting for her at the end of the drive in less than an hour.

She'd told no one of her plans, although she wondered if Magnus suspected something. He'd looked at her strangely when he'd come to the kitchen for breakfast that morning. Sometimes she had the feeling he could read her mind.

She told herself she was glad he'd gone into Rutherford for the day so he wouldn't be here when she left. But some part of her wanted one last glimpse of that kind, handsome face.

She left her apron on the peg next to the sink where she'd been hanging aprons since she was a child. Then she walked through the house for the last time.

A chilly gust of air accompanied Kit as she came in through the front door. "That wind has some bite to it. I'm going to make chowder for dinner tonight."

Sophronia forgot that such things were no longer her responsibility. "It's nearly five o'clock," she scolded. "If you wanted chowder, you should have told me earlier. Patsy already made a nice okra pilau."

Kit jerked off her woolen jacket and shoved it irritably onto the newel-post. "I'm sure she won't mind if I add chowder to the menu." She began to stomp up the stairs.

"People in this house would appreciate it if you smiled once in a while."

Kit paused and looked down at Sophronia. "What's that supposed to mean?"

"It means that you've been grouchy for months now, and it's getting contagious. You've even got me snapping at Patsy."

It wasn't the first time Sophronia had reprimanded Kit for her behavior, but today Kit couldn't muster the energy to come to her own defense. She'd been feeling edgy and listless, not sick exactly, but not entirely well, either. She sighed wearily. "If Patsy doesn't want chowder on the menu tonight, I'll make it tomorrow."

"You'll have to tell her yourself."

"Why's that?"

"Because I won't be here."

"Oh? Where are you going?"

Sophronia faltered. Kit had asked the question so innocently. "Let's go into the sittin' room for a few minutes so we can talk."

Kit looked at her curiously, then followed her down the hallway. Once inside, she sat on the settee. "Is something wrong?"

Sophronia remained standing. "I—I'm going away to Charleston."

"You should have told me earlier. I have some shopping to do, too. I could have gone with you."

"No, it's not a shopping trip." Sophronia clasped her hands in front of her butternut wool skirt. "I—I'm goin' for good. I won't be coming back to Risen Glory."

Kit stared at her uncomprehendingly. "Not coming back? Of course you're coming back. You live here."

"James Spence bought me a house."

Kit's forehead knitted. "Why would he do that? Are you going to be his housekeeper? Sophronia, how could you even think of leaving here?"

Sophronia shook her head. "I'm not goin' to be his housekeeper. I'm goin' to be his mistress."

Kit gripped the arm of the settee. "I don't believe you. You'd never do anything so horrible."

Sophronia's chin shot up. "Don't you dare judge me!"

"But this is wrong! What you're talking about is wicked, plain and simple. How could you even consider such a thing?"

"I'm doin' what I have to," Sophronia said stubbornly.

"You don't have to do this!"

"That's easy for you to say. But did you ever think I might want some of the same things you want—a house, pretty clothes, being able to wake up in the morning knowing nobody can hurt me?"

"But nobody can hurt you here. The war's been over for three years. Nobody's bothered you."

"That's just because everybody assumed I was sharing your husband's bed." At Kit's sharp look, she added, "I wasn't. Still, nobody except Magnus knew that." The sculptured lines of her face set into bitter planes. "Now that you're married, everything's different. It's just a matter of time before somebody decides I'm free for the picking. That's the way it is for any black woman doesn't have a white man lookin' out for her. I can't go through the rest of my life like that."

"But what about Magnus?" Kit argued. "He's a good man. Anybody with eyes can see that he loves you. And no matter how much you pretend otherwise, I know you have tender feelings for him. How can you do this to him?"

Sophronia's mouth formed a straight, stubborn line. "I have to look out for myself."

Kit jumped up from the settee. "I don't see what's so wonderful about having a white man watching out for you. When you were a slave, my father was supposed to be watching out for you, and look what happened. Maybe Mr. Spence won't be able to protect you any more than my father could. Maybe he'll look the other way the same as my father. Did you ever think about that, Sophronia? Did you?"

"Your father didn't *try* to protect me!" Sophronia cried. "He didn't try, do you understand what I'm telling you? It wasn't just a matter of not seeing what was happenin'. *He* was the one who was giving me away for the night to his friends."

Kit felt a stabbing deep in the walls of her stomach.

Now that the truth was out, Sophronia couldn't stop herself. "Sometimes he'd let them throw dice for me. Sometimes they'd race their horses. I was the prize in the games they played."

Kit ran to Sophronia and took her in her arms. "I'm sorry. Oh, I'm so very, very sorry."

Sophronia's back was rigid under her hands. Kit stroked her, blinked away tears, muttered apologies that weren't hers to make, and tried to find the argument that would convince Sophronia not to leave the only home she'd ever known. "Don't let what happened ruin the rest of your life. As awful as it was, it happened a long time ago. You're young. Lots of slave women—"

"Don't you tell me about slave women!" Sophronia jerked away, her expression ferocious. "Don't you dare tell me about slave women! You don't know nothin' about it!" She took a deep gulp of air, as if she were strangling. "He was *my* father, too!"

Kit froze. Slowly, she shook her head. "No. It's not true. You're lying to me. Even he wouldn't give away his own daughter. Damn you! Damn you for lying to me!"

Sophronia didn't flinch. "I'm his daughter, no different from you. He took my mama when she was only thirteen and kept her right in this house, right under your mama's nose. Kept her there until he found out she was carryin' a baby, then he tossed her back to the slave cabins like a piece of trash. At first, when his friends came sniffin' after me, I thought maybe he might have forgotten I was his. But he hadn't forgotten. He just didn't attach any significance to it. Blood had no meaning because I wasn't human. I was property. Just another nigger gal."

Kit's face was chalk-white. She couldn't move. Couldn't speak.

Now that her secret was no longer locked inside her, Sophronia was finally calm. "I'm glad my mama died before it all started. She was a strong woman, but seeing what was happening to me would have broke her." Sophronia reached out and touched Kit's immobile cheek. "We're sisters, Kit," she said softly. "Didn't you ever feel it? Didn't you ever feel that tie between us, binding us so tight nothing could ever pull us apart? Right from the start, it was the two of us. Your mama died after you were born, and my mama was supposed to take care of you, but she didn't like to touch you because of what had happened. So I took care of you, right from the beginning. A child raising a child. I can remember holding you in my lap when I couldn't have been more than four or five myself. I used to set you next to me in the kitchen when I was working and play doll babies with you in the evening. And then Mama died, and you were all I had. That's why I never left Risen Glory, not even when you went away to New York City. I had to make sure you'd be all right. But when you came back, it was like you were a different person, part of a world I couldn't belong to. I've been jealous, and I've been scared, too. You've got to forgive me for what I'm goin' to do, Kit, but you have a place in the world, and now it's time for me to find mine." She gave Kit a swift hug and fled.

Not long after, Cain found Kit there. She was still standing in the center of the room. Her muscles were rigid, her hands knotted into fists.

"Where the hell is every— Kit? What's wrong?"

In an instant he was beside her. She felt as if she'd been pulled from a trance. She sagged against him, choking on a sob. He took her in his arms and led her to the settee. "Tell me what happened."

His arms felt so good around her. He'd never held her like this—protectively, with no trace of passion. She began to cry. "Sophronia's leaving. She's going away to Charleston to be...to be James Spence's mistress."

Cain swore softly. "Does Magnus know about this?"

"I—I don't think so." She tried to catch her breath. "She just told me... Sophronia's my sister."

"Your sister?"

"Garrett Weston's daughter, just like me."

He stroked her chin with his thumb. "You've

lived in the South all your life. Sophronia's skin is light."

"You don't understand." She clenched her jaw and spat out the words through her tears. "My father used to give her away to his friends for the night. He knew she was his daughter, his own flesh and blood, but he gave her away just the same."

"Oh, God..." Cain's face grew ashen. He pulled her tighter and rested his cheek against the top of her head as she cried. Gradually she filled in the details of the story for him. When she was done, Cain spoke viciously. "I hope he's burning in hell."

Now that she'd poured out the story, Kit realized what she had to do. She leaped up from the settee. "I have to stop her. I can't let her go through with this."

"Sophronia's a free woman," he reminded her gently. "If she wants to go off with Spence, there's nothing you can do about it."

"She's my sister! I love her, and I won't let her do this!"

Before Cain could stop her, she raced from the room.

Cain sighed as he uncoiled himself from the settee. Kit was hurting badly, and as he knew only too well, that could lead to trouble.

Outside, Kit hid in the trees near the front. Her teeth chattered as she huddled in the damp, wintry shadows waiting for Cain to come out. He soon appeared, as she'd known he would. She watched him descend the steps and look toward the drive. When he didn't see her, he cursed, turned on his heel, and headed for the stable.

As soon as he was out of sight, she ran back into the house and made her way to the gun rack in the library. She didn't expect too much trouble from James Spence, but since she had no intention of letting Sophronia go off with him, she needed the gun to add weight to her arguments.

Several miles away, James Spence's crimson-and-black buggy swept past the buggy Magnus was driving. Spence was in an all-fired hurry to get wherever he was going, Magnus thought as he observed the vehicle disappear around the bend. Since there wasn't much along this road except Risen Glory and the cotton mill, Spence must have business at the mill.

It was a logical conclusion, but somehow it didn't satisfy him. He gave the horses a sharp slap with the reins. As he hurried toward Risen Glory, he considered what he knew about Spence.

Local gossip reported that he'd managed an Illinois gravel quarry, bought himself out of the draft for three hundred dollars, and headed South after the war with a carpetbag stuffed full of greenbacks. Now he had a prosperous phosphate mine and a hankering for Sophronia.

Spence's buggy had already stopped at the bottom of the drive when Magnus got there. The businessman was dressed in a black frock coat and bowler, with a walking stick in his gloved hand. Magnus barely spared him a glance. All his attention was fixed on Sophronia.

She stood at the side of the road with her blue woolen shawl wrapped around her shoulders and a satchel at her feet.

"Sophronia!" He pulled up the buggy and jumped out.

Her head shot up, and for an instant he thought he saw a flicker of hope in her eyes, but then they clouded over, and she clutched the shawl tighter. "You leave me alone, Magnus Owen. This doesn't have anything to do with you."

Spence stepped around from the side of the carriage and looked at Magnus. "Something the matter, boy?"

Magnus tucked a thumb into his belt and glared at him. "The lady's changed her mind."

Spence's eyes narrowed beneath the brim of his bowler. "If you're talking to me, boy, I suggest you call me 'sir.' "

As Sophronia watched the confrontation, prickles of dread crept along her spine. Magnus turned to her, but instead of the gentle, soft-spoken man she knew, she saw a tight-lipped, hard-eyed stranger. "Get back to the house."

Spence stepped forward. "Now see here. I don't know who you think you are, but—"

"Go away, Magnus." Sophronia could hear her voice tremble. "I've made up my mind, and you can't stop me."

"I can stop you, all right," he said stonily. "And that's exactly what I'm goin' to do."

Spence sauntered over to Magnus, his

walking stick with its golden knob firmly in hand. "I think it might be better for everybody if you went back to wherever you came from. Now come along, Sophronia."

But as he reached for her, she was abruptly snatched away. "You're not touching her," Magnus snarled, shoving her firmly behind him. Then he clenched his fists and stepped forward.

Black man against white. All Sophronia's nightmares had come true. Fear shot through her. "No!" She clutched Magnus's shirt. "Don't hit him! You hit a white man, you'll be hanging from a rope before morning."

"Get out of my way, Sophronia."

"The white man's got all the power, Magnus. You leave this be!"

He set her aside, but the gesture of protecting her cost him. Behind his back, Spence lifted his walking stick and, as Magnus turned, slammed it into his chest.

"Stay out of things that don't concern you, boy," Spence growled.

In one swift movement, Magnus snatched the cane and broke it across his knee.

Sophronia gave an outcry.

Magnus tossed the cane aside and landed a hard blow to Spence's jaw that sent the mine owner sprawling onto the road.

Kit had reached the line of trees just in time to see what was happening. She rushed out, raised her rifle, and leveled the barrel. "Get out of here, Mr. Spence. Doesn't seem you're wanted."

Sophronia had never been more grateful

to see anyone, but Magnus's face grew rigid. Spence slowly rose, glaring at Kit. Just then a deep, drawling voice intruded.

"Looks like things are getting a little out of hand here."

Four sets of eyes turned as Cain climbed down off Vandal. He walked toward Kit with the loose, easy swagger that was so much a part of him and extended his hand. "Give me the rifle, Kit." He spoke so calmly he might have been asking her to pass bread across the dinner table.

Giving him the rifle was exactly what Kit wanted to do. As she'd discovered once before, she had no stomach for holding a gun on anyone. Cain would see to it that Magnus came to no harm, and she gave him the rifle.

To her astonishment, he didn't turn it on Spence. Instead, he took Kit's arm and pulled her, none too gently, toward Vandal. "Accept my apologies, Mr. Spence. My wife has an excitable temperament." He shoved the rifle into the scabbard that hung from his saddle.

She saw Spence's eyes grow shrewd. The cotton mill made Cain an important man in the community, and she could see his mind working as he decided it was to his advantage to have Cain as a friend. "Don't mention it, Mr. Cain." He reached down to dust off his trousers. "I'm sure none of us can predict the ways of our little womenfolk."

"Truer words have never been spoken," Cain replied, oblivious to Kit's glare.

Spence picked up his black bowler and

jerked his head toward Magnus. "Do you value this boy of yours, Major?"

"Why do you ask?"

He gave Cain a man-to-man smile. "If you was to tell me you valued him, I'd assume you wouldn't be too happy to see him dangling from the end of a rope. And seeing as how we're both businessmen, I'd be more than willing to forget what just happened here."

Relief made Kit's knees wobble. Cain's eyes locked with Magnus's.

They stayed that way for several long, hard seconds before Cain looked away and shrugged. "What Magnus does is his own business. It doesn't have anything to do with me, one way or the other."

Kit gave a hiss of outrage as he scooped her up onto Vandal, mounted himself, and spurred the horse back up the drive.

Sophronia stared after them, bile rising in her throat. The major was supposed to be Magnus's friend, but he wasn't a friend at all. White stood together against black. That was the way it always had been, the way it always would be.

Despair overwhelmed her. She darted her eyes toward Magnus, but Cain's betrayal didn't seem to bother him. He stood with his legs slightly apart, one hand lightly balanced on his hip, and a strange light shining in his eyes.

The love she'd refused to admit burst free inside her, breaking all the invisible shackles of the past and sweeping away the rubble in a great cleansing rush. How could she have denied her feelings for so long? He was everything a man should be—strong, good, kind. He was a man of compassion and pride. But now, through her actions, she'd put him in peril.

There was only one thing she could do. She turned her back on Magnus and forced herself toward James Spence.

"Mr. Spence, it's my fault what's happened here today." She couldn't make herself touch his arm. "I been flirtin' with Magnus. Makin' him believe he meant somethin' to me. You got to forget all this. I'll go with you, but you got to promise you won't let any harm come to him. He's a good man, and all this is my fault."

Magnus's voice came from behind her, as soft and mellow as an old hymn. "It's no good, Sophronia. I won't let you go with him." He moved up beside her. "Mr. Spence, Sophronia is goin' to be my wife. You try to take her with you, I'll stop you. Today, tomorrow, a year from now. Doesn't make any difference. I'll stop you."

Sophronia's fingers turned icy.

Spence licked his lips and shot a nervous glance in the direction Cain had disappeared. Magnus was the bigger man, taller and more muscular, and Spence would be the loser in a physical match. But Spence didn't need that kind of fight to win.

With a sense of dread, Sophronia watched the play of emotions on his face. No black man could get away with hitting a white man in South

Carolina. If Spence didn't get the sheriff to do something about it, he'd go to the Ku Klux Klan, those monsters who'd begun terrorizing the state two years ago. Images of whippings and lynchings filled her mind as he walked confidently over to his buggy and climbed up onto the seat.

He picked up the reins and turned back to Magnus. "You've made a big mistake, boy." And then he regarded Sophronia with a hostility he didn't try to hide. "I'll be back for you tomorrow."

"Just a minute, Mr. Spence." Magnus bent over to pick up the broken halves of the walking stick. As he made his way to the buggy, he walked with a confidence he had no right to feel. "I consider myself a fair man, so I think it's only right I tell you what kind of risk you'd be taking if you got any ideas about coming after me. Or maybe you might decide to send your acquaintances in bedsheets here. But that wouldn't be a good idea, Mr. Spence. Matter of fact, it'd be a real bad idea."

"What's that supposed to mean?" Spence sneered.

"It means I've got a talent, Mr. Spence, that you should know about. And I've got three or four friends with the same talent. Now, they're only black men like me, you understand, so you might not think their talent is worth your notice. But you'd be wrong, Mr. Spence. You'd be dead wrong."

"What're you talking about?"

"I'm talking about dynamite, Mr. Spence.

Nasty stuff, but real useful. I learned to use it myself when we had to blast some rock to build the mill. Most people don't know too much about dynamite, since it's so new, but you strike me as a man who keeps up with new inventions, so I'll bet you know a lot about it. I'll bet you know, for example, just how much damage dynamite could cause if somebody set it off in the wrong place in a phosphate bed."

Spence regarded Magnus incredulously. "Are you threatening me?"

"I guess you might say I'm just trying to make a point, Mr. Spence. I've got good friends. Real good friends. And if anything was to happen to me, they'd be mighty unhappy about it. They'd be so unhappy they might set off a load of dynamite in the wrong place. Now, we wouldn't want that to happen, would we, Mr. Spence?"

"Damn you!"

Magnus put his foot up on the step of the buggy and rested the broken pieces of the stick on his knee. "Every man deserves his happiness, Mr. Spence, and Sophronia's mine. I intend to live a good, long life so we can enjoy each other, and I'm willing to do whatever's necessary to make sure we have that. Now whenever I see you in town, I'm going to take off my hat and say, 'Howdy, Mr. Spence,' real polite. And as long as you hear that 'Howdy, Mr. Spence,' you'll know I'm a happy man wishing you and your phosphate mine all the best." Drilling his eyes directly into Spence's, he extended the broken halves of the walking stick.

Taut with anger, Spence snatched them away and grabbed the reins.

Sophronia could barely take it in. What she'd just witnessed ran contrary to everything she believed, and yet it had happened. She'd just seen Magnus stand up against a white man and win. He'd fought for her. He'd kept her safe...even from herself.

She threw herself across the border of dry, wintry grass that separated them and tumbled into his arms, repeating his name over and over again until its rhythm became one with the beating of her heart.

"You're a trial to me, woman," he said softly, cupping her shoulders in his hands.

She lifted her gaze and saw eyes that were steadfast and true, eyes that promised both goodness and strength. He lifted one hand and moved his index finger over her lips, almost as if he were a blind man staking out the boundaries of a territory he was about to claim. Then he lowered his head and kissed her.

She accepted his lips shyly, as if she were a young girl. He made her feel pure and innocent again.

He pulled her closer, and his kiss grew more demanding, but instead of feeling afraid, she thrilled to its power. This man, this one good man, was hers forever. He was more important than a house in Charleston, more important than silk dresses, more important than anything.

When they finally drew apart, Sophronia saw his eyes glistening. This strong, hard man who had been coolly threatening to blow up a phosphate mine had turned soft and gentle as a lamb.

"You've been giving me a lot of trouble, woman," he said gruffly. "Once we're married, I won't stand for any more nonsense."

"Are we gettin' married, Magnus?" she inquired saucily. And then she splayed her long, elegant fingers along the sides of his head and pulled him back for another deep, lingering kiss.

"Oh, yes, honey child," he replied when he finally caught his breath. "We're gettin' married for sure."

19

"*I* figured you for a lot of things, Baron Cain, but I never figured you for a coward!" Kit stormed out of the stables at Cain's heels. "Magnus is going to be a dead man, and it'll be on your conscience. All you had to do was nod your head, just nod your head, and Spence would have made himself forget that Magnus hit him. Now give me that rifle back right now! If you're not man enough to defend your best friend, I'll do it myself."

Cain turned, the carbine across his chest.

"You even look like you're going back there, and I'll lock you up and throw away the key."

"You're hateful, do you know that?"

"So you keep telling me. Has it once occurred to you to ask me about what happened instead of throwing accusations around?"

"What happened was obvious."

"Was it?"

Suddenly Kit felt unsure of herself. Cain was no coward, and he never did anything without a reason. The edges of her temper cooled, but not her anxiety. "All right, suppose you tell me what you had in mind when you left Magnus with a man who wants to see him lynched."

"You've made me just mad enough, I'm going to let you figure it out for yourself."

He began walking toward the house, but Kit jumped in front of him. "Oh, no, you're not getting away that easily."

He shifted the carbine to his shoulder. "Magnus hated your interference, and he'd have hated mine, too. There are some things a man has to do for himself."

"You might as well have signed his death warrant."

"Let's just say I have more faith in him than you seem to have."

"This is South Carolina, not New York City."

"Don't tell me you're finally admitting your native state isn't perfect?"

"We've talked about the Klan," she said. "The last time you were in Charleston, you tried to get the federal officials to take action against them. Now you act like the Klan doesn't exist."

"Magnus is his own man. He doesn't need anybody to fight his battles. If you knew half as much as you think you know, you'd understand that."

From Magnus's viewpoint, Cain was right, but she didn't have any patience with that kind of male pride. It only led to death. As Cain walked away, she thought of the war, which had once seemed so glorious.

She fumed and stomped around for most of an hour until Samuel appeared, a grin on his face and a note from Sophronia in his hand.

Dear Kit,
Stop worrying. Spence is gone, Magnus is fine, and we're getting married.

Love,
Sophronia

Kit stared at it with a mixture of joy and bemusement. Cain had been right. But just because he was right about this didn't mean he was right about anything else.

Too much had happened, and all her feelings about Sophronia, about Risen Glory, and about Cain tumbled around inside her. She headed for the stable and Temptation, then remembered that Cain had ordered her not to ride the horse. A small voice told her she had only her own recklessness to blame, but she refused to listen. She had to settle this with him.

She stalked back to the house and found Lucy in the kitchen peeling potatoes. "Where's Mr. Cain?"

"I heard him go upstairs a few minutes ago."

Kit shot down the hallway and up the steps. She threw open the bedroom door.

Cain stood by the table picking up some papers he'd left there the night before. He turned to her, his expression quizzical. He saw that she was seething and lifted one eyebrow. "Well?"

She knew what he was asking. Would she break the unwritten rule between them? The rule that said this bedroom was the one place where they didn't argue, the one place that was set aside for something else, something as important to both of them as the air they breathed.

She couldn't break that rule. Only here did her restlessness fade. Only here did she feel... not happy...but somehow right.

"Come here," he said.

She moved toward him, but her resentment about Temptation wasn't forgotten. Her fear that he would still put a road to the mill across her land was not forgotten. His high-handedness and stubbornness were not forgotten. She stuffed it all inside to boil while she gave in to lovemaking that was growing less satisfying and more necessary every day.

* * *

The next morning, even the happiness of Sophronia and Magnus couldn't keep Cain and Kit from snarling at each other. It had become their pattern. The more passionate the night, the worse they treated each other the next day.

Do not expect daylight to bring a change in me... I will give you my body, but do not, dare not, *expect more.*

As Kit watched Magnus and Sophronia move in a blissful daze through the next week while they got ready for their wedding, she found herself wishing she and Cain could have such a happy ending. But the only happy ending she could imagine for them would have Cain riding away, leaving her alone at Risen Glory. And that didn't seem right at all.

On Sunday afternoon, Sophronia and Magnus took their vows in the old slave church with Kit and Cain beside them. After hugs, tears, and slices of Miss Dolly's wedding cake, they were finally alone in Magnus's house by the orchard.

"I won't press you," he said as the December night fell deep and peaceful outside the windows. "We can take our time."

Sophronia smiled into his eyes and feasted on the sight of his beautiful brown skin. "We've had too much time already." Her fingers trailed to the top buttons of the beautiful silk dress Kit had given her. "Love me, Magnus. Just love me."

He did. Tenderly and completely. Driving away all the ugliness of the past. Sophronia had never felt so safe or so loved. She would never forget what had happened to her, but the nightmares of her past would no longer control her. Finally she understood what it meant to be free.

As December gave way to January, the lovemaking between Cain and Kit developed a primitive, ferocious edge that frightened them both. Kit left a bruise on Cain's shoulder. Cain left a mark on her breast, then cursed himself afterward.

Only once did they speak the truth.

"We can't go on like this," he said

"I know." She turned her head into the pillow and pretended to fall asleep.

The treacherous, most female part of her longed to give up the struggle and open her heart before it burst with feelings she couldn't name. But this was a man who gave up his books and his horses before he could grow too attached to them. And the devils of her past were powerful.

Risen Glory was all she had—all she'd ever had—the only part of her life that was secure. People disappeared, but Risen Glory was everlasting, and she'd never let her tumultuous unnamed feelings for Baron Cain threaten that. Cain with his cold gray eyes and his spinning mill, Cain with his unchecked ambitions that would eat up her fields and spit them out like so many discarded cotton seeds until nothing was left but a worthless husk.

"I told you, I don't want to go." Kit slammed down her hairbrush and stared at Cain in the mirror.

He threw aside his shirt. "I do."

All arguments stop at the bedroom door. But this one wasn't. And what difference did it make? Their lovemaking had already turned this bedroom into another war zone.

"You hate parties," she reminded him.

"Not this one. I want to get away from the mill for a few days."

The mill, she noted, not Risen Glory.

"And I miss seeing Veronica," he added.

Kit's stomach knotted with jealousy and hurt. The truth was, she also missed Veronica, but she didn't want Cain to.

Veronica had left Rutherford six weeks earlier, shortly before Thanksgiving. She'd settled in a three-story mansion in Charleston that Kit had learned was already turning into a center of fashion and culture. Artists and politicians showed up at her front door. There was an unknown sculptor from Ohio, a famous actor from New York. Now Veronica intended to celebrate her new home with a winter ball.

In her letter to Kit, she'd said she was inviting everyone in Charleston who amused her, as well as several old acquaintances from

Rutherford. In typically perverse Veronica fashion, that included Brandon Parsell and his new fiancée, Eleanora Baird, whose father had taken over the presidency of the Planters and Citizens Bank after the war.

Normally Kit would have loved attending such a party, but right now she didn't have the heart for it. Sophronia's new happiness had made her conscious of her own misery, and as much as Veronica fascinated her, she also made Kit feel awkward and foolish.

"Go by yourself," she said, even though she hated the idea.

"We're going together." Cain's voice sounded weary. "You have no choice in the matter."

As if she ever did. Her resentment grew, and that night, they didn't make love. Nor the next. Nor the one after that. It was just as well, she told herself. She'd been feeling ill for several weeks now. Sooner or later, she needed to stop fighting it and see the doctor.

Even so, she waited until the morning before they left for Veronica's party to make the trip.

By the time they reached Charleston, Kit was pale and exhausted. Cain left to attend to some business while Kit was shown to the room they'd share for the next few nights. It was light and airy, with a narrow balcony that looked down upon a brick courtyard, appealing even in winter with its green border of Sea Island grass and the scent of sweet olives.

Veronica sent up a maid to help her unpack and prepare a bath. Afterward, Kit lay down on the bed and closed her eyes, too drained of emotion even to cry. She awakened several hours later and numbly put on her cotton wrapper. As she knotted the sash, she walked over to the windows and pushed back the drapery.

It was already dark outside. She'd have to get dressed soon. How would she get through the evening? She lay her cheek against the chilly window glass.

She was going to have a baby. It didn't seem possible, yet even now a small speck of life grew inside her. Baron Cain's baby. A child who would bind her to him for the rest of her life. A child she desperately wanted, even though everything would become so much more difficult.

She forced herself to sit down in front of the dressing table. As she fumbled for her hairbrush, she noticed the blue ceramic jar resting next to her other toiletries. Lucy had packed it as well. How ironic.

The jar contained the grayish-white powders Kit had gotten from the Conjure Woman to keep her from conceiving. She'd taken it once and then never again. At first there'd been the long weeks when she and Cain had slept apart, and then, after their nighttime reconciliation, she'd found herself reluctant to use the powders. The contents of that blue jar had seemed almost malevolent, like finely ground bones. When she'd heard several women talking about how difficult it had been for them to conceive, she'd justified her carelessness by deciding the risk of pregnancy wasn't as great as she had feared. Then Sophronia had discovered the jar and told Kit the powders were worthless. The Conjure Woman didn't like white women and had been selling them useless prevention powders for years. Kit ran her finger across the lid of the jar, wondering if that was true.

The door flew open so abruptly, she jumped and knocked over the jar. She leaped up from the stool. "Couldn't you just once enter a room without tearing the door from its hinges?"

"I'm always much too eager to see my devoted wife." Cain tossed his leather gloves down on a chair, then spotted the mess on the dressing table. "What's that?"

"Nothing!" She grabbed a towel and tried to wipe it up.

He came up behind her and settled his hand over hers. With his other hand, he picked up the overturned jar and studied the powder that remained inside. "What is this?"

She tried to pull her hand from beneath his, but he held it there. He set down the jar, and his measured stare told her he wouldn't let her go until she told him the truth. She started to say it was a headache powder, but she was too tired to dissemble, and what was the point anyway?

"It's something I got from the Conjure Woman. Lucy packed it by mistake." And then, because it didn't make any difference now: "I—I didn't want to have a baby."

A look of bitterness flashed across his face. He released her hand and turned away. "I see. Maybe we should have talked about it."

She couldn't quite keep the sadness from her voice. "We don't seem to have that kind of marriage, do we?"

"No. No, I guess we don't." With his back to her, he took off his pearl-gray coat and tugged at his cravat. When he finally turned, his eyes were as remote as the North Star. "I'm glad you were so sensible. Two people who detest each other wouldn't make the best parents. I can't imagine anything worse than bringing some unwanted brat into this sordid mess we call a marriage, can you?"

Kit felt her heart break into a million pieces. "No," she managed. "No, I can't."

"I understand you own that new spinning mill out past Rutherford, Mr. Cain."

"That's right." Cain stood at one end of the foyer next to John Hughes, a beefy young Northerner who'd claimed his attention just as he'd been about to go upstairs to see what was keeping Kit.

"Hear you're doing a good business there. More power to you, I say. Risky, though, don't you think, with the—" He broke off and whistled softly as he gazed past Cain's shoulder to the staircase. "Whoa, now! Would you look at that? There's a woman I'd like to take home with me."

Cain didn't need to turn around to know who

it was. He could feel her through the pores of his skin. Still, he had to look.

She wore her silver-and-white gown with the crystal beads. But the dress had been altered since he'd last seen it, the way she'd altered so many of her clothes recently. She'd cut away the white satin bodice to just below her breasts and set in a single fine layer of silver organdy. It rose up over the soft curves to her throat, where she'd used a glimmering ribbon to gather it into a high, delicate ruffle.

The organdy was transparent, and she wore nothing beneath. Only the crystal bugle beads she'd taken from the skirt and placed in strategic clusters over the transparent fabric protected her modesty. Crystal spangles and warm, rounded flesh.

The gown was outrageously lovely, and Cain had never seen anything he hated more. One by one, the men around him turned to her, and their eyes greedily devoured flesh that should have been his alone to see. She was an ice maiden set afire.

And then he forgot his jealousy and simply lost himself in the sight of her. She was savagely beautiful, his wild rose of the deep wood, as untamed as the day he'd met her, still ready to stab a man's flesh with her thorns at the same time she enticed him with her spirit.

He took in the high color smudging her delicate cheekbones and the queer, voltaic lights that glittered in the deep violet depths of her eyes. He felt his first prickle of uneasiness. There was something almost frenetic lurking inside her tonight. It pulsed from her body like a drumbeat, straining to break loose and run free and wild. He took one quick step toward her and then another.

Her eyes locked with his and then deliberately drew away. Without a word, she swept across the foyer to another neighbor from Rutherford who'd been invited.

"Brandon! My, don't you look handsome tonight. And this must be your sweet fiancée, Eleanora. I do hope you'll let me steal Brandon from you every once in a while. We've been friends for so long—like brother and sister, you understand. I couldn't possibly give him up entirely, even for such a pretty young lady."

Eleanora tried to smile, but her lips couldn't hide either her disapproval or the knowledge that she looked dowdy next to Kit's exotic beauty. Brandon, on the other hand, gazed at Kit in her shocking dress as if she were the only woman in the world.

Cain appeared. "Parsell. Miss Baird. If you'll excuse us..."

His fingers sank into Kit's organdy-draped arm, but before he could pull her across the foyer to the steps and force her to change her dress, Veronica glided toward them in a jet-black evening gown. There was a slight lift to her forehead as she took in the small drama being played out before her.

"Baron, Katharine, just the two I was looking for. I'm late as usual, and for my own party. Cook's ready to serve dinner. Baron, be a darling and escort me into the dining room. And, Katharine, I want you to meet Sergio. A fascinating man and the best baritone New York City has heard in a decade. He'll be your dinner partner."

Cain ground his teeth in frustration. There was no way he could remove Kit now. He watched a much too handsome Italian eagerly step forward and kiss Kit's hand. Then, with a soulful look, he turned it over and pressed his lips intimately to her palm.

Cain moved quickly, but Veronica was even quicker. "My dearest Baron," she cooed softly as she dug her fingers into his arm, "you're behaving like the most boring sort of husband. Escort me into the dining room before you do something that will only make you look foolish."

Veronica was right. Nevertheless, it took all his will to turn his back on his wife and the Italian.

Dinner lasted for nearly three hours, and at least a dozen times during the meal, Kit's laughter rang out as she divided her attention between Sergio and the other men who sat near her. They all flattered her outrageously and showered her with attention. Sergio seemed to be teaching her Italian. When she spilled a drop of wine, he dipped his index finger into the spot and then touched it to his lips. Only Veronica's viselike grip kept Cain from leaping across the table.

Kit was waging a battle of her own. She'd perversely asked Lucy to pack the crystal-and-silver dress after Cain had told her he disliked it. But she hadn't really intended to wear it. Yet when the time came to don the more appropriate jade-green velvet, Cain's words had haunted her.

I can't imagine anything worse than bringing some unwanted brat into this sordid mess we call a marriage...

She heard Cain's laughter echo from the other end of the table and observed the attentive way he listened to Veronica. The ladies left the gentlemen to their cigars and brandy. Then it was time for the dancing to begin.

Brandon abandoned Eleanora to her father and asked Kit for the first dance. Kit gazed into his handsome, weak face. Brandon, who talked of honor, was willing to sell himself to the highest bidder. First to her for a plantation, then to Eleanora Baird for a bank. Cain would never sell himself for anything, not even his cotton mill. His marriage to her had been retribution and nothing less.

As she and Brandon moved out onto the dance floor, she saw Eleanora at the side of the room looking unhappy, and she regretted her earlier flirtatiousness. She'd drunk just enough champagne to decide she needed to settle a score for all unhappy women.

"I've missed you," she whispered as the music began.

"I've missed you, too, Kit. Oh, Lord, you're so beautiful. It's nearly killed me to think of you with Cain."

She pushed closer to him and whispered mischievously, "Dearest Brandon, run away with me tonight. Let's leave it all, Risen Glory and the bank. It will only be the two of us. We won't have money or a home, but we'll have our love."

She concealed her amusement as she felt him stiffen beneath the cloth of his coat.

"Really, Kit, I—I don't think that would be—would be wise."

"But why not? Are you worried about my husband? He'll come after us, but I'm certain you can take care of him."

Brandon stumbled. "Let's not—that is to say, I think, perhaps—too much haste—"

She hadn't wanted to let him off the hook so easily, but a bubble of rueful laughter escaped her.

"You're making fun of me," he said stiffly.

"You deserve it, Brandon. You're an engaged man, and you should have asked Eleanora for the first dance."

He looked confused and a bit pathetic as he tried to regain his dignity. "I don't understand you at all."

"That's because you don't really like me very much, and you certainly don't approve of me. It would be easier for you if you could just admit that all you feel for me is a most ungentlemanly lust."

"Kit!" Such unvarnished honesty was more than he could accept. "I beg your pardon if I've offended you," he said tightly. His eyes caught on the crystal-spangled bodice of Kit's gown. With great effort, he tore his gaze away and, smarting with humiliation, went in search of his fiancée.

With Brandon's departure, Kit was quickly claimed by Sergio. As she took his hand, she glanced toward the far end of the room, where her husband and Veronica had been standing a moment before. Now only Veronica was there.

Her husband's indifference prodded Kit to the limits of what even she considered acceptable behavior. She whirled from one partner to the next, dancing with Rebel and Yankee alike, complimenting each one extravagantly and letting several hold her too closely. She didn't care what any of them thought. Let them talk! She drank champagne, danced every dance, and laughed her intoxicating laugh. Only Veronica Gamble sensed the edge of desperation behind it.

A few of the women were secretly envious of Kit's bold behavior, but most were shocked. They looked around anxiously for the dangerous Mr. Cain, but he was nowhere in sight. Someone whispered that he was playing poker in the library and losing badly.

There was open speculation about the state of the Cain marriage. The couple had not once danced together. There'd been rumors that it was a marriage of necessity, but Katharine Cain's waistline was as slim as ever, so that couldn't be.

The poker game folded shortly before two. Cain had lost several hundred dollars, but his black mood had little to do with money. He stood in the doorway of the ballroom, watching his wife sail across the floor in the arms of the

Italian. Some of her hair had come loose from its pins and tumbled in disarray around her shoulders. Her cheekbones still held their high color, and her lips were rosy smudges, as if someone had just kissed her. The baritone couldn't seem to look away from her.

A muscle twitched in the corner of Cain's jaw. He pushed past the couple in front of him and was about to stride onto the ballroom floor when John Hughes caught at his arm.

"Mr. Cain, Will Bonnett over there claims there wasn't a bluecoat in the whole Union army could outshoot a Reb. What d'ya think? You ever meet a Reb you couldn't pick off if you set your mind to it?"

This was dangerous talk. Cain tore his eyes away from his wife and turned his attention to Hughes. Even though nearly four years had passed since Appomattox, social interaction between Northerners and Southerners was still tenuous, with talk of the war pointedly avoided when they were pushed together.

He looked over at the group of seven or eight men made up of former Union soldiers as well as Confederate veterans. It was obvious that they'd all had more than enough to drink, and even from where he was standing, he could hear that their discussion had progressed from polite disagreement to open antagonism.

With a last glance toward Kit and the Italian, he walked with Hughes to the men. "War's over, fellows. What do you say we all go sample some of Mrs. Gamble's fine whiskey?"

But the discussion had gone too far. Will Bonnett, a former rice planter who had served in the same regiment as Brandon Parsell, punched his index finger in the direction of one of the men who worked for the Freedmen's Bureau. "No soldier in the world ever fought like the Confederate soldier, and you know it."

The angry voices were beginning to catch the attention of the other guests, and as the argument grew louder, people stopped dancing to see what the commotion was about.

Will Bonnett spotted Brandon Parsell standing with his fiancée and her parents. "Brandon, you tell 'em. You ever see anybody could shoot like our boys in gray? Come on over here. Tell these bluebellies how it was."

Parsell moved forward reluctantly. Cain frowned when he saw that Kit had moved up, too, instead of remaining in the back with the other women. But what else had he expected?

By this time Will Bonnett's voice had reached the musicians, who gradually put down their instruments so they could enjoy the argument. "We were outnumbered," Bonnett declared, "but you Yankees never outfought us, not for a minute of the war."

One of the Northerners stepped forward. "Seems like you got a short memory, Bonnett. You sure as hell got outfought at Gettysburg."

"We didn't get outfought!" an older man standing next to Will Bonnett exclaimed. "You got lucky. Why, we had boys twelve years old could shoot better than all your officers put together."

"Hell, our *women* could shoot better than their officers!"

There was a great roar of laughter at this sally, and the speaker was slapped heartily on the back for his wit. Of all the Southerners present, only Brandon didn't feel like laughing.

He looked first at Kit and then at Cain. The injustice of their marriage was a splinter under his skin. At first he'd been relieved not to be married to a woman who didn't behave as a lady should, even though it meant the loss of Risen Glory. But as the weeks and months had passed, he'd watched Risen Glory's fields bursting white with bolls and seen the wagons laden with ginned cotton head for Cain's spinning mill. Even after he'd become engaged to Eleanora, who'd bring him the Planters and Citizens Bank, he couldn't erase the memory of a pair of wicked violet eyes. Tonight she'd had the audacity to poke fun at him.

Everything in his life had soured. He was a Parsell and yet he had nothing, while they had everything—a disreputable Yankee and a woman who didn't know her place.

Impulsively he came forward. "I believe you do have a point about our Southern women. Why, I once saw our own Mrs. Cain shoot a pinecone out of a tree from seventy-five yards, even though she couldn't have been more than ten or eleven at the time. There's talk to this day that she's still the best shot in the county."

Several exclamations met this piece of information, and once again Kit found herself the object of admiring masculine eyes. But Parsell hadn't finished. It wasn't easy for a gentleman to settle a score with a lady and remain a gentleman, but that was exactly what he intended to do. And he'd settle with her husband at the same time. It would be impossible for Cain to go along with what Brandon was about to propose, but the Yankee would still look like a coward when he refused.

Brandon fingered the edge of his lapel. "I've heard that Major Cain is a good shot. I guess we've all heard more than enough about the Hero of Missionary Ridge. But if I were a betting man, I'd put my money on Mrs. Cain. I'd give about anything to send Will across the street for his matching set of pistols, place a row of bottles on Mrs. Gamble's garden wall, and see just how good a Yankee officer can shoot against a Southern woman, even if she does happen to be his wife. Of course, I'm sure Major Cain wouldn't permit his wife to take part in a shootin' contest, especially when he knows he has a pretty good chance of coming out the loser."

There were hoots of laughter from the Southern men. Parsell had put that Yankee in his place! Although none of them seriously believed a woman, even a Southern one, could outshoot a man, they'd enjoy seeing the match all the same. And because she was only a woman, there'd be no honor lost to the South when the Yankee beat her.

The women who'd gathered nearby were deeply shocked by Brandon's proposal. What could he be thinking of? No lady could make such a public spectacle of herself, not in Charleston. If Mrs. Cain went along with this, she'd be a social pariah. They glared at their husbands, who were encouraging the match, and vowed to curtail their consumption of spirits for the rest of the evening.

The Northerners urged Cain to accept the challenge. "Come on, Major. Don't let us down."

"You can't back out on us now!"

Kit felt Cain's eyes on her. They burned like fire. "I can't permit my wife to engage in a public shooting contest."

He spoke so coldly, as if he didn't care at all. He might have been talking about a mare he owned instead of a wife. She was merely another piece of property.

And Cain gave away his property before he could become attached.

The wildness claimed her, and she came forward, sparking fires in the beads of her gown. "I've been challenged, Baron. This is South Carolina, not New York. Even as my husband, you can't interfere in a matter of honor. Fetch your pistols, Mr. Bonnett. Gentlemen, I'll face my husband." She shot him a challenge. "If he declines, I'll face any other Yankee who'd care to shoot against me."

The shocked gasps of the women went unheard beneath the triumphant whoops of the men. Only Brandon didn't join in the joviality. He'd meant to embarrass them both, but he hadn't meant to ruin her. After all, he was still a gentleman.

"Kit—Major Cain—I—I believe I was somewhat hasty. Surely you cannot—"

"Save it, Parsell," Cain growled, his own mood now as reckless as his wife's. He was tired of being the conciliator, tired of losing the battles she seemed determined to thrust them into. He was tired of her distrust, tired of her laughter, tired even of the expression of concern he glimpsed too often in her eyes when he came in exhausted from the mill. Most of all, he was tired of himself for caring so damned much about her.

"Set up your bottles," he said roughly. "And bring as many lamps as you can find into the garden."

With a great deal of laughter, the men moved off, Northerner and Southerner suddenly drawn together as they figured the odds on the match. The women fluttered with the excitement of being witnesses to such a scandal. At the same time, they didn't want to get too close to Kit, so they drifted farther away, leaving husband and wife standing alone.

"You've got your match," he said stonily, "just like you've gotten everything else you've wanted."

When had she gotten anything she wanted? "Are you afraid I'll beat you?" she managed to ask.

He shrugged. "I figure there's a pretty fair

chance of it. I'm a good shot, but you're better. I've known that since the night you tried to kill me when you were eighteen."

"You knew how I'd react when you forbade me to shoot, didn't you?"

"Maybe. Or maybe I figured that champagne you've been drinking has tilted the odds in my favor."

"I wouldn't count too much on the champagne." It was false bravado. Although she wouldn't admit it, she had drunk too much.

Veronica descended on them, her habitual amusement cast aside. "Why are you doing this? If this were Vienna, it would be different, but this is Charleston. Kit, you know you'll be ostracized."

"I don't care."

Veronica spun on Cain. "And you…how can you be a party to this?"

Her words fell on deaf ears. Will Bonnett had reappeared with his pistol case, and Kit and Cain were swept out through the back doors into the garden.

20

*D*espite the moonless night, the garden shone as brightly as if it were daylight. Fresh torches had been lit in the iron brackets, and kerosene lamps had been brought outside from the house. A dozen champagne bottles perched along the brick wall. Veronica noticed that only half of them were empty and gave hurried orders to the butler to replace the others. Honor might be at stake, but she wouldn't see good champagne wasted.

The Southerners groaned when they saw the matching guns Bonnett had produced. They were the Confederate version of the Colt revolver, plain and serviceable, with walnut grips and a brass frame instead of the more expensive steel frame of the Colt. But they were heavy, designed for wartime use by a man. This was no gun for a woman.

Kit, however, was accustomed to the weight and barely noticed it as she took the gun nearest to her from the box. She inserted six of the paper cartridges Will had provided into the empty chambers of the cylinder and pulled the loading lever down each time to press them into place. Then she fitted six copper percussion caps at the other end of the cylinder. Her fingers were smaller than Cain's, and she was done first.

The distance was marked off. They would stand twenty-five paces from their target. Each would fire six shots. Ladies first.

Kit stepped up to the line that had been scratched in the gravel. Under normal circumstances, the empty champagne bottles would have held little challenge for her, but her head swam from too many glasses of champagne.

She turned sideways to the target and lifted

her arm. As she sighted through the notch and bead, she made herself forget everything except what she had to do. She pulled the trigger, and the bottle exploded.

There were surprised exclamations from the men.

She moved on to the next bottle, but her success had made her careless, and she forgot to take those extra glasses of champagne into account. She fired too quickly and just missed the second target.

Cain watched from the side as she picked off the next four bottles. His anger gave way to admiration. Five out of six, and she wasn't even sober. Damn, but she was one hell of a woman. There was something primitive and wonderful in the way she stood silhouetted against the torch flames, her arm extended, the deadly revolver forming such marked contrast to her loveliness. If only she were more manageable. If only...

She lowered the revolver and turned to him, her dark brows lifting in triumph. She looked so pleased with herself that he couldn't quite suppress a smile.

"Very nice, Mrs. Cain, although I believe you left one."

"That's true, Mr. Cain," she replied with an answering smile. "Make sure you don't leave more than one."

He inclined his head and turned to the target.

A hush had fallen over the crowd as the men became uneasily aware of what Cain had known from the start. They had a serious match on their hands.

Cain lifted the revolver. It felt familiar in his hand, just like the Colt that had seen him through the war. He picked off the first bottle and then the second. One shot followed another. When he finally lowered his arm, all six bottles were gone.

Kit couldn't help herself. She grinned. He was a wonderful shot, with a good eye and a steady arm.

Something tight and proud caught in her throat as she gazed at him in his formal black-and-white evening dress, the copper lights from the torches glinting in his crisp, tawny hair. She forgot about her pregnancy, she forgot her anger, she forgot everything in a rush of feeling for this difficult and splendid man.

He turned to her, his head tilted.

"Good shooting, my darling," she said softly.

She saw the surprise on his face, but it was too late to snatch back the words. The endearment was a bedroom expression, part of a small dictionary of love words that formed the private vocabulary of their passion, words that were never to be used in any other place, at any other time, yet that was what she'd done. Now she felt naked and defenseless. To hide her emotions, she tossed her chin high and turned to the onlookers.

"Since my husband is a gentleman, I'm certain he'll give me a second chance. Would someone fetch a deck of cards and pull out the ace of spades?"

"Kit..." Cain's voice held a brusque warning note.

She turned to confront him and wipe away her moment of defenselessness. "Will you shoot against me? Yes or no?"

They might have been standing alone instead of in the midst of dozens of people. The onlookers didn't realize it, but Cain and Kit knew the purpose of the contest had shifted. The war that had raged for so long between them had found a new battleground.

"I'll shoot against you."

There was a deadly quiet as the ace of spades was fastened to the wall. "Three shots each?" Kit asked as she reloaded her gun.

He nodded grimly.

She lifted her arm and sighted the small black spade at the exact center of the playing card. She could feel her hand trembling, and she lowered the revolver until she felt steadier. Then she lifted it again, sighted the small target, and fired.

She hit the top right corner of the card. It was an excellent shot, and there were murmurs from the men as well as from the women who'd gathered to watch. Some of them even felt a secret burst of pride at seeing one of their own sex excel at such a masculine sport.

Kit cocked the hammer and adjusted her aim. This time she was too low, and she hit the brick wall just below the bottom of the card. But it was still a respectable shot, and the crowd acknowledged it.

Her head was spinning, but she forced herself to concentrate on the small black shape at the center of the card. She'd made this shot dozens of times. All she needed was concentration. Slowly she squeezed the trigger.

It was nearly a perfect shot, and it took the point off the spade. There was a trace of disquiet in the subdued congratulations of the Southern men. None of them had ever seen a woman shoot like that. Somehow it didn't seem right. Women were to be protected. But this woman could do that for herself.

Cain lifted his own weapon. Once again the crowd fell silent, so that only the sea breeze in the sweet olives disturbed the quiet of the night garden.

The gun fired. It hit the brick wall just to the left of the card.

Cain corrected his aim and fired again. This time he hit the top edge of the card.

Kit held her breath, praying that his third shot would miss, praying that it wouldn't, wishing too late that she hadn't forced this contest upon them.

Cain fired. There was a puff of smoke, and the single spade in the center of the playing card disappeared. His final shot had drilled it out.

The onlookers went wild. Even the Southerners temporarily forgot their animosity, relieved that the natural law of male superiority had held firm. They surrounded Cain to congratulate him.

"Fine shootin', Mr. Cain."

"A privilege to watch you."

"Of course, you were only firin' against a woman."

The men's congratulations grated on his ears. As they pounded him on the back, he looked over their heads at Kit, standing off by herself, the revolver nestled in the soft folds of her skirt.

One of the Northerners shoved a cigar into his hand. "That woman of yours is pretty good, but when all's said and done, I guess shootin' is still pretty much a man's game."

"You're right there," another said. "Never much doubt about a man beating a woman."

Cain felt only contempt for their casual dismissal of Kit's skill. He thrust the cigar back and glared at them.

"You fools. If she hadn't been drinking champagne, I wouldn't have had a chance against her. And neither, by God, would any of you."

Turning on his heel, he stalked out of the garden, leaving the men gaping after him in astonishment.

Kit was stunned by his defense. She thrust the revolver at Veronica, picked up her skirts, and ran after him.

He was already in their bedroom when she reached it. Her brief happiness faded as she saw him throw his clothing into a satchel that lay open on the bed.

"What are you doing?" she asked breathlessly.

He didn't bother to look up at her. "I'm going to Risen Glory."

"But why?"

"I'll send the carriage back for you the day after tomorrow," he replied, without answering her question. "I'll be gone by then."

"What do you mean? Where are you going?"

He didn't look at her as he tossed a shirt into the satchel. He spoke slowly. "I'm leaving you."

She made a muffled sound of protest.

"I'm getting out now while I can still look myself in the eye. But don't worry. I'll see a lawyer first and make sure your name is on the deed to Risen Glory. You won't ever have to be afraid your precious plantation will be taken away from you again."

Kit's heart was pounding in her chest like the wings of a trapped bird. "I don't believe you. You can't just walk away. What about the cotton mill?"

"Childs can manage it for now. Maybe I'll sell it. I've already had an offer." He grabbed a set of brushes from the top of the bureau and shoved them inside with the rest. "I'm done fighting you, Kit. You've got a clear field now."

"But I don't want you to go!" The words sprang spontaneously from her lips. They were true, and she didn't want to take them back.

He finally looked up at her, his mouth twisted in its old mockery. "That surprises me. You've been trying your best to get rid of me one way or another since you were eighteen."

"That was different. Risen Glory—"

He slammed the open palm of his hand against the bedpost, making the heavy wooden spindle vibrate. "I don't want to hear about Risen Glory! I don't ever want to hear that name again. Damn it, Kit, it's just a cotton plantation. It isn't a shrine."

"You don't understand! You've never understood. Risen Glory is all I've ever had."

"So you've told me," he said quietly. "Maybe you should try to figure out why that is."

"What do you mean?" She grabbed the bedpost for support as she closed in on him.

"I mean that you don't *give* anything. You're like my mother. You take from a man until you've bled him dry. Well, I'll be damned if I end up like my father. And that's why I'm leaving."

"I'm not anything like Rosemary! You just can't accept the fact that I won't let you dominate me."

"I never wanted to dominate you," he said softly. "I never wanted to own you, either, no matter how many times I said it. If I'd wanted a wife I could grind under my bootheel, I could have gotten married years ago. I never wanted you to walk in my dust, Kit. But, by damn, I won't walk in yours, either."

He closed the satchel and began fastening the leather straps. "When we got married—after that first night—I had this idea that maybe it could somehow be all right between us. Then it went bad right away, and I decided I'd been a fool. But when you came to me in that black nightgown, and you were so scared and so determined, I forgot all about being a fool and let you creep right back under my skin."

He released the satchel and straightened up. For a moment he gazed at her, and then he closed the small distance left between them. His eyes were full of a pain that pierced through her as if it were her own. A pain that *was* her own.

He touched her cheek. "When we made love," he said huskily, "it was as if we stopped being two separate people. You never held back. You gave me your wildness, your softness, your sweetness. But there wasn't a foundation underneath that lovemaking—no trust or understanding—and that's why it turned sour."

He rubbed his thumb gently over her dry lips, his voice barely a whisper. "Sometimes when I was inside you, I wanted to use my body to punish you. I hated myself for that." He dropped his hand. "Lately I've been waking up in a cold sweat, afraid that someday I'd really hurt you. Tonight, when I saw you in that dress and watched you with those other men, I finally realized that I had to go. It's no good between us. We started out all wrong. We never had a chance."

Kit clutched his arm and gazed at him through the haze of her own tears. "Don't go. It's not too late. If we both tried harder—"

He shook his head. "I don't have anything left in me. I'm hurting, Kit. I'm hurting bad."

Bending down, he pressed his lips to her forehead, then picked up the satchel and walked out of the room.

* * *

True to his word, Cain was gone when she returned to Risen Glory, and for the next month Kit moved like a sleepwalker through the house. She lost track of time, forgot to eat, and locked herself away in the big front bedroom she'd once shared with him. A young lawyer appeared with a stack of documents and a pleasant, unassuming manner. She was shown papers that gave her clear title to Risen Glory as well as control over her trust fund. She had everything she'd ever wanted, and she'd never been more miserable.

He gives away his books and his horses before he can grow too attached to them…

The attorney explained that the money Cain had taken from her trust fund to rebuild the cotton mill had all been repaid. She listened to everything he said, but she didn't care about any of it.

Magnus came to her for orders, and she sent him away. Sophronia scolded her to eat, but Kit ignored it. She even managed to turn a deaf ear to Miss Dolly's fretting.

One dreary afternoon in late February, as she sat in the bedroom pretending to read, Lucy appeared to announce that Veronica Gamble was waiting for her in the sitting room.

"Tell her I'm not feeling well."

Veronica, however, wasn't so easily put off. Brushing past the maid, she climbed the stairs and entered the bedroom after knocking.

She took in Kit's uncombed hair and sallow complexion. "How Lord Byron would have loved this," she said scathingly. "The maiden withers like a dying rose, growing more frail each day. She refuses to eat and hides away. What on earth do you think you're doing?"

"I want to be left alone."

Veronica shrugged off an elegant topaz velvet cloak and tossed it on the bed. "If you care nothing for yourself, you could at least consider the child you're carrying."

Kit's head shot up. "How do you know about that?"

"I met Sophronia in town last week. She told me, and I decided to come see for myself."

"Sophronia doesn't know. No one knows."

"You don't imagine something that important could get past Sophronia, do you?"

"She shouldn't have said anything."

"You didn't tell Baron about the child, did you?"

Kit mustered her composure. "If you'll go down to the sitting room, I'll ring for tea."

But Veronica wouldn't be distracted. "Of course you didn't tell him. You're much too proud for that."

All the fight left her, and Kit sagged into the chair. "It wasn't pride. I didn't think of it. Isn't that odd? I was so stunned by the fact that he was leaving me that I forgot to tell him."

Veronica wandered over to the window, pushed back the curtain, and stared outside. "Womanhood has been hard coming to you, I think. But then, I suppose it's hard coming to all of us. Growing up seems easier for men, maybe because their rites of passage are clearer. They perform acts of bravery on the battlefield or show they're men through physical labor or by making money. For women, it's more confusing. We have no rites of passage. Do we become women when a man first makes love to us? If so, why do we refer to it as a *loss* of virginity? Doesn't the word 'loss' imply that we were better off before? I abhor the idea that we become women only through the physical act of a man. No, I think we become women when we learn what is important in our lives, when we learn to give and to take with a loving heart."

Every word Veronica uttered settled in Kit's heart.

"My dear," Veronica said softly as she walked over to the bed and picked up her cloak, "it really is time for you to take your final step into womanhood. Some things in life are temporal and others are everlasting. You'll never be content until you decide which are which."

She was gone as quickly as she had arrived, leaving only her words to linger. Kit heard the carriage move off down the drive, then grabbed the jacket that went with her riding habit and threw it over her rumpled woolen dress. She slipped out of the house and made her way to the old slave church.

The interior was dim and chilly. She sat on one of the rough wooden benches and thought hard about what Veronica had said.

A mouse scratched in the corner. A branch tapped at the window. She remembered the pain she'd seen on Cain's face before he'd left, and at that moment the door she'd kept so tightly shut on her heart swung open.

No matter how much she'd tried to deny it, no matter how hard she'd fought it, she'd fallen in love with him. Her love had been written in the stars long before that July night when he'd pulled her down off the wall by her britches. All of her life since birth had shaped her for him, just as all his life had shaped him for her. He was the other half of herself.

She'd fallen in love with him through their battles and arguments, through her stubbornness and his arrogance, through those sudden surprising moments when they'd each known they were seeing the world in the same way. And she'd fallen in love with him through the deep, secret hours of the night when he'd stretched her and filled her and created the precious new life inside her.

How she wished she could do it over again. If only during those times when he'd softened toward her, she'd opened her arms and met his softness with her own. Now he was gone, and she'd never spoken the words of her love. But neither had he. Maybe because his feelings didn't run as deeply as hers.

She wanted to go after him, to start all over again, and this time she'd hold nothing back. But she couldn't do it. She was the one responsible for the pain she'd seen in his eyes. And he'd never pretended he wanted a wife, let alone a wife like her.

Tears ran down her cheeks. She hugged herself and accepted the truth. Cain was glad to be rid of her.

But there was another truth she needed to accept. The time had come to get on with her life. She'd been mired in self-pity long enough. She could cry in the privacy of her bedroom at night, but during the day she needed to keep her eyes dry and her head clear. There was work to be done and people who depended on her. There was a baby who needed her.

The baby was born in July, four years almost to the day since the hot afternoon Kit had arrived in New York City to kill Baron Cain. The child was a girl, with fair hair like her father's and startling violet eyes fringed with tiny, black lashes. Kit named her Elizabeth and called her Beth.

Kit's labor had been long, but the birth had gone without complications. Sophronia had stayed by her side the entire time, while Miss Dolly had fluttered about the house, getting in everyone's way and shredding three of her handkerchiefs. Afterward, Kit's first visitors had been Rawlins and Mary Cogdell, who seemed pathetically relieved to see that a baby had finally been produced from the Cain marriage, even though it had taken twelve months.

Kit spent the rest of the summer regaining

her strength and falling deeply in love with her new daughter. Beth was a sweet, good-natured baby, happiest when she was in her mother's arms. At night, when she would awaken to be fed, Kit would tuck her close in bed, where the two of them would doze until dawn—Beth content with the milky-sweet breast of her mother and Kit full of love for this precious infant who'd been God's gift to her when she'd most needed it.

Veronica wrote her regular letters and occasionally visited from Charleston. A deep affection grew between the two women. Veronica still spoke outrageously about wanting to make love to Cain, but Kit now recognized her statements as none-too-subtle attempts to prod Kit's jealousy and keep her feelings for her husband alive. As if she needed anything more to remind her of her love for her husband.

With the secrets of the past swept away, Kit's relationship with Sophronia deepened. The two still bickered out of habit, but Sophronia talked freely now, and Kit took comfort from her presence. Sometimes, though, Kit's heart would ache as she watched Sophronia's face soften with a deep, abiding love when she caught sight of Magnus. His strength and goodness had laid to final rest the ghosts of Sophronia's past.

Magnus understood Kit's need to talk about Cain, and in the evenings while she sat on the piazza, he told her all that he knew about her husband's past: his childhood, the years of drifting, his bravery during the war. She took it all in.

The beginning of September found her with renewed energy and a deeper understanding of herself. Veronica had once said that she should decide which things in life were temporal and which were everlasting. As she rode through the fields of Risen Glory, she finally understood what Veronica meant. Now it was time to find her husband.

Unfortunately, that proved easier in theory than in practice. The lawyer who handled Cain's affairs knew he'd been in Natchez, but hadn't heard from him since. Kit learned that his profits from the sale of the cotton mill were lying untouched in a bank in Charleston. For some reason, he'd left himself virtually penniless.

She made inquiries throughout Mississippi. People remembered him, but no one seemed to know where he'd gone.

By the middle of October, when Veronica arrived from Charleston for a visit, Kit was in despair. "I've inquired everywhere, but no one knows where he is."

"He's in Texas, Kit. A town called San Carlos."

"You knew where he was all this time and you didn't tell me? How could you do this?"

Veronica ignored Kit's temper and took a sip of tea. "Really, my dear, you never asked me."

"I didn't think I had to!"

"The reason you're so angry is because he wrote me instead of you."

Kit wanted to slap her, but, as usual, Veronica was right. "And I'm sure you've been sending him all sorts of seductive messages."

Veronica smiled. "Unfortunately not. This was his way of keeping in touch with you. He knew if anything was really wrong, I'd tell him."

Kit felt sick. "So he knows about Beth, but he still won't come back."

Veronica sighed. "No, Kit, he doesn't know about her, and I'm not certain I did the right thing by not telling him. But I decided it wasn't my news to share. I couldn't bear to see either of you hurt any more than you have been."

Her anger forgotten, Kit pressed Veronica. "Please. Tell me everything you know."

"The first few months he traveled the riverboats and lived on what he won at the poker tables. Then he moved on to Texas and rode shotgun for one of the stagecoach lines. A beastly job, in my opinion. For a while he herded cattle. And now he's running a gambling palace in San Carlos."

Kit ached as she listened. The old patterns of Cain's life were repeating themselves.

He was drifting.

21

Kit reached Texas the second week of November. It was a long journey, made all the more arduous by the fact that she hadn't traveled alone.

The uninhabited space of Texas was a surprise to her. It was so different from South Carolina—the flat east Texas prairie and then the rougher country farther inland, where twisting trees grew from jagged rocks and tumbleweed chased across the harsh, hilly terrain. She was told that the canyons flooded when it rained, sometimes washing away entire herds of cattle, and that in the summer, the sun baked the earth until it hardened and cracked. Yet there was something about the land that appealed to her. Perhaps the challenge it posed.

Still, the closer she came to San Carlos, the more uncertain she became about what she'd done. She had precious responsibilities now, yet she'd left the familiar behind to search for a man who'd never said he loved her.

As she climbed the wooden steps that led to the Yellow Rose Gambling Palace, her stomach twisted into tight, painful knots. She'd hardly been able to eat for days, and this morning not even the mouthwatering smells that drifted up from the dining room of the nearby Ranchers Hotel had been able to tempt her. She'd dallied while she dressed, fixing her hair one way and then another, changing outfits several times, and even remembering to check for any unfastened buttons or hooks that might have escaped her notice.

She'd finally decided to wear her dove-gray dress with the soft rose piping. It was the same outfit she'd worn on her return to Risen Glory. She'd even added the matching hat and veiled her face. It comforted her somehow, the illusion that she was starting over again. But the dress fit differently now, clinging tighter to her breasts as a reminder that nothing remained the same.

Her gloved hand trembled slightly as she reached for the swinging door that led into the saloon. For a moment she hesitated, and then she pushed hard against it and stepped inside.

She'd learned that the Yellow Rose was the best and most expensive salon in San Carlos. It had red-and-gold wallpaper and a crystal chandelier. An ornately carved mahogany bar ran the length of the room, and behind it hung a portrait of a reclining nude woman with titian curls and a yellow rose caught between her teeth. She'd been painted against a map of Texas, so that the top of her head rested near Texarkana and her feet curled along the Rio Grande. The portrait gave Kit a renewed kick of courage. The woman reminded her of Veronica.

It wasn't quite noon, and only a few men sat inside. One by one, they stopped talking and turned to study her. Even though they couldn't see her features clearly, her dress and her bearing indicated she wasn't a woman who belonged inside a saloon, even the elegant Yellow Rose.

The bartender cleared his throat nervously. "Can I help you, ma'am?"

"I'd like to see Baron Cain."

He glanced uncertainly toward a flight of curving stairs at the back and then down at the glass he was polishing. "There's no one here by that name."

Kit walked past him and made her way toward the stairs.

The man dashed around the edge of the bar. "Hey! You can't go up there!"

"Watch me." Kit didn't slacken her pace. "And if you don't want me invading the wrong room, maybe you should tell me exactly where I can find Mr. Cain."

The bartender was a giant of a man, with a barrel chest and arms like ham hocks. He was accustomed to dealing with drunken cowboys and gunslingers out to make a reputation for themselves, but he was helpless in the face of a woman who was so obviously a lady. "Last room on the left," he mumbled. "And there's gonna be hell to pay."

"Thank you." Kit climbed the stairs like a queen, shoulders back and head held high. She hoped none of the men watching could guess just how frightened she was.

The woman's name was Ernestine Agnes Jones, but to the men at the Yellow Rose, she was simply Red River Ruby. Like most people who had come West, Ruby had buried her past along with her name and never once looked back.

Despite powders, creams, and carefully rouged lips, Ruby looked older than her twenty-eight years. She'd lived hard, and it showed. Still, she was an attractive woman with rich chestnut hair and breasts like pillows. Until recently, little had come easy for her, but all that had changed with the convenient death of her last lover. Now she found herself the owner of the Yellow Rose and the most sought-after woman in San Carlos—sought after, that is, by every man except the one she wanted for herself.

She pouted as she looked across the bedroom at him. He was tucking a linen shirt into a pair of black broadcloth trousers that fit him just closely enough to renew her determination. "But you said you'd take me for a ride in my new buggy. Why not today?"

"I have things to do, Ruby," he said curtly.

She leaned slightly forward so that the neck of her red, ruffled dressing gown fell farther open, but he didn't seem to notice. "Anybody would think you was the boss around here instead of me. What do you have to do that's so important it can't wait?"

When he didn't answer her, she decided not to press him. She'd done that once before, and she wouldn't make that mistake again. Instead, as she walked around the bed toward him, she wished she could break the unwritten rule of the West and ask about his past.

She suspected there was a price on his head. That would account for the air of danger that was as much a part of him as the set of his jaw. He was as good with his fists as he was with a gun, and the hard, empty look in his eyes gave her a chill just looking at them. However, he could read, and that didn't fit with being a man on the run.

One thing for sure, he wasn't a womanizer. He didn't seem to notice that there wasn't a woman in San Carlos who wouldn't lift her petticoats for him if she got the chance. Ruby had been trying to get into his bed ever since she'd hired him to help her run the Yellow Rose. So far, she hadn't been successful, but he was about the handsomest man she'd ever seen, and she wasn't going to give up yet.

She stopped in front of him and put one hand over his belt buckle and another against his chest. She ignored the knock at the door to slip her fingers inside his shirt. "I could be real nice to you if you'd give me the chance."

She wasn't aware that the door had opened until he lifted his head and looked past her. Impatiently she turned to see who'd interrupted them.

The pain hit Kit in a wave. She saw the scene before her in separate pieces—a gaudy, red, ruffled dressing gown, large white breasts, a brightly painted mouth open in indignation. And then she saw nothing but her husband.

He looked years older than she remembered. His features were thinner and harder, with deep creases at the corners of his eyes and near his mouth. His hair was longer, hanging well over the back of his collar. He looked like an outlaw. Was this the way he'd been during the war? Watchful and wary, like a piece of wire drawn so taut it was ready to snap?

Something raw contorted his features as he saw her, and then his face closed like a locked door.

The woman rounded on her. "Who the hell do you think you are, bargin' in like this? If you come here lookin' for a job, you can just drag your tail downstairs and wait till I get to you."

Kit welcomed the anger that rushed through her. She pushed up the veil of her hat with one hand and shoved the door back on its hinges with the other. "You're the one who needs to go downstairs. I have private business with Mr. Cain."

Ruby's eyelids narrowed. "I know your type. High-class girl who comes West and thinks the world owes her a livin'. Well, this is my place, and there ain't no la-de-da lady gonna tell me what to do. You can put on airs back in Virginny or Kentucky or wherever you come from, but not in the Yellow Rose."

"Get out of here," Kit said in a low voice.

Ruby tightened the sash of her dressing gown and moved forward menacingly. "I'm gonna do you a favor, sister, and teach you right off that things are different here in Texas."

Cain spoke quietly from across the room.

"My best piece of advice, Ruby—don't tangle with her."

Ruby gave a contemptuous snort, took another step forward, and found herself looking down the barrel of a snub-nosed pistol.

"Get out of here," Kit said quietly. "And close the door behind you."

Ruby gaped at the pistol and then back at Cain.

He shrugged. "Go on."

With a last assessing glance toward the lady with the pistol, Ruby hurried from the room and slammed the door.

Now that they were finally alone, Kit couldn't remember a word of the speech she'd rehearsed so carefully. She realized she was still holding the pistol and that it was pointed at Cain. Swiftly she shoved it back into her reticule. "It wasn't loaded."

"Thank God for small favors."

She'd imagined their reunion a hundred times, but she'd never imagined this cold-eyed stranger fresh from another woman's arms.

"What are you doing here?" he finally asked.

"Looking for you."

"I see. Well, you've found me. What do you want?"

If only he'd move, maybe she could find the words she needed to say, but he stood stiffly in place, looking as if her simple presence was inconveniencing him.

Suddenly it was all too much—the grueling

journey, the horrible uncertainty, and now this—finding him with another woman. She fumbled inside her reticule and drew out a thick envelope. "I wanted to bring you this." She put it on the table next to the door, then turned and fled.

The hallway seemed to go on forever, and so did the stairs. She tripped halfway down and barely managed to catch herself before she fell. The men at the bar craned their necks to watch her. Ruby stood at the bottom of the stairs, still wearing her red dressing gown. Kit brushed past her and made her way toward the swinging doors of the saloon.

She'd nearly reached them when she heard him behind her. Hands clasped her shoulders and spun her around. Her feet left the ground as Cain swept her up into his arms. Holding her against his chest, he carried her back through the saloon.

He took the stairs two at a time. When he reached his room, he kicked the door open with his foot and then closed it the same way.

At first he didn't seem to know what to do with her; then he dumped her on the bed. For a moment he stared at her, his expression still inscrutable. Then he crossed the room and picked up the envelope she'd left for him.

She lay quietly as he read it.

He glanced through the pages once, very quickly, and then went back to the beginning and read them through more carefully. Finally he gazed over at her, shaking his head. "I don't believe you did this. Why, Kit?"

"I had to."

He looked at her sharply. "Were you forced to?"

"Nobody could force me to do that."

"Then why?"

She sat up on the edge of the bed. "It was the only way I could think of."

"What do you mean by that? The only way to do what?"

When she didn't immediately answer him, he threw down the papers and came toward her. "Kit! Why did you sell Risen Glory?"

She stared down at her hands, too numb to speak.

He thrust his fingers through his hair, and he seemed to be talking as much to himself as to her. "I can't believe you sold that plantation. Risen Glory meant everything to you. And for ten dollars an acre. That's only a fraction of what it's worth."

"I wanted to get rid of it quickly, and I found the right buyer. I had the money deposited in your account in Charleston."

Cain was stunned. "My account?"

"It was your plantation. Your money put Risen Glory back on its feet again."

He said nothing. The silence stretched between them until she thought she would scream if it weren't filled.

"You'd like the man who bought it," she finally said.

"Why, Kit? Tell me why."

Was she imagining it, or could she detect a slight thawing in his voice? She thought of

Ruby pressed up against him. How many other women had there been since he'd left her? So much for all her dreams. She'd look like a fool when she explained it to him, but her pride no longer mattered. There'd be no more lies from her, spoken or unspoken, only the truth.

She lifted her head, fighting the lump forming in her throat. He stood in the shadows of the room. She was glad she didn't have to see his face while she talked.

"When you left me," she said slowly, "I thought my life was over. I felt so much anger, first at you and then at myself. It wasn't until you were gone that I realized how much I loved you. I'd loved you for a long time, but I wouldn't admit it, so I hid it away under other feelings. I wanted to come to you right away, but that wasn't—it wasn't practical. Besides, I've acted impulsively too often, and I needed to be sure about what I was doing. And I wanted to make certain that when I did find you, when I did tell you I loved you, you'd believe me."

"So you decided to sell Risen Glory." His voice was thick.

Kit's eyes filled with tears. "It was going to be the proof of my love. I was going to wave it under your nose like a banner. Look what I did for you! But when I finally sold it, I discovered that Risen Glory was only a piece of land. It wasn't a man who could hold you and talk to you and make a life with you." Her voice broke, and she rose to her feet to try to cover her weakness. "Then I did something very foolish. When you plan things in your head, they sometimes work out better than they do in real life."

"What?"

"I gave Sophronia my trust fund."

There was a soft, startled exclamation from the shadows of the room, but she barely heard it. Her words were coming in short, choppy bursts. "I wanted to get rid of everything so you'd feel responsible for me. It was an insurance policy in case you told me you didn't want me. I could look at you and say that whether you wanted me or not, you'd have to take me because I didn't have anyplace to go. But I'm not that helpless. I'd never stay with you because you felt responsible for me. That would be worse than being apart."

"And was it so horrible being apart from me?"

She lifted her head at the unmistakable tenderness in his voice.

He stepped out of the shadows, and the years seemed to have fallen away from his face. The gray eyes that she'd always thought cold overflowed with feeling.

"Yes," she whispered.

Then he was beside her, catching her up, pulling her to him. "My sweet, sweet Kit," he groaned, burying his face in her hair. "Dear God, how I've missed you. How I've wanted you. All I've dreamed about since I left was being with you."

She was in his arms again. She tried to take a deep breath, but it turned into a sob as she drew in his familiar clean scent. Feeling his body against hers after so many months was almost more than she could bear. He was the other part of herself, the part that had been missing for so long. And she was the other part of him.

"I want to kiss you now and make love with you more than I've ever wanted anything," he said.

"Then why don't you?"

He gazed down into her upturned face, a sense of wonder in his expression. "You'd let me make love with you after you just found me with another woman?"

The pain was a sharp, keen stab, but she fought it down. "I guess I'm partly responsible for that. But it better never happen again."

"It won't." His smile was soft and tender. "You love just like you do everything else, don't you? Without condition. It took you a lot less time than it took me to figure out how to do it right." He drew back. "I'm going to let you go now. It won't be easy, but there are some things I have to say to you, and I can't think straight when I'm holding you like this."

He released her with agonizing slowness and stepped just far enough away so he was no longer touching her. "I knew long before I left that I loved you, but I wasn't as smart as you. I tied strings to it and made conditions. I didn't have the guts to go to you and tell you how I felt, to put everything on the line the way you just did. Instead, I ran. Just like I've done all my life when I felt somebody or something getting too close to me. Well, I'm tired of running, Kit. I don't have any way to prove this to you. I don't have a banner to wave under your nose. But I love you, and I was coming back to fight for you. I'd already made up my mind. As a matter of fact, I was just getting ready to tell Ruby I was leaving when you barged in that door."

Despite the unmistakable message of love she was hearing, Kit couldn't help but wince at the mention of the saloonkeeper's name.

"Get that fire out of your eyes, Kit. I have to tell you about Ruby."

But Kit didn't want to hear. She shook her head and tried to fight the notion that what he'd done while they were apart was a betrayal.

"I want you to listen," he insisted. "No more secrets, even though this part isn't easy for me." He drew a deep breath. "I—I haven't been the world's greatest lover since I left you. I haven't...I haven't been any kind of lover at all. For a long time I stayed away from women, so I didn't think much about it. Then I came to work at the Yellow Rose, and Ruby was pretty determined, but what you saw today was all one-sided on her part. I never touched her."

Kit's spirits rose.

He shoved a hand in his pocket and turned slightly away from her, some of his former tension coming back. "I guess to you, Ruby doesn't look like much, but it's a little different for a man. It had been a long time for me, and she was making it easy—coming to my room all the time dressed like she was dressed today and letting me know what she wanted. But I didn't *feel* anything for her!"

He stopped talking and looked at her as if he expected something. Kit was beginning to grow confused. He sounded more like a man confessing infidelity than one confessing fidelity. Was there more?

Her confusion must have shown, because Cain spoke more sharply. "Don't you understand, Kit? She offered herself to me in every way she could, and I didn't want her!"

This time Kit did understand, and happiness burst inside her like the whole world had been made anew. "You're worried about your virility? Oh, my darling!" With a great whoop of laughter, she threw herself across the room and into his arms. Pulling his head down, she pressed her mouth to his. She talked, laughed, and kissed him all at the same time. "Oh, my dear, dear darling...my great, foolish darling. How I love you!"

There was a hoarse, tight sound deep in his throat, and then he trapped her in his embrace. His mouth came alive with need. Their kiss was deep and sweet, full of love that had finally been spoken, of pain that had finally been shared.

But they'd been apart for too long, and their bodies weren't content with kisses. Cain, who only moments before had doubted his manliness, now found himself aching with desire. Kit felt it, yearned for it, and, in the last instant before she lost her reason, remembered that she hadn't told him everything.

With her last ounce of will, she pulled back and gasped out, "I didn't come alone."

His eyes were glazed with passion, and it was a moment before he heard. "No?"

"No. I—I brought Miss Dolly with me."

"Miss Dolly!" Cain laughed, a joyous rumble that started in his boots and grew louder as it rose upward. "You brought Miss Dolly to Texas?"

"I had to. She wouldn't let me go without her. And you said yourself that we were stuck with her. She's our family. Besides, I needed her."

"Oh, you sweet... My God, how I love you." He reached for her again, but she stepped back quickly.

"I want you to come to the hotel."

"Now?"

"Yes. I have something to show you."

"Do I have to see it right away?"

"Oh, yes. Definitely right away."

Cain pointed out some of the sights of San Carlos as they walked along the uneven wooden sidewalk. He kept his hand tightly clasped over hers where it rested in the crook of his elbow, but her absentminded responses soon made it evident that her thoughts were elsewhere. Content merely to have her beside him, he fell silent.

Miss Dolly was waiting in the room Kit had taken. She giggled like a schoolgirl when Cain picked her up and hugged her. Then, with a quick, worried look at Kit, she left to visit the general store across the street so she could make some purchases for the dear boys in gray.

When the door closed behind her, Kit turned to Cain. She looked pale and nervous.

"What's wrong?" he asked.

"I have a—a sort of present for you."

"A present? But I don't have anything for you."

"That's not," she said hesitantly, "exactly true."

Puzzled, he watched her slip through a second door leading to an adjoining room. When she came back, she held a small white bundle in her arms.

She approached him slowly, her expression so full of entreaty it nearly broke his heart. And then the bundle moved.

"You have a daughter," she said softly. "Her name is Elizabeth, but I call her Beth. Beth Cain."

He looked down into a tiny valentine of a face. Everything about her was delicate and perfectly formed. She had a fluff of light blond hair, dark slivers of eyebrows, and a dab of a nose. He felt a tight prickling inside him. Could he have helped create something this perfect? And then the valentine yawned and fluttered open her pink shell lids, and he lost his heart to a second pair of bright, violet eyes.

Kit saw how it was between them right

away and felt that nothing in her life could ever be as sweet as this one moment. She pushed away the blanket so he could see the rest of her. Then she held their child out to him.

Cain gazed at her uncertainly.

"Go on." She smiled tenderly. "Take her."

He gathered the baby to his chest, his great hands nearly encompassing the small body. Beth wriggled once and then turned her head to look up at the strange new person who was holding her.

"Hello, Valentine," he said softly.

Cain and Kit spent the rest of the afternoon playing with their daughter. Kit undressed her so her father could count her fingers and her toes. Beth performed all her tricks like a champion: smiling at the funny noises that were directed toward her, grabbing at the large fingers put within her reach, and making happy baby sounds when her father blew on her tummy.

Miss Dolly looked in on them, and when she saw that all was well, she disappeared into the other room and lay down to take her own nap. Life was peculiar she thought as she drifted toward the edge of sleep, but it was interesting, too. Now she had sweet little Elizabeth to think about. It was certainly a responsibility. After all, she could hardly count on Katharine Louise to make certain the child learned everything she needed to know to be a great lady. So much to do. It made her head spin like a top. It was a tragedy, of course, what was happening at Appomattox Court House, but it was probably all for the best. She would be far too busy now to devote herself to the war effort....

In the other room, Beth finally began to fret. When she puckered her mouth and directed a determined yowl of protest toward her mother, Cain looked alarmed. "What's wrong with her?"

"She's hungry. I forgot to feed her."

She picked Beth up from the bed, where they'd been playing, and carried her over to a chair near the window. As she sat down, Beth turned her head and began to root at the dove-gray fabric that covered her mother's breast. When nothing happened right away, she grew more frantic.

Kit gazed down at her, understanding her need, but suddenly feeling shy about performing this most intimate of acts in front of her husband.

Cain lay sprawled across the bed, watching them both. He saw his daughter's distress and sensed Kit's shyness. Slowly he rose and walked over to them. He reached down and touched Kit's cheek. Then he lowered his hand to the cascade of gray lace at her throat. Gently he loosened it with his fingers to expose a row of rose-pearl buttons beneath. He unfastened them and pushed apart the gown.

The blue ribbon on her chemise surrendered with a single tug. He saw the trickles of sentimental tears on Kit's cheek and leaned down to kiss them away. Then he opened the chemise so his daughter could be nourished.

Beth made a ferocious grab with her tiny mouth. Cain laughed and kissed the chubby folds of her neck. Then he turned his head and touched his lips to the sweet, full breast that fed her. As Kit's fingers coiled in his hair, he knew he finally had a home and nothing on earth would ever make him give it away.

There were still promises that had to be sealed between them in private. That evening, with Beth safely tucked in bed where Miss Dolly could watch over her, they rode out to a canyon north of town.

As they rode, they talked about the lost months between them, at first only the events, and then their feelings. They spoke quietly, sometimes in half sentences, frequently finishing each other's thoughts. Cain spoke of his guilt at deserting her, overwhelming now that he knew she'd been pregnant at the time. Kit spoke of the way she'd used Risen Glory as a wedge to drive them apart. Sharing their guilt should have been hard, but it wasn't. Neither was the forgiveness each of them offered the other.

Tentatively at first, and then with more enthusiasm, Cain told her about a piece of land he'd seen to the east, near Dallas. "How would you feel about building another cotton mill? Cotton's going to be a big crop in

Texas, bigger than any state in the South. And Dallas seems like a good place to raise a family." He gazed over at her. "Or maybe you want to go back to South Carolina and build another mill there. That'll be all right with me, too."

Kit smiled. "I like Texas. It feels like the right place for us. A new land and a new life."

For a while they rode in silent contentment. Finally Cain spoke. "You didn't tell me about the man who bought Risen Glory. Ten dollars an acre. I still can't believe you let it go for that."

"He was a special man." She regarded him mischieviously. "You might remember him. Magnus Owen."

Cain threw back his head and laughed. "Magnus owns Risen Glory and Sophronia has your trust fund."

"It only seemed right."

"Very right."

The deep, cool shadows of evening fell over them as they entered the small, deserted canyon. Cain tied their horses to a black willow, drew a bedroll from behind his saddle, and took Kit's hand. He led her to the edge of a lazy creek that meandered through the floor of the canyon. The moon was already out, a full, shining globe that would soon bathe them in silver light.

He looked down at her. She wore a flat-brimmed hat and one of his flannel shirts over a pair of fawn britches. "You don't look much different than you did when I pulled you down off my wall. Except now, nobody could mistake you for a boy."

His eyes traveled to her breasts, visible even under his oversized shirt, and she delighted him by blushing. He smoothed out the bedroll and took off first her hat, then his own. He tossed them both onto the mossy creek bank.

He touched the small silver studs in her earlobes and then her hair, coiled in a thick knot at the nape of her neck. "I want to take your hair down."

Her lips curved in gentle permission.

He took the pins out, one at a time, and set them carefully inside his own hat. When the shining cloud of her hair finally fell free, he caught it in his hands and brought it gently to his lips. "Dear God, how I've missed you."

She put her arms around him and gazed up. "It's not going to be a fairy-tale marriage, is it, my darling?"

He smiled softly. "I don't see how. We're both hot-tempered and stubborn. We're going to argue."

"Do you mind very much?"

"I wouldn't have it any other way."

She pressed her cheek to his chest. "Fairy-tale princes always seemed dull to me."

"My wild rose of the deep wood. Things between us will never be dull."

"What did you call me?"

"Nothing." He stilled her question with his lips. "Nothing at all."

The kiss that began gently grew until it set them both on fire. Cain plowed his fingers through her hair and cupped her head between his hands. "Undress for me, will you, sweet?" he groaned softly. "I've dreamed of this for so long."

She knew at once how she would do it, in the way that would give him the most pleasure. Tossing him a teasing grin, she rid herself of her boots and stockings, then peeled off her britches. He groaned as the long flannel shirttail fell modestly below her hips. She reached beneath it, pulled off her white pantalets, and dropped them next to her.

"I don't have anything on under this shirt. I seemed to have forgotten my chemise. On purpose."

He could barely keep himself from leaping up and taking her. "You're a wicked woman, Mrs. Cain."

Her hand traveled to the top button of her shirt. "You're about to find out just how wicked I am, Mr. Cain."

Never had buttons been opened so slowly. It was as if each unfastening could be accomplished with only the most leisurely of movements. Even when the shirt was finally unbuttoned, the heavy material kept it together in the front.

"I'm going to count to ten," he said huskily.

"Count all you want, Yankee. It won't do you a bit of good." With a devil's smile, she peeled away the shirt, slow inch by inch, until she finally stood naked before him.

"I didn't remember it right," he muttered

thickly. "How beautiful you are. Come to me, love."

She sped across the chilled ground toward him. Only when she reached him did she wonder if she could still please him. What if having a baby had changed her in some way?

He caught her hand and pulled her beside him. Gently he cupped her fuller breasts. "Your body is different."

She nodded. "I'm a little scared."

"Are you, love?" He tilted up her chin and grazed her mouth with his own. "I'd die before I'd hurt you."

His lips were soft. "Not that. I'm afraid...I won't please you anymore."

"Maybe I won't be able to please you," he breathed softly.

"Silly," she murmured.

"Silly," he whispered back.

They smiled and kissed until the barrier of his clothing became too much for them. They worked at it together so that nothing was left between them, and as their kisses deepened, they fell back onto the bedroll.

A wisp of cloud skidded over the moon, casting moving shadows on the ancient walls of the canyon, but the lovers didn't notice. Clouds and moons and canyons, a baby with a valentine face, an old lady who smelled of peppermint—all of it ceased to exist. For now, their world was small, made up of only a man and a woman, joined together at last.